For Nickie,

T.L. WILLIAMS

ZERO DAY
CHINA'S CYBER WARS

All the Best!

T.L. Williams

First Coast Publishers

Also by T.L. Williams

Cooper's Revenge

Unit 400: The Assassins

Acknowledgements

The author and publisher wish to acknowledge all of those whose expertise and generosity of time made this work possible. To my editor, Emily Carmain, whose skillful application of her craft unfailingly produces a more polished final product. To Carol, my first reader and love of my life, whose instincts on writing style and substance have a positive influence on my writing. To my brother, Jim Williams, whose technical expertise proved invaluable as I struggled to capture fictional cyber hacking scenarios in a realistic and factual way. To Mark A. Stokes, Jenny Lin and L.C. Russell Hsiao of the Project 2049 Institute, whose groundbreaking 2011 paper on China's Cyber infrastructure provided invaluable background. To U.S. civilian and military intelligence professionals engaged in offensive and defensive cyber efforts, without whom, our nation would be in dire straits. To my design team at Expert Subjects, Heather Upchurch, who produced the striking cover and Catherine Murray who designed the book interior. To the Central Intelligence Agency Map Library for their generous consent to use the China Transportation map found herein. But most of all I would like to thank you, my readers, without whom all of this would not be possible.

T. L. Williams
Ponte Vedra Beach, Florida

To my mother,

Betty Lee
1927 – 2008

With love

Publisher's Note
This is a work of fiction. The people, events, circumstances, and institutions depicted are fictitious and the product of the author's imagination. Any resemblance of any character to any actual person, whether living or dead, is purely coincidental.

The publisher is not responsible for websites (or their content) that are not owned by the publisher.

Library of Congress Cataloging-in-Publication Data

Names: Williams, T. L.
Title: Zero day : China's cyber wars / T.L. Williams.
Description: Ponte Vedra Beach, FL : First Coast, 2017.
Identifiers: LCCN 2015900997 | ISBN 978-0-9884400-6-7 (pbk.) | ISBN 978-0-9884400-7-4 (ebook)
Subjects: LCSH: Cyberterrorism--Fiction. | United States. Central Intelligence Agency--Fiction. | Intelligence officers--Fiction. | Espionage, Chinese--Fiction. | BISAC: FICTION / Thrillers / Espionage. | FICTION / Thrillers / Suspense. | GSAFD: Spy stories. | Suspense fiction.
Classification: LCC PS3623.I5643 Z47 2017 (print) | LCC PS3623.I5643 (ebook) | DDC 813/.6--dc23.

Epigraph

*"In war, the way is to avoid what is strong,
and strike what is weak."*

Sun Tzu on the Art of War

CHINA

Novosibirsk

ASTANA

Barnaul

RUSS

Qaraghandy
(Karaganda)

KAZAKHSTAN

ULA

Lake
Balkhash

Karamay

MC

BISHKEK

Almaty

Ürümqi

KYRGYZSTAN

Korla

TAJ.

Kashi

AFG.

PAK.

Hotan

Indian
claim

Golmud

La

Aksai
Chin

1972 Line of
Control

One of
Actual
Control

NEW
DELHI

Ch

Lhasa

NEPAL

BHUTAN

INDIA

KATHMANDU

THIMPHU

Ledo

BANGL.

INDIA

Myitkyina

Kunm

Mandalay

BURMA

Nay Pyi Taw
(administrative
capital)

Chiang
Mai

RANGOON

THA

BANC

Andaman
Sea

	International boundary
	Expressway
	Road
	Railroad
	Canal
★	National capital
✈	Major airport
⚓	Major port

0   500 Kilometers

0   500 Miles

Scale 1:30,000,000

LAMBERT CONFORMAL CONIC PROJECTION; STANDARD PARALLELS 18°00'N 46°00'N

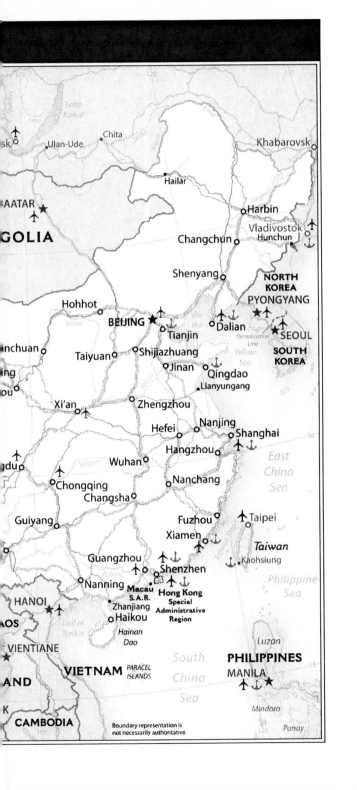

Chapter 1

The tip of the man's cigarette glowed like something feral in the muggy darkness, marking the spot where he squatted on his haunches beneath the protection of an ancient plane tree. Had it not been for the harsh smell of the tobacco smoke wafting up into the night air, accompanied by an occasional nervous cough, Logan Alexander would have bet even money that he was the only living soul for miles in any direction.

He had observed the tentative figure approaching their meeting site thirty minutes earlier, cautious, head swiveling to confront every sound. Now, he strained to make out the man no more than seventy yards away who had settled in to wait until Logan signaled that it was secure to initiate contact.

The lanky operations officer lay stretched out on his stomach, motionless in a shallow depression in the earth, most likely carved out by a wild animal. There was a stench in the air emanating from the makeshift pigsty attached to a windowless hovel about sixty yards east of his position. He'd been in place for forty-five minutes, and by his reckoning it was at least an hour until daybreak. There was no stirring from the direction of the farmer's hut. Only the occasional night sounds of woofing and grunting from the pigs' enclosure broke the silence.

Logan had crossed over the border from Hong Kong into China's New Territories three days ago, and had been making his way by train, bus, and on foot to this meeting site, a farm just outside of Chongqing in Szechuan Province. This area had been inhabited for millennia and even today was known as Banan District in honor of the ancient Ba State founded in the eleventh century BC.

Logan thought back to the area familiarization course he'd taken at Langley in preparation for his assignment to Hong Kong. In his previous life as a Navy SEAL, everything he'd studied had been geared towards the Middle East, mostly Iraq and Afghanistan. But this time it had been different. The focus had been on China. He remembered his Chinese culture professor, Dr. Wang, solemn in his frayed pinstripe suit and muted silk rep tie, superior in manner despite his sartorial shortcomings. Squinting through thick tortoise-shell bifocals, Wang had held forth on China's three thousand years of history, never failing to take a jibe at the U.S., which he described as an upstart, not even a quarter of the way through its first millennium.

Logan gritted his teeth as his left leg cramped up; the muscle spasm was painful, but his mind was preoccupied with the shadowy figure up ahead. The cramping intensified, forcing him to shift his weight slightly to relieve pressure on the muscle.

He hadn't been the same since the day his SEAL team had been ambushed in Afghanistan. He'd been lucky that it was only a short helicopter ride from the battlefield to the military hospital in Kandahar and that SEAL Team 8's medic was one of the best in theater. Triage and timing had saved his leg that day, but ultimately did little to sway the medical evaluation board's decision, despite eighteen months of rehab, that his Navy career was finished.

He allowed his thoughts to dwell for a moment on the scene at MacDill Air Force Base, Special Operations Command, firmly etched in his mind even though it had been five years ago. Admiral Sylvester, the senior medical officer in charge of the review, had delivered the board's verdict – separation from the Navy. He'd walked out of the room with a sense of loss so profound that he felt his life would never be the same.

Logan tensed as he realized with a start that the satisfied grunts emanating from the pigsty had given way to shrill squealing. Staring in that direction he was dismayed to see the bobbing headlights of two jeeps bouncing down the rutted dirt path that passed for a road. They clattered to a stop just short of the farmer's hut. A half-dozen public security officers spilled out. The Ministry of Public Security's (MPS) Public Security Bureau, the PSB, he surmised, as one approached the hut and began banging on the makeshift wooden door with a clenched fist. Moments later it opened and a stooped figure emerged, rubbing his eyes and hitching up baggy trousers as he stared in astonishment at the PSB officers roiling around the farmyard.

There was a rapid-fire exchange as the policeman questioned the bewildered farmer. The latter gestured vaguely with one hand and ran the other through his hair, as he seemed to ponder what the PSB officer was saying.

Logan shifted his attention back to the reason he was here in the first place –the man crouched beneath the tree. The shadowy figure had extinguished his cigarette and was no longer waiting there. His head was down, and keeping low to the ground, he was scrambling away from the direction of the police. There was a thicket of dense shrubs roughly two hundred feet away. With any luck he would make it there, giving him a chance to blend into the landscape and disappear.

The patrolmen were milling around the farmyard while the one who had hammered on the door continued to harangue the peasant with questions. Logan's mind was churning as he assessed the situation, wondering if this had been a set-up from the very beginning.

He thought back to the message he'd received from Langley two weeks ago. In it they had described a letter that had been slipped into the open window of the regional security officer's (RSO) vehicle, a short distance from the American Consulate in Chengdu, the capital of Szechuan province. It had happened so fast that the RSO had not been able to get a description of the person. The missive had been written in Chinese and was translated by an officer working on the China desk at Langley.

"Dear Sir,

"Please deliver this message to the appropriate authorities of the Central Intelligence Agency.

"I have important information to share with your government. It is dangerous for me to communicate with you here but I am unable to leave China at this time because of my position in public security. It is even risky for me to put this letter in the car of an American official, but I am desperate.

"Your country is under attack. But the weapons being used to accomplish this are not guns and bullets. No. The attack comes from the cyber world, and is on such a scale that you would not be able to fathom it.

"To prove my access to this information I will reveal one project that we initiated before this year's G-20 meetings in Europe. Our group identified senior staff members in the various U.S. departments supporting your Secretary of State's trip and sent them a malicious virus encoded in an email entitled EU_Economic_Options_in_Asia.

"When the email was opened it executed a malicious code to their personal computers and through it we were able to read all of their correspondence. We knew your negotiating positions on a wide range of issues before the conference even started! I have much more to share with you."

The letter was unsigned and gave no indication of the author's identity, other than his obvious access to sensitive information, but it had provided instructions to meet at this site on this date and at this time, and had even provided a backup meeting site. The volunteer had gone on to elaborate on half a dozen of the U.S. Administration's policy positions for the G-20 summit, two of which had not come up during the meetings and which, to date, had not been made public.

A small interagency team of cyber experts had been assembled to evaluate the letter's contents. After three days of feverish activity, including liaison with the affected departments and forensic analysis of staff computers, the consensus was that the write-in was for real. From the information he had provided it was impossible to tell where he fit into the scheme of things, but it was certain that he, or someone he knew, had accessed U.S. classified information.

FBI's Cyber Division was appointed to take the lead on the case and the special agent in charge had been given free rein to set up a commercial entity through which the FBI could monitor the main computer server that the hackers were using to gain access to the targeted computers. The Chinese must have become aware of the U.S. monitoring of their actions because within days all activity on the targeted server ceased; the hackers had moved on but the FBI had no idea where to.

After an eleventh-hour meeting at FBI headquarters, chaired by the head of Cyber Division, the task force had decided there was too much at stake to ignore the letter, despite concerns that it might be a Chinese provocation. The volunteer had to be met to get to the bottom of the hacking operation against the Secretary of State.

Candidates to make the meeting were proposed; the CIA devised a detailed plan to meet with the write-in. Logan had been selected to make the meeting because he was already deployed to the region, and had no overt affiliation with the United States Government. As head of the Hong Kong branch of a Boston-based company, Alexander Maritime Consulting, he could operate without attracting the attention of Chinese authorities. Logan had opened the Hong Kong office in September, and to date there was no indication that he was under surveillance or even on the radar of Chinese security officials.

The MPS, with over two million active duty officers nation-wide, had relegated the responsibility for keeping tabs on embassy and consulate officers in China to local public security bureaus, raising the risk of having someone whose name was on the diplomatic or consular list meet an unvetted volunteer. Since Logan was in Hong Kong working for a legitimate company, it was easier for him to blend into the woodwork.

Who was this guy? Logan scowled as the best chance for answering that question made it to the hedgerow and pushed through until he was out of sight. Turning his attention back to the scene in the farmyard, Logan continued evaluating the situation and his own escape and evasion options. He figured that he had about five minutes at most to make it out of Dodge, before all hell broke loose. While he had no definitive proof that this activity was aimed at him, he had long ago stopped believing in coincidences.

The police sure weren't getting anything out of that *'tubaozi'* from the farmhouse. He grinned despite the circumstances. *Tubaozi*, literally *dirt dumpling* in Chinese, was a term meant to describe a country hick. This guy sure fit the bill.

Returning to the question at hand, Logan reasoned that the volunteer himself might be a provocateur. Maybe the whole thing was a set-up designed to embarrass the U.S. But why would the Chinese give away the fact that they were having some success against U.S. cyber security?

No, it made more sense that if the MPS were behind this charade, they would allow the meeting to take place. Then, depending upon how it went down, the Chinese would have any number of options available to them, the most attractive being to run the asset as a double agent and feed disinformation to the CIA.

They might also try recruiting the American handler, biding their time until they had enough assessment data to determine how to finesse their pitch. That tactic had always been given a low probability of success, though, by most foreign security services because of the belief that CIA officers were impervious to recruitment pitches. That fiction had been put to rest in 1985 after CIA officer Edward Lee Howard defected to Russia. Russian successes against two other more senior CIA case officers, Aldrich Ames and Jim Nicholson, followed in the 1990s and further tarnished the Agency's reputation, leaving the impression that its officers could be purchased.

Logan began crawling south, away from where the policemen were milling around. It was crucial to put distance between him and what was going on down there. He'd scouted out an emergency egress route from overhead imagery when he'd planned for this meeting, but the one unknown had been where the volunteer would be coming from. And, more problematically, as it turned out, where he'd gone.

Until proven otherwise, his assumption must be that the volunteer was legitimate, and that the MPS presence had nothing to do with a planned provocation or ambush. That meant that he had to take every precaution to protect the volunteer's life, which would make his egress out of the area a bit tricky. Not knowing exactly where the volunteer had gone meant that they could still unintentionally cross paths. And with the area heated up, it was best that there be no contact between them, at least for now.

He'd continued moving south and soon a change in elevation shielded him from view of the security patrol. He rose, and set off at a six-minute-mile pace. As a SEAL he'd done this with a full rucksack and his weapon. Running without all of that gear to weigh him down, he moved without effort. The stink from the pigsty had filled his nostrils when he set off, but as he moved away, the strong smell dissipated and he was left with a not unpleasant earthy odor. He ran along the edge of the rutted road so that he could move to cover if the search party came his way. His breathing was easy and he concentrated on putting distance between him and the nerve-racking scene he'd just left behind.

After forty minutes of running at this pace he came to a major road, which he recognized from his earlier reconnaissance as Chongqing Ring Road. Traffic was light at this hour, but he managed to flag down a taxi heading in the direction of Chongqing center and told the driver to take him to the Chongqing New World Hotel.

"You mean the one on Congbai Road, over by the river?"

"Yes. The one built into the cliffs near the business center of town."

"All right. Where are you from? Are you American?" The cab driver was eyeing him suspiciously in the rear view mirror. There was a strong smell of garlic in the closed cab that made breathing unpleasant.

Logan was also having trouble with the driver's strong Bashu-accented Mandarin, but he was getting sixty percent of it. "Yes, American. I'm here on business."

"Business? What business brings you out here so early?"

Logan stuck with the cover story he had concocted before beginning his trip. "I build boats, and my company is scouting out a location for a boat yard near Chongqing. Anyway I like to see a place at all hours to get a good feeling for it before I make an investment. I hired a car to take me out here, but then the driver ran off and left me."

"Did you pay him first?"

Logan tried his best to look sheepish, and then admitted that he had. "Yes, he insisted that I pay him when I got out to have a look around."

"Did you tell him to wait for you?"

"Of course. I told him I'd only be five or ten minutes."

The driver cackled with barely suppressed glee. "You got screwed. How much did you pay him?"

Logan was irked by the obvious pleasure the driver was taking in his less than ideal circumstances. In the short time he'd been in Asia he knew that Chinese valued a bargain, and that they also were of the view that they were far superior to anyone else when it came to negotiating a deal.

"Two hundred *yuan*." China's currency is the *renminbi*, called RMB, which for years exchanged at the rate of eight-point-five to one U.S. dollar, but the word *yuan*, which is China's basic monetary unit, is more often used than RMB.

The driver did the mental calculation, and the smirk on his face told Logan what he was thinking.

They were approaching the Changjiang Bridge, which spans the Yangtze River in Chongqing. Outside the left window Logan could see the expansive International Convention and Exhibition Center. He made a mental note to stop in there while he was in Chongqing to reinforce his cover story.

A boat yard in Szechuan Province wasn't that farfetched a scenario for his cover business. The Yangtze River, known in Chinese as the Changjiang or "Long River," at roughly

4,000 miles in length, is the third longest river in the world and the longest in all of Asia. Originating in the Qinghai-Tibet Plateau, it flows through much of Szechuan and then east to Wuhan, not far from Shanghai. The area around Chongqing is popular with tourists, especially those looking for river cruises that take sightseers through the scenic Three Gorges, where towering peaks and ancient temples dot the landscape. With the boom in river tourism, Logan had a made-to-order cover story for his business.

His driver pulled up to the hotel and Logan hurried inside. It was almost seven-thirty a.m. and he had a lot to do to get ready for his back-up meeting later that night.

Chapter 2

Li Jiang barreled through the underbrush, forcing his way through the hedge. The MPS officer was panting from the exertion the short sprint to reach cover had cost him. Now, out of sight of his colleagues converging on the farm-house behind him, he paused to catch his breath and contemplate his next move.

He remembered the day he decided to offer his services to the Americans. It was a year ago, while leading his father's funeral procession down Shiyuan Street to the Martyrs' Cemetery. He'd been exhausted that day because the wake preceding the funeral had gone on for three days. White chrysanthemums and ornate banners had filled his parents' apartment and the white envelopes stuffed with cash had spilled over onto the floor.

Black-clad mourners filled the streets that morning, and his frail mother had clung to his arm as they walked the few blocks to the cemetery. He'd hired a local band to precede them on the funeral route to keep ghosts and spirits away from his father's coffin as he made his final journey. The band's shrill, clanging notes would do more than that, he remembered thinking. It was deafening enough to wake the dead.

His father had died in shame, months after Chongqing Communist Party chief Bo Xilai unceremoniously evicted him from the apartment he had shared with his wife of fifty-five years, during an anti-corruption campaign dubbed *Da Hei* or "Striking Black," Bo's popular crackdown against organized crime.

The problem was that his eighty-four-year-old father not only was not a crook, he was a war hero in his own right.

As an eighteen-year-old artilleryman in 1943, he had fought with "Vinegar Joe" Stilwell, the American general who, over a six-month period in 1943-1944, drove the Japanese Army out of Burma and opened up the Burma Road to China.

Stilwell had accomplished this despite his open hostility towards General Chiang Kai-shek, founding member of the Kuomingtang (KMT), who, during the second Sino-Japanese War, was named Supreme Commander of Allied Forces in China, and later went on to become President of the Republic of China.

Li's father had seen the writing on the wall though, and in 1945 had joined the Communist-backed People's Liberation Army, where he was assigned to the Central Plains Field Army. There he had the good fortune to become acquainted with a fellow Szechuan native, Deng Xiaoping, who at that time was the political commissar.

The elder Li distinguished himself during the Huaihai Campaign in 1948-1949, during which the PLA defeated the KMT forces, in large part contributing to Chiang Kai-shek's decision to abandon the mainland for Taiwan, where he set up his provisional government.

His father's relationship with Deng had served him well over the years, although the elder Li had never gained the level of national prominence that his mentor had. He had held a number of important positions in Szechuan before he retired in 2000 as the director of a research institute funded by the government, ensconced in one of Szechuan Province's premier institutions of higher learning, the Chongqing University of Posts and Telecommunications.

There was some commotion from the farmhouse behind him, and Li squinted in the early morning light to see what was happening. The police sergeant had braced the old man against a wall. He thrust his face inches from the farmer's, all the while barking orders at his subordinates. Two of them entered the hut with weapons drawn while the others set up a perimeter around the farmyard. The two who had gone in to search the building emerged moments later empty-handed except for their weapons.

Their report seemed to enrage the sergeant, who turned his venom on the old man. He backhanded him across the face, causing the old fellow to slump against the wall. When he straightened, trembling before his assailant, Li could see a stain spreading across the front of his pants and down his leg. The officer leapt back, castigating the old man as the others pointed and doubled over in laughter. In his fear, the peasant had pissed himself.

Li was close enough to read the contempt in the sergeant's eyes. He stood, legs apart, arms akimbo, surveying the scene around him. He spat at the feet of the old man, and slowly swiveled his head left to right, taking in the scene before him. He stood that way for a moment before snarling orders to his men to clear the area. Five minutes later they were gone, leaving only fear and dust in their wake.

Li waited for another thirty minutes before setting off across a flooded rice field. It was the most direct route to the place where he had concealed his bicycle, a Flying Pigeon relic that he'd owned for over a decade. Despite his senior rank as a superintendent, 2nd grade in the MPS's Chongqing office of the PSB, his income was modest and although he enjoyed certain perks at work, he lived frugally.

He cursed his bad luck as he slogged through the paddy. A thick fog was settling in and as it enveloped the area it made it nearly impossible for him to see. Soon he was navigating by feel alone. He'd grown up in Chongqing, and was familiar with many of the villages and townships in the sub-districts that surrounded the city. At this point he was less concerned about getting lost than stumbling into the police patrol or someone else who might question what he was doing out at this hour.

Li lurched, nearly losing his footing as he emerged from the rice field. He was an unassuming figure, with angular features and delicate hands. His teeth were nicotine stained and a dark mole presided over his bushy left eyebrow. Despite his humble demeanor, Li possessed great physical courage, bolstered, in this case, by the strength of his convictions.

He had not confided his plans for the evening to his wife, Xiao Mei. She and their son were visiting her grandmother for the weekend, and he had determined not to burden her with the knowledge of his treachery. She would be furious with him for putting their family at risk. Xiao Mei was a statistics professor at Yangtze Normal University and had recently been nominated to chair the Wujiang Economic and Cultural Research Center.

Li found his bike where he had left it, and paused to brush himself off before beginning the long slog back into town. He was beginning to wonder if all of this was a mistake. He had bided his time following his father's fall from grace, plotting his revenge so that there would be no direct association between his actions and the attack by Bo and his clique against his father.

The fog began to lift as the sun rose, brightening his dampened spirits. He was still shaken by the events of the past two hours and as he pedaled homeward his mind was churning over what he had witnessed. What about the American? Had he been there, concealed somewhere in the shadows? There had been no sign of him at the meeting site. Just as well, he reasoned. If the foreigner had blundered into the police patrol it would be all over, especially with that brute of a squad leader in charge. His treatment of the farmer had been despicable. Li shuddered. He could only imagine how he would have handled a traitor.

How could the PSB have found out about his meeting? He felt certain that he had not been observed slipping the letter into the car of the official from the consulate. And he suspected that China had not cracked America's sensitive diplomatic communications, their recent success against the Secretary of State notwithstanding. Besides, the CIA had a reputation for being professional. They would have recognized right away what he was offering and would have rushed to secure it.

And then it hit him. He remembered a Signals Intelligence (SIGINT) report that had crossed his desk two weeks ago. The SIGINT dispatch documented plans by a cell of Uighurs from Xinjiang Province, believed to have been trained by Al Qaeda, who were attempting to establish a network of supporters within greater China. The MPS had disseminated the report to PSB police tactical units nation-wide, and he had heard back informally that the PSB and the People's Armed Police (PAP) were planning to conduct surprise raids in neighborhoods that they suspected might be sympathetic to the Muslim extremists' agenda.

Li felt his body relax as the memory sank in. While he didn't have definitive proof that the police raid was part of this anti-Uighur campaign, he was increasingly confi-dent that it had nothing to do with his meeting with the Americans.

He began pedaling with greater purpose back into the city. He would be at the back-up meeting site tonight. And, with any luck, the American CIA officer would be there too.

Chapter 3

Desmond Magarity (Des to his friends) drained his draft, grabbed a handful of peanuts in his beefy paw and shoved them into his face. He wiped his mouth with the back of his sleeve and burped with pleasure as he scanned the room. The Emerald Lounge was a dive in Springfield, Virginia, off Backlick Road. The smoking bar was buzzing and a handful of people were beginning to trickle into the non-smoking dining room. It was Des's home away from home.

He was a dying breed of FBI agent, being third generation and all. His grandfather had joined the force under Mr. Hoover himself, working bootlegging and smuggling matters out of the Chicago Field Office during prohibition. He'd regaled young Des with stories of the criminal cases he'd worked on, the most famous being the arrest and conviction of Al Capone, nicknamed Scarface.

Grandpa had been the first FBI agent on the scene of the St. Valentine's Day Massacre, where Capone's gang allegedly machine-gunned seven members of the rival Bugs Moran gang in 1929. The victims were slaughtered at the SMC Cartage Company, a warehouse owned by Moran.

Even though the Feds had given their best shot to get a conviction for the killings, they weren't able to pin the attack on Capone. It wasn't until two years later that they finally nailed him on tax evasion charges.

Des chuckled as he recalled the time in high school, when the old man had warned him off of premarital sex. He'd told Des that Capone, known as Old Scarface, had been promiscuous all his life and had died of neurosyphillis. His bushy eyebrows had come together as his eyes bored into Des's.

15

"You keep your pecker in your pants, boy, and you'll keep your wits about you," he'd admonished.

Des had heeded his grandfather's advice. He channeled all his youthful testosterone into sports. He'd wrestled and played football in high school and then, just like the old man and his father, he'd gone on to Notre Dame, where he did more heavy lifting in the bars around South Bend than in Hesburgh Library.

He hadn't been good enough to play in the house that Rockne built, but he did wrestle for the Fighting Irish while they still had a wrestling program. He managed to maintain a three-point-zero GPA, and that, coupled with his family legacy, had been enough to gain him a slot in the 1977 New Agent training class at Quantico, Virginia, home of the FBI Academy.

At Notre Dame he'd overlapped his junior and senior years with Rudy Ruettiger, who went on to become a football legend for the Fighting Irish. Still, the tenacious little bastard hadn't fared so well after college, Des ruminated as he signaled the bartender for another beer.

"Hey, Moe. You remember that Rudy fellow? Played football for Notre Dame? You know, the one they made the movie about?"

"Yeah, Rudy. What about him?" Moe slid the frothy lager across the bar and lazily wiped away a wet spot.

Des raised the glass and took a long draw. He set the glass down, burped again, and leaned forward on his arms. "After all the awards, the movie, honorary degrees, he goes and commits securities fraud," Des scoffed.

"No! I didn't know that."

"Yep. SEC nailed his ass for almost $400,000 dollars in fines. Little scammer didn't have to do time, but it cost him a bundle."

"Man, why'd you have to tell me that? I watched that movie with my kid. You know, to motivate him."

"I'll motivate him," Des growled.

Moe moved away to tend to another customer.

"You're such a hard ass, Des. You gotta lighten up."

"Yeah, yeah," Des grumbled.

"Trouble with parents today is you're too soft on your kids." His phone vibrated and he squinted in the dim light to read the text message.

"Where are you?" It was from his deputy, Rick Wheeler.

"Moe's place," he texted back.

"You alone? I'm five minutes out. Need to talk to you."

"All right. See you in five."

Five minutes later Rick slid into the booth that Des had moved to and signaled to Moe for a draft.

"We got problems."

"What?" For the past three weeks Des had been working a Chinese cyber security case for Cyber Division out of the Washington Field Office (WFO). Rick had played point for him in setting up an undercover operation out of a safehouse in Arlington, Virginia. They had brought in a team of computer security analysts to try and identify the server in China behind an apparent cyber attack on the Secretary of State.

"I got a call from one of my contacts at Langley. They heard from their man in China. It seems he was about to make the meeting with their volunteer when company showed up. A whole squad of PSB goons crashed the meeting site, just before he was going to establish contact."

Des's eyebrows shot up and he let out a low whistle. "Son of a bitch. What happened to them?"

"There weren't a lot of details. But it seems as though the case officer and the volunteer were both at the meeting site. The C/O hadn't established contact up to that point because he was waiting to make sure the coast was clear. He was just about to go for it when the cops showed up. He never exposed himself to the volunteer, but he was able to watch him leave the area without coming to their attention. Then he hightailed it out of there himself without being seen."

Des toyed with his empty glass while he chewed on his lower lip, thinking it through. What a goat rope, he thought to himself. Leave it to the CIA to make his life difficult. He'd been hoping that the volunteer was the real deal and that

17

they'd get some additional insights into who was behind the hacking operation. Of course this never would have happened in the first place if those idiot staffers at the State Department hadn't opened up the infected emails.

"So what's next?"

"Wait and see. The C/O's supposed to have another shot at this guy within twenty-four hours. He couldn't explain the presence of the PSB at the meeting site. But there's no way it was just a coincidence. From the way the volunteer cleared out of there, though, it didn't seem like he was part of the set-up, if that's what it was. He looked nervous, according to the C/O."

Des looked at his watch. "You want to get something to eat?"

"No. Marge is expecting me. You want to come over for dinner?"

Des looked at his deputy with sympathy. Despite his own Catholic upbringing, he wasn't a big believer in the sacrament of marriage. Three trips to the altar in thirty years and nothing left to show for it but three hostile exes, two sullen daughters, and a son that wouldn't talk to him. Oh, yeah, and an empty bank account.

"Nah, go ahead. Tomorrow we need to start thinking about breaking down the safe house in Arlington. I have a sneaking suspicion that if we ever do meet this guy in China we're going to need a whole lot more than one measly undercover op to put the screws to the Chinese.

"I'm thinking we need to leverage the NCCIC on this." The National Cybersecurity and Communications Integration Center was run 24/7 by the Department of Homeland Security, the DHS.

"We should be joined at the hip," Des said. "Working with them, we ought to be able to get ahead of the next attack. You know, go on the offensive instead of waiting for them to stick it to us."

The problem was that the U.S. always seemed to be playing catch-up when it came to protecting its cyber infrastructure. The nation's love affair with the Internet and the prevalence of computers at every level of society had created a perfect storm waiting to happen.

It used to be, when personal computers first came out, that they were strictly desktops. Now every Tom, Dick and Harry with a smartphone had a computer in his hand, sometimes with multiple Internet accounts linked back to laptops, tablets and desktops at home and work.

And then the perfect storm did hit, on September 11, 2001, when Al Qaeda terrorists were able to coordinate their horrendous attacks from locations inside U.S. borders. Security and law enforcement were caught flat-footed because the tools to mitigate those kinds of risk weren't yet in place.

Following the attacks, President George Bush created the first "cyber czar" position in the government, naming Richard Clarke to the position of special advisor to the President on Cybersecurity. The emphasis in the early days was on securing national infrastructure from threats of terrorism and cyber attacks. The President's advisors had told him that as bad as the bombing of the World Trade Center had been, with the tragic loss of so many innocents, it would have been catastrophic if cyber terrorists had taken out the U.S. banking system, or destroyed the power grid.

Over the next decade the White House and national security agencies made every effort to secure the nation's critical infrastructure and in the process went through a succession of cyber czars. The focus these days was on getting the private sector on board with the government's Cybersecurity Framework, a plan that emphasized standards and practices that would lessen the risk to the nation's critical infrastructure from hostile cyber attacks.

"I want you to set up a meeting tomorrow morning with Jim Baylow over at NCCIC's Computer Emergency Readiness Team," Des said. "We need to find out if they're tracking any other Chinese hacking cases. Things have gone kind of quiet with them since that meeting we had last month."

"Who do you want to go?"

"Just me. No, wait a minute." Des thought for a moment. "Tell that new analyst that just transferred in from Kansas City, what's her name? Lois. Yeah. Lois Caldwell. Have her come by my office in the morning and we'll take a car over there. I want her to meet Baylow's team."

Des had pegged Caldwell as a real talent when he first met her last week. With a master's in computer science from MIT, she had geek written all over her. She was smart, and he had a feeling they were going to need all the smarts they could muster on this one.

Chapter 4

Logan was eight hours into his second surveillance detection run in as many days. Doubts about the fiasco before dawn this morning had been gnawing at him all afternoon. Trust the tradecraft, his surveillance instructors had drilled into him during training. And he had, during endless hours of practice exercises, where he had gone up against some of the best. But no matter how good you thought you were, there was always a nagging doubt that you had missed something, had failed to detect your adversary.

In surveillance detection you have to force the enemy to show his hand, in a sophisticated game of cat and mouse. Who's the prey and who's the predator? Logan liked to think of himself as the latter, a wolf on the prowl. He was stealthy and he owned the street. He had learned how to manipulate surveillance, to force its hand, but never in a grotesque, heavy-handed way, rather in a lulling courtship where the opposition comes to believe that he was innocence itself.

But now he had to make a critical decision. All afternoon and evening he'd been on the run, in a carefully orchestrated scenario, cataloging events, and memorizing a jigsaw puzzle of vehicle descriptions, license plate numbers and images of suspects. As he rode through the early evening dusk he was dissecting every anomaly, asking himself if anything he'd experienced was aimed at him, or was simply part of Chongqing's natural rhythm. It was a city of 31 million after all.

He exited the metro at the Xiaoshenzi Station and walked west on Datong Street. It was humid, and a thin sheen of perspiration was smeared across his skin. The light windbreaker he wore clung to his otherwise bare arms. At seven o'clock, the street churned with throngs of shoppers and workers returning home from their jobs. As he put distance between him and the metro station, the crowds began to thin out and he breathed more easily, knowing that fewer people on the street would make it easier for him to determine if he was truly "black," that is, surveillance-free.

If he had the slightest doubt, he'd call off the meeting, go back to his hotel and book a flight to Hong Kong as soon as possible. But if he *was* black, he'd have several more hours of work to do before he committed to the meeting site. The hardest part was staying black. It meant having minimal one-on-one contact with people inclined to report their spotting of a foreigner, where he had no business being, to the authorities. He had to steer clear of security cameras and hot spots.

Logan walked through a narrow passageway to an open-air market, taking in a cacophony of sounds and images in a glance. Mounds of fresh noodles in bamboo baskets, sheets of dried bean curd and rows of dumplings vied for space with stalls displaying heaps of golden apples, tamarinds and dragon fruit.

He cut behind a kiosk where a barber was busy cleaning a customer's ears, tuning forks, feathers, scoops and knives, laid out on a small table beside him.

As he moved past the market, Logan crossed an alley, walked a hundred meters and came out on a narrow lane. He gave a hard look behind him, scrutinizing the few pedestrians walking there, none of whom seemed the slightest bit interested in him. He was black. Removing his windbreaker and donning a cap, he walked for ten more minutes, emerging finally on Minzu Road, where he flagged down a taxi. Twenty minutes later he had the driver drop him off near the south gate to Fotuguan Park.

As the taxi drove away Logan hurried into the park. He searched for a secluded area off one of the main trails and, once there, conducted the first of what would be three clothing changes. Stripping off his pullover he removed a long-sleeved cotton shirt from his backpack, followed by a pair of hiking shorts and sneakers. He finished changing and stuffed the clothing he had removed into his pack. He was certain that no one had followed him into the park, but these extra precautions were his insurance policy.

Four hours and two more clothing changes later, he stood in the shadows, not far from the rear entrance to the Fortune Garden Duck Restaurant. The establishment was closed and the alley deserted, but Logan still felt conspicuous standing there in the dark.

It was eleven forty-five and he had fifteen minutes before the meeting. He used the time to review his agenda. He and the volunteer would need a good cover story in the event they were seen together or worse yet, stopped by public security. He didn't know enough about the man to concoct anything that would hold up under scrutiny, so for now the explanation of a casual encounter would have to do.

He had a whole laundry list of things he needed to find out, but they wouldn't have much time to get through it. Fifteen, twenty minutes max. Any more than that and they'd be inviting the prying eyes of passers-by, or worse yet, security patrolling the neighborhood.

Logan was on high alert as he spotted a shadowy figure turning into the alley. He didn't have a description of the volunteer and last night's sighting didn't give him much to work with. Besides that, there had been no way to establish oral *bona fides* to ensure that he was talking to the right person. It was a good thing the alley was otherwise empty, because a false move could ruin everything.

As the person drew closer, Logan saw that it was a man, perhaps in his late forties to early fifties. He was of average height and on the thin side. He hesitated as he approached Logan, who had stepped out of the shadows so that he would be able to see him more clearly.

The man spoke first in Bashu-accented Mandarin.

"Do you speak Chinese?"

"Yes, some."

"Where are you from?" The man glanced nervously behind him.

"I'm from the U.S." Logan wanted to hear something more definitive before revealing anything else, but decided that he would have to lead with something.

"Do you know anything about the G-20 meetings in Europe?"

The man visibly relaxed and replied, "I do know something about the EU's economic options for Asia."

Bingo. He had referred to something the volunteer had specifically addressed in his letter.

"We got your message. But just to make sure, can you tell me where you left this information?"

"Yes, of course. I wrote a letter that I put through the window of a U.S. Consulate vehicle a few weeks ago. My name is Li."

"You can call me Logan. Nice to meet you, Mr. Li. Let's keep walking down this alley so we don't attract too much attention. How much time do you have?"

"My wife is out of town for the weekend visiting her grandmother, so there's no rush."

"How'd you get here tonight?"

"I rode my bicycle. It's parked nearby."

"What happened yesterday?"

"Oh, so you were there? I was worried when the PSB patrol showed up. I didn't see you there but I was glad because it would complicate things if they had spotted you."

Good instincts, Logan thought. "That reminds me, if anyone should question us tonight we should just tell them that we met on the street and I was asking you if Chongqing is a good place for foreigners to do business.

"So what did happen with that patrol?"

"It was bad luck that they were there. We had reporting that Muslim Uighurs might be making trouble in this area. The PSB and PAP planned to respond by conducting random spot checks in suspect areas. I think that's what it was."

A couple turned into the alley and began walking towards them. Logan held his finger to his lips and did not speak until they had passed by. His Chinese was pretty good but his foreign accent would be a giveaway. When they were alone again he continued.

"We were surprised to receive your letter. What made you decide to contact us?"

"It's a long story. Perhaps someday I will share it with you. Let's just say for now that the Chinese government is corrupt and they've hurt many people who deserve better. My father was one of those people."

Logan had been planning to get to the bottom of Li's decision to volunteer. His motivation appeared to be revenge for his father's mistreatment at the hands of the Chinese government.

He'd take revenge as a motivator any day. People volunteered to the Agency for any number of reasons – greed, ideology, thrills, and need were a few of the more common. But revenge, sweet revenge, was best. With the avengers it always seemed that the need for revenge was proportionate to the hurt that had been inflicted, if not on them personally, then on a loved one. And China was rife with corruption, so revenge was not an uncommon motivator.

"You mentioned that you were in the Ministry of Public Security."

"Public Security Bureau."

Logan whistled to himself. Langley had never succeeded in recruiting a senior PSB officer. If Li were for real, it would be significant. He knew that since the late 1970s there had been limited cooperation between the U.S. and the Chinese, and that as recently as the 2008 Olympics in Beijing, China and the U.S. had worked together to make sure that security for the Olympics was bullet proof. He'd done a little research on the PSB and had discovered that there were over 1.9 million police officers, under the auspices of the MPS, nationwide.

These officers worked in a variety of areas, such as national security, border control, criminal investigations, counter terrorism, economic crime, and a host of other mundane police functions. Washington suspected, and hoped that Li could confirm, that within the national security portfolio, the MPS had set up a Cyber Security unit.

Logan hadn't really followed the MPS and its subordinate units, but he knew that there was a big difference between a sanctioned liaison relationship with the police and a penetration of the MPS. While you couldn't always be sure your agent was giving you everything he knew, it was a given that your police contacts weren't.

Li drew a pack of cigarettes from his pocket and offered one to Logan.

"No, thanks."

Li tugged one out of the pack, lit it and took a long drag. He looked tense as he exhaled. "Yes, Logan. I'm the head of a PSB tactical unit in Chongqing."

Logan did his best to maintain a neutral expression as they meandered through the alley. They had just passed the rear of a fish market and the stench from the waste nearly gagged him.

"You know, your information caused quite a stir in Washington."

"I thought it might, but it's just the tip of the iceberg. We have many programs, some of them so compartmented that even I don't know the full extent of their activity." He reached into his pocket and withdrew a thumb drive, which he held up for Logan to examine.

"I'm going to give this to you. It's very technical, and unless you're a specialist, it won't mean anything to you. Give it to your analysts. They will understand."

"How did you obtain it?"

"This describes one of the programs my office is responsible for. I took it from our internal files, removing all the classification and office designations. It's classified 'Top Secret.'"

"Can you tell me what unit you're in?"

"I thought you might ask. On that thumb drive there's a photo of my PSB ID card. It has my picture, name and office designation. That should help your analysts figure out where I fit in. So you'll know, I head up a special cyber task force that is subordinate to a PSB Tactical Unit headquartered in Chengdu."

They had come to the end of the alley and Logan wanted to wrap it up. He and Li had been walking for fifteen minutes and he didn't want to push his luck. But he needed to figure out how he was going to re-contact Li and whether he was even amenable to continued contact.

"There's a lot more I'd like to ask you, but it's not safe for us to meet like this. We don't have an office in Chengdu or Chongqing. Do you have any possibility of travel abroad?"

"Not normally, but something just came up last week. I will be going to Bangkok in two weeks as part of a cyber crimes delegation. You know that China and Thailand have enjoyed a close security relationship since the late 1980s. We've conducted joint training and now our minister is interested in expanding this to joint operations during these training exercises."

"Do you know the dates you'll be there?"

"Three days, 27-30 September. Our delegation will be staying at the Sheraton Hotel. These are just planning meetings. We won't be doing any actual operations in the field."

"Will you have any free time?"

"I think so. There will be at least one banquet one evening and possibly a return banquet from the other side. I am the senior officer from our side, so I will have some flexibility about our schedule. But we must be careful."

Logan made a quick decision. "I'll be in Bangkok to meet you. After you check in to the hotel, locate a house phone away from the lobby to find out what room I'm in. Ask for Logan Crowley. I'll be there waiting for you." Logan decided that he would check into the Sheraton in his Crowley alias. It would be safer for him and Li if he didn't reveal his true identity.

"One more thing. Is there anything you need? Anything I can do for you?" This was touchy. Logan had cash to pass to Li if he needed it. He'd brought $5,000 to give him, and he wanted to let him know that there was more where that came from.

"No. I have everything I need. I'll see you in Bangkok."

The two men shook hands, and Li departed first, taking a right out of the alley. Logan waited a few minutes for him to clear the area and then turned left, walking thirty minutes until he hailed a passing taxi to take him back to his hotel.

Chapter 5

Frank Sisler finished studying Logan's readout from the initial meeting with Li Jiang. Picking up the report, he walked down the hall to Ellen Sanders' office. Ellen was one of the smartest Cyber analysts working the China account at Langley. In her early sixties, she knew more about the structure of China's public security apparatus than most people had forgotten. She was a national treasure and he was lucky enough to have her working for him.

Frank was no slouch either. He had made a name for himself as a young cyber sleuth in the early '90s when he helped the CIA build its espionage case against Jim Nicholson. The Russians had recruited Nicholson, a turncoat CIA operations officer, during an assignment to Kuala Lumpur. At the time he was the highest-ranking CIA officer ever recruited. The damage he did to the Agency was irreparable.

He closed the door and tossed the report onto Ellen's desk.

"Have you seen this yet?"

Ellen looked up from the file she was reviewing. She had been diagnosed with breast cancer earlier in the year and had just completed an aggressive regimen of chemo. As tough as it had been on her, she had wasted no time getting back in the saddle, even though Frank had encouraged her to recuperate for as long as she needed. She was thin, and her pale complexion and hollowed face belied the intelligence behind deep violet eyes. Work had been her antidote, her *raison d'être*. It fueled the drive that had made her a legend in Cyber Division and earned her praise from across the intelligence community and even the White House.

Glancing at Logan's report, she handed it back to him. "Read it first thing this morning. It was at the top of my queue. Seems that our Mr. Alexander has a live one on his hands."

"Maybe. What did you think about the PSB patrol showing up at the meeting site? I think it reeks of a set-up. Think it was a trap?"

Ellen rummaged around on her desk until she found what she was looking for. "Here, take a look at this. That was my initial thought too. But I did a little research and came across this. It's not definitive but it does track with what Li told Logan."

Frank took the report from her, sat down and began reading. It was a SIGINT intercept from China's Ministry of Public Security requesting that regional Public Security Bureaus and People's Armed Police units initiate spot checks throughout the rural Muslim communities in Szechuan Province thought to be sympathetic to Uighur activists. The report was dated ten days ago.

"The Hui minority is the biggest Muslim group in Szechuan, but I'm not sure that anyone has linked them to Uighur extremism. And the Huangsheng Mosque in Chengdu is active, but again I haven't seen anything indicating they're conspiring with the Uighurs." Ellen reached into a drawer safe next to her desk and pulled out a folder.

"I was going over the first report we had from Li. When he dropped his letter into the RSO's car in Chengdu. Do you think it's possible the PSB picked up on him from the get-go?"

"There's a lot we don't know. Is Li already on their radar for something going on in his life? He seems desperate to make contact with us. We don't know how he targeted the RSO's vehicle in the first place or what kind of precautions he took when he collected the info he provided. We don't even know if anyone saw him put the letter in the car and reported it to the authorities.

"One thing I feel pretty comfortable about though is how his information was handled once the RSO got it. I remember briefing him personally on the security threat in China before he transferred to Chengdu last year. We even talked about how to handle something like this. He would have taken the letter right into the Consulate and secure faxed it to us," Frank said.

"Let's put together a laundry list of questions for Logan to ask Li if he does show up for the meeting in Bangkok. Li looks like the real deal, but we need to make sure he hasn't been compromised from the outset, or worse yet, isn't playing us."

"You mean something like this?"

Ellen pulled a three-page questionnaire from a folder on her desk and handed it to him. Frank perused the questions and shook his head in admiration.

"You must have been reading my mind."

"Come on, Frank. Just say it."

"Okay, Ellen. You're brilliant, just brilliant."

She beamed as he walked out of the office. Calling back over his shoulder he said, "I have a ten o'clock briefing with the DDO, to talk about next steps. Why don't you come with me?"

"All right. I'll come by your office and we can go up together."

* * *

Meanwhile, Lois Caldwell was schooling Des, on their way over to NCCIC for a nine o'clock meeting with Jim Baylow. She gave him a rundown of her graduate work at MIT's Electrical Engineering and Computer Science (EECS) Department. He was beginning to regret having asked her what she had studied.

"I was in the Communication and Network Group at EECS."

"What was your field?"

"Optical communications systems and networks."

Des suppressed a yawn and feigned interest he did not feel.

"Did you have to do a thesis?"

"Yes. I developed a new set of algorithms to enhance vertex connectivity on networks."

Des scrunched up his eyes and gave her a dubious look. Maybe it had been a mistake to bring her with him. She sounded like a real egghead, one of those ivory tower types. He'd talked to the special agent in charge at the Kansas City Field Office when her application to work for Cyber Division in Washington had come in. Kansas City had nothing but high praise for her. She was a team player and got along with pretty much everyone.

"You're kidding me, right? I don't even know what that means."

"My idea was to see if I could develop new communication protocols that would boost bandwidth across networks. Take the Bureau for example. There's a need for more and more bandwidth here every day. By enhancing vertex connectivity it might be possible to eliminate bandwidth limitations."

"What good would that be?"

"We could improve our workflow, handle more data, and increase efficiency."

"That's all good. But let's take a step back. What the heck is vertex connectivity?"

"Okay. Are you familiar with graph theory?"

Des sighed, and admitted that he was not.

"In computer science we use graphs to depict the relationship between nodes and edges. The study of these is called graph theory."

"That's great, but what are nodes and edges?"

"It's an abstract way for mathematicians to look at objects that are connected. On a graph these are called vertices and the links that connect them are called edges.

"We can use graphs to map out networks, depict how data is managed and so on. For example, a more detailed network graph might include things like all of the equipment on the network, like computers, servers, and printers." Lois was warming to her subject.

"When you look at this relationship between vertices and edges, two variants come into play – edge connectivity and vertex connectivity."

"All right, you're losing me again."

Lois looked out the passenger window, took a deep breath and continued.

"Basically what you're trying to understand with these numbers is how many edges or vertices can be removed from the network before it fails. A lot of work has been done in the area of edge connectivity over the years, but not as much on vertex connectivity."

Des guided the black Ford Taurus onto Interstate 395 south and minutes later exited onto Washington Boulevard in Arlington. Traffic in and around the District was a nightmare, but Des knew his way around.

The Cybersecurity Operations Center was located in a commercial office building in Arlington. It had been constructed in just ninety days in 2009 when DHS decided it needed to get serious about the increasing number of cyber attacks against government and private sector computer networks.

A protective security officer checked their credentials at the entrance to the parking garage and directed Des to a VIP parking spot, one of the perks of being a member of the Bureau's Senior Executive Service.

Moments later they were being welcomed into the operations center. It was Lois's first visit to the NCCIC, and Jim Baylow began by showing her around.

"Des, good to see you again. Lois, nice to meet you. Welcome to the NCCIC. We're standing in the heart of the ops center. Along this front wall you see half a dozen screen and monitor arrays."

Lois looked around. The operations center had the shape and feel of a small amphitheater, its dimly lit expanse offering clear views of two large rear-projected screens on the front wall, with smaller screens and monitors strategically located for easy viewing. These displayed different graphs, data streams, news feeds and a banner indicating the current threat level: YELLOW.

A dozen semicircular rows ascended toward the upper reaches of the amphitheater, each having a half-dozen workstations complete with swivel chairs and double monitors enclosed within consoles. The entire scene resembled NASA's flight control center, only nicer.

"What kind of data feeds do you get?" Lois asked.

"We can pull feeds from the National Cybersecurity Center, other federal cyber centers, DHS's Office of Intelligence, and private industry. When we were set up, the idea was to integrate cyber security efforts across the government and the private sector. Everything you see is real time."

"Very impressive."

"The Secretary's vision was to create a unified operations center. One where there would be seamless interoperability between all the participants."

Baylow led them into his office. Two analysts from the Internet Traffic Inspection analytic team joined them.

Des had warned Lois not to mention the source of the information behind their hacking investigation to Baylow. At CIA's request, the FBI was playing that card close to the vest. Meeting a volunteer inside China was risky, especially for the volunteer, and the fewer people who knew about him, the less chance that he would be compromised.

"Lois is going to be working China cyber for us and I wanted to bring her over and introduce her to you." Des took a sip of coffee from the Styrofoam cup in front of him.

"She's been going over everything we have on the attack against Sec State. I thought a fresh set of eyes would be good." Des shrugged. He'd been baffled by the persistence of the Chinese attack and how easily they had penetrated their target.

"After the Chinese figured out somebody was on to them they went quiet. They got in, got what they wanted and then shut it down. When they want to I'm sure they'll pop up somewhere else."

"Are you aware of the scale of Chinese hacking against the U.S.?" Baylow asked them.

"I know it's a lot, but it's not something I've followed. We got called into this because the attack was against Sec State."

Lois piped up. "I remember reading somewhere that the

Chinese are stealing hundreds, maybe even thousands of terabytes of data a year."

"I don't even know what a terabyte is," Des growled.

"Tera is the fourth power of 1,000," one of Baylow's analysts replied. Des cast him a withering look.

"One terabyte," Lois continued, "is one trillion bytes. That's a trillion bytes of U.S. intellectual property, proprietary information from American businesses, defense contractors, and think tanks, not to mention the government, going out the back door every year.

"Some economists estimate that we lost over $300 billion last year just from Chinese cyber hacking."

Des frowned. The number was so big he was having trouble getting his arms around it.

"That answers one question we came over to see you about."

"What's that?" Baylow asked.

"I'm trying to visualize this thing. You know, how big is it?"

"China's cyber-hacking efforts are systematic and pervasive. They're so voracious they make a school of piranhas look like a bunch of guppies. Mark my words. If we don't figure this out and put a stop to it, one day we'll be facing a cataclysmic attack," Baylow said. "You remember when Iran's nuclear program got shut down?"

"You mean Operation Stuxnet?" Lois asked.

"Yeah. Imagine an attack on that scale against our transportation system, water supply, satellites, banking system, energy, you name it."

Des looked grim. "They could take us out."

"It's not a matter of could," Baylow said. "Unless we get our arms around this, it's just a matter of when."

Chapter 6

Logan, Norm Stoddard and Bruce Wellington led the pack in the Saturday morning Hash House Harriers run. The Hash is an international running club with chapters everywhere runners congregate. The three-mile round-trip stretch between Magazine Gap Road and Happy Valley is flat, giving runners a breather before taking on the grueling climb to Victoria Peak.

Known as "the Peak" by locals, Victoria Peak is home to the city's most exclusive neighborhood, offering stunning vistas of Hong Kong Harbor and Kowloon far below.

Stoddard and Wellington were former Special Forces operators Logan had recruited five years earlier to destroy a terrorist training camp in Bandar Deylam, Iran, after terrorists from the camp killed his younger brother, Cooper, in an IED attack in Iraq. Also on that team was Zahir Parandeh, the team's interpreter, who later went on to marry Logan.

The incursion into Iran had been a success by all accounts, but a year later, following an exposé on Iran's role in international terrorism in the *Wall Street Journal*, assassins from Unit 400, an elite Qods Force hit team, retaliated by killing team member Hamid Al Subaie, son of a Kuwaiti billionaire.

After the Qods Force killed Hamid, Logan's team mounted an operation to track down the assassin. Following an exhaustive search on three continents, things came to a head when the killer surfaced in Boston, where he was killed in a shootout at Logan's office.

After the dust settled, Logan planned to put all of his energy into building up his new company, Alexander Maritime Consulting, but a funny thing happened to change his plans.

William Channing Jr. from the CIA's Directorate of Operations showed up on his doorstep with a compelling offer.

The Agency had figured out that Logan and his team were behind the Bandar Deylam attack and the operation against the Unit 400 assassins. During a follow-up meeting in Washington, Channing pitched a concept to Logan designed to tackle some of the Agency's toughest problems.

The idea was to use Alexander Maritime Consulting as a CIA front company. Channing's concept, however, went way beyond that of a run-of-the-mill non-official cover operation.

"The idea is a field office on steroids, a company that can do legitimate business in the real world, but if necessary, has personnel with the requisite paramilitary skills if we need them," he'd said.

"Covert action?" Logan asked.

"Yes. Sometimes the President needs the flexibility to conduct military-type operations when it's in our national interest, without committing boots on the ground.

"The way your team went after the Qods Force is a perfect example. You went in, got the job done and had complete deniability."

Logan had said yes after talking it over with Zahir. It had taken them three years to pull it together, with training at CIA covert facilities around the country, Chinese language studies and area familiarization. Wellington, Stoddard and Logan's secretary, Alicia, had also readily signed up when Logan pitched the idea to them.

Logan put on a burst of speed as he neared the Peak. The last time they had run this route the "rabbit" who laid out the trail had left a very subtle chalk mark on a restaurant wall showing the way and it had taken the group fifteen minutes to get back on track.

"Where the hell did he leave it?" Stoddard grumbled as he searched near Lugard Road.

"On, on!" The telltale shout came from another runner who had found the sign pointing the way down Pok Fu Lam Reservoir Road.

Logan and the others set off down the wooded path after him at a moderate pace. When they reached Pok Fu Lam Country Park minutes later, Logan spotted the "rabbit" standing next to an ice chest of cold beers, the signal that the run was over and the drinking was about to begin. He was an Aussie and he'd stocked the cooler with an assortment of his favorite brews.

Logan mopped the sweat off of his face, snagged an icy Fosters from the cooler and wandered over to where Stoddard stood taking in the view.

"You all set for your trip to Bangkok?"

Logan looked around to make sure no one was within earshot.

"I think so. I've got all of headquarters' requirements. They really want this guy."

"What do you think? Is he the real deal?"

Logan thought back to his meeting with Li. "I'm going to go out on a limb and say yes. We've got a lot of ground to cover with him though."

"The analysts were pretty impressed with the info on the thumb drive he gave you." Wellington stripped off his tee shirt and used it to mop his face.

"I know. They're still scrambling to translate everything. They were meeting with NSA and DHS to compare notes on the MPS's Cyber capabilities.

"Li claims that China has reorganized its Cyber program, and that because the MPS is so pervasive in Chinese society, at the national, regional and district levels, it has an enlarged role in all of this, even in areas like cyber network exploitation, which they never used to do."

"So they're like the FBI?"

"Not entirely. I'm not sure if there's a direct equivalent. They've co-opted a lot of rogue cyber groups to work for them."

"Where are you going to meet him?"

"At the Sheraton in Bangkok. That's where his delegation's staying."

"Isn't that risky?"

"It's not the best-case scenario, but he's not going to be able to break away for a meeting outside. He'll come to my room."

"Did you give Bangkok a heads-up?"

"Yeah. They already knew about the delegation. They have a penetration inside the Thai police that told them about this new relationship with the Chinese.

"Their guy's going to be in on the meetings with the Chinese delegation, so they'll get the take from that."

Stoddard looked thoughtful. "Maybe their asset will tell us something useful about your man."

"I thought about that. Obviously we can't task him because that would show our hand, but we can have his contact ask him general questions about the members of the delegation and get his take. We can also use it as a chance to vet Li's reporting on their meetings with the Thais too."

"Who in the office there knows about Li?"

"Just the chief. He may bring in his deputy, but it's supposed to be close hold."

Stoddard leaned forward to stretch out a cramped hamstring and noticed Wellington chatting up a leggy blond.

"Check out Bruce."

Logan glanced in the direction Stoddard pointed and could see Bruce talking to one of the female runners.

"She's cute."

"Yeah. I think Bruce wants to ask her out. She's Swedish. Works for a telecom company."

"Ericsson?"

"Yeah, I think that's it."

Bruce finished his conversation with the woman and made his way over to where Logan and Norm were standing.

"Hey, guys."

"Hey, Bruce. Who's your friend?"

"Adèle. She's Swedish, and a heck of a runner. She's done six marathons in Europe. Said she's only been in Hong Kong for a couple of months. We're going out for Mongolian barbecue tonight."

"Nice. You taking her to Nomads?"

Yeah. The one on Kimberley Road."

"Get the noodles. They're amazing."

"You and Zahir up for Mongolian?"

"No, thanks. I'm taking off for Bangkok tomorrow, so I want to spend some time with her and Cooper." Cooper was Logan and Zahir's five-year-old son.

"Have a safe trip. Hope everything goes all right. You need us to take care of anything for you while you're gone?"

"See what you can find out about Abercrombie and York here in Hong Kong. They've been doing Yangtze River cruises since the 1980s."

"Anything in particular you want to know?"

"I'd like to find out where they're sourcing their river cruisers. I saw one in Chongqing that's definitely at the high end of the market. They bill it as a luxury river cruiser. I'd like to know if they're building them in China."

Logan finished his beer and headed back up to the Peak. He and Zahir were renting an apartment on Barker Road, not too far from the Peak Tram. The owners, a wealthy Chinese family from Singapore, were happy to have an American family in the apartment and had given them a good price.

Zahir and Cooper hadn't missed a beat settling in to life in Hong Kong. Zahir was on a leave of absence from Boston University's Academy for Arabic Teachers, where she had been teaching advanced Arabic courses. She had finished her doctorate in Arabic studies at BU, and received her degree in the spring.

Hong Kong University's School of Modern Languages and Cultures had offered her a teaching position in its Arabic Department soon after they arrived.

Logan took the stairs to their third floor apartment and let himself in. It was quiet, but then he remembered that Cooper was taking a swimming lesson at the American Club in Stanley. There was a note from Zahir saying that they'd be home by two.

He decided to pack his bag for Bangkok. He'd probably be spending most of his time in the hotel room, waiting for

Li to establish contact. He planned to do some cover business while he was in Bangkok, though, to justify his trip to the Thais or anyone else that might be watching. For that he'd need some business casual attire.

Just after two, the front door opened and Cooper Alexander charged into the room.

"Daddy!"

"Hey, buddy." Logan wrapped him in a bear hug and swung him around.

"How was swimming?" He looked over Cooper's head as Zahir came into the room.

"It was neat." Cooper wriggled loose from Logan's arms.

"He's like a fish." Zahir walked over to Logan and kissed him. She bent down and tousled her son's hair.

"Maybe we have a future SEAL on our hands," Logan said.

Zahir gave him a disapproving look.

"I don't think so."

Logan gave her a hug. "That's a long ways off. Not something we have to think about right now."

"Are you packed yet?"

"Just about done."

They spent the rest of the afternoon baking chocolate chip cookies and then walked over to Mt. Austin Playground for a picnic. At this hour the playground was relatively quiet. It was one of the few places in the congested city where it was possible to relax without huge crowds.

After they ate and gave Cooper time to run around, they walked back home. While Zahir was getting their son ready for bed, Logan powered up his laptop to see if Washington had sent him any last-minute instructions for his meeting.

There was a message from Frank Sisler, verifying Li's claim that the Chinese government was worried about Muslim extremism and had begun cracking down on suspect groups all around the country, including Szechuan Province. The PSB was conducting random checks in neighborhoods suspected of supporting these extremists.

One of the DO's analysts, Ellen Sanders, had also included three pages of questions about Li's background. This would help headquarters verify Li's claims about his past and his current access. Asset validation was key to establishing the credibility of a reporting source. But it wasn't something you did just one time at the beginning of the recruitment. It was ongoing throughout the course of the relationship.

During his training Logan had reviewed a number of case studies designed to show how hostile security services use volunteers to penetrate the opposition. These services sometimes go to great lengths to establish a volunteer's credibility, even to the point of giving away sensitive intelligence.

The opposition understands that at times they must give up something to get something. Their goal is to identify foreigners working against China and learn something about their tradecraft. But more than anything, they hope that through this they will learn the identity of the spies the enemy had recruited.

Logan's gut told him that Li was not a provocation. No, he was acting on his own. The look in Li's eyes when he talked about his father had been enough to convince him of the man's genuine contempt for the corrupt system that was the Chinese Communist Party.

Logan shut off his computer and double-checked his bag to make certain he had everything he needed for his trip. He had an early flight in the morning and needed a good night's sleep to prepare for the week ahead.

Chapter 7

Li Jiang entered Deputy General Commissioner Gu Yan's office with hesitation. Gu had recently been named as Deputy Minister of the MPS. He had ordered Li to headquarters, located in a sprawling compound on East Changan Avenue, near Tiananmen Square, for preliminary talks in anticipation of Li's upcoming trip to Bangkok. Li wasn't quite sure what to expect. His recent contact with the American in Chongqing had him second-guessing even the most mundane encounter at work. Were they on to him?

MPS shared its headquarters building with the Ministry of State Security (MSS). Outwardly the two organizations gave the impression of collegial cooperation, but in reality they were frequently at odds with each other as they vied for resources from the central government. The MPS had lost some ground and prestige to the MSS over the years, but recently had found favor because of their successes in several high profile cyber security operations.

As Li walked into Gu's office, an assistant arrived to deliver two steaming cups of tea. He set them down on a small sideboard and excused himself. After the door closed behind him, the deputy minister turned his attention to Li.

"*Cui Jian* tea," Gu said, gesturing toward the table and the cups of Jade Sword tea. "Grown near my village in Fujian."

Gu took Li's arm and steered him to a rosewood settee. There was an ornate area carpet on the floor, and reproductions from the *Book of Chrysanthemums* by renowned Fujian artist Weng Lian Gui were hung around the room.

"Superintendent. Nice to see you. I knew your father years ago when he was about to retire from the military and take that university job in Chongqing. He was quite a man. I was very sorry to hear about his death last year."

"Thank you, sir. It came as a shock to all of us."

"And that business with Bo Xilai." Gu shook his head. A hint of aggravation ruffled his otherwise neutral demeanor.

Gu had a reputation for being a straight shooter. It was unusual, although not unheard of, for one to rise so high up the MPS ranks based solely on merit. That had certainly been the case with his father in the military, Li reminisced. He turned his attention back to the deputy minister.

"Yes, it was unfortunate that he got caught up in all of that. I think the shame and embarrassment of losing his home led to his failing health and ultimately his death."

"How's your mother doing?"

"She's not well. She moved in with my sister after our father died. She's not physically ill, but suffers from depression."

"Please convey my condolences."

Gu removed the lid from the porcelain cup and slurped his tea. Setting it aside he withdrew a pack of *Zhonghua*-brand cigarettes from his breast pocket and offered one to him. Li drew a lighter out of his tunic, proffered a light to his host and then lit his own.

"This trip you're taking to Thailand is more important than you may realize." Gu blew a cloud of smoke to one side.

"I imagine you want me to lay out my expectations for expanded cyber cooperation with the Thais. I have no doubt that you grasp the significance of a close partnership with them. I won't insult your intelligence by overstating the obvious. No, I brought you here to discuss something else." Gu gave Li a penetrating look before continuing.

"As you know, over the last decade we've been working very hard to build up our security cooperation with the Thais. Of course this cuts both ways. They want to modernize their police force. Their leadership sees us as a regional partner who can supply them with more affordable technology and training than they can get anywhere else.

"For years Thailand has depended upon U.S. aid. These days the Americans are bogged down with the war on terror and all the upheaval in the Middle East. They've left the impression that Thailand is not as important to them as it once was. That, and the fact that the U.S. Congress is slow to authorize foreign aid expenditures, has put a strain on their bilateral relationship."

Li was beginning to wonder where Gu was going with this monolog. He was loath to voice his question, surmising that Gu would get to the point when he was ready. He didn't have to wait long.

"It's in China's national interest to diminish U.S. influence in Asia. We shouldn't antagonize the Americans by blatantly challenging them, but where we can, we should make every effort to undermine their influence.

"Thailand's relationship with the U.S. dates to the early 1800s. I believe Thailand was the first Asian country to establish diplomatic ties with the U.S."

"That pre-dates our own first dealings with the U.S.," Li remarked.

"Yes. During the Qing Dynasty."

"Deputy Minister, what would you like me to do?"

"As Lao Tzu said, 'The journey of a thousand miles begins beneath one's feet.'

"I want you to keep your ears open while you're in Bangkok. Find out who our friends are on the security side. I'm looking for people that can influence their leadership. Time is on our side, though, so don't come across as overly eager."

Gu asked for Li's agenda with the Thais. Li dug it out of the folder he'd brought with him and handed it over. Gu took his time reading it, pausing to ask for clarification on a couple of points. When he finished reviewing it he nodded and handed it back.

"This looks fine. Good luck, and don't forget what I said about the big picture."

Gu pushed back from his desk and rose, indicating that the meeting was over. Li got to his feet and shook hands.

"Of course, sir. I'll do my best."

As he walked out of Gu's office, Li stopped by reception to retrieve his bag. Glancing at his watch, he saw that it was ten o'clock. Good, he thought. Just enough time to catch his noon flight to Bangkok.

His driver picked him up a few minutes later in front of the headquarters building. Li settled into the back seat and let his thoughts wander. His face was expressionless as he stared out the window. They were passing Tiananmen Square, the world's largest central square, capable of holding a million people. Bright red flags rustled atop the Great Hall of the People. A lengthy line of tourists snaked around the outside of Chairman Mao's Memorial Hall.

But it was the massive portrait of Mao Zedong that held his attention as they passed by. The Chairman's eyes seemed to follow him as they rolled in front of Tiananmen Gate (The Gate of Heavenly Peace.) The oil portrait, which measures roughly 18 by 14 feet, had been hanging in that spot for as long as Li could remember. Hung above the entrance to the Imperial City, it was a tribute to the man who had left his mark on China like no other, before or since.

Li was thoughtful as the driver sped out of the city towards the airport. Gu's plan to undermine the Americans in Thailand was part of a larger pattern that Li had observed in China's, sometimes testy, relationship with the U.S. He flinched as he thought about what Gu would do to him if he knew that he was in secret contact with the Americans. Spies did not generally fare well in China. A bullet to the brain and the family name forever disgraced was the standard fare for betrayal.

"I hope that you know what you're doing, Logan Crowley," was his silent supplication as the car picked up speed.

* * *

Logan left the apartment before Zahir and Cooper were up. Zahir had given him a drowsy goodbye kiss and fallen back asleep. He had checked on Cooper, grabbed his bag, and taken the elevator downstairs. His taxi was already waiting for him, engine idling, when he exited the apartment building.

"Hong Kong Station, please."

The driver nodded and after a nail-biting fifteen-minute race through empty streets, pulled up in front of the station in Central. Logan breathed easier as he grabbed his suitcase from the trunk, tipped the man and set off for the Airport Express customer service center.

"That guy should try out for the Grand Prix," he muttered to himself.

He checked his bag for the eight o'clock Cathay Pacific flight and in moments was hurtling towards Hong Kong International Airport.

Twenty-four minutes later he was checking in at Terminal 1. He paid the HK$120 departure tax and then endured a thirty minute delay before making it through security. Once inside the departure lounge he found a Starbucks, ordered a French roast and then hurried over to his gate.

The two-hour flight to Bangkok was uneventful save for a patch of air turbulence somewhere over the Vietnamese coastline that was so bumpy, it had passengers all around him grabbing for their "barf bags."

Logan went over the upcoming meeting scenario in his mind. He had a lot to cover and he hoped that Li could spend enough time with him to get through everything. He tried not to think about the possibility that Li wouldn't be able to get away from his group, or worse yet, hadn't even made it to Bangkok.

These things could be hit or miss, depending on the other delegation members. Sometimes a minder from the local Chinese Embassy was assigned to an official delegation. It was usually a security officer, whose job it was to make sure the group stuck together, didn't stray too far from the official meeting venues and most importantly, didn't have any unauthorized contact with foreigners.

Often, it was the senior member of the delegation who set the tone on these visits. If he was confident, he might let his charges have some free time for shopping or other diversions, and not require them to go out in pairs, which for years had been the norm when Chinese delegations traveled abroad.

The plane landed on schedule and Logan cleared customs and immigration in record time. On the immigration form he'd written that he was staying at a friend's apartment in Sukhumvit Road. In reality he was going to do a four-hour surveillance detection run, conduct a document swap with a station contact, and then check into the Sheraton in his Crowley alias.

He had traveled to Bangkok on his true name documents since he lived in Hong Kong and could not risk that the security officials would pick up on his extracurricular activities.

He knew when he gave Li the Crowley alias that it was going to complicate the logistics of his trip, but he couldn't take the chance that Li was being directed by the security service. If he was, and they learned his true identity, it would be game over. His team would have to pull up stakes in Hong Kong before they'd even begun.

It was raining when he left the airport. Bangkok's traffic is notorious for being out of control. Thailand has the highest motor vehicle fatality rate per capita in the world. On average, more than one person dies every hour of every day in motorbike or *tuk tuk* (Bangkok's popular motorized rickshaws) accidents alone.

Logan exited the cab, after a white-knuckle dash through heavy traffic. He ducked for shelter under an overhang and pulled a rain jacket out of his bag. He was lugging a convertible carry-on that doubled as a backpack. Temperatures were in the mid-eighties with probably ninety percent humidity. The good news was that the rain was beginning to taper off.

Four hours later, drenched in sweat and light-headed from exhaust fumes, Logan turned down an alley east of Princess Mother Memorial Park. As he made the turn he spotted his contact, a seasoned officer by the name of Craig

Longley, walking towards him. The casual observer would have seen nothing untoward. Logan dropped his true name identification into Craig's open bag with his left hand and in one motion received an envelope with his alias documents in his right. He secured it in his inside pocket and kept on walking.

Logan knew that Bangkok took these exchanges seriously. It would take the better part of Craig's day making sure that he was free of surveillance, before committing to the document exchange. He had to spend a fair amount of time on the street before he went back to the embassy too, but not nearly as much as before.

Logan checked behind him and saw that the coast was clear. He did three more taxi switches over the next hour and then flagged down a cab and instructed the driver to take him to the Sheraton Hotel. It was three-thirty when the driver dropped him off for check-in.

Now the fun would begin, Logan thought to himself, as he took his room key from the petite receptionist and headed for the lobby elevators. All he could do now was wait for Li's call.

Chapter 8

It was eight-fifteen when Des Magarity, Rick Wheeler and Lois Caldwell walked into the 10th Street entrance of the J. Edgar Hoover Building. Moments later they were filing into the waiting room outside of FBI Director Greg Mitchell's office. Des had scheduled the meeting to brief Mitchell on the status of the Washington Field Office's China cyber-espionage investigation.

FBI headquarters occupies two blocks of prime northwest Washington real estate. Despite its choice Pennsylvania Avenue location, the building is considered by many to be the most forbidding government building in Washington. Not even forty years old, most agreed that the Bureau's headquarters was in dire need of a makeover.

Director Mitchell had made it a priority of his tenure to resolve the building issue. As the trio was ushered into his office, they passed by a table laden with blueprints and drawings for the new structure. Everyone from county government officials to real estate mogul Donald Trump had jumped at the opportunity to bid on the project.

Des rolled his eyes as they trooped past the plans.

"We're getting our lunch handed to us by the Chinese, and he's picking out wallpaper," he bristled to himself.

Mitchell had been on the job for less than a month. He was three weeks into a ten-year term as FBI director, and by all accounts had yet to hit his stride. It was generally believed by those in the know that he was a lightweight. As a consequence, the other members of the President's national security team, who expected everyone to pull their own weight, gave him a wide berth.

The assessment was not entirely fair. Mitchell was a Yale Law School grad who had worked for over twenty years in the private sector. After making a pile of money as a trial attorney, he had been named to the U.S. Circuit Court of Appeals for the District of Columbia.

There he developed a reputation as a first-class schmoozer. With fifteen years on the court, most expected him to finish his career on the bench. But in April the President nominated him to the top FBI post after the previous director, Harry Sullivan, dropped dead from a heart attack. Mitchell had breezed through the confirmation hearings and was installed at the beginning of September.

After they were all seated around the director's conference table, Des began by distributing a handout.

"Sir, we felt this was a good time to bring you up to speed on our Chinese hacking investigation. I've brought along my deputy, Rick Wheeler, and Special Agent Caldwell, who's a computer network security specialist, to answer any questions you might have.

"This summarizes where we are, based in part on current intelligence from a new Chinese source." Des gestured towards the report he had handed the director.

"It explains the role the MPS plays in these cyber network attacks.

"You'll recall that we were called in to investigate an attack against Sec State's staff computers after we got a tip from this source. From him we learned that hackers inside China had infected a number of these computers with a virus."

"How the hell were they able to get into staff computers? Did they have physical access to any of them?" Mitchell looked up from the document.

"You mean from staff travel or something like that? No, Sir. They used social engineering to draw them in."

"How do you mean?"

"All they had to do was put out an email with an enticing subject line. They knew the staff was preparing the Secretary for G-20 meetings in Geneva. So they concocted this phony email that alluded to the EU's economic strategy for Asia."

"And once that email was opened?"

"A malicious virus spread throughout the system."

"What have you learned from your undercover operation?" Mitchell was already toying with his cuff links.

"Rick?" Des turned to his deputy.

"Sir, they were on to us pretty quick. We were able to trace the attack back to China. Once we identified the server the attack was coming from, they shut it down. They just went off the grid.

"Meanwhile, we got word from the Agency a couple of weeks later that they were planning to meet their new source inside China. The expectation was that he would be able to shed more light on all of this."

"Who's the source?"

"If he's telling the truth, he's a Public Security Bureau officer. They come under the Ministry of Public Security."

"How does he fit into the hacking attack?"

"Lois?" Des indicated that she should answer the director's question.

"Sir, we don't know his exact position. We're still waiting for the case officer to clarify it. What we do know is that the PSB has many functions. National security is one of them. They don't usually play an intelligence role, but there has been reporting that they are becoming more involved in network attacks through a newly created cyber component. They have access to a lot of cyber criminals who they press into service."

"Have we demarched the Chinese officially, or are we just assuming they're the ones behind this?"

"State has not gone in with a formal demarche. The consensus in the cyber community though is that the Chinese government or some elite hackers are behind this," Lois replied. "We've had a few bumps in the road with the Chinese over the years. I'm not sure you'd get a straight answer from them if you did demarche them.

"Such as?"

Lois looked up from her notes.

"The EP-3 incident on Hainan Island in 2001 was significant. The EP-3 is an electronic warfare reconnaissance aircraft. This one was on a routine reconnaissance mission over international waters when a Chinese Navy F-8 fighter collided with it, forcing the crew to land on Hainan Island."

"I take it that's Chinese territory?"

"Yes, sir. In fact they crash-landed at a military airfield. The Chinese pilot didn't make it. He went down in the South China Sea.

"The EP-3 crew was able to destroy much of the sensitive gear on board before they landed, but they didn't have time to get rid of everything before the Chinese got there," she said.

"The Chinese held our crew for eleven days and kept the plane for several months. It caused a major rift in Sino/U.S. relations, especially after they found documentation for the army's electronic order of battle on board.

"Relations were tense for months. Just when it seemed that we were getting back to normal, China found out we had bugged a Boeing 767 they had ordered from the U.S. for their President."

"Who the hell let the CIA pull off a stunt like that?"

"Actually, sir, it was a joint NSA/FBI operation."

Mitchell grimaced. "Please continue."

"From CIA's source we're beginning to get a handle on how the MPS might play in China's offensive cyber program. This is new for them, even though their top priority is national security. And we could all agree that protecting cyber infrastructure is a key national security objective.

"We don't know if this is some kind of rogue operation, or if the MPS has been co-opted by China's Cyber Executive to act on their behalf. Just like us, China has a muddy playing field when it comes to figuring out who's doing what on the cyber front.

"If you look at the handout in front of you, you'll get a sense of the importance China places on information assurance. Not just going out offensively after new information, but securing their own, and disrupting the opposition's access to information." Lois raised her hand and ticked off each of the key points with her fingers.

"We still don't fully understand where CIA's source fits into the big picture," she reiterated. "We just found out that he is going to travel to Thailand this month, and the case officer will try to meet him there. With any luck, he'll be able to fill in some of the gaps." Lois paused a few seconds, looking thoughtful, before she continued speaking.

"One thing's for certain right now. The attack against Sec State's computers is not new in terms of methods employed or persistence. It's getting a lot of attention because of the high profile target. But in reality, we've been hemorrhaging data across our networks for years. Private sector and government networks are being hacked at a mind-boggling rate."

"When you say mind-boggling, what exactly do you mean? Can you quantify it?" Mitchell gave her a skeptical look.

"Just to give you one example, there are over 10 million cyber attacks against the computers at the National Nuclear Security Administration, every day."

"And these are all Chinese attacks?" Mitchell looked incredulous.

"Not necessarily. And truth be told, many of the attacks could be from 'bots' deployed by other hostile governments or malicious hackers."

Des could tell from the vacant look on Mitchell's face that Lois had lost him.

"What the hell is a 'bot'?" the director asked.

Lois looked flustered by the abruptness of Mitchell's question, but continued. "It's a software application that hackers use in cyber attacks, a type of malware used to automate certain tasks. Think of it as a kind of Internet robot. The bots infect individual computers, and depending on their objective, hackers can program them to do many different tasks; send spam, steal passwords, propagate themselves, or even deny service to a network by infecting thousands of computers that they turn into 'zombies.'"

"Zombies?"

Mitchell was beginning to shift around in his seat and Des knew that they were about to lose him. He made a motion to Lois to cut it short.

"Yes, zombies. Computers that have been infected and then put to work by the hackers, who establish command and control through a master computer, directing tens of thousands of zombies to carry out their tasks at the same time. This way a hacker can overwhelm a single website by requesting a simultaneous connection, crashing the website. Imagine 10,000 computers hitting one website at the exact same time, and the webmaster unable to drop the bad connection because they're distributed from all over the world, which is why it's called a distributed denial of service attack or DDoS.

"Hackers would love nothing better than to get control of our nukes. That's just one area though. It's an important area, but every government agency, the military, defense contractors, the entire financial system, the power grid. No one's safe. Look what happened to Sony," Lois pointed out, referring to a massive hacking attack against the entertainment giant. "All of them are being bombarded."

"And you think it's primarily the Chinese who are carrying out these attacks?"

"They're huge players, but they're not the only ones. The Russians, Iranians, North Koreans, and non-state cyber criminals are very active too. Attribution's a tricky thing, because the Internet is mostly anonymous, with hackers taking stealthy routes to their target. In fact, many of them use hop points right here in the U.S., mostly at institutions of higher education where Internet bandwidth is widely available and computing power is abundant. It's easy to get many hacking tools. Elite hackers have access to these same tools and methods, plus their own special private tools.

"In this case we knew it was the Chinese because we had a source. Without the Agency's informant we might still be trying to figure out who was behind it."

"I want a seamless lash-up with the Agency on this. Who else are you working with?"

Des spoke up. "As far as we can tell, CIA's playing straight with us. I think we're getting everything they've got. We're also working with Jim Baylow's shop at Homeland Security, and the military."

Mitchell stood up, indicating the meeting was over.

"Keep me updated on this, Des. The President has made cyber security one of his top priorities. It's a minefield right now, though, because of the scrutiny the intelligence community is getting following the NSA leaks."

"Snowden?"

Mitchell nodded, looking grim. "He's done more damage than we'll ever know. If Congress has its way, they'll have NSA and the rest of the intelligence community on a short leash before the end of the year. Big changes are coming."

As they walked out of the office, Des was going over the meeting in his mind. Mitchell had appeared engaged and had asked some relevant questions.

"Boss, I'm going to stop in Cyber Division to talk to some of the China analysts."

"All right, Lois. See you back at the office." Des pressed the down button for the elevator as Lois headed for the stairwell.

"You did a good job in there today, Caldwell. Keep it up."

Lois turned to flash them a smile, gave a little wave and disappeared down the stairs.

"What do you think?" Rick tilted his head in the direction Lois had gone as they both entered the elevator.

"I think Agent Caldwell is going to work out just fine," Des smiled. "Just fine."

* * *

Ellen Sanders studied the enlarged copy of Li's ID. She had spent days researching Chinese identification documents and had come to the conclusion that Li's was authentic.

She took a bite from the tuna sandwich that she'd picked up from the employee cafeteria and turned back to her notes. For years, the Ministry of Public Security had issued PSB officers ID cards. A 1985 document entitled "Regulations of the People's Republic of China Concerning Resident Identification Cards" laid out a new policy that the Sixth National People's Congress Standing Committee had adopted.

At the time it was issued, it appeared that police officers were being penalized, or at a minimum, would not have the same civil rights as civilians, under the new policy.

Article 9 of the edict provided that "Citizens who are enlisted in active police service shall hand in their resident identity cards when going through the formalities to cancel their resident registration; when they retire from active service, they shall have their resident identity cards back or apply for new ones."

In 2003, the government instituted a new law on identification cards to rectify the disparity and by 2008 most police officers, but not all, had begun carrying civilian ID cards.

As she pulled her notes together, Frank Sisler poked his head into her office.

"What you working on?"

"I was just going over my notes on Li's ID card. I'm feeling pretty good about it." Ellen gave Frank a rundown of her findings.

"The Chinese are doing some interesting things with national identity cards."

"Like what?"

"In 2012 they added fingerprints to all national IDs."

"Think that would go over here at home?"

"Are you kidding? The whole idea of a national ID card gives people the creeps. Especially in this environment, where everyone feels government has overstepped its bounds."

Frank came into the room and sat down. "Privacy, as we once knew it, is an illusion. With so many people using social media, their personal lives are out there for anyone to see."

"The Chinese are taking it to a whole different level. They've even been experimenting with gene ID cards since 2002."

"You're talking about having your DNA on your ID?"

"Right. I came across several articles in Chinese media reporting on it. In Szechuan, Shaanxi, and Jiangsu Provinces.

"The scientists decide how many loci they want to include in an individual's ID."

"What do they mean by loci?"

"Those are markers or particular areas of the DNA that scientists analyze. The more markers they evaluate, the more definitive the result. The examples I read about in China had as few as thirteen and as many as twenty-four.

"The Bureau did a lot of research on this here at home in the late '90s when they developed DNA typing technology for the National DNA Databank. What's amazing is that, unless you have an identical twin out there somewhere, that gene ID definitively differentiates you from anyone else on the planet."

Frank nodded. "Nice work, Ellen. I'm beginning to get a little warm and fuzzy about this guy, but we need to make sure Logan spends the time to validate everything he gets from him. If the MPS is behind this, you know they could dummy up an ID card to make Li look like the real deal.

"For that matter he could be the genuine article, and still be working for them. We just need to be smart about this. How many times have we been sucked in because we couldn't believe the Chinese would dangle information that sensitive in front of us?"

Ellen took a last bite of her sandwich and washed it down with a swig from the water bottle she kept on her desk.

She told Frank that she was now going over the organization chart that Li provided. She had already been in touch with the FBI's Cyber Division, NSA's Information Assurance people, CIA's own Directorate of Digital Innovation's Analysis Group, as well as the Office of East Asian Pacific Affairs, EAP.

"What did they have to say?"

"You'd be surprised how much is out there in public on China's cyber capabilities.

"Ted Owens in the Directorate of Digital Innovation pointed me to a 2012 DIA white paper called 'Roaring Dragon.' It's an unclassified study on China cyber." Ellen rummaged through a file folder and pulled out the document.

"What's interesting is that it goes through a list of the usual suspects that you'd expect to find involved in cyber operations. Goes into some detail describing their mission, organization and, to a lesser extent, personnel. There's very little about the PSB's role in China's Cyber program. One report from three year ago said that the Minister of Public Security had expressed interest in getting the PSB into computer operations. Most analysts discredited it at the time."

"My warm and fuzzy just got cold."

"I know. Li's information doesn't go much beyond the DIA study."

Frank handed the folder back to Ellen and stood up. "Logan will have to be sharp for this meeting. Did the DI come in with requirements for him?"

"Five pages of questions. I hope he has time to get through all of it. The Intel piece is obviously important, and so is asset validation. If we get that far, we need to figure out if Li's interested in a long-term relationship with us, and how we're going to meet him if he is."

"Right. For all we know this trip to Thailand is a one-off, although it sounds like the Chinese are interested in expanding their security relationship with the Thais. If they're serious about beefing up their security cooperation, Li might be able to travel a few times a year."

"That would be ideal. Otherwise we might want to start thinking about whether or not we would want to meet him inside," Ellen said.

"A lot riding on this meeting," Frank said as he headed for the door.

"That's all right," she smiled. "Logan can handle it."

"I hope you're right."

Frank closed the door behind him. He looked at his watch. He had a one o'clock meeting with Rick Wheeler at the WFO. He stopped by his office to pick up a jacket and hurried out the Original Headquarters Building East entrance to the shuttle bus stop. As he settled into the mini-van he went over his conversation with Ellen.

They needed to button this thing down if they were going to meet Li inside China. That would take their relationship to a whole new level.

Chapter 9

Logan paced about his tenth floor suite at the Sheraton Hotel. He paused before the windows offering a view of the boats plying the Chao Phraya River far below. Commuter ferries, rice barges and longboats glided past makeshift houses on stilts, floating markets and tourist attractions. It was ten-thirty p.m., yet he sensed a restless rhythm to the river, even from his elevated perspective.

"Where the hell is Li?" he muttered.

A dozen scenarios raced through his mind, most of which he dismissed outright. The most likely explanation was that Li was tied up with his delegation and was unable to break away. More sinister was the possibility that everything had somehow unraveled and Li had been detained in China. Perhaps at this very moment he was being interrogated.

Logan shrugged off the thought and pulled the curtains closed. Settling into an armchair he switched on the TV and tinkered with the remote until he found a local English-language news channel. He was half paying attention when he saw something on the screen that made him sit upright.

There, on the tarmac next to an Air China carrier was a group of Asian men in civilian clothing being greeted by a Thai police escort. And at the very front of the group was Mr. Li.

"He made it. That takes a load off," Logan exhaled, suddenly aware that he had been holding his breath. He turned up the volume.

"Planning for annual discussions between the Royal Thai Police and China's Ministry of Public Security got underway today as this MPS delegation arrived at Bangkok International Airport from Beijing.

"Earlier today we spoke with Commissioner General Niran Meesang, regarding Thailand's relationship with the MPS."

The camera switched from the airport arrival scene to Royal Thai Police Headquarters, where Commissioner Meesang, a short, round figure with an owlish expression, held forth on the burgeoning Sino/Thai security cooperation.

Logan listened to the interview and made a mental note to include the sighting of Li at the airport in his report. The film footage and press conference would help substantiate Li's story that he was traveling to Thailand on official business.

It was possible that Li had checked into the hotel earlier in the day, and was waiting for an opportunity to contact him.

Logan decided to check his classified email account one more time in the event there were any new requirements from Headquarters. There was a message from Frank Sisler. As he scanned it his eyes grew wide. According to a sensitive report provided by analysts in the Directorate of Digital Innovation, Li was in fact a Superintendent in one of Szechuan Province's Public Security Police Tactical Units (PTU). At the PTU, he headed up a group of elite hackers involved in computer network operations against the U.S.

Whoa. This is huge, he thought to himself. His reverie was broken by the jingle of the telephone.

"Hello?"

"Yes?"

Logan recognized Li's voice. Without acknowledging his name over the open phone line, Logan simply spoke his room number.

"Room 1032."

Li repeated the number, and then said; "I'll see you in five minutes."

Logan replaced the receiver and lowered the volume on the TV so that it was just loud enough to provide masking for his conversation with the volunteer, in the event his room was bugged.

Moments later there was a faint knock on the door. Logan looked through the peephole, saw that it was his man, and welcomed him into the room. He seemed tense, but gave Logan a vigorous handshake as he walked into the room. He was dressed in a conservative blue two-piece suit, red silk tie and black oxfords.

"We had a welcome banquet this evening," he said, explaining his attire.

"Make yourself comfortable." Logan gestured for him to take off his jacket and tie.

He removed his jacket and loosened his tie before taking a seat on the sofa.

"How'd it go today?" Logan asked.

"Both sides are putting a lot of emphasis on these discussions."

"I can see how the Thais are hoping to get something from China, but what's in it for the MPS?"

Li paused as if considering how to respond to Logan's question. He then recounted his meeting with Deputy Minister Gu earlier that morning.

"Thailand is in China's back yard. With these kinds of exchanges, we believe that gradually we will undermine the U.S. role in Asia. Given our proximity, it's simple for us to expedite requests from the Thais. Also, we know the U.S. currently places greater emphasis on its 'War on Terror' than other foreign policy concerns. Thailand is feeling that perhaps it is no longer so important to your country. Our leaders feel that these distractions give us an opening to expand our security relationships and influence in the region.

"We hope to fill that vacuum by providing training, conducting more joint exercises and sourcing police equipment. The expectation is that eventually Thailand will come to view China as a more reliable partner than the U.S."

"Let's come back to this in a second. How much time do you have?"

"My men are busy preparing for our meetings tomorrow. I told them not to bother me until morning. They will obey my orders."

"Would you like something to drink?"

"Do you have any scotch?"

"Yes. How would you like it?"

"Straight, please."

Logan poured their drinks and then sat down across from Li. The latter took an appreciative sip from his glass and visibly relaxed. He pulled a pack of cigarettes from his jacket and offered one to Logan.

"No, thanks. I don't smoke."

Li lit up, inhaled and then blew tendrils of smoke through his nostrils.

"We shouldn't be interrupted, but if we are, our story is that we met in the bar and I was telling you about my consulting business. When I found out that you were MPS, I invited you up to my room so that I could give you one of my business cards. I'm looking for opportunities to do business with the PSB."

Logan didn't plan to give Li his true name just yet. Given that he had originally requested a meeting with the CIA, chances were that he assumed Logan was Agency. Still, there was just enough ambiguity with the Crowley alias to give him cover until headquarters made up its mind whether or not Li was the real deal.

Logan spent the next hour going over the information Li had provided during their walking meeting in Chongqing. He needed to narrow down the sourcing for headquarters.

"Tell me more about the relationship between the provincial level security bureaus and the tactical units. Do they all come under the Ministry of Public Security?"

"Technically, yes. But our unit is unique. We are the only tactical unit set up to deal with offensive and defensive cyber operations. Most of the other tactical units have more traditional police capabilities like anti-terrorism assault squads, or SWAT teams.

"The Governor of Szechuan Province is a good friend of the Minister of Public Security. He convinced the minister that the MPS should get on the Cyber bandwagon, because it's high profile. If we have big successes it might improve the Minister's position on the State Council and maybe even move him up to the Politburo."

"So in Chongqing...?"

"Our tactical unit comes under the Chongqing MPS."

"Is it accurate to say that your unit's main target is the U.S.?" This was a loaded question, because Logan knew from his reading over the past several weeks, that this was not the case.

"Our emphasis has shifted since we were set up three years ago. Traditionally, we would not even be involved in cyber operations. There are other groups outside of the MPS involved in collection against U.S. targets. They get a lot of attention and resources from the leadership because the U.S. target is so important.

"A few years ago, our unit developed a close working relationship with China's Cyber Executive after the governor approached the minister of public security during a State Council meeting in Beijing."

"What was the basis of that?"

"Like I said. It's a kind of cronyism. The idea was to provide more visibility for the minister of public security so that he would get promoted. After that meeting we had all the resources we needed to exploit vulnerabilities in U.S. cyber communications. What we have done in the last three years is build an elite cyber hacking unit. We've pulled in several rogue hackers who otherwise would be wasting away in a Chinese prison without access to an Internet connection."

"Bear with me." Logan poured a generous share of scotch into Li's glass and then replenished his own.

"I was under the impression that another department actually had the lead on computer network operations."

"It's not that straightforward. Under our doctrine of Integrated Network Electronic Warfare, China's Cyber Executive has urged all relevant departments to work closely together. Generally speaking, one department focuses on offensive attacks and another is responsible for intelligence collection and China's own network assurance."

Li crossed his legs and withdrew another cigarette from the pack on the end table. He tamped it down as he searched for his lighter, which had slipped between the cushions.

"Three years ago we created a team made up of thirty-five elite civilian hackers, most of them proficient in English. Our mission was to go after the highest priority targets using our most advanced tools and, of course, to exploit the intelligence from these attacks. We set this team up in Chongqing to give it more visibility because that way our activities are not administered at the provincial level, rather by the central government itself. The central government also administers the PSBs in Shanghai, Tianjin and Beijing, but so far as I know, only Chongqing has a Cyber program." Li paused to light his cigarette.

"The effort against your Secretary of State was only one of many successful operations we conducted this year. There have been others. A great number in fact." He tapped the ash from his cigarette into the ashtray and leaned forward, waving his hand in an expansive gesture.

"A top priority from the beginning has been your military's C4ISR."

"Command, Control, Communications, Computers, Intelligence and Surveillance."

"Yes. Because the Pentagon relies so heavily on civilian defense contractors to handle sensitive military projects, we've been able to hack into many of these companies' computer networks.

"Much of the information we've obtained from Cyber operations is valuable to the central government because it's proprietary commercial information that helps keep down our own R&D costs." Li took one last drag on his cigarette and ground it into the ashtray.

"So that's it? China's interest in hacking is all about gaining a commercial advantage over U.S. manufacturers?"

"You don't really believe that, do you?" Li looked skeptical.

"No, but I'd like to hear it from you."

"In *The Art of War*, Sun Tzu said 'In war, the way is to avoid what is strong, and strike what is weak.'

"China cannot win a conventional war against the United States." Li jumped up from his seat and paced around.

"Take our navy for example. China has only one aircraft carrier, which we didn't even build."

"The Varyag? Didn't a travel agency in Hong Kong pay $20 million for it so they could turn it into a floating casino?"

"That's the one, although it's been renamed the Liaoning, after the province. They bought it from the Ukraine. I suspect our navy was working with them behind the scenes all along. The buyers have close ties to the military.

"The U.S. has ninety years of experience conducting these kinds of operations. China is training its very first group of carrier pilots this year. There's no comparison. We would be foolish to take on your Navy."

"And?"

"If you accept Sun Tzu's logic then it follows that China should focus on the areas where the U.S. is weak. Our leaders believe that weakness lies in the cyber world."

"Even if that were true, how is China going to strike America's cyber infrastructure in any meaningful way?"

Li stopped pacing and stood in front of Logan. "We haven't shown you anything yet. Most of the computer attacks that we mount have more than one objective. Obviously an important element is to collect proprietary information. But more important than that, each of these attacks is a probe, designed to measure U.S. capabilities and responsiveness to these actions.

"Last year China conducted a distributed denial-of-service attack against several major U.S. financial institutions."

"Are you talking about the attacks against Wells Fargo, Bank of America and Citigroup?"

Li nodded.

Logan looked skeptical. "Most of the experts I've talked to believe Iran was behind that. In fact, a group claimed responsibility for them. Cyber Fighters of Izz ad-din Al Qassam."

Li replied with a thin smile. "Yes, they did."

"You mean…?"

"Things are not always what they seem. Cyber Fighters is only one group. There are thousands of other hackers working for us. It's not in our interest to admit that we're the ones behind it."

"What's the end game, Mr. Li? What does China hope to accomplish by this?"

Li was grim-faced. "Nothing less than China replacing the U.S. as the number one economy in the world."

Chapter 10

Des Magarity checked the time. He'd been looking forward to a relaxed night at home watching the Washington Nationals and Atlanta Braves slug it out. A six-pack of icy cold Bud was the only companionship he needed.

But when he'd checked his voice mail he discovered that one of his Chinese sources had called for an unscheduled meet at nine-thirty. It was eight o'clock. Just enough time to change, grab a sandwich and head over there.

"So much for that," he grunted, as he walked into the bedroom and stripped off his suit. His communications plan with Mr. Ji normally worked pretty well, with dates and times prescheduled and out-of-the-way meeting sites preselected. Tonight's meeting would be by the Aquatic Gardens near Kenilworth Park.

Des wasn't big on skulking around in the dark. That was for the spooks over at CIA. Even though the Bureau owned the District, he had to be careful meeting Ji in public, particularly since in his job as the S&T counselor at the Chinese Embassy he had no business meeting with the FBI.

There were more Chinese running around Washington stealing sensitive information than you could shake a stick at. They could be found prowling around Chinatown, but they were in the suburbs too. Hell, you couldn't go anywhere near Fairfax County, Rockville or Bethesda without bumping into one of them.

Des pulled on a running suit and sneakers. He stuffed his FBI-issue Glock-23, his FBI credential and wallet into a fanny pack and hustled into the kitchen. He hadn't done any food shopping in the last week and his stomach rumbled as he sniffed the disagreeable odor of rotting leftovers that greeted him when he opened the refrigerator. He slammed the door shut in disgust, making a mental note to clean up the mess when he got back home.

Des lived in a decaying apartment building in Old Town Alexandria, a couple of blocks from the King Street Metro. He took the stairs to the ground floor and walked out into the early October evening.

As he approached the station he heard the whoosh of opening doors and a voice announcing the arrival of the northbound Yellow Line train for Fort Totten. Des pushed through the turnstile and made it onto the car just before the doors closed.

At L'Enfant Plaza he switched to the Orange Line and rode it seven stops to Deanwood Metro station in Kenilworth. Northeast D.C. wasn't his usual stomping ground, but it was one of the few places in the District the Chinese didn't frequent. The area was mostly African-American with a growing population of sub-Saharan immigrants.

It was dark, as he exited the pedestrian tunnel onto the Deanwood underpass, and headed up Kenilworth Avenue towards Anacostia Avenue. The Aquatic Park closed at dark, so he wasn't entirely sure where Ji would be waiting.

Des slid his fanny pack around so that it was stretched taut and low across his stomach. He wasn't expecting trouble, but this area had one of the highest crime rates in Washington.

He spotted the squat Chinese S&T officer hustling down the sidewalk towards him. He appeared skittish, peering over his shoulder as he walked. He saw Des and rushed over to where he was waiting.

Des hadn't totally made up his mind about Ji. He'd been on the books for two years, agreeing to work with the Bureau after he'd been caught "in flagrante" in the back seat of his car with a female cultural attaché from the Taipei Economic and Cultural Representative Office.

Ji had initially attempted to dismiss the indiscretion but when Des had explained that Beijing would likely not take kindly to the news of Ji's extracurricular activities, he had been more forthcoming.

That said, nothing Ji had provided to date had been of earth-shattering importance. Details of his attempt to wine and dine an ethnic Chinese nuclear scientist; a list of S&T delegations planning travel to the U.S.; and notification of the travel itineraries of several suspect Intelligence officers attempting to gain access to proprietary high-tech Intel in Silicon Valley.

At their last meeting, Des had directed Ji to be on the lookout for anything related to Chinese hacking or cyber security. Given the hacking operation against Sec State, and information he'd picked up at DHS, he was more sensitized to the fact that there was an all-out cyber push by China, and he suspected the S&T officer would know about it.

"How you doing, Ji?"

"I've had better days," Ji replied.

"This better be good." Des was still miffed about missing his ball game.

"We weren't scheduled to meet again until the end of the month, but I thought this would be something you'd be interested in."

"So what have you got?" Des gave him a quizzical look.

"Our Commercial Counselor received a request yesterday to set up meetings for a wealthy Hong Kong investor interested in purchasing some commercial real estate."

"Nothing against Hong Kong investors putting their money into U.S. real estate. What's so special about this guy?"

"He's only interested in large commercial properties in the Dulles Technology Corridor. Specifically, Ashburn, Virginia. And I know for a fact that he's close to the Communist party chief in Szechuan."

Des's ears pricked up at the mention of Ashburn. *The Washington Post* had recently reported that Loudon County was home to millions of square feet of data centers. The area had seen exponential growth ever since the early nineties when a group of area network providers banded together to form the Metropolitan Area Exchange-East (MAE-E).

Internet service providers like ATT, Verizon, British Telecom and Cisco use the MAE-E to exchange Internet content. The *Post* had made it sound like Ashburn was the hub of all this activity. Interesting, but the fact that a Chinese investor with deep pockets was looking for prime real estate there was yesterday's news.

"So what makes this guy so special?"

"By itself, it's no big deal. But I happened to be talking to one of my embassy colleagues about it."

"Song?" Des recalled the name Ji had given him last year.

"Yes. Song. He has a group of three engineers, supposedly from the Internet company, Taixun, coming in at the same time. He knows for a fact that one of the engineers doesn't work for them." Ji fished a paper with the names of the three engineers out of his pocket and handed it to Des.

"Where's he from?" Des asked, as he studied the note.

"They worked together in a sensitive S&T Intelligence Bureau that comes under China's Cyber Executive. Before that they both were at Qinghua University, so they're pretty good buddies. About the time Song was selected to come to Washington, his friend got a job at this secret research institute in Szechuan Province. Someplace near Chengdu."

"Sounds pretty harmless. What's it called?"

"The Institute of Applied Computer Science. And it's not. This place is actually a sensitive research facility. Supposedly they got a big budget from the central government a few years back to develop software and hacking tools for our Cyber warfare program work."

"Which one is he?"

"Pan Chengong."

"What's this research institute actually do?"

"Information security. I asked Song what meetings he's setting up for them and he said they don't have a fixed schedule. They're shipping a bunch of equipment in the pouch, renting some vans and leaving their itinerary wide open."

"When are they supposed to get here?"

"They're flying direct from Beijing on the 9th of October."

"How about your visitor?"

"He gets in a day later."

Des pondered what Ji had just said. It sounded as though the Chinese were planning a technical operation in one of the busiest Internet hubs in the world.

They've got a lot of balls coming in here and screwing around in our back yard, he muttered to himself. What the hell were they up to? He clasped Ji on the shoulder.

"Nice work, Ji. I want you all over this. Let me know if you pick up anything else, especially if their schedule changes or they ask for any meetings."

Ji murmured his understanding and the two men shook hands and parted ways. Des watched him stride away and then turned back towards Kenilworth Avenue.

His jaw was set as he hurried towards the metro. The Bureau was going to be all over this delegation. They wouldn't be able to take a piss without him knowing about it.

Chapter 11

Frank Sisler tugged at his lip as he re-read Logan's write-up of his Bangkok meeting with Li. Li's assertion that China was planning to marginalize the U.S. economy through cyber warfare had sounded like hyperbole, but the grim reaction the report had elicited from China-watchers was nothing short of surprising.

According to banking analysts, the People's Bank of China, China's Central Bank, was making policy decisions that would position the *renminbi* as a future global reserve currency within the next decade. They pointed to a late 2013 Bank for International Settlements survey that made a startling revelation — the *renminbi* now ranked ninth amongst the ten most actively traded currencies worldwide.

"Not only that," Preston Phillips, senior economist, had added, "since 2010, China's been aggressively pursuing international currency agreements with trading partners that historically maintained dollar-denominated accounts.

"China currently has, or is working on, currency exchange deals with six key trading partners: Australia, Brazil, Japan, Russia, Turkey and the United Arab Emirates."

"How extensive is trade with just those six countries?" Ellen Sanders had asked.

Phillips looked down at his notes and did the mental math.

"You're probably looking at in excess of half a trillion dollars in annual trade this year alone. We've done some trend analysis, and at the rate China's pursuing these bilateral currency exchanges, you could be looking at $3 trillion inside of five years."

Frank had exhaled, letting out a low whistle. "That much!" he exclaimed.

T. L. Williams

"Now mind you, the Intel community's probably a little more bullish on this than the private sector. I'm not sure Goldman or HSBC have given enough weight to the impact China's trade in emerging markets will have on all this."

As usual, Ellen had drawn the conclusion that everyone else was mulling over but had not yet voiced.

"If China's able to stir up mistrust in our banking system by creating uncertainty or worse yet, through cyber attacks, cripple our financial networks, they may believe financial markets will gravitate towards a more stable currency."

"The *renminbi?*" Frank had asked, incredulous. "I can't believe that anyone in his right mind would dump the dollar in favor of the *renminbi*," he had protested.

"When I took my first trip to China in the early '80s, the masses were getting around on bicycles. I couldn't have imagined that today there would be entrepreneurs riding around Shanghai in Lamborghinis, living in faux French villas. It's a different China." Phillips had shaken his head in wonder and the meeting had ended on a somber note.

Frank put the paper down and called Ellen on the intercom to come to his office. Minutes later she poked her head in.

"What's up?"

"I had a call from Rick Wheeler this morning. Magarity met Ji last night."

"I didn't think they were scheduled to meet until the end of the month."

"Ji called for an unscheduled meeting. After the cyber attacks against Sec State, Magarity told Ji that he wanted a heads-up on the slightest activity that smelled of cyber.

"Apparently Ji has a request from a Hong Kong investor with deep pockets who wants to look at commercial properties in Ashburn."

"Right in the middle of the Dulles Technology Corridor."

"It gets better. Song, who's also in the S&T Office, has a group of engineers coming in at the same time. They all supposedly work for Taixun but Song told Ji that at least one of them works at the Institute for Applied Computer Science."

75

"Information assurance?"

"Right. On the crypto and technology side."

"What are they up to?" Ellen looked apprehensive.

"I don't know, but I'm from the school that believes the best defense is a damn good offense."

"What are you thinking?"

"I'm not sure, but remember when we set up Alexander Maritime Consulting we did it with the idea that it would be able to do more than your run-of–the-mill Intel collection platform."

Ellen nodded. "Covert action? My God, Frank. The last time we ran a covert action operation against the Chinese, Eisenhower was President."

"Not true, although Ike did encourage CIA to think big in the '50s. That's when the Nationalist government still thought it had a chance to take the mainland back. We were training guerilla forces on the islands off Taiwan so they could infiltrate the mainland.

"And don't forget our support for the Dalai Lama in the '60s and '70s. We trained hundreds of Tibetan rebels right here in the U.S., supplied them with arms and ammunition and sent them back to collect Intel against China."

"Right. I forgot about Tibet. But there hasn't been anything since Nixon's trip to China in '72."

There was a glint in Frank's eyes.

"Maybe it's time we did something about that. Let's get Logan back here for consultations and put our heads together."

"Are you thinking about targeting them here or on their own turf?"

"As far as I'm concerned, all options are on the table. In some ways an operation in China would be less complicated than trying to do one here."

"You mean the Bureau?"

The CIA and the FBI operate under a Memorandum of Agreement that assigns responsibility for operations in the foreign field to the CIA and domestic operations to the FBI, in keeping with their respective charters.

This might have worked in a simpler time, but in an era of transnational crime, terrorism and cyber warfare, it's sometimes difficult to determine where one agency's responsibilities end and the other's begin. Often they overlap.

Fast-moving operations leave little room for the institutional myopia that more often than not characterizes fractured FBI/CIA interactions.

Fortunately there are broad-minded individuals in both organizations who care about the work, and can see beyond the petty turf wars that so often rupture relations between the two.

"Our lash-up with Cyber Division is pretty good," Frank said. "But that's getting ahead of the game. The director needs buy-in from the Administration before we do anything."

"What are our chances?"

"If we were talking boots on the ground, I'd say zero to nil. We'd be skewered if it ever came out. But for something like this... You should have been there yesterday when we briefed the President on Logan's meeting with Li."

The President was an avid supporter of the Agency, in particular the DO. Occasionally, case officers are invited to accompany the DDO to the President's daily brief to provide a detailed read-out of a breaking development. The President clears the room and it's just him and the Agency team in the Oval Office.

"He asked a lot of good questions. You could tell that he'd read the Intel.

"I think now's as good as it's going to get. We just had this high-profile attack against Sec State, and now this Intel from Li that basically says China is doing everything it can to undermine international support for the dollar."

"All right. Do you want me to take a crack at drafting a memo for the Seventh Floor?"

"Let me get on the DDO's schedule tomorrow and I'll brief him on the concept, just to make sure he's behind it. If we get the green light from him, we can go ahead and circulate a memo internally and then send it over to the National Security Council (NSC).

"Oh, I wanted to give you this." Frank handed Ellen an envelope that was sitting on his desk.

"Li's code name came in this morning. From now on he'll be known as 'Phoenix.'" They'd have to get used to referring to the MPS officer by his new code name when discussing the case or corresponding with Logan, to better protect their new asset's identity.

"Risen from the ashes."

"Someone in registry was feeling creative, I guess."

* * *

Lois Caldwell was frustrated. She had walked the names of the three engineers that Ji had given to Des over to a China analyst in Cyber Division to see if they had any information on them. Two of the names drew a blank, but they were luckier with the third. Pan Chengong was on loan from the Institute for Applied Computer Science. His résumé was posted on the university website.

Pan had a PhD in computer science from Stanford, she learned. His undergraduate course work was in software development, but his graduate work focused almost entirely on telecommunications and network security and risk management.

She thanked the analyst who had pulled Pan's bio off the university website and walked back to her office at the Washington Field Office. It was just before noon and a jazz quartet was setting up to play during the lunch hour in front of the Navy Memorial.

Signal flags rustled as a gentle breeze blew through the plaza. Lois paused in front of the statue of the Lone Sailor and let her mind wonder as she went over the information she'd just received.

It had only taken one call to gain FBI access to Pan's student records at Stanford. He'd been an honor student from his first semester and there was nothing in his early course work that would arouse any concerns.

During graduate school, Pan had spent the majority of

his time at Stanford's Security Laboratory. Lois was becoming increasingly concerned as she read through Pan's transcripts. Virtually all of his time during his last two years was spent working on two projects – Web Security and Protocols, where he had delved into the characteristics of network protocols.

Most of what Pan had done at Stanford was ultra-geeky. He was a key innovator in the use of protocol composition logic to understand the security properties of network protocols. Through his work, Pan would have developed incredible insights into state-of-the-art computer network security standards in the U.S.

In fact, Pan's work was so advanced, he had been invited to lead a workshop entitled "Formal Methods in Security Engineering" at the Institute of Electrical and Electronics Engineers' annual meeting in 2004.

"What are you up to, Mr. Pan?" Lois asked herself.

And then it hit her, sending an icy sensation coursing through her veins. Pan's understanding of U.S. network security standards made him an expert in network vulnerabilities. Pan wasn't your run-of-the-mill hacker, exposing weaknesses in the system and then exploiting them with malware. No, his would be a Zero Day cyber attack. Something spectacular, and on a scale never before seen.

Lois clenched her teeth and turned away from the plaza.

"Not if I have anything to say about it," she swore. Pan had no idea what he was up against.

Chapter 12

Logan exited the MTR at Kowloon's Mong Kok Station. His ten o'clock appointment with Abercrombie and York's Hong Kong director, Andrew Gao, was in the nearby Langham Place Office Tower. Logan was following up on a query that Norm Stoddard had made for him while he was in Thailand.

Gao's office suite was situated on the twentieth floor. It was plush, but that was to be expected given Abercrombie's high-end clientele. Gao's secretary ushered him into a small conference room and took his order for a cappuccino. From the photos on the walls it looked as though Abercrombie had a fleet of four river cruisers operating in China.

"That's the Jade Empress," Gao said, as he stepped into the room.

Logan turned away from the photo to look at the man. He was in his forties, urbane and exuded old-school money.

"Good morning, Logan Alexander." He withdrew a name card from his breast pocket and handed it to Gao.

"Alexander Maritime Consulting. Are you from the States?" Gao guided him over to a set of leather chairs where they sat down.

"Yes, Boston. We've just set up a branch office in Hong Kong and are open for business. We specialize in consulting and maritime design, but are exploring the possibility of opening a small shipyard on the mainland with a view to entering the luxury yacht market.

"I was recently in Chongqing and saw two of your ships on the Yangtze River. One of them was the Jade Empress. I was so impressed with her lines that I asked your captain if he would mind giving me a tour. He was nice enough to accommodate me."

"We're proud of what we've created. Our brand is 'luxury boutique.' We're not trying to compete with the large cruise lines of the world. Seabourn and Uniworld are our chief competitors in Asia. As you're probably aware, Abercrombie got its river cruising start in Europe but we've been in Asia for three decades."

"Who else are you competing with here?"

"Besides those two I would say Silversea."

"Where are you having your ships built?"

"Ten, twenty years ago we were using European ship-yards, but about four years ago we contracted with a ship-yard in Wuhan to build the Jade Empress, and were very pleased with the results.

"We decided to take a page from McDonnell Douglas's playbook. They established a joint venture in Shanghai in the 1980s to assemble MD-11 passenger planes from kits.

"When those MD-11's started coming off the line, aircraft inspectors were amazed that they were of a higher quality than the ones coming out of Long Beach. Why? You ask. Because labor costs were so low that they could afford to be painstaking," Gao said.

"When we started, the idea was to bring in virtually all the components, and use inexpensive skilled labor to assemble them. Except for the hull, we imported essentially everything – major systems like propulsion and navigation – materials, furnishings. The works."

"Did you have any problems importing all that material?"

"No. The Chinese take the long view in these ventures. While they could shut us down because they control so many critical elements – labor, supplies, facilities, and power – it's in their interest to have it go smoothly. In ten years they'll be producing luxury yachts on their own and all of the components will be made in China.

"Wuhan was attractive to us, too, because of its university. It has a reputable maritime engineering program that turns out a steady stream of graduates looking for jobs. There's also no shortage of skilled labor in the city.

"The shipyard experienced some initial growing pains, but one thing that helped us early on was convincing Lloyd's Register to establish an office nearby. As you know, they're the gold standard when it comes to design and safety.

"Lloyd's worked closely with our marine engineers to approve some of the innovations you saw on the Jade Empress. Also, as a leader in green technology, we looked to Lloyd's expertise in this area to certify our new hybrid propulsion system."

Logan was growing restless. Although he was actually interested in what Gao had to say, given his degree in naval architecture from Annapolis, he was chafing to get back to work on his cyber operation.

Time spent on cover business could pay dividends down the road, he conceded to himself. Most Ops officers have a strong distaste for cover work because, more often than not, it does little to advance their careers.

In this case, meeting with Andrew Gao, he was enhancing Alexander Maritime's cover as a legitimate company. And with any luck he might develop business opportunities that would provide legitimate cover for travel to China.

"Take a look at this." Gao rose to dim the lights and an overhead projector began flashing a slide show of the stunning interior of the Jade Empress. There were twenty three-hundred-square-foot suites with balconies offering panoramic vistas and nearly as many one-hundred-fifty-square-foot suites for passengers traveling by themselves.

"Do all of the cabins face outside? I don't remember."

"Yes, everything is geared towards optimizing our clients' experience."

The slide show went on to highlight the fitness center, spa, hair salon, wood-paneled library and richly furnished common areas. Those accustomed to traveling in style would want for nothing.

When the show was over, Logan thanked Gao for taking the time to discuss their fleet. The two men shook hands and promised to stay in touch.

Logan took the elevator down to the ground floor and walked over to the Star Ferry terminal in Tsim Sha Tsui. The ferry had been a fixture in Hong Kong for over a hundred and twenty years, plying the waters of Victoria Harbor between Kowloon and Central.

I wish I had this gig, Logan thought. Let's see — 70,000 passengers a day according to Fodor's at about a buck a trip. $70,000 a day comes out to more than $25 million a year.

He was meeting Zahir for lunch at the China Club in Central. Located in the old Bank of China Building, the club was the last bastion of British colonial rule up until the UK handed the reins back over to China in 1997.

He'd be happy getting a bowl of noodles from one of the food vendors on Graham Street, but Zahir liked the atmosphere of the club. There was rich wood paneling in the dining rooms. Ceiling fans moved the still air and white-gloved waiters moved efficiently amongst the tables. You got the feeling that you had stepped back in time. Way back.

Zahir was waiting for him in the lobby. He smiled when he saw her. They'd had an unlikely courtship five years ago. She'd been working on a DoD contract in Iraq as a civilian Arabic language translator, and had been assigned to his younger brother Cooper's unit. She and Cooper had fallen in love and Zahir had become pregnant just before Cooper was killed in an IED attack.

Logan initially had mistrusted Zahir, because of an experience he had while serving in Afghanistan with his SEAL unit. His Arabic translator set the team up for an ambush and Logan was severely wounded.

Over time Zahir had gained his trust, while accompanying Logan's team on his Iran mission as their Farsi linguist, and then his love.

After they'd been seated and the waiter took their order, Logan leaned forward and made an announcement.

"Looks like I have to go to Washington next week. I was thinking we could make it a family trip, get up to Montpelier to visit Mom and Dad for the weekend, and when I have my meetings in Washington, we could visit with your parents."

"I think I can manage that. I'll have to get somebody to cover my classes for the week, but that shouldn't be a problem. A couple of the teaching assistants are always looking for extra hours.

"It's a long trip for Cooper though. He has trouble sitting still that long."

"He'll be all right. The grandparents don't get a chance to see him very often with us over here."

Zahir knew there were times that Logan was operational with the CIA and was using her presence to provide cover for action, but for the most part she was not aware of his specific operations.

During his operational training, Zahir had received several briefings on the life of an operations officer and had even participated in some surveillance training for spouses so she would be able to recognize surveillance when she had it.

"I think I had surveillance on my way to the club."

"What!"

"Don't turn around now, but there are two guys seated three tables behind us." She described what they were wearing. "I spotted them near the Peak Tram, and they followed me into the restaurant. It was a pretty straight hike so it may be nothing."

Zahir was very observant, and Logan had come to trust her operational judgment from the time they had infiltrated the terrorist training camp in Iran. If she thought she had spotted surveillance, she probably had. The question was why? And if so, why now?

The trip to China may have caught somebody's attention. He didn't like the timing and it was probably wrong to link it, if it was surveillance, to his recent operational activity. Even so, there was no such thing as a coincidence in the spy business. He decided to take a look.

Logan got up to wash his hands in the men's room. He was nonchalant as he walked past the suspects' table.

Although the dress code in the dining room called for jacket and tie for men, these two were dressed more casually. Both were wearing button-down shirts and dark trousers. Lightweight black leather bomber jackets hung from their chair backs.

Logan glanced in their direction as he walked by. They both appeared to be in their early thirties, and sat slouched back in their chairs smoking. Their unblinking eyes stared back as he looked their way. He could feel their eyes boring into his back as he moved past the table.

"Looks like security," he thought to himself as he stepped into the men's room and walked over to the row of sinks. He heard the door open behind him and, glancing in the mirror was surprised to see one of the two men come in.

The man walked over to a sink next to his and turned on the water. He began lathering his hands with soap, all the while turning his head this way and that scrutinizing his reflection. He allowed his gaze to settle on Logan for an instant, gave him a menacing look and then turned back to his hand washing.

When he was done he dried his hands, grunted and then turned and sauntered out of the restroom.

When Logan stepped out a moment later the two men were gone. He returned to the table and Zahir gave him a questioning look.

"I saw him go in after you. What happened?"

"It was bizarre." He described his encounter with the suspect public security officer.

"It was almost like counting coup."

"What's that?"

"It was a native American thing. The Great Plains warriors used to have these things called coup sticks and they felt that the bravest thing in battle was to touch the enemy with a stick or their hand and escape unharmed.

"This was like an old-style KGB move. The Russians didn't care if their target knew they were there. In fact, a lot of times they would go out of their way to show themselves as a form of intimidation.

"Chinese security has always been much more subtle. They don't want you to know they're out there. If those two guy were public security it wasn't standard MO."

"And if they weren't?"

"It was just weird. I'll report it, and we'll definitely have to keep our eyes open. But we'll have to be careful. If they get the sense that we're surveillance-conscious or they think I'm taking evasive measures, they'll know I'm up to no good."

Logan didn't meet agents or do anything operational on the streets of Hong Kong. It was imperative for his cover and for Li's safety that he look like nothing more than an American maritime consultant.

The waiter brought their food, and Logan pushed the encounter out of his mind for now. If the Chinese thought they could spook him by sending two goons in to intimidate him, they didn't know what they were dealing with. It would take a lot more than that to rattle Logan Alexander.

Chapter 13

Superintendent Li Jiang awoke from a restive slumber. Rubbing his eyes, he sat up in bed and glanced down at his wife. They had known each other since middle school. Her parents were intellectuals – both had been teachers at the Chongqing Technology and Business University, but were now retired.

Xiao Mei's family had lived in university-provided housing on Xuefu Avenue, near the foothills of Nan Shan Mountain, not far from the PLA-provided apartment where the Li family dwelled.

As college students Li and Xiao Mei had often packed picnic lunches to take on their weekend hikes in the mountains. She delighted in preparing his favorite dishes – baked Hoisin chicken wings, and potato salad. In the spring they would walk in the lush green foothills and spread their blanket on the ground. There they would stare up at the sky and dream about their future together.

Li grunted as he slipped out of bed. Xiao Mei was sleeping in this morning. Their son, Xiao Jun, had already left for his morning *taiqi* class. Li dressed quietly and slipped out of the apartment. He mounted his bicycle and rode a half-mile to a side street lined with food vendors.

He dismounted near one of the mobile noodle carts and ordered a bowl of beef noodle soup and a hot bean juice from the peddler. The old woman shuffled to a mound of fresh egg noodles, scooped up a handful, and in a single motion tossed them into a basket that she lowered into boiling water. When they were ready she drained them, shaking the basket with a vigorous motion, and dumped them into a large plastic bowl. She added several thin strips of beef, poured in a seasoned broth, and added a sprig of cilantro for garnish.

She handed the steaming bowl across the counter and then ladled out a portion of hot bean juice. She accepted the six *renminbi* he handed her without comment and then turned to wait on another customer.

Li took his breakfast to a card table set up on the sidewalk and watched Chongqing come to life as he slurped his noodles. He belched in appreciation, wiped his mouth on a paper napkin and moments later re-mounted his bicycle for the two-mile ride to his office.

It had been a welcome surprise three years ago when his boss tasked him to recruit a group of hackers proficient in English to set up a computer network exploitation unit in Chongqing, targeting leadership communications in the U.S. government. He and Xiao Mei had grown weary of Chengdu, where he had been assigned, and had looked forward to returning to their hometown, where they would be closer to their parents. He hadn't realized at the time that this chance to reunite with his father would be so short-lived.

Most outsiders felt that Chengdu was overwhelming, swarming with a population of 13 million. Chongqing, which had recently been named a municipality, had more than twice that number.

Li loved the city with its boundless, abrasive energy. Poised at the confluence of two great rivers, it had neighborhoods bordering the waterways while still others could only be reached by ascending dramatic staircases 1,400 feet to Nan Shan Park.

Ten minutes later he turned into his building. The MPS had taken advantage of a glut in commercial real estate in Chongqing to put a long-term lease on this commercial office building downtown. They had retrofitted the office space to fit their particular needs, installing an OC3 fiber optic line to handle their high-speed computing requirements.

When he walked into his office, his assistant, Sergeant Shi, handed him a sealed envelope, marked Top Secret - Urgent.

"This just arrived, sir."

"Thank you. Anything else need my immediate attention?"

"You're meeting with the new group of civilian employees this morning."

Li nodded. He sat down at his desk and opened the envelope. Inside was a message from the Deputy Minister of Public Security ordering him to attend a meeting with China's Cyber Executive in Chengdu the next day to be briefed on a project of the highest priority.

Li asked Sergeant Shi to take care of his travel arrangements. He'd take a morning train and return to Chongqing late in the afternoon. The trip was only two hours each way. Today he'd spend the morning meeting with a new group of elite civilian hackers who had just joined the program. He had found that spending time with new employees at the beginning of their service paid dividends in productivity.

Most of these young hackers were involuntary workers. Since hacking in China is illegal, those who are caught can face stiff fines – up to several years of jail time, although the MPS rarely enforced it.

When it suits the government's purpose they round up these cyber criminals and transform them into cyber warriors. From the outset they are obligated to two years of service. They are read in on some of the most sensitive Cyber operations and, when they leave the program, must pledge a vow of secrecy.

Li walked into a small conference room down the hall from his office. A dozen young men were sprawled around the table, chattering. They straightened in their seats when he entered the room and looked at him in anticipation.

"Good morning." Li set some notes down on the table and took a seat.

"I'm Superintendent Li, and I'm in charge of this facility." He looked around at the expectant faces.

"This is one place where you won't get into trouble for being a good hacker." There was an eruption of nervous laughter from the group. After it had subsided he picked up a page from the desk and scanned it.

"Which one of you is Wu?" he asked, studying the faces.

An undersized youth with prominent glasses that kept sliding down his nose gave an apprehensive wave of his hand.

Li returned to the sheet of paper in front of him.

"Mr. Wu is with us because of his creation of the virus, W43/XDocCrypt.d. This virus is capable of infecting executable files within the Microsoft Office suite of programs.

"But where Mr. Wu proved to be most proficient was in his entrepreneurial abilities. He sold over 1,000 copies of the virus online before it came to the prosecutor's attention."

The other men in the room regarded Wu with newfound respect. Li turned back to his notes and thumbed through them without comment. After a minute he looked up at the attentive faces.

"Mr. Zhang?" He eyeballed the group and caught sight of a slender young man with alert eyes and a suave demeanor, who acknowledged Li with a vague wave.

"Mr. Zhang is the designer of '2004 Tsunami,' a Trojan horse that attacks primarily Microsoft computers. This worm spreads through email and then tasks infected computers to join a botnet.

"Mr. Zhang was apprehended before he had the opportunity to implement his attack, but it goes without saying that we are very interested in Tsunami's potential."

Li waved the file in front of him.

"There are many more examples of your collective creativity in here. I won't belabor the point because I think you can see where I'm going with this. We are an elite Public Security Tactical Unit. Our Bureau comes under the command of the Central Government." He had their attention now. They sat tall in their seats, eyes fixed on him.

"I believe you'll find the working conditions here quite good. We have an OC3 line servicing our building, so I assume you'll find computing speed a bit faster than what you're accustomed to." He gave the men a wry smile.

"I'm going to turn you over to my deputy, Superintendent Bai, who will provide you with a security briefing, give you a tour of our spaces and show you where you will be working. You'll each be assigned a mentor, someone who came into the program because they ran afoul of law enforcement through their criminal hacking activities. They will be here to answer your questions and make sure you get off to a good start.

"I'll be meeting with each of you one on one during the first week and we'll talk about your individual assignments then. Most of you will be working in teams, but there are one or two who will be working on their own projects. How many of you are proficient in writing code?"

Everyone's hand shot up.

"Good. Are there any questions?"

The men looked around at one another and shifted in their seats. No one spoke up.

"All right then. I'll turn you over to Mr. Bai."

Li returned to his office. "Interesting group," he thought, as he picked up the phone to call Xiao Mei.

"Hi. I just wanted to let you know that I have to go to Chengdu tomorrow morning."

"Will you be spending the night?"

"No. It's just a day trip. I should be home in time for dinner."

"Don't forget, your mother's coming over tomorrow night."

"Yes, I remember. Do you need me to pick up anything while I'm out?"

"No. I just thought I'd make a hot pot."

"She likes that. See if you can find some fresh squid. That's her favorite. I'll be home by six tonight."

"Okay. See you then. *Bao bei?*" It was her usual affectionate term, meaning sweetheart.

"Yes?"

"Oh, never mind. I'll see you tonight."

"Bye."

Li hung up and then spent the rest of the afternoon working at his desk. His initial anxiety over the clandestine meetings with the Americans had given way to a sense of relief and acceptance. There was no evidence that he was under suspicion at work. All of his colleagues continued to treat him per usual.

Not for the first time though, he felt a pang of guilt when he acknowledged that he had not discussed his actions with Xiao Mei before going down this path. They had shared their deepest feelings since childhood. This was the first time he had kept her in the dark, especially about something that could impact her so deeply. It was for her own safety, he reasoned. She would be fearful for their family and furious with him if she knew what he'd done.

Recently he'd been giving serious thought to a new plan – that one day soon he would take the family to America. Of course it was out of the question as long as he remained on active duty. But after he retired, their son could go to college there and he and Xiao Mei would move far away from the rot that had destroyed his father.

His mood turned black as his thoughts wandered back to his father's rapid fall from grace and the sense of helplessness that had enveloped the family as they watched his abrupt decline in health.

In moments of weakness, when he questioned the wisdom of his decision to offer his services to the Americans, all he had to do was recall the frail shadow of a man who had once been admired for his battlefield exploits. Too embarrassed to be seen in public after Bo's clique tarnished his reputation, he had kept to himself those last few months of his life.

Li decided to wrap things up early. With their busy schedules, it seemed he and Xiao Mei had little time to spend together. They should plan a picnic in Nan Shan Park, as they had years ago. He reminded Bai that he would be in Chengdu all day tomorrow.

Twenty minutes later he wheeled his bicycle into the courtyard of his apartment building. He was anxious to tell Xiao Mei about his idea to have a picnic in the park. He knew she would be pleased.

There were no lights on in the apartment. It was dark and quiet as he walked down the hallway to their bedroom. Perhaps Xiao Mei was taking a nap. She had been busy with exams in her graduate statistics class. But, no, there was a light on shining under the door.

Xiao Mei was sitting in a chair by the window. A book was in her lap, and she was curled to one side, napping.

"Xiao Mei?"

She did not stir, and as he walked over to the chair he was surprised that she had not awakened, because she normally was a very light sleeper. As he reached for her shoulder he glanced down and saw that Xiao Mei's wrist was slit, dangling to one side. There was blood everywhere. The razor blade she had used lay on the floor next to the chair.

"Xiao Mei!"

He touched her face and felt for a pulse on her neck. She was cold and he could feel no heartbeat. He knew then that she was dead. Rigor mortis had not yet set in. It was likely she had not been there for all that long.

"Xiao Mei!" he wailed. "What have you done?" He slumped to his knees and buried his face in her lap. Convulsed with sobs he raised his head and stared into his wife's pallid face. His heart was thudding in his chest and his mind was racing to understand what could have led her to do this.

He reviewed his conversation with her earlier in the day to see if there had been any clue that she was contemplating suicide. But, no, she had seemed quite normal. It had sounded as though she was looking forward to hosting his mother for hot pot.

She must have left a note. He tore through the apartment looking for something, anything. But everything seemed to be in order. There was nothing.

Li looked at the time, and remembered that Xiao Jun was going to chess club after classes and would not be home until later. He didn't want their son to find his mother like this.

He called the PSB chief and Bai to report what had happened. He asked Bai to contact Chengdu to explain the circumstances and to cancel his travel plans. Then he called his sister, Huiling, and Xiao Mei's parents.

Within the hour the apartment was swarming with Public Security officers, who treated the area as a crime scene. After they finished examining Xiao Mei's body they released it to the Szechuan Sixth People's hospital, where it would be placed in the mortuary. Normally, the body would be kept at home and a wake would be arranged, but given the circumstances, the police wanted the body preserved until they had completed their investigation. After the police left, the family gathered in the kitchen.

"I don't understand why she would do this," Li spread his hands and looked around the table. Xiao Mei's parents were huddled together and Huiling was busy putting a kettle on for tea. Moments later his son arrived home from chess club.

"Ba, what's going on?" he asked, as he looked around the kitchen. "Where's Ma?"

Li dreaded the words he was about to speak.

"There's been an accident, Xiao Jun. Mother passed away sometime this afternoon." He couldn't bring himself to utter the word "suicide" although he knew that he would have to tell Xiao Jun soon enough. How could you explain to a child that his mother had chosen death over life? It was the consummate form of rejection.

Huiling wrapped her arms around Xiao Jun as he began to sob out of control. She looked over his shoulder into the eyes of her brother and shook her head. Li knew that she and Xiao Mei had never been as close as sisters, but neither had there been any differences between them.

No one felt like eating. They drank tea and talked until ten o'clock, when his sister and in-laws took their leave. Exhausted, Li and his son went to their rooms and collapsed in their respective beds.

The rest of the week flew by in a hazy blur of activity. Huiling took charge of the funeral arrangements. Public Security released Xiao Mei's body on Wednesday and there followed three days of mourning at the Li residence. She was cremated on Sunday and Li, grasping for anything to dull his grief, left for Chengdu on Monday. Work would have to be his antidote for sorrow.

Li walked into Commissioner Fang's office in the Chengdu Public Security headquarters building at ten-thirty Monday morning. By eleven o'clock he was being read into a compartmented project by three engineers the Cyber Executive had brought in from the Institute for Applied Computer Science. They were outlining an operation so bold that it had sent his mind racing. Pan Chengong, the lead engineer for the project, was speaking.

"Through a sensitive source, we've identified three buildings in Ashburn, Virginia, that house Internet relays for critical communications from the major financial institutions in the United States.

"This system was set up following the attacks on the World Trade Center in 2001. Each of these buildings functions essentially as a server farm, housing thousands of computers, switches and routers.

"After our denial-of-service attack against major U.S. banks last year, we discovered that, at the urging of the U.S. cyber czar, financial institutions have developed a sophisticated traffic rerouting scheme, designed to insulate their most sensitive transactions and avoid tampering from hackers."

Pan turned on an overhead projector and displayed a diagram depicting the scheme. Using a laser pointer, he highlighted one area.

"This is where the fiber optic trunk line servicing these three buildings resides. A sensitive source has confirmed that fiber optic lines transmitting the most sensitive Internet communications pass beneath all three buildings. But they all feed off of this trunk line.

"Because of the high number of subscribers, when the network engineers set this up, they had to devise a secure means of routing traffic to all of them. The solution? Install beam splitters in the fiber optic trunk. This way they were able to run individual fiber optic lines off the beam splitters and into the three buildings. From there the traffic is distributed all over the U.S. and internationally.

"Last week the three of us visited Washington under the auspices of a commercial venture funded by Taixun, the Internet company. While there we visited Ashburn, and identified this office building, ostensibly for Taixun."

Pan went to the next slide, which showed a nondescript three-story commercial building. He then pulled up a final slide depicting all four buildings on a map. The Taixun property was adjacent to, and less than a hundred feet from the building above the fiber optic trunk.

Li gave Pan a knowing look.

"What does your plan call for?"

"We're going into the fiber optic trunk. In this first phase we'll be sampling what's coming across the trunk. We'll be tasking your unit to help us exploit the Intel take."

"And then?"

"When we get the okay from leadership, we're going to take down their banking system."

"Everything?" Li blurted out.

"Everything," Pan repeated. "Everything."

Chapter 14

Logan chuckled as he watched Cooper scramble through a pile of leaves that his grandfather, Harry Alexander, had just raked together, scattering them every which way. Cooper screeched as Harry feigned anger and began chasing him around the backyard.

The Alexanders had arrived at the family homestead in Montpelier, Vermont, late Friday night, following an exhausting flight from Hong Kong. Two cups of black coffee had done little to soothe his jet lag, but Logan could feel the caffeine starting to kick in.

His mother, Lise, and Zahir had taken their coffee outside and were deep in conversation, curled up in a chaise on the deck. His sister, Millie, and her husband, Ryan, were coming up from Boston later in the morning to spend the weekend with them.

Logan was moved by a surge of nostalgia as he gazed out at the familiar tableau. He, Millie, and their kid brother, Cooper, had spent hours playing in this back yard. He felt a lump in his throat as a flood of memories crowded his thoughts. It had been five years ago, in this very house, that two U.S. Army National Guard officers had shattered their world with news of Cooper's death in Iraq.

He sighed as he refilled his coffee cup and took it outside. Cooper lived on through his son, who was the spitting image of his father. Logan's cell phone rang and he recognized from the caller ID that it was an ops number Frank Sisler used to call him when he was in the U.S.

"Hey. What's up?"

"Just checking to make sure you got in okay."

Despite the fact that Frank used an encrypted phone not linked to the Agency or to him personally, their conversations were always cryptic. Logan knew that Frank would be calling from Baltimore or someplace far from CIA Headquarters, and that the call would be rerouted through cities as far-flung as San Francisco, Miami and Duluth before it ever got to him, just in case someone was trying to track his whereabouts.

"Listen, I wanted to let you know that we had a message from your friend."

Li must have activated the rudimentary communications plan that was issued to him in Bangkok. The PSB officer was still considered an un-vetted asset, and despite the tantalizing Intel he was providing, Langley wouldn't risk compromising its most sensitive covert communications systems with him until he had proven himself beyond a doubt.

Logan had given Li a post office box number located in Ames, Iowa. A support asset there was supposed to check the box weekly and would expedite delivery of any communications to Frank's unit at Langley.

He'd made Li memorize the address, so that when he returned to Chongqing, he wouldn't have any incriminating evidence on his person when he went through security. He'd told him to mail his letter from an international mailbox, to use a bogus return address, and to avoid any content in the message itself that the authorities could link back directly to him.

"It was vague, but it pretty much confirms information that our friends downtown got ten days ago."

Must be the Bureau, Logan thought to himself. They're under the gun to deliver on the cyber threat.

He knew that there was an all-out effort to counter what the Chinese were doing. Li's op against Sec State had been a wake-up call to just how good the Chinese hackers really were.

"Do you need to see me sooner than Monday?" Logan asked.

"No. Let's stick with our original schedule. I'm working on something that I think you'll find is right up your alley."

"Can't wait. See you then."

The rest of the weekend flew by. After a quiet day at home on Saturday, everyone wanted to go for a drive, because Vermont in the fall is something special. They headed out Sunday morning after breakfast and Mass, driving along Route 2 where the leaves, painted in shades of red and orange, dangled like ornaments from Christmas trees.

They meandered through quaint villages, distinguished by tall, slender church spires and historic covered bridges. Near Shelburne they were pleasantly surprised to find a working sugar shack out of season. The farmer told them he had so many trees that he was tapping five hundred this fall just to satisfy the tourist trade. His busy season was normally in the spring, when the temperatures rise above freezing and the sap begins to run. Zahir bought a maple cream pie to take back to Montpelier for desert.

Millie and Ryan headed back to Boston following an early dinner. After they had left, Logan put Cooper down and he and Zahir joined his parents in the family room for a couple of hands of whist before going to bed.

They were up before daybreak in order to get an early start for the airport. They had a light breakfast and then loaded the rental car with their bags. Logan hugged his parents and then walked around to the driver's side.

"Mom and I are talking about coming out to Hong Kong in December." Harry leaned into the back seat to check that Cooper's seat belt was snug and gave him a kiss.

"This little guy's growing so fast we won't recognize him."

Elise squeezed Zahir's arm. "Safe travels," she said, sniffling. Goodbyes were always hard.

"Thanks for everything, Mom and Dad," Logan and Zahir said in unison. "We'll plan on seeing you in December. Love you."

"Bye. We love you," the parents chorused, standing in the driveway, waving until the car was out of sight.

The drive up I-81 to Burlington International was uneventful. Logan left Zahir and Cooper in front of the departures area and then circled back around to drop off the rental car.

Their U.S. Airways flight to Reagan National was on time, and ninety minutes later the Capitol dome and the Washington Monument came into view as their pilot descended through the clouds and lined up his visual approach along the Potomac River.

Zahir's parents, who were retired and lived in nearby Arlington, met them at baggage claim. Their bags were delayed but when they finally spilled out onto the conveyer belt Logan lugged them to the short-term parking area where he piled everything into the Parandehs' Escalade.

Zahir and Cooper were going home with her parents and Logan was going to pick up a rental car and try to make his eleven o'clock meeting with Frank Sisler.

"I'll see you tonight, sweetheart." He kissed Zahir goodbye.

"Call me if you think you'll be late."

"Okay. Love you." He tickled Cooper under the chin, shut the rear door, and waved goodbye to his in-laws as the car pulled away.

Avis upgraded him to a Chrysler 300. He tossed his briefcase onto the back seat, hung his suit jacket on the rear passenger side and steered the rental towards Vienna. He fiddled with the radio until he found his favorite country station, 98.7 WMZQ. Tapping his hand on the steering wheel to the beat of the music, his mind shifted to work. He wondered who, beside Frank, would be at the meeting. They would be meeting at safehouse "Boral," an office suite in a commercial building near the Vienna Metro Station.

Twenty minutes later, Logan pulled into the Lincolnwood's parking lot. The safehouse was on the top two floors of the eight-story building. For security purposes, the Agency preferred to control the space on all sides of these commercial safe sites. That way there was less risk of hostile penetration by hostile foreign intelligence services.

The solid wood exterior door leading into the office bore the name Hathaway and Sons, Geothermal Engineers, inscribed in gold block lettering.

Logan buzzed himself in and was greeted by Penelope Kieper, an Agency staffer from the Office of Security.

"Good morning, sir," she smiled. "Mr. Sisler and the others just got here. You can go on in," she gestured down the hall.

Penny looked like a bookworm sitting there behind the receptionist desk. But Logan knew for a fact that she had aced her last firearms qualifications test and two years ago had earned a black belt in taekwondo.

"Hey, Penny. How've you been? Still going out with that lawyer in the Office of General Counsel?"

She laughed and shook her head. "Negative. When he said he wanted me to stop competing in martial arts, I knew he didn't really get me. There wasn't much of a future there."

She pulled a picture out of her wallet, and offered it to Logan.

Logan let out a low whistle of appreciation when he saw the picture. Penny was standing next to a hulk of a man that Logan recognized as Gary Rivers, starting left wing for the Washington Capitals.

"We've been going out for a month."

He nodded in appreciation as he handed the picture back. "Nice. Don't let him get out of line."

Penny laughed. "Not much chance of that happening."

Logan could hear the murmur of voices coming from the conference room as he drew near.

"Wonder who Frank's got in there. Probably the Bureau since they've got the lead on foreign cyber attacks," he speculated.

Even though he was under deep cover, he wasn't too worried about meeting with the Bureau. They all had SI/TK security clearances, and outside of Frank and Ellen, no one even knew his real name. In settings like this, the rule of thumb was to call him Jake. No last name.

Entering the conference room, Logan spotted Frank Sisler and Ellen Sanders. He didn't recognize the man and woman on the other side of the table, although he'd bet even money that the guy was FBI, because of the blue suit, button-down white shirt and muted tie.

"Jake!" Frank leapt up from the table and reached out to clasp his hand. Ellen smiled and patted his arm as he walked around her to a vacant seat at the table.

"I'd like to introduce Special Agents Des Magarity and Lois Caldwell. Des is running the cyber investigation at the Bureau and Lois is a computer scientist specializing in optical communications systems and networks."

Des and Lois both acknowledged Logan and looked to Frank to kick things off.

"I took the liberty of having lunch brought in, so we could work straight through. Penny's going to bring it in – deli sandwiches, chips and sodas. We've got bottled water if anyone prefers that."

After the food was delivered and everyone had fixed a plate, Frank asked Des to recount his meeting with Mr. Ji.

"I don't trust this guy a hundred percent," Des confided. "We had our eye on him for a couple of years and we got lucky. Caught him in a compromising position and leaned on him, threatening to take it to his ambassador if he didn't cooperate. So far his info's checked out."

He went on to recount Ji's report on the delegation purportedly from the Internet company, Taixun.

"Lois was able to dig up the skinny on one of the other S&T officers, Mr. Song, who told Ji that Pan really works for the Institute for Applied Computer Science. He has ties to China's Cyber executive." Des took a swipe at a dollop of mustard that had squirted onto his tie, and swore.

"We got this message from Phoenix after Song's group had come and gone," Frank said. He handed a translation of Phoenix's letter to Logan, who read it in silence. When he finished reading he looked around the room.

"What do you think it means?"

Lois Caldwell spoke up. "We're not exactly sure what they're after, but I have an idea."

She gave him a rundown of her research into Pan Chengong's background, emphasizing his expertise in U.S. network security standards.

"I think China's planning a Zero Day cyber attack. Something that goes beyond anything we've experienced to date."

"We have an idea where they might be headed, but it's so outrageous it strains credibility," Frank said.

He went on to describe his and Ellen's meeting with analysts in Cyber Division and their concerns about China's feverish race to secure *renminbi* currency agreements with their most important trading partners.

"China's currency deals have marginalized the dollar in those markets. Analysts project that within the next five years over $3 trillion in Chinese trade will be conducted using the *renminbi* as the preferred currency over the dollar. The world is experiencing non-dollar-denominated currency transactions on a scale never before seen. Certainly as it relates to China."

"But that's ridiculous," Logan protested. "You can't tell me the Chinese really believe the *renminbi* is going to replace the dollar as the most stable trading currency." He looked in disbelief at the somber faces staring back at him.

"Right now it's a working hypothesis," Ellen said. "But China's effort to change the status quo vis-à-vis the dollar in foreign trade is indisputable."

"And," Lois added, "we're identifying more aggressive, persistent cyber attacks by the Chinese against the homeland than at any other time in recent memory. Banking, the electric power grid, sensitive government networks like the Office of Personnel Management (OPM), and the entire military industrial complex. They're all under attack.

"Take the repeated theft of consumer credit card data and the denial-of-service attacks against major banks. If these intrusions cause a loss of confidence in the banking system at home, China will have succeeded in undermining one of the strongest underpinnings of U.S. national security. Our economy."

Ellen Sanders turned on an overhead projector and displayed a map of Northern Virginia.

"Based on information from the Bureau's source, we identified the target building Pan and his so-called Taixun buddies were going after."

She clicked to the next slide and a head shot of a Chinese male appeared on the wall.

"This is Jason Wu. He's a wealthy Hong Kong businessman with ties to the Minister of Public Security. We've kept a file on him since 2009. He seems to be the go-to guy the MPS uses when they're trying to conceal their hand. Some of our officers have taken a run at him over the years but he's never shown any vulnerabilities."

"We had surveillance on Wu and the engineers the whole time they were here," Des interjected.

"They shipped a load of equipment in through the pouch. And they weren't carrying anything out of the ordinary in their personal luggage. We had someone in baggage claim at Dulles check their bags before they came out."

"What were you looking for?" Logan asked.

"We weren't sure. Ji didn't know, but he said Song seemed to think they were going to do some kind of survey in Ashburn."

Ellen clicked to the next slide. "We now know this is the target building based upon FBI surveillance reports on Jason Wu's activity over several days. It's clear that he was laying down a smokescreen because he had a realtor from Coldwell Banker take him around to a dozen commercial properties, not just in Ashburn, but Reston, Vienna, Leesburg and Chantilly."

"And he never physically hooked up with the team of engineers." Des had a dour look on his face. He leaned back in his chair and stabbed a finger at Lois.

"Tell them what we found out, Lois."

"The engineers kept a low profile until last Thursday evening. Around eleven p.m. they left their hotel in a Ryder van and went to this commercial building." She highlighted the Ashburn property.

"They used underground parking to gain access to the building. We had guessed, correctly as it turns out, based in part on the Phoenix information, what their target was."

"It also helped that the realtor that Jason Wu was using is a retired Army colonel who is cooperating with us. We approached him earlier in the week and asked him to notify us if Wu closed on a property. He gave us a heads-up that Wu is interested in the Ashburn deal," said Des.

"He didn't bat an eye when we requested access to the property so that we could we set up a surveillance camera in the underground parking garage near the cabinet housing the trunk line."

"We had the equipment up and running a day before this video was taken," Lois remarked.

She clicked on a video file on her laptop, and a grainy surveillance video began to play. It showed the three engineers driving into the garage, unloading several bags near the large green cabinet, and beginning the work of installing an optical tap.

"They have a number of options since they have direct access to the fiber in the trunk line. But from what we can see here and what we now know, it looks like they were set up to do a survey, not a permanent tap.

"Our engineers went in after Pan and his crew left the country. They checked the box and ran some diagnostics, and their best estimate is that that they did not install a permanent tap.

"If all Pan's group wanted to accomplish was a survey of the line, all they had to do was put a bend in the fiber, which allows them to divert some light and then use a receiver and computer with packet-sniffer software to identify key data that can be stored and analyzed at a later date."

"Did you consider wrapping Pan and his crew up, before they could finish their survey?" Logan asked.

"We did," Des replied. "But there's some risk that it would blow back on Ji and your asset if we did. Frank and

I briefed the senior leadership of the Intel committees on the Hill last week and both our directors briefed the NSC Friday. Everyone agreed that we should let this play out a little longer."

They chatted for a few more minutes and the meeting broke up. After Des and Lois left for another meeting downtown, Frank asked Logan to stay behind.

"This morning the President signed off on a Covert Action finding against China, specifically as it relates to cyber warfare."

"What does it authorize?" Logan queried.

"Whatever it takes to put an end to China's hacking. And guess what? You and Phoenix are going to play point on this."

Chapter 15

Li Jiang and Xiao Jun had settled into a numb coexistence following Xiao Mei's funeral. It had only been two weeks since he had found her lifeless body curled up with an open book in her lap. He remained baffled by her decision to take her own life. Was her despair so great that she had seen no way out of her personal hell?

In the evenings he had been searching the Internet for clues. Anything that would help him understand what led people to commit suicide. He was shocked to discover that recently, authorities had estimated over 100 million Chinese suffered from mental illness. And tens of millions more had serious mental health issues that largely went untreated.

Traditionally, mental health had been treated as a family issue in Chinese culture. We don't institutionalize our loved ones, Li reflected. We keep them at home and care for them ourselves.

He had to admit that Chinese families today were experiencing overwhelming societal pressures. Long-simmering grudges against rampant official corruption, competition for children to get into the best schools, and a rapidly diminishing safety net of traditional government services were creating levels of stress not felt since the Cultural Revolution. Many people couldn't deal with the burden and simply buckled under the weight of it all, he concluded.

Xiao Jun had become withdrawn, and Li himself was so depressed that he usually retired to his own room after dinner. He had the presence of mind to ask Huiling if she could check in on his son daily to see how he was doing. Huiling had always been more than just an aunt, almost like a second mother to him.

Work took his mind off of his personal struggles and so more and more he was practically living at the office. He had even traveled to Chengdu again, following Pan Chengong's successful survey of the fiber optic trunk line in Ashburn, to be briefed on the survey team's findings.

Pan had provided his unit with the files recovered from the survey, and his network exploitation group had been busy assessing the data. The linguists had been going through the material using keyword searches to identify items of interest. Today, he was back in Chengdu to brief one of his many bosses, Fang Guili, who had once been a secretary to the Minister of Public Security, but last year, had been assigned to work out of the governor's office to oversee special projects for the minister.

Fang kept him waiting for ten minutes while he dealt with a personnel issue. When Li was finally ushered into his office he could tell by the tight-lipped scowl on Fang's face that he was not having a particularly good day.

"What do you have, Li?" was his curt greeting.

"Sir, my men have been analyzing the data Mr. Pan's people collected off the fiber optic trunk line in Virginia."

"And?"

"One of the most interesting things we've discovered is that everything we've examined so far is unencrypted." Inwardly he winced as he uttered these words. He had volunteered to help the Americans, but they weren't doing much to help themselves.

"Our linguists are conducting keyword searches so that we can prioritize what's been collected. Once we rank order everything, I'll have them write summaries and then we'll solicit input from the analysts as to which documents merit full translation."

"Give me an idea of what you're seeing so far." Fang called his assistant to bring in two mugs of tea. After it had been delivered, he removed the porcelain lid on his mug and sniffed in appreciation. "Jasmine," he announced. "Go on." He made an impatient gesture with his hand.

Li sorted through the papers in his file. "One point that stands out is the number of subscribers on this network. They include most of the major commercial and investment banks, brokerages, credit unions, insurance companies, underwriters, trust companies, and mortgage companies." Li waved the list. "It goes on and on."

"What sort of data are they transmitting?"

Li shuffled through his papers until he found the one he needed. "There's a range. Quarterly reports, annual reports, cash flow statements, balance sheets, income statements, credit and debit card lists, business credit reports."

"And you say everything you've examined thus far is unencrypted?"

"So far we've been able to read everything in clear text."

"Typical arrogance from the Americans. We would never admit to it of course, but their leaders know we're at war with them. A cyber war.

"Knowing that, arrogance aside, why do you think they leave their networks so vulnerable to attack?" Fang asked.

"Their cyber czar has been trying to drum up support in the private sector for legislation that would strengthen cyber security on a national level. It's unlikely he'll have any success even though Congress passed the so-called Cyber Intelligence Sharing and Protection Act, CISPA in 2015.

"Corporate America isn't convinced the government will back them up with this new law. Under CISPA, corporations are required to disclose to the government, threats that they detect, and actual security breaches of their networks. By doing so they open themselves up to potential lawsuits from customers who may feel that their privacy has been violated. And there could be other liabilities if data passed to the government is mishandled and somehow results in actual losses."

"So this is what democracy buys you," Fang snorted.

"This law won't do anything for America's cyber security if the private sector doesn't get on board," Li responded.

"Leaving the door wide open for us to continue exploiting their weakness."

Fang signaled that the meeting was over. "Keep me posted on any developments." He paused before continuing. "I recall that you were briefed on our larger strategic goals for this operation in your first meeting with Pan. We haven't set a definitive timeline for our Zero Day attack but I feel certain that it will be within the next three to six months.

"Meanwhile, we can exploit what we've collected here. Once Taixun has taken over occupancy of the property in Virginia, we'll have our work cut out for us."

"Yes, sir."

Li left Fang's office and hailed a taxi to take him to Chengdu Railway Station on North Second Road. He didn't envy Fang's proximity to power. The former governor had been accused of graft last year and was removed from office. This new governor had the backing of the Minister, and at least for now, good standing with the State Council.

He had a couple of hours to kill before his train to Chongqing was scheduled to depart and he decided to walk around an old neighborhood near the station that he and Xiao Mei had frequented when they lived in the capital.

He stopped at a stall selling spicy dragon prawns, and ordered a bottle of Blue Sword, a local beer. It was still early and as he sat savoring his snack and watching the crowd he felt his cell phone vibrate.

He didn't recognize the caller ID, but the 28 area code indicated that it was a Chengdu phone number. His pulse raced when he heard the voice on the other end. He looked around, but there was no one sitting within earshot and the cook was squatting by the curb busy cleaning his utensils.

"Is this a good time?" the man asked.

He hesitated before answering. "Yes, but I don't have much time to talk. I have to catch a train in an hour."

"Where are you going?"

"Back home. I'm in Chengdu right now."

There was a momentary pause and Li detected a palpable sense of surprise in the caller's reply.

"I just arrived in Chengdu this morning, and am on my way to your hometown this afternoon. Are you traveling by yourself?"

"Yes."

They talked for another thirty seconds. Li confirmed his departure time and then ended the call. He noticed with surprise that his hands were shaking and that he was sweating profusely. He drained his beer and stood up, looking around him to see if anyone was watching. Everything seemed normal. He set out for the train station, which was about a fifteen-minute walk from where he was. As he walked his mind was churning. He was desperate to find out what Logan Crowley was doing in Chengdu.

Chapter 16

Logan didn't hesitate to act when Li told him that he was in Chengdu getting ready to board a train for Chongqing. He knew that Chinese trains typically have four classes of cars – hard and soft seat, and hard and soft sleeper classes. He wasn't aware of anyone having met a Chinese asset on a train before, but he was confident that if he was able to purchase a soft sleeper ticket, he could meet Li securely, out of the public's eye. If not, he would simply revert to his original plan to meet him in Chongqing.

Logan hadn't expected to be in China again so soon, but when Frank Sisler outlined what he had in mind for the Agency's covert action operation against China's cyber hacking program, he knew that Li would most likely play a key role in its planning and implementation phases. This was a lot to ask of someone who had only recently volunteered and had no track record with the Agency to speak of. It was imperative that he contact Li as soon as possible to get a reading on how he was doing.

Logan's original plan had been to travel to Chongqing and trigger a meeting with the PSB officer at site "Magnolia," located in a residential area distant from the teeming city center. But this opportunity to meet on the train was too good to pass up. He had already done a six-hour surveillance detection run before calling Li's cell phone, and he was confident that he was not being followed.

When they met in Bangkok, Logan had told Li that there was a possibility he might travel to China on short notice. If so, he would need to let him know that he was in town so they could arrange to meet. But Headquarters wouldn't approve one of its state-of-the-art communications packages for the volunteer until he was vetted. So, for now, Logan had to use off-the-shelf technology available to anyone, to establish contact. Hence the cell phone. It wasn't the most secure means of communicating, given China's pervasive public security apparatus, but it would have to do.

With over a billion mobile phone users in China, the likelihood that a thirty-second cryptic call from a cell phone could be linked back to him seemed pretty remote, Logan reasoned.

Logan began walking. He pulled the prepaid SIM card from the device and slipped it into his pocket to dispose of later. He turned a corner and when he was certain that no one was watching, he crushed the cheap Xiaocai X6 cell phone under his heel and ground it into the pavement, leaving a trail of broken glass, and crushed phone parts. He kicked it into the gutter and then flagged down a taxi to take him to the train station. He had two spare phones and extra SIM cards in his bag for later use. At thirty dollars and change each, the Chinese-made mobile devices were cheap and easy to procure.

Logan reached the station forty-five minutes before the train's scheduled departure time. The attendant at the ticket booth on the main concourse looked bored. She barely acknowledged him as she took his money. She made change, handed him his ticket and pointed vaguely towards the gate. Before he turned away she already had her nose back in the glossy fashion magazine that held her rapt attention.

Logan walked through the main terminal in the direction of his gate. A voice came over the loudspeaker announcing that train K652 to Chongqing would begin boarding in five minutes. Logan kept his eyes peeled for any sign of Li amongst the hoard of passengers milling around the terminal. Even though the volunteer knew he was there, the last thing he wanted to do was to spook him.

Moments later Logan climbed aboard the deluxe soft sleeper car and made his way to his compartment. There were two seats that converted into beds, plus a private bathroom. A small table between the two seats would serve as their workspace.

He stepped into the bathroom to wash his face and hands and from outside could hear the conductor announce the final "all aboard." Seconds later, a shrill whistle signaled their departure. As they picked up speed, the figures on the platform began to blur. Within minutes they were speeding east away from the capital.

Logan pulled a duplicate of the Xiaocai X6 cell phone he had destroyed in Chengdu out of his bag, inserted a new prepaid SIM card, and punched in Li's number. It rang several times before he picked up.

"Hello?" Logan thought he detected a note of wariness in the muted response.

"Car three, number 15," he said.

"I'll see you in five minutes," Li replied.

Minutes later he heard a faint rattle outside the compartment. When he opened the door a crack, a visibly agitated Li jostled Logan as he practically dove into the sleeping car, craning his neck to look behind him as the door slammed shut.

Logan caught a glimpse down the corridor before the door closed, and could see that it was empty. He locked the door and then turned to face his agent.

"What's this about? Your call took me by surprise." Li fidgeted as he confronted the lanky case officer.

"Have a seat." Logan gestured toward one of the seats and then sat down on the other side. He leaned forward and fixed his gaze on the agitated PSB officer. He wasn't certain, but something about the man was off kilter. Maybe it was the surprise call that had him out of sorts.

"I'm sorry if I gave you a scare, Mr. Li. Remember when we met in Bangkok we talked about the possibility that this might happen.

"I received the letter you mailed. It got people's attention in Washington big time." He wasn't about to tell Li that the Bureau had been all over Pan's delegation like white on rice from the get go. If he did, Li might figure out that the Bureau had a source inside the Chinese Embassy who had been reporting on Pan's activities. And if Li was being controlled, his suspicions would be duly reported to his handlers and the Bureau's source could kiss his career and his ass goodbye.

He planned to selectively use what he knew from the FBI surveillance to draw Li out. He'd have to be careful not to reveal too much, though. This much he did know. Li had been briefed on the Ashburn operation. It wasn't clear how much he knew, but Logan figured he could weigh what Li had to say against the FBI surveillance take to see if there were any discrepancies. If there weren't, it was just possible that Li was the real deal. On the other hand, if his information didn't track, they might have a bigger problem on their hands.

"I should have known that my letter would cause a reaction. I guess I didn't think through the possibility that you would come back so soon."

"This was the first we knew of the Ashburn operation," Logan lied. "We're trying to figure out what the hackers are up to. Your letter was cryptic, and that's good because it keeps you safe. But we need more details."

Li pulled a pack of cigarettes from his pocket.

"Do you mind?"

"No, go ahead." Actually Logan did mind but he knew Li was on edge and the cigarette would help to calm him down.

Li lit up and blew a cloud of smoke through his nostrils. "I didn't find out about the Ashburn operation until after Pan's team had already gone and come back. If I had known earlier I would have told you."

"Is Pan part of your operation in Chongqing?"

"No. He runs a program for the Cyber Executive out of the Institute For Applied Computer Science. Most of what he does has to do with cryptology and technology related to information security."

"Where are they located?"

"They're in Mianyang, north of Chengdu, but the briefing I attended was in Chengdu."

"How does that fit in with what your group does?"

"We do both attacks and exploitation. We have the capability, with our English language specialists, to translate the data we collect. In this case, I was briefed on the operation so that I could direct the necessary language resources to it. It has the highest priority."

"And why's that? What makes this particular target so important?"

There was a knock on the door and Li blanched. Logan motioned him to go into the bathroom, and then answered the door. A squat, barrel-chested service attendant no more than five feet tall, looked up at him.

"Ticket?"

Logan handed him his ticket. He masked his tension with a nonchalant nod.

The man punched the ticket, handed it back to Logan and moved down the corridor to the next compartment. After he had closed the door, Logan pressed his ear against it to see if he could hear the conversation next door, but all he heard was the clickety clack of the wheels as the train raced down the track.

Logan tapped on the bathroom door and Li poked his head outside. He motioned for the skittish agent to return to his seat.

"No problem. Just the service attendant," he murmured.

Li nodded and sat down. He had already smoked one cigarette down to the filter and was fumbling with the pack to pull out another. Logan noticed that his hands were trembling.

"Is everything all right?"

"Yes. Yes. I knew that it was risky to contact the CIA in the first place. I guess I didn't anticipate how much it would affect me. I'm a dead man if we're caught together."

"Your security is the most important thing in this relationship. We would never do anything to compromise you." Logan went on to explain the measures he had taken with the phone and how he had ascertained that he wasn't being followed before establishing contact.

"We were talking about the target in Ashburn. Do you know what they're after? Why's it so important?"

"Pan completed his undergraduate and graduate degrees at Stanford in telecommunications and network security. He became an expert on risk management.

"He was there after 9/11 and found out about some of the changes the U.S. was making to protect its cyber infrastructure, in particular as it relates to the financial sector."

"What kind of changes?"

"For example, there was an effort to create more redundancy and alternate routes to transmit sensitive financial information. That's when he learned about the fiber optic network that goes through Ashburn.

"Pan's team did a survey at the target site. They collected roughly one terabyte of data. My men have been going through it, using a program to identify key words. We've done summaries of some of the information and have tasked the analysts to prioritize everything so that we can focus on the most important files."

As Li narrated his story, Logan was thinking back to his meeting in Washington. So far, everything Li had said tracked with what he had heard there.

"In your briefings, did anyone talk about the end game? What are they trying to do? Why just a survey instead of a permanent tap?"

"The point of the survey is to verify what's coming across the network. So far we have not been disappointed." He described the range of financial documents his men had been translating.

"These documents in and of themselves are quite interesting to our people. A financial analyst told our office that he had never before had access to sensitive financial information of this caliber on such a scale.

"But that is not where the true value lies. There was always the possibility that we would come up empty-handed. Our work so far has confirmed the validity of the original targeting study. It sets in motion the next phase."

"And what's that?"

"Taixun will take over the spaces in the next month. They will be doing real business, but several of the engineers on staff will be from the Institute for Applied Computer Science. They plan to stage their operation from there."

"What operation?"

"They're going to mount a Zero Day attack that's going to take down the entire financial network."

"You're kidding, right?"

"I'm dead serious. The thinking is that there will be so much concern in the markets about stability, that there will be massive capital flight out of the country."

"When is this supposed to happen?"

"I don't have a definite date. I don't think they know. But my boss told me this morning that it would be in the next three to six months."

Logan's jaw hardened as he heard Li out.

"That gives us a window of opportunity," he said. "So here's what we're going to do."

Chapter 17

Des Magarity groaned as he rolled over and stabbed at the alarm. He'd been holding court at the Emerald Lounge until midnight the night before with a half-dozen new agents fresh out of Quantico. They'd pretty much stuck to beers, mostly Millers on tap, but his bar tab had still been over two hundred dollars.

He staggered into the bathroom and turned the shower on full blast, the icy needles punishing him as he slumped forward, braced against the wall, arms extended. He gasped as the water cascaded down his back and stood that way until the dull ache from the frigid stream had driven the thudding in his head back to wherever it is hangovers go.

"I'm getting too old for this shit," he grumbled. He toweled off, dressed and was out the door in twenty minutes. He had to be on the range at Quantico by nine o'clock for his quarterly weapons qualification. The Bureau had recently revised its firearms test to place more emphasis on close-range encounters, and drawing a concealed weapon. He'd be firing sixty rounds – forty from between three and seven yards, and the rest from between fifteen and twenty-five.

Des pulled into a Starbucks drive-thru on Jeff Davis Highway and ordered a black venti coffee of the day. He took a tentative sip and for the first time that morning began to feel almost human.

The drive to Quantico wasn't bad. At this hour, traffic on I-95 was backed up in the northbound lanes headed into the District. The southbound lanes slowed briefly at the Mixing Bowl in Springfield where I-95, I-395 and the Beltway come together, but then picked up again near the Occoquan.

If he had some time before his test he might check out VirtSim, the Bureau's new Virtual Simulator Tactical Training system. One of the rookie agents from last night's beer fest had been talking about it. He'd gone on about how VirtSim is modeled after the same wireless technology Hollywood uses to capture motion. With it, firearms instructors set up scenarios that capture the full body motion of the agent, assailant and even bystanders or hostages in a virtual setting.

Thinking about Quantico made Des nostalgic. He remembered the first time he'd set foot on the grounds of the FBI Academy, a sprawling 547-acre campus in rural Virginia, forty miles south of D.C. Quantico Marine Corps Base, which houses the academy, had already been there fifty-five years when the Bureau took up residence in 1972.

There'd been five months of PT, operational training, case studies, weapons training and academics before he was sworn in as a newly-minted special agent. Some of his best friends today dated back to that original training class.

He got off of I-95 in Dumfries and ten minutes later pulled up to Hogan's Alley, a lifelike mockup of a small town, where the Bureau simulates real-life scenarios that agents are likely to encounter day in and day out.

Jack Nolton, the Bureau's range master, strolled out of one of the classrooms and greeted Des.

"Well, look what the cat dragged in," he exclaimed with a broad smile. Jack had been training new agents at Quantico for twenty-five years. A Vietnam War vet who hailed from South Carolina, there wasn't much he hadn't seen.

"Hey, Jack. How you been?" He gripped Jack's hand in his, but was careful not to squeeze too hard. He knew that Jack's arthritis had been bothering him for some time. If he wasn't so ornery, he would have retired on a medical disability years ago.

Jack winced despite Des's gentle handshake. He withdrew his hand and searched a clipboard that he was holding. "I see we've got you down for a quarterly qualification. You good to go?"

"Yeah. Let's do it."

They walked down to the range. Des picked up his hearing protection from the shooting bench and pulled his Glock-22 .40-caliber pistol from its holster. As he did so he noticed a slender Asian male turn the corner behind one of the buildings in Hogan's Alley. He was jogging at a pretty good clip and carrying a firearm in his right hand.

Des swiveled his head to look at Jack, and then turned back to face the man, who was about fifty yards away and closing fast. Normally the Bureau didn't include scenarios in the quarterly qualification tests, so he was surprised by the sudden appearance of the young man.

Jack consulted his clipboard. He had a puzzled look on his face as he ran his finger down the schedule.

"What the—?" He glanced back up and a look of alarm registered on his face.

"Take cover, Des! This guy's—"

Before he could finish his sentence, the man raised his pistol and began firing in their direction. Des crouched behind the shooting bench while Jack hit the deck, rolling over as he pulled his weapon from its back holster. The shooter was closing fast. He was spraying rounds all around them, a grim look on his face.

Des waited until the man was about twenty yards away, and then squeezed off a round. Missed right! He shot again and the Winchester 180-grain bonded hollow-point round tore into the shooter's shoulder, stopping him cold. He tumbled over and lay writhing on the ground.

Des stood and circled around to where the shooter lay cursing. He had lost his grip on the pistol when he fell down. Des kept him covered and then kicked the pistol out of reach. He bent down and with practiced ease slapped cuffs on the assailant and frisked him. Nothing but a wallet and a set of car keys.

Jack was on his cell phone, speaking with security. Within minutes, members of the Bureau's Hostage Rescue Team, which is based at Quantico, were fanning across the campus to see if the threat had been contained. No one knew if the shooter was acting alone or was part of a larger group.

"I recognize him," Jack said, staring down at the figure on the ground. "He's one of our role players in Hogan's Alley. Name's Fred. Fred Liang." He scratched his head. "He's been here going on two years. Quiet guy." Jack shook his head.

He bent down to get a better look at Liang's face. The shooter was lying in a fetal position, eyes closed. "What the hell, Fred? What were you thinking?"

Liang looked up and gave Jack a baleful stare, but remained silent. He turned his head to one side, averting his eyes. His breathing was shallow. Des removed a handkerchief from his pocket, crouched down and placed it over Liang's wound and applied pressure.

Twenty minutes later an ambulance from Stafford Hospital, running silent, lights flashing, pulled up. The two EMTs exited their rig and walked over to where the shooter lay. They began working on him; one holding his c-spine while the other checked his vitals. After they had applied gauze and tape to the wound, they rolled him onto a long board, secured a c-collar around his neck and loaded him into the back of the ambulance.

An Office of Security special agent had appeared and was talking to Jack. "I'll ride with him in the ambulance," he said. "We'll sort out jurisdiction with local law enforcement later. We need to keep an eye on this guy for now."

Two members of the Hostage Rescue Team walked out of Hogan's Alley. As they approached, Des could tell from their grim faces that they had bad news. "We found three victims back there," one of them said as he stopped in front of Jack. "One male and two females." He spat on the ground. "Looks like he was working alone. They were all inside, within a couple of yards of each other."

"What building were they in?" Jack asked.

"The Dogwood."

Jack grimaced. "I was just over there earlier this morning setting up a special role play for a group of Homeland Security agents that we're training. I was briefing one of their senior agents. A guy by the name of Baylow."

"Baylow?" Des repeated. "Not Jim Baylow?"

"Yes. Jim Baylow. You know him?"

"We're working on a case together. But he's not a field agent. He runs the NCCIC."

"I know he does something on cyber security. What's NCCIC?"

"The National Cyber Security and Communications Integration Center. Baylow's a computer geek."

"Maybe now, but I know he went through Federal Law Enforcement Training in Brunswick. He started out as a field agent and worked fraud investigations for years."

Jack turned to the Hostage Rescue Team officer. "Do we have definitive ID on the victims?"

"Yes, sir. They all had ID on them. Mr. Baylow was the male victim, like you said. The other two females were role players in Hogan's Alley." He consulted a note card. "Janet Price and Juanita Aquino."

Jack slumped with a resigned look on his face. Des knew that the deaths had hit him hard. It was Jack's facility and he ran a very tight ship. There had never been anything like this in the history of the Bureau.

They started walking over to the Dogwood. As they walked, Des's thoughts turned back to the gunman. "Do you know much about the shooter? Liang?"

"Like I said, he's been with us for a couple of years. He washed out of a special agent training class two years ago, and was trying to find a way to get back into operations.

"I know his grandfather immigrated from China in '49 when the Communists took over. His dad started some kind of import/export business in China when things opened up and Fred has been over there with him a few times. He even lived in Shanghai one summer in college, working for his dad's company."

"How the hell did he ever pass his background investigation?"

"We get applicants from all over the place. It's nearly impossible to get into the Bureau if you're first-generation coming out of a place like China, but Fred was born here. Los Angeles. Hell, his father was born here."

A bad feeling was beginning to gnaw at Des. It was just a hunch, but he'd learned a long time ago to pay attention to his gut instincts. He picked up his cell phone and punched in his deputy's number.

"Rick? Des. There's been an incident at the range."

"I know. It's all over the news. I'm watching CNN right now. They haven't ID'd the shooter or any of the victims. Waiting to get word to next of kin."

Des didn't bother to tell him that he'd taken down the shooter. "Look, I need you to see if we have anything on the shooter. He's a role player down here. Works for Jack. Name's Fred Liang."

"Got it."

"Check with personnel. He washed out of a special agent class two years ago, so they should still have a file on him. Find out who's got the lead on the investigation. I don't want to step on anybody's toes, but we need to be in the loop on this thing. I want to find out everything there is to know about Mr. Liang.

"Also, run this by Langley. See if they've got anything on him. I've got a bad feeling about this guy."

Des ended the call. They had reached the Dogwood Inn, already being marked off as a crime scene. A police officer directed them to the restaurant, in reality a classroom, where the bodies of the three victims lay. He stared down at Baylow, who was slumped over a table, a spilled cup of coffee pooling with blood oozing from a wound in his chest.

He hadn't known Baylow well. He knew that he was married and had a couple of kids in high school. Lived in Falls Church. He shook his head in anger. Those kids would grow up without their dad. And for what?

Jack walked with him back to where his car was parked. Both men were subdued.

"We'll get you back down here after this has blown over," Jack said.

"Maybe next week." They shook hands and Des climbed into his car, taking one last look at the Dogwood before retracing his route back to I-95 north. He turned on the radio, where one station was already reporting the shootings.

Des pulled out his phone and punched in the direct number of his boss, the director of Cybersecurity Division, Arthur Grady. Bureau policy requires an agent to report any incident involving the discharge of his firearm to his immediate supervisor as soon as possible.

Grady picked up on the first ring.

"Grady," he growled.

"Hey, boss. Have you heard?"

"Yeah. Rick was in here a few minutes ago to brief me. I assume it was you who took down the shooter?"

"Yes, sir."

"Nice job, Des. It could have been a lot worse if you hadn't nailed that guy. We've already advised Internal Affairs Division. When you get in stop by and give them your statement."

"All right. I should be back in about a half-hour."

"When you're done, come see me."

"Okay. Talk to you later."

By the time he had briefed Internal Affairs on the incident and stopped in to talk to Grady, it was time for lunch. He realized that he was famished. All he'd had today was a cup of coffee. His stomach growled as if to remind him. He called Rick and asked him to meet him at the Potbelly sandwich shop in Chinatown.

Fifteen minutes later he was tucking into a meatball sandwich dripping in marinara sauce and oozing provolone cheese.

"Ahh," he sighed in contentment.

Rick had ordered a Caesar salad with chicken. "I called Sisler to see if the Agency had anything on Liang. The name didn't ring a bell with him but he was going to talk to Ellen and get back to us this afternoon at the latest.

"I was able to pull Liang's personnel folder." He pulled a thin file out of a briefcase and slid it across the table to Des.

Des wolfed down the last bite of his sandwich and began to thumb through Liang's record. There were the usual personnel actions, medical records, training reports, evaluations, and transcripts. Nothing he read set off any alarms. Liang had even navigated the Bureau's polygraph exam without a hitch.

"Too bad about Baylow," Rick said. He ordered a refill on his ice tea.

Des put the file down and rubbed his eyes. The stress of the shooting was beginning to catch up with him. "Yeah, it doesn't make any sense. I had this crazy idea going through my head when I heard that Liang had a China connection. He'd just shot Baylow and it looked like he was coming after me.

"I mean, there's no way he would have known that Baylow and I were working on a China cyber case, or that we would both be at the range this morning for that matter."

"Just to play devil's advocate, he would have had access to the schedule, which was probably posted two weeks ago," Rick said. "I seriously doubt that he would have known what you and Baylow were working on though.

"The other thing is, even if Liang had been recruited by the Chinese to infiltrate the Bureau it seems like a real stretch that they would order a hit like that. It's not their MO. They're all about stealing technology."

"Yeah, I have to agree with you. It doesn't make any sense. And the other thing I can't figure out is why he washed out of training."

They paid their bill and walked back to the office. There was a message from Frank Sisler asking Rick to give him a call.

Rick walked over to his phone, selected a secure line, and dialed the number to Langley.

"Hello?"

"Frank? Rick here. I've got Des with me. Let me put him on." Rick handed the phone to Des and motioned for him to take a seat at his desk.

"Hey, Frank. How you doing?"

"Sorry to hear about Jim. Sounds like it was a close call."

"Yeah, well, these things happen. It's a shame with his kids and all. You guys come up with anything on Liang?"

"Ellen found a report from a case officer who met this American businessman, who, coincidentally, knew Liang when he was in Shanghai. They played tennis together. Liang had complained to this guy that the PSB was all over him, calling him in about his visa and asking him about his Chinese contacts. They even threatened to make trouble for him if he didn't cooperate.

"The PSB likes to keep tabs on Chinese-Americans because they play the 'motherland' card with them. According to the report, Liang pretended to be receptive to their approach so they would get off his back. He met with them several times that summer. The PSB considered him to be a source."

"What!"

"Yeah. The last reporting we had from our case officer said that the PSB was going to put him on ice when he got back to the States and then activate him when necessary."

"Why didn't that come out in the background investigation?"

"Who knows? We sent a cable to the SAC/Los Angeles and FBI director advising them of what we had learned.

"Now remember, at this point, Liang was just a private citizen. The LA Field Office was going to send a couple of agents out to interview him, but we never got a copy of their report. I suspect they treated it as a local matter, checked the box and moved on to put out the next fire."

"If Liang convinced them he was clean, and they didn't open a case against him, there might not have been any paperwork."

Des thanked Frank for the report and hung up. There was a glint in his eye, and his mouth was set in a tight line. "I need to have a little chat with Mr. Ji."

Chapter 18

Li Jiang was sweating profusely as he exited Chongqing North Railway Station. He had remained in Logan's car until they passed Shapingba, on the outskirts of Chongqing District. The terminal there had been reduced to rubble, demolished in 2013 to make way for a modern underground complex forming part of the new high-speed Chongqing-Chengdu Intercity Railway.

As Logan had instructed, he did not linger in the station but moved with some alacrity to distance himself from the CIA officer. They had coordinated their movements away from there beforehand so that their paths would not cross. Logan was flying back to Hong Kong the next day, but there was no plan for them to meet again before he departed.

Li relaxed as he turned down a side street. The acidic smell of diesel fumes filled his nostrils. He passed a food alley where the pungent odor of chili peppers sizzling in a wok made his mouth water, making him realize how hungry he was. He looked at his watch and saw that it was only four o'clock. Enough time to stop by the office and check in with his deputy.

He hailed a taxi and twenty minutes later he was there. Occupying a commercial office building meant that there were no People's Armed Police guards posted outside, and all the employees wore civilian clothes, better to disguise the fact that they were a PSB tactical unit.

When he reached his office, Li greeted his assistant, who was crouched down in front of a filing cabinet, putting away correspondence. "Sergeant Shi, have Mr. Bai report to me in ten minutes."

"Yes, sir. Welcome back, sir. He's been having one-on-one meetings with the new people. Right now he's meeting with Mr. Zhang." Shi groaned as he stood up. He had a bad back, the result of a parachuting accident that had ended his budding career with the Army Special Operations Forces. Fortunately, he had an uncle who was in the PSB and he had arranged a transfer.

"That's fine. Have him come see me when he's done. By the way, how are they all settling in?"

"This morning Mr. Bai paired them up with their mentors. They've been shadowing them all day. This afternoon he met with the older guys to get their feedback. Based on what they had to say, he's in the process of assigning them their duties."

"Thank you, Sergeant. Please bring me a cup of tea and see that I'm not disturbed until Mr. Bai is ready."

"Yes, sir."

Li closed the door behind his aide and then called his sister. "Hi. I just got back from Chengdu. How's it going?"

"Oh, *Da Ge*." He knew when she called him "big brother," in that tone that she was especially troubled. "I'm so worried about Xiao Jun. I checked on him this morning before class and he was still in bed, staring at the ceiling. I made him get up, but he wouldn't eat any breakfast. You need to spend more time with him," she chastised.

"I know. It's just…" His voice trailed off and he remained silent as he contemplated how he had allowed his own sorrow to drown out his son's silent pleas for help.

"Why don't you both come for dinner tonight? I'm making a crispy orange beef and a spicy bean curd. Nothing special."

"Ah, Huiling. You're so good to us. It's too much bother."

"No, not at all. I'll see you at six-thirty. And make sure Xiao Jun is there. He needs to eat."

"All right. We'll see you then."

There was a knock on the door, and Bai came in. "Sir? You wanted to see me?"

"Sergeant Shi was just filling me in on our charges. How are they doing?"

Bai took a seat next to Li's desk. "I'm impressed with them. I just finished talking to Zhang. You remember him, don't you?"

"Yes. He's the one who designed 2004 Tsunami."

"Right. I think he's the best hacker in the group. It's still too early to tell for sure, but he may be one we'll want to turn loose to work on his own."

"What do you have in mind?" Li was interested, because he had mentioned the young hacker to Logan, who had seemed interested in his background.

"I thought we could get him to work on his 2004 Tsunami design. Once a computer is infected with this Trojan horse, the hacker owns it. We could create a massive botnet. Zhang has some ideas. No one's ever done anything like what he has in mind. I'll let him explain it to you." Bai bounced in his chair, excited.

"All right. Now you've piqued my curiosity."

Li recounted his conversation with Fang. "The Cyber Executive wants to implement the Zero Day attack sometime in the next three to six months. I don't know if they're locked into a specific approach, but it seems to me that Tsunami could do some very serious damage to the Americans.

"Let's talk about it some more tomorrow." He dismissed his deputy and spent an hour working on correspondence before calling it a day. Sergeant Shi was still at his desk as he left the office.

"I'll see you in the morning, Sergeant."

"Good night, sir."

Li took a taxi to his apartment. It was six o'clock and beginning to grow dark. There were no lights on inside. He showered, put on a clean shirt and then called Huiling to see if she had heard from Xiao Jun.

"He just got here," she murmured.

"I'll be there in ten minutes," he said. Huiling and her husband lived just three blocks away. He locked the apartment and hurried out the front door.

Passing under a streetlight he paused to watch three men from the neighborhood, crouched on their haunches, betting on a cricket fight. Two other players were readying their fighters, stroking their respective cricket's whiskers with miniature straw brushes to goad them into battle. The men placed the crickets in a fighting container, separated by a thin screen partition. When the combatants were ready to clash, one of the men lifted the screen and the frisky gladiators charged out. The first one to turn away from the fight or stop chirping would lose the contest. Li watched the first match; it was over in less than ten seconds.

He smiled as he continued on his way. His grandfather had kept fighting crickets, he reminisced. He used to spend hours shopping for paraphernalia; gourds, pots, whisks and cages, all used to keep or train his crickets. Grandfather had bought only the best male crickets to groom for battle. Li had treasured those trips to the teeming cricket market, listening to his grandfather barter for this or that one.

It was an even bigger treat to accompany Grandfather to the Saturday afternoon cricket fights. These were raucous affairs, replete with judges and bettors exchanging substantial sums of money as they placed their wagers and urged on their favorites.

Li felt himself tensing as he approached Huiling's apartment. His trepidation, he realized, was the result of his own feelings of inadequacy as a parent. His father had been a larger-than-life figure who had commanded respect and obedience. Li gritted his teeth and vowed to bend over backward to help his son.

Xiao Jun and Huiling's husband, Wang Gang, were in the living room, watching a replay of the most popular Chinese reality show, called 'Dad, Where Are We Going?' In it, a group of celebrity fathers and their young children are sent on a three-day adventure to exotic locales, where they use their survival skills to compete against one another.

Li winced inwardly as he sat down next to Xiao Jun, who barely acknowledged him. Wang nodded, but kept his eyes fixed on the TV. The show had become a social phenomenon in China. Voted the best TV program last year, it had generated a nationwide discussion on the role of fathers in the family. Traditionally, mothers were the most visible caregivers in Chinese families, with fathers coming in a distant second. Maybe he and Xiao Jun could compete as a team if the producers did a spin-off with everyday fathers and their adolescent offspring, he mused.

"Where's Mom?" he called to his sister.

"She's visiting a friend who invited her over for hot pot. She said not to wait for her."

"That's good that she's getting out," Li said.

"I know. Dinner's ready." She began bringing food out to the table. "Xiao Jun, would you fill the rice bowls?"

Xiao Jun shrugged and trudged into the kitchen. He emerged a couple of minutes later with four rice bowls and they all sat down to eat. Conversation was strained, although Huiling tried her best to engage the young teen.

"Have you begun studying for the Gao Kao?" she asked, while heaping spicy bean curd into his bowl.

The Gao Kao is China's National Higher Education Entrance Exam, a mind-numbing two-day test that takes place in June at the end of a student's senior year. The budding scholars are tested in Chinese, math, a foreign language and two optional subjects, drawing from the liberal arts and hard sciences.

Achieving a high score on the Gao Kao is the most important requirement for admission to one of China's prestigious state universities. Students have been known to spend their entire senior year cramming for the exam.

Some things never change, Li thought to himself. Nearly fifteen hundred years ago, candidates for China's Civil Service spent months studying for the Keju, the imperial examination system that had its beginnings during the Sui Dynasty. The Gao Kao is an outgrowth of the Keju, producing many of the same results; an over-reliance on rote learning, which in turn stifles creativity.

It hasn't held back my hackers, he marveled. They were creative, although they all possessed a destructive bent that made them decidedly sociopathic.

He nudged his son. "Your aunt asked you a question," he leaned over and whispered.

Xiao Jun poked at his food with his chopsticks. "Why bother? Nothing matters anyway."

"But you have your whole life before you, Xiao Jun."

"No," he said under his breath. "My life is over." He put his head down and began to sniffle.

Li wanted to take his son in his arms and comfort him. But something held him back. He was too embarrassed to display his emotions.

Huiling rose from her seat and came around the table. She knelt next to Xiao Jun and hugged him as he sobbed out of control. Li looked away. His hand trembled as he reached for the beer glass, draining it in one gulp. Wiping his mouth he glanced down at his son, who was struggling to control his emotions.

They finished eating in silence. After Huiling had cleared the table, he decided to call it a night. "Come," he said. "We should be going. Thank you, little sister. Wang Gang." He gripped his brother-in-law's hand and then ushered Xiao Jun out the door.

They were silent as they walked back to the apartment. Xiao Jun was wordless as he walked into his room and closed the door. Li sat up for another hour before retiring. His thoughts turned to his plan to leave China for the U.S. Maybe he and Xiao Jun could get a fresh start in America when this was all over. His heart was heavy as he thought how much Xiao Mei would have enjoyed the adventure. His eyes narrowed. There was much work to be done before he went anywhere. He fell asleep, dreaming that he and Xiao Mei were holding hands, walking in the foothills of Nan Shan Mountain.

The next morning he awoke later than usual. Xiao Jun had already left for school. He yawned as he brushed his teeth and got ready for work. One of the first things he wanted to get done today was to talk to the young hacker who had designed 2004 Tsunami.

For a moment he reflected on its namesake, the actual 2004 Tsunami in the Indian Ocean. It had started as an underwater earthquake and by the time it was over more than 230,000 people had died. Some scientists had estimated that it had generated more than 550 million times the energy created when the Americans bombed Hiroshima in World War II.

He and Logan had talked in detail about the persistence of China's warfare against U.S. computer network operations and the likely form the Zero Day attack would take. It was possible, although uncertain, that his unit would be tapped to work with Pan's group to write the code for the malware attack against U.S. financial networks. The Zero Day attack.

When Li arrived at his office he asked Sergeant Shi to call Zhang. Moments later the young man entered his office. He remained standing until Li directed him to a couch and joined him there. Zhang didn't seem as self-assured as he had in the group meeting the other day. He sat ramrod straight and avoided looking directly at him.

Li studied the young hacker for a moment before speaking. "We briefly talked about your work on 2004 Tsunami the other day. I wanted to learn more about it. I'm also interested in knowing if you think it's still viable, and if so, what we could do to maximize its potential."

Zhang thought for a moment before replying. "As you know, I initially developed it as a Trojan horse that would eventually infect enough computers to create a botnet, which in turn would spread the virus around. The idea was to attack both individual computers and servers.

"When I was programming it, my end goal was to be able to conduct a distributed denial-of-service attack, a so-called DDoS."

"Did you have a particular target in mind?"

"Not really. What I was hoping to do was find a buyer for the program and just let them run with it.

"The thing is, so many networks have unprotected portals, that once you harness all that computing power in the botnet you've created, you can amp up the attack and direct it at those unprotected portals."

"You're talking about a reflective DDoS."

Zhang looked at Li with new respect. "You know your stuff," he said with undisguised admiration.

"Well, I've been doing this for a few years."

"Tsunami is like a lot of bots in some respects. With it I would be able to maintain command and control on a remote server, and then direct the attack as I choose. It becomes something like a chess match between me and the target's network security team. Typically they'll come up with a fix, but by then I've moved on to my next target."

Talking about his work had energized Zhang. He was leaning forward and clenching his fist. "There are DDoS attacks going on all the time. What makes Tsunami unique, is that I've found a way to incorporate 'Blue Waters' into my attack."

"You're talking about the supercomputer center in Illinois?"

"Yes. It's one of the supercomputer centers that the National Science Foundation, the NSF, has funded over the years. This one is at the National Center for Supercomputing Applications in Urbana.

"The NSF has been working with the private sector since the 1980s to set up these centers. Originally they were meant to give major research universities high-speed interconnectivity. They were designed to be closed networks."

Li nodded his head. "Right. I've followed their progress. 'Blue Waters' is one of their fastest centers."

Zhang nodded. "Their original plan was to build these supercomputers that would be part of a closed network between a hundred or so universities and research institutes. But I found a weak spot in their system.

"Last year I was looking for ways to hack into the supercomputer centers. I stumbled across this research physicist in Illinois who uses Blue Waters. He's in Urbana, at the center. I discovered that he was experimenting with applications that require Blue Waters to go online."

"You mean...?"

"Yes. I was able to plant a virus on his computer. I can use it to pull Blue Waters into a DDoS attack." Zhang rubbed his hands together in glee. "It works at a speed of thirteen petaflops per second."

That's a quadrillion floating point operations per second. My God! Li thought. The Americans will never know what hit them.

Chapter 19

Dragonair Flight 841, destined for Hong Kong, boarded at five p.m. Logan settled into his business class seat and ordered a scotch on the rocks from the flight attendant.

He'd spent the day on cover work in Chongqing to create the impression that he was, in fact, conducting legitimate business in China. Most of that time he'd been in meetings with representatives from the China Shipbuilding Industry Corporation. They'd been generally bullish on China's shipbuilding prospects in the years ahead. Quoting from a Ministry of Industry and Information Technology report, one of the reps had gone so far as to predict that China's domestic shipbuilders would reach sales of $190 billion within a year.

Sixty percent of that business was projected to be domestic, despite the fact that new orders were down fifty percent from the previous year because of overcapacity in the market, he'd pointed out. And exports showed a sluggish trend line because the global economy remained generally lackluster.

Logan doubted the Agency was interested in investing big bucks to build ships in China. For now, creating the impression that Alexander Maritime was exploring new business opportunities on the mainland would buy him credibility in the local business community, give him the flexibility to move around the country and hopefully keep the PSB off his back.

His mind turned back to his meeting the week before in Washington with Frank Sisler and Ellen Sanders. When Frank had told him that the President had authorized a covert action finding against China's cyber program it had blown him away.

The U.S. had protested Chinese government cyber hacking for decades, to no avail. Faced with repeated denials from Beijing, the attorney general had recently taken the unprecedented step of filing charges in federal court against several Chinese officials involved in the government-directed attacks. The indictment listed the officials by name, charging them with theft of proprietary information from a wide range of private sector and government organizations by means of unauthorized hacking into their internal networks.

China claimed that it was doing everything it could to stem the tide of rogue cyber attacks against the U.S. Just months ago the PSB had claimed that it had arrested 15,000 suspects for supposed cyber crimes. The alleged crimes included fraud, hacking and the sale of personal information. Many analysts believed that there had been no arrests, that China was making these claims to stem the building wave of anti-Chinese sentiment in the U.S.

Cyber Division had pulled together a team of computer scientists from the Directorate of Science and Technology, ops officers from the Directorate of Operations, and intelligence specialists from the Directorate of Analysis experienced in analyzing offensive computer network attacks, to brainstorm an approach that would deter or, better yet, derail the Chinese hacking activity.

In a nod to inter-agency cooperation, Frank had invited Lois Caldwell from the FBI to attend these meetings. Congress had criticized the Agency over the years for being stove-piped and for failing to share sensitive intelligence more broadly amongst U.S. intelligence and law enforcement agencies. Maybe the gesture would persuade the naysayers in Congress that the Agency had finally turned the corner on sharing.

Truth be told, the Agency might have done a better job of sharing intelligence more broadly, but it has a statutory and moral obligation to protect its sources and methods. If intelligence is actionable, meaning someone is going to be arrested by the FBI or taken out of circulation in a Special Forces-type operation, based upon that information, then there's a danger that the sensitive source who risked his life to provide it will be exposed. It's a slippery slope, because the Agency isn't in the business of collecting intelligence just so that it can gather dust on a shelf.

Congress has no business pointing fingers, Logan mused as he accepted his scotch and settled back for the two-hour flight. They'd reached new lows of dysfunction and partisan quarreling on Capitol Hill. Washington was in perpetual gridlock as Congress and the Administration lurched from one crisis to the next.

It's a good thing the President grants the CIA broad authorities under covert action findings, he thought. The Agency would be able to push forward without worrying that the initiative would die in committee or get derailed by some member with an axe to grind.

On something this significant, the CIA director is required to brief the Gang of Eight – the majority and minority leaders in the Senate and House, and the chairs and ranking minority members of the Senate Select Committee on Intelligence and the House Permanent Select Committee on Intelligence. Other than that, he pretty much has free rein to run with it.

They would have to move fast, whatever they did, Logan reasoned. If Li's information proved correct, the Chinese were going to mount their Zero Day attack sometime in the next six months. That wasn't much time to put a plan in place.

He had felt slightly reassured when he received Frank's readout of the cyber team's first meeting, in which Lois Caldwell had come off as some kind of a rock star. She had done her homework on Pan Chengong, the computer scientist from the Institute for Applied Computer Science.

"Pan has a PhD in computer science from Stanford," she had reported to the group. "He has spent more time analyzing the weaknesses in U.S. computer networks than possibly anyone else in the Chinese government.

"Because he's an expert with respect to web security and protocols he understands what our telecommunications and network security teams are likely to be doing to mitigate risk.

"Also, Pan isn't some ivory tower academic. In grad school he spent virtually all of his time at Stanford's Security Laboratory. So, although his primary focus was network protocols, he would also have been exposed to a wide range of security-related research being conducted at the lab."

Lois had also tapped into Bureau and Agency databases to track Pan's attendance at professional meetings, seminars and symposia over the years. He had been a regular attendee at the Information Security Conference, the IEEE's annual Symposium on Security and Privacy, Applied Cryptography and Security Conference, the Network and Distributed System Security Symposium and more.

Over time, law enforcement and intelligence officers, trolling for future recruits, had documented Pan's attendance at these conferences. From these reports it appears that Pan took a vacuum cleaner approach to collecting scientific papers, handouts and business cards.

"At all of these conferences, Pan would have made contacts," Lois had pointed out. "It's anybody's guess how big his Rolodex is. Academics thrive on an environment of open sharing and peer review. It's a safe bet that Pan has been plumbing his graduate school contacts for information ever since he returned to China."

Logan's attention shifted back to the present. The plane had dropped through the clouds and now the seatbelt sign came on as the pilot announced their imminent arrival in Hong Kong. Their approach was from the southwest. Logan could make out the shimmering lights on Lantau Island to his left as the plane descended, lining up to land on the north runway.

Touchdown was bumpy, but the passengers burst into applause as the plane slowed and then turned towards the terminal. Logan grinned as the applause died down. He didn't know if the passengers were being polite or were just relieved to have made it down in one piece. He took his phone off airplane mode and called Zahir.

"Hi, sweetheart. I just got in."

"Hi. I was just wondering when you were going to call. How was your trip?"

"Not bad. I had a good meeting at China Shipbuilding in Chongqing. Chengdu was a bust. My meeting there got canceled. How's Cooper?"

"I just put him down. He missed you." They talked for a couple of minutes as Logan deplaned. He said goodbye as he approached immigration, which he navigated without incident. With only a carry-on, he bypassed baggage claim and headed for the Airport Express kiosk.

"One-way to Central, please." He slid the one hundred HK$ fare across the counter, took his ticket and made his way to the platform. He didn't have to wait long. Ten minutes later, passengers began boarding the sleek train. Once aboard, he settled into his seat for the twenty-minute ride into Central.

Glancing around the car he was surprised to see one of the suspect PSB officers who'd tailed Zahir into the Hong Kong Club and then followed him into the men's room a couple of weeks back. The man boarded the car without looking his way and took a seat three rows back from where he was sitting.

He was certain that it was the same guy. Identical leather bomber jacket, slick hair combed to the side, sunglasses and a sullen look, with downturned mouth and slack features.

Logan was careful not to let on that he'd seen him, shifting his gaze back to the front of the train. Without having done a surveillance detection run, it was hard to determine if 'Bomber Jacket' was following him. He hadn't spotted the man's partner from the restaurant, but that didn't rule out the possibility that he was out there somewhere or that a larger team was following him.

The worst-case scenario would be that the PSB had checked his itinerary and had a team waiting for him at the airport when he arrived. It was public information that he had traveled to China. Because of circumstances, he hadn't done an extensive surveillance detection run before he met

Li on the train. He had been confident no one had seen them together, especially since they had taken precautions to depart separately. What if they'd been out there, though? He was beginning to doubt his instincts.

He'd report seeing this guy again. Langley wouldn't like it, but it was what it was. He remembered during training reading a report about an ops officer who had come under regular surveillance by the PSB in China, but no one could figure out why. It wasn't until years later when a high-profile double-agent operation unraveled, that Langley learned the FBI's agent had passed the ops officer's name to Chinese authorities. He'd have to do some probe surveillance detection runs to see if they were on him. But he'd have to be careful not to look like he was surveillance-conscious. Normal businessmen don't behave that way.

Logan got off the train in Central and took a taxi to the Peak. 'Bomber Jacket' melted into the crowd and Logan didn't see him again as the car began the steep climb up Garden Road.

When he opened the door to the apartment, he caught a whiff of savory Persian food cooking. Walking into the kitchen he found Zahir busy preparing one of his favorite meals, kebab morgh and a Shirazi salad. It was simple – skewered broiled chicken and a cucumber and tomato salad.

He put his bag down and walked over to give Zahir a kiss. As he pulled her to him she put down the bottle of olive oil and ran her hands along his back. They stood that way for a moment. She pulled away and gave him an impish grin. "Maybe after dinner…"

He reached over and turned off the broiler. "How about before dinner?" He picked her up and carried her into their bedroom, closing the door behind them.

An hour later they wandered back into the kitchen. They had both changed into running shorts and tee shirts. Logan marveled that after five years of marriage and one child, Zahir was as sexy as ever. He opened a bottle of pinot noir as she tried to salvage their meal.

"This chicken is ruined," she groused. "I don't think I can heat it up. It'll be too tough."

"It's fine. Let's have it cold." He set the table and then put on an old Simon and Garfunkel album. As the strains of "Bridge Over Troubled Water" took them back to another time, they sat down to eat.

Logan had poured the wine into a decanter. He reached over to fill Zahir's glass, but she held up her hand, a mischievous look on her face.

"No wine for me," she said, putting her hand on top the wineglass to make her point.

"I can open something else. I thought you liked this pinot." Zahir appreciated a good wine almost as much as he did, even though she'd been raised in a conservative Shia family.

"I do. But Dr. Morely said I shouldn't have any alcohol."

"Who's Dr. Morely?"

"A colleague of Dr. Collins." Dr. Collins was Cooper's pediatrician at Hong Kong Adventist Hospital.

"Is he a pediatrician?"

"He specializes in prenatal care."

"But…" His jaw fell open as the implications of what Zahir was saying dawned on him. "Are you…?"

"Yes. I'm pregnant."

He jumped up from the table, almost spilling his wine. Zahir tilted her head up, eyes dancing as he reached for her. He took her face in his hands and kissed her.

"When?"

"June."

"How long have you known?"

"I realized I was a week late, just before you took off on your trip. I didn't want you to worry while you were gone, so I didn't say anything. That afternoon I went to Watsons and bought a pregnancy test."

"Are they accurate?"

"According to their literature, yes. Something like ninety-nine percent accurate. That was enough for me to call Dr. Collins. He referred me to Dr. Morely. I called his office and spoke with a nurse. She scheduled my first prenatal visit in December."

Logan sat down next to her and placed his ear against her stomach, as if listening. "Hello in there. Anybody home?"

Zahir giggled and ran her fingers through his hair. "Silly. I can't wait to tell Cooper he's going to be a big brother."

"Yeah. He's going to be so excited. Do you think we should wait?"

"You mean the first trimester? I think so. Just in case…"

"Yeah." He lifted her tee shirt and kissed her on the stomach. "Ready for bed?"

"Let me clean up first."

"No. I'll get it. You get ready. This'll just take a couple of minutes."

Logan began clearing the table, whistling under his breath as he moved around the kitchen.

Chapter 20

Des turned onto Hospital Center Boulevard in Stafford and took a right turn into the Stafford Hospital visitor's parking lot. It had been three days since Fred Liang had terrorized Hogan's Alley, killing Jim Baylow and two others.

The Naval Health Clinic at Quantico isn't equipped to deal with emergency care, so Liang had been transported to the trauma center in Stafford to care for his shoulder wound.

An officer from the Stafford County Sheriff's department was standing guard outside of Liang's room. He examined Des's FBI credential and stepped aside to allow him in.

Liang was propped up in bed watching television. He turned when he heard the door open. His faced turned pale when saw the burly FBI officer barrel into the room. His eyes stayed fixed on Des's face as he strode over and stared down at him.

Des had met with his Chinese Embassy source, Mr. Ji, to follow up on the Agency's reporting that the MPS had recruited Liang. Well, maybe not the MPS, but the PSB. Technically they were part of the same outfit although the PSB, which was subordinate to the MPS, could be protective of its autonomy.

Ji had disavowed any knowledge of Liang's supposed recruitment. Which wouldn't be that unusual, Des reasoned. The Chinese could compartment information along with the best of them, especially when it came to sharing sensitive intelligence with their foreign service officers.

Ji had gone on to say that it wouldn't be that uncommon for the PSB to keep the details of the recruitment of an American penetration of the FBI from the MPS, except perhaps at the highest levels.

Ji had said something else that night that got his attention. From his PSB contacts he knew that the Chinese definition of what constituted a recruitment was very different from that used by the CIA or the Bureau. Just the fact that the PSB had met with Liang in Shanghai a number of times could lead them to believe that he was recruited. And, if it turned out that the PSB had tasked Liang to kill Baylow, it would represent a whole new level of Chinese activity in the U.S.

"You!" Liang spat out the word as his eyes darted around the room.

"That's right, dickwipe." Des pulled a chair up next to the bed and sat down. "I got a few questions I want to ask you. And if you don't play it straight with me, I'm going to be your worst nightmare."

"Talk to my lawyer."

"Oh yeah? You lawyered up already? You haven't even had your initial court appearance."

Liang looked uncertain. "Well, I'm getting a lawyer."

Des knew that Liang had been read his Miranda Rights on day one. He was hoping that he would make a voluntary statement to him that would shed some light into his motivation for murdering Baylow and those two women.

"Look. You're damn right you're going to need a lawyer. You're looking at murder one right now. In Virginia that means you're going to fry. If you help me out though, I'll think about recommending a plea bargain to the prosecutor. Life without parole is probably the best deal you can make."

Liang took this in with a sullen look on his face. He grimaced as he shifted his weight. "What do you want to know?"

"For starters, what were you doing in China a few years back?"

Liang appeared surprised by the question. "Working for my father in his import/export business."

"How many times have you been over there?"

"Four, five. I spent one summer in college living in Shanghai."

"When did you start working for the Chinese?"

"I wasn't working for the Chinese. I was working for my dad."

"You know what I mean."

Liang appeared confused by the question. "He had a Chinese partner, but I didn't work for him."

"I'm not talking about that kind of work. I'm talking about spying for the Chinese."

"Spying?"

"Yeah. Spying."

"I don't know what you're talking about."

"Are you telling me the Chinese didn't recruit you and task you to try and get a job with the Bureau?"

Liang's mouth gaped open. The look of incredulity on his face gave Des pause. Either Liang was one hell of a liar, or he didn't have a clue what Des was talking about.

"Let me spell it out for you. Two guys show up at your apartment and have a little chat with you. They appeal to your Chinese heritage and talk about how you can do something special for the motherland. They might even suggest that they could make it easier for your dad's business if you help them out. Starting to sound familiar?"

"There were a couple of security types who came around a few times when I was living there that summer. I told them I was just a student and didn't know anything. They didn't mention the Bureau. They wanted me to stay in touch with them when I got home, but I never did. I told them I'd think about it just to get them off my back."

Des leaned forward and his eyes bored into Liang's. "So you're telling me they didn't push you to apply to the Bureau? They didn't have anything to do with this hit on Jim Baylow?"

Liang's eyes opened wide. "No," he stuttered. "It wasn't like that."

"How was it then, Fred?" Des cocked his head and appraised his bewildered captive. "Why did you kill those people?"

Liang closed his eyes and his lips trembled as he fought to control his emotions. He took a deep breath. "A couple of years ago I tried to get a job at the Bureau, but I washed out of the special agent class, so I decided to apply for a job with Homeland Security. Baylow chaired a panel that reviewed my application. Based on his recommendation, I didn't get the job. He felt that if I wasn't good enough for the FBI, then I wasn't good enough for DHS." Liang's eyes narrowed and he scowled as he looked up at Des.

"I tried to appeal, but once the decision was made, it was final. Because of Baylow, the only government job I was ever going to get was as a role player in Hogan's Alley."

"You killed him for that? Over a job?" Des looked incredulous.

"I didn't mean to kill him." Liang turned a plaintive face up to Des. "We get the training rosters at the Academy so we can tailor our scenarios to individual requirements. I saw that Baylow was coming to meet Jack. I thought I'd just scare him a little. I waited for my chance.

"When he and Jack finished talking, Baylow sat down with Janet to go over the role play scenario. When I pulled my gun, Baylow just laughed at me. I told him to shut up, but he just called me a loser."

"What happened then?"

"Juanita walked in on us. I was yelling at Baylow and had my gun in his face. She tried to run away and I shot her. The rest is a blank. I must have panicked and shot Baylow and Janet. Then I started running. That's when I saw you and Jack." Liang gripped his head and stared down at his lap.

Des was starting to believe that Liang just might be telling the truth. In a way he was relieved that Baylow's death had nothing to do with the Chinese. Still, it infuriated him that this worthless piece of shit had destroyed three lives and caused irreparable damage to their families and friends. And for what?

Des stood up. "I can't guarantee what the U.S. attorney's going to do. It'll be hard for your defense to prove that this wasn't premeditated, seeing as you brought a loaded firearm onto government property. I'll tell the prosecutor about our little talk. Then it'll be up to him."

Personally, Des didn't give a rat's ass if Liang fried for what he'd done. He deserved it. At 1,300 executions, Virginia had carried out the death penalty more than any other state in the union save Texas. The Commonwealth even had the dubious distinction of carrying out the first known execution in the New World in 1607 when Captain George Kendall, a Jamestown councilman, was led before a firing squad on trumped-up charges. With any luck Liang would make it 1,301.

Des thanked the sheriff's deputy and left the hospital. He was pensive on the drive back to Washington. After he got back to his office he walked down the hall to talk to Rick.

"Is Lois around?" He slumped into a chair by the desk.

"I think so. She had a meeting at Langley with the cyber team this morning, but she thought she'd be back by lunch. I'll have her come up.

"You want to ride together to the wake tonight?"

Des swore under his breath. He'd forgotten that Baylow's viewing was this evening and the funeral service tomorrow. "Yeah. Where is it?"

"Bethesda. Rayner and Sons on Wisconsin."

Rick picked up his phone and spoke briefly with Lois. He hung up and eyed his boss. "She'll be up in a minute."

"Good. I'd like to hear what's going on with her cyber group."

"You feeling all right? How'd your meeting with Liang go?"

"Yeah, I'm okay. I was just thinking how pointless this whole thing is." He proceeded to give Rick a rundown of his conversation with Baylow's killer.

"I have to tell you. I came away feeling a lot better that we're not dealing with some rogue PSB agent. I know they're interested in penetrating the Bureau, but the thought that they'd order a hit on Baylow because of our own cyber countermeasures seemed way out there."

"The stakes are only going to get higher. We're not seeing them back away from these attacks." Rick picked up a report on his desk. "We just got this in this morning. All these Washington think tanks are reporting aggressive phishing from what looks like Chinese hackers."

Des took the report from him and read through the list. "Rand, CATO Institute, Heritage Foundation, Brookings, Council on Foreign Relations." He threw it down in disgust.

"What the hell are they after this time?"

"Our people have been talking with security analysts in two of the cyber security firms contracting with the think tanks. It appears that most of these recent attacks are against Middle East experts."

"That's a switch from their usual targeting."

"Right. Normally they're all over the senior Asian experts, figuring they'll get the inside scoop on our Asian foreign policy."

"They'd be wrong. I'm sure there are a lot of staffers who read what these folks write, and there are some really smart people working in these think tanks who probably do influence foreign policy. But their ability to drive policy decisions is limited."

At that moment, Lois Caldwell burst into the room. She plopped down next to Des and drained the bottle of water she was carrying. "Sorry, I just got back from Langley." She picked up a newspaper off the desk and fanned herself.

"Rick and I were just talking about this report." He handed it to her.

Lois scanned the first page and looked up. "I talked to one of the security analysts at Paragon Cyber this morning. She said that they're seeing a very sophisticated method to these attacks. Instead of installing viruses on the target computers through phishing, the hackers are using Power Shell scripts to make the intrusions look like regularly scheduled tasks on the computers."

Des had a pained look on his face. "What are Power Shell scripts?"

Lois gave him a derisive look as if to ask, "You're kidding me, right?"

"OK. A shell is the command prompt, and on your computer it looks like this: C:/." She grabbed a pencil and wrote the prompt on a pad of paper. "Every Microsoft operating system has it, but most people never see it or use it. Power Shell's a tool that Microsoft developed a few years back, putting the command prompt on steroids with added power to help network administrators manage complex, repetitive tasks. They're text files written with a particular script, line by line.

"Users write one-line commands with command lets, or cmdlets for short, to execute these tasks. Microsoft included it in its last few Windows versions, but it's so powerful that it can be devastating if a hacker starts using your own Power Shell against you. Hackers using a simple text script can bypass antivirus scanners and get a computer to work against itself.

"These Chinese hackers know that a lot of system administrators never operate beyond the graphic user interface. Some may not even know that Power Shell exists. So, with these intrusions, the hackers went into Power Shell and wrote specific scripts that appeared as normal, scheduled tasks on the targeted computers. That way they were able to stay under the radar."

"One of these days the Chinese are going to piss off enough people that Congress will pass a cyber security bill with some teeth in it." Des slammed his hand down on the desk.

"They did pass the Cyber Information Sharing Act," Rick noted with satisfaction.

"I'll be surprised if it does any good," Des responded. "The private sector can't get over concerns about privacy protections."

"We'll see. There have been a bunch of high-profile cyber attacks in the last year," Rick conceded. "Sec State. Sony. OPM. Now this. Then there were those five hackers we indicted late last year. It's been nonstop. It's true. People are fed up."

Des turned his attention to Lois. "How's it going with the Agency's Covert Action plan?"

Lois's face brightened as she answered his question. "I never understood how much power the President gives the

CIA when he signs one of these Covert Action findings. And the director delegates a lot of that down, so this team I'm working on, the China Cyber team, has a lot to work with.

"One of the things that's become clear from the get-go is that we need better Intel on what Pan has planned for his Zero Day attack. Frank wants the case officer to go back to China to meet with Phoenix. He wants to see if we can hack into the computers at the Institute for Applied Computer Science. That's where Pan is working on his attack."

"Can he go back into China so soon?" Des looked dubious.

"Ellen Sanders researched the travel patterns of U.S. expats living in Hong Kong, to China. She found that it varied, but in many cases people were traveling once a week or every other week.

"The risky part is that Phoenix isn't a validated agent. Besides that, meeting him so often is dangerous. It increases the chances that they'll get caught."

"Normally, they're mostly concerned about their agent getting wrapped up," Rick interjected. "Hell, they won't even tell us his real name. But in this situation the case officer doesn't have diplomatic immunity. If he gets caught he could end up in a Chinese prison."

"You ever hear about those two Agency officers who got shot down over China in the '50s?" Des asked.

"Yeah. Downey and Fecteau. John Downey and Richard Fecteau. They were paramilitary officers," Rick said.

"I remember that," Lois jumped in. "The *Post* did a story on them a few years ago. They were supporting a Chinese 'Third Force,' trying to put Chinese agents the CIA had trained in touch with sympathetic Chinese generals who opposed the communists.

"Downey and Fecteau were trying to extract one of their agents using an aerial pickup, but their plane crashed. They survived the crash, but were captured by the communists and spent twenty years in Chinese prisons."

"Whew," Rick exclaimed. "That's some price to pay."

"Frank thinks it's worth the risk. The sooner we understand what Pan's group is planning, the better off we'll be.

One of the possibilities we're exploring involves something called the 'Boomerang Effect.'"

"What's that?" Des asked.

"Turning a Chinese cyber-weapon back on them. By studying their cyber attacks, we're confident that we can reverse engineer the tools they're using and turn them back against China.

"Frank told us one of the key tenets of U.S. covert action policy is that there should be no public recognition of United States government involvement. In diplomatic and military engagements, our involvement is obvious. With covert action the law says 'it's intended that the role of the United States Government will not be apparent nor acknowledged publicly.'"

"This Boomerang idea sounds plausible," Des conceded. "But will it work?"

"We'll have to see," Lois replied. "Theoretically I don't see why not. But the more time we have to experiment with their tools the better off we'll be."

Des stood up, signaling that the meeting was over. "Keep me in the loop, Lois. I have a feeling that when this thing comes down, it's going to come down hard. I hope that crowd over at CIA knows what the hell they're doing."

Chapter 21

Logan felt the familiar surge of adrenalin as he re-read Frank Sisler's cable. The cyber team urgently needed information on the computer network at the Institute for Applied Computer Science, Pan Chengong's computer lab in Mianyang.

Predictably, despite all indications that Phoenix was committed to the relationship with CIA, headquarters didn't trust him sufficiently to collect the information they needed. They wanted Logan to penetrate the facility and survey the IT infrastructure there.

There was no way he was going to be able to just waltz into Pan's institute on his own. The State Council had implemented a plan in 2000 designed to turn Mianyang into a National Science and Technology City. It had grown into a major defense, S&T and manufacturing center. There were over eighteen scientific research institutes, several state-sponsored R&D complexes, and six universities, of which the Southwest University of Science and Technology was the most well known.

Logan recalled that Li had reported that Pan's institute was on the Board of Governors for the university. Pan had a lab at the university and a team of computer scientists staffing it.

A plan was beginning to take shape in his mind. He reasoned that it would be easier to get onto the campus of a university, especially one that had an international student body, than it would be to penetrate a sensitive institute dedicated to work for the Cyber Executive. If Pan was working on the Zero Day attack at his university lab, it would greatly simplify his task. He needed to verify this with Li.

He and Wellington were meeting at noon to exercise –
a five-mile run in Hong Kong's Mid-levels district. They
usually ran down Bowen Road to where it dead-ends into
Stubbs Road and back. He liked the route because there were
few cars. Also, because it was so lush and green you almost
forgot you were in a city of over seven million people.

They met at noon on Cotton Tree Drive next to Hong
Kong Park in Central.

"Hey, Bruce. How you been?" Wellington had been TDY
in Manila for the past week, meeting a Chinese Foreign
Ministry asset who had resurfaced after a ten-year break in
contact. He'd been recruited in Indonesia and was run suc-
cessfully there but had refused to be met inside China when
he was reassigned to Beijing. He didn't trust the Agency to
run a case internally under the nose of the MPS.

When he'd left Indonesia he was given a re-contact plan
and told to call a certain number the next time he traveled
abroad. It had been so long since he was last met that his
recruiting case officer had retired, and Bruce, as one of the
few Chinese-speaking case officers in the region (but not in
China), had been tapped to meet and debrief him.

"Good. My man showed up. He's done all right for himself since the last time we met him. He's the ambassador to the
Philippines. Headquarters was definitely interested in him,
mainly because he's pretty tight with some people high up
in the Chinese leadership. They want me to handle him out
of Hong Kong until they can get a Chinese speaker out there
permanently." They took off running at a moderate pace.

"We'll have to figure out how to cover your travel to
Manila," Logan replied, breathing easy.

"I've already been thinking about that. I did a little research while I was there. The Philippines is a major ship-
builder. They're like fourth in the world in terms of orders,
behind China, Japan and South Korea.

"Most of what they build isn't relevant to what we're
doing. It's container ships, bulk carriers and passenger ferries. But I think I can do enough cover work while I'm over
there to stay under the radar."

"How about the ambassador? It sounds like he has a healthy bent towards self-preservation," Logan said, referring to the latter's chariness about being met inside China. "I imagine he's pretty high profile in Manila, especially given China's maritime disputes with their neighbors in the South China Sea."

"That came up when we spoke. I used to think it was just the Spratly Islands, but China claims some other maritime boundaries too."

"Like what?"

"Boundaries north of Borneo, the Luzon Strait, and an Exclusive Economic Zone determined by the UN Convention on the Law of the Sea."

They were breathing harder as they climbed. Logan could see the gleaming Bank of China tower, with its commanding views of Hong Kong's skyline, up ahead. Cotton Tree Drive turned into Garden Road and then swerved onto Magazine Gap Road. Bowen Road was ahead on the left.

"Run into any security issues while you were there?"

"No. Ran into some hot Filipinas at the hotel bar."

"Yeah?"

"I'll tell you, those Filipina chicks are a turn-on."

Logan glanced sideways at Wellington. He didn't have to remind him about the Agency's non-frat policy. If he'd been playing grab-ass with anybody, even if it was a one-night stand in Manila, he knew that he was required to report it to headquarters, through his chain of command.

The Agency isn't opposed to its employees fooling around with foreigners, although they do draw the line on those from criterion countries. These include the usual suspects: China, Russia, Iran, North Korea and Belarus. The list is fairly consistent and reflects the counterintelligence concerns CIA has about hostile security services targeting its officers.

"How'd you like to take a trip with me next week to Mianyang?" Logan asked.

"In Szechuan?"

"Yeah."

"What's going on?"

Logan gave him a brief rundown of Frank Sisler's cable. "I'm going to have to go to Chongqing first and track down Phoenix." Logan was still getting used to Li's new code name, which he was expected to use when discussing the case, even with people who were read in on the operation. "I need to get some details from him. Confirm Pan's working out of his lab at the university and see how much he can tell us about the location of the lab, security, and staffing.

"The university has a Chinese language program for foreigners. I was thinking we could visit under the pretext of scouting out the language school for my American employees."

"Isn't that a bit of a stretch?" The former Navy SEAL from Custer City, Oklahoma, raised a skeptical eyebrow. "I mean, there are Mandarin and Cantonese language schools right here in Hong Kong. Why would you go all the way to Szechuan?"

"As an immersion experience. There are so many English speakers here that it's almost impossible to have a complete language immersion. The Foreign Service Institute (FSI) tried something like this in the early '90s. Back in the day, they trained their people in Washington for a year and then shipped them out for language study at an FSI school in Taiwan.

"They did that for decades, but then in 1994 they worked with Johns Hopkins University to set up a Center for Chinese and American Studies at Nanjing University. It's a much more intense experience, for both the Chinese and the Americans. They still use the FSI school but Nanjing is more of an immersion.

"You want to crank it up a notch?"

"I'm game if you are," Wellington replied.

Logan stepped up the pace to a six-minute mile. They reached Stubbs Road minutes later and turned around. Logan checked his watch when they reached the finish line at Hong Kong Park. Thirty-five minutes. Not bad, but he wasn't going to win any races clocking six-minute miles. He wiped his face with his shirt and got a drink from a water fountain.

"See you back in the office in an hour. I told Zahir I'd be home for lunch."

"All right. See you then."

Logan hurried home. He had enough time to shower and grab lunch before heading back for a two-thirty meeting with Stoddard and Wellington. He was alarmed to see that the door to their apartment was ajar and when he stepped inside he could hear muffled cries coming from the study. He raced into the room and found Zahir lying on the floor. She was curled up into a ball, sobs wracking her body.

"Zahir!" He crouched down next to her and was shocked to see that the front of her dress was stained with blood. He cradled her head and tried to comfort her as his mind raced.

"What happened?"

She whimpered but managed to speak. "I came home early because classes were canceled. When I came in I heard a noise and thought it was an intruder. I started to call the police, but he... he..." Her voice caught and she started sobbing.

After a moment she settled down and continued. "It was one of those two men from the restaurant. He was trying to get onto the computer. When he saw me, he knocked me down and ran out. I fell hard and could feel myself starting to bleed. I was afraid to move, because of the baby." She began crying again.

The bleeding was not profuse, but she needed to see a doctor immediately. He made her comfortable and called 999, giving the emergency dispatcher their address. Moments later he could hear the wail of a siren as the responders pulled up outside their apartment. The EMTs settled Zahir into the ambulance and allowed him to ride in the back with her. He held her hand and tried to keep her calm.

Logan instructed the ambulance driver to take them to Hong Kong Adventist Hospital, which was only fifteen minutes away. As he began driving, the other EMT was busy checking Zahir's vital signs.

Minutes later they pulled up to the urgent care facility and two orderlies rushed out to meet them. They lifted Zahir onto a stretcher and wheeled her into an examination room.

Logan called Wellington to let him know that he had an emergency and would have to cancel their meeting. Then he called one of their regular babysitters to see if she was available to take care of Cooper when he got home from school.

Waiting seemed like an eternity. He had time to let his mind wonder. What the hell was that guy doing in their apartment? His blood began to boil as he contemplated the possibility that they might lose the baby.

The doctor came out about an hour later. "Mr. Alexander? Your wife is resting comfortably. She had quite a scare. I did a pelvic exam. She's spotting and her cervix is dilating. These are signs of possible miscarriage but it's not definitive.

"I ordered a trans-vaginal ultrasound to check on the fetal heartbeat, although they're inconclusive through the first seven weeks of pregnancy. In this case we did not detect a heartbeat."

"What's that mean?"

"Again, nothing definitive. Under normal circumstances we wouldn't even do an ultrasound until ten weeks. We're doing blood tests to check her hormone levels. I'm prescribing bed rest for a week and will see her again in ten days to do another blood test and administer another ultrasound.

"Meanwhile, if she experiences any pain or the bleeding increases and shows signs of clotting, bring her in immediately. We'll have her ready to go in a few minutes."

While he was waiting, Logan's thoughts returned to the man who'd broken into their apartment. He was almost certain that he was PSB and not some criminal. His behavior was beyond brazen. That wasn't unusual in Beijing, where the PSB was known to conduct full-coverage surveillance operations and home intrusions against embassy officers. But they rarely went after foreign businessmen unless they were involved in a financial dispute with a Chinese business partner.

He needed to get to the bottom of this and find out why the Chinese were giving him so much attention. The problem was, unless CIA had a penetration of the MPS it was unlikely he'd ever find out why they were interested in him.

A nurse wheeled Zahir out of the emergency room a few minutes later. She was pale and subdued. Evidence of her unpleasant experience weighed heavily on her features.

Logan and Zahir rode down the elevator in silence. They only had to wait a couple of minutes before one of Hong Kong's red-and-white taxis pulled up to where they were waiting. Logan helped Zahir into the back seat and rolled the wheelchair over to an attendant.

When they got home, Logan made her comfortable in the living room. Cooper climbed up onto the sofa to cuddle with her while he went into the kitchen to see about putting some dinner together. He didn't normally do a lot of cooking because Zahir was such a good cook, but he knew his way around the kitchen.

As he began making a salad he reminded himself to send Frank a message later on, letting him know that he planned to postpone his trip for a few days until Zahir was feeling better. Also he needed to change the locks on the doors in case that goon was thinking about another visit. He gritted his teeth. If he ever got his hands on that guy he'd regret what he'd done.

Chapter 22

Logan delayed his trip to China for a week. Although Zahir was getting restless staying cooped up in the apartment, she had taken the doctor's admonition to refrain from any physical activity seriously. She'd had no more spotting and was eager for her follow-up appointment.

Logan and Wellington had flown into Chongqing the day before. He'd introduced Wellington to his contacts at China Shipbuilding and they'd been offered a tour of the Chongqing shipyard. Afterwards the Chinese hosted a lunch for everyone at the Crowne Plaza Riverside. Wellington had taken a late afternoon train to Chengdu, and then on to Mianyang, where the plan was for him to meet up with Logan the following day.

At the moment it was ten-thirty p.m. and Logan was set to meet Li in fifteen minutes. He had called him on a throw-away cell phone at five-thirty and confirmed his availability to meet at ten-forty-five that night at the site they had agreed to during their last encounter, an alley off of Xingdong Road behind Huang's Foot Massage Parlor.

At ten-forty he entered the alley. There was little foot traffic here and in the dark, he could barely discern the features of the few pedestrians who walked through. Then one of them spoke to him.

"Logan?"

"Li? How are you?" He shook the PSB officer's hand. He was relieved to see his familiar features.

"Not bad. I'm surprised to see you again so soon."

Before addressing this comment, Logan went through their cover story for the meeting, and gave Li directions to their next meeting site. When he had finished, Li raised a question that often comes up early in a clandestine relationship.

"When we're done I want to take my son to the United States. Can you arrange this for me?"

"You mean for a visit?"

"No, to live."

"What about your wife?" Logan asked.

Li paused before responding. "She died."

Logan was shocked by Li's muted response. He hadn't mentioned anything about his wife being ill in their previous encounters.

"What happened?" Logan tried to read the PSB officer's expression, but his face remained blank.

"She took her own life," he whispered.

Logan didn't know what to say. "I'm sorry." He searched his asset's face and then continued. "It must be hard for you."

Li remained noncommittal, waiting for Logan to answer his question.

"I'll do what I can," Logan said. Getting Li and his son out of China would be no easy feat, particularly if he had not reached retirement age. The Ministry of Public Security wasn't about to let an active-duty senior officer pull the plug and move to the States. It would be easiest to secret Li away if he traveled abroad again on official business, but getting the son out would be the hard part. "I promise," he said.

"We don't have much time. I need to ask you some questions. Do you know if Pan Chengong is working on his attack scenario in the lab at Southwest University of Science and Technology?"

Li looked surprised by the question. "Yes, he is. Why do you ask?"

"I need to get inside his lab."

Li frowned. "That's not so easy. The university has roving security patrols, and the labs are alarmed. Why do you need to get in there? It would be easier if I went. Let me do it."

"No. It's too dangerous." Li didn't argue with him.

"When are you thinking about going?"

"Tomorrow."

He turned pale. "So soon?"

"Does it matter?"

"No. It's..." Li's voice trailed off.

Logan spent the rest of the meeting plying him with questions about the specific location of the lab, layout of the facility, security system, and types of computers the cyber hackers were using.

"You must be careful, Logan. I have to tell you about something else." He began talking about Zhang's attack on Blue Waters, the supercomputer center in Illinois.

"If we are successful using Blue Waters in a DDoS attack against U.S. financial institutions, it will be unlike anything you've seen to date."

Logan looked grim. "That's why we have to stop it now!"

They parted ways at eleven-fifteen. Logan returned to his hotel and spent a restless night tossing and turning as he went over the details the Chinese volunteer had provided.

Early the next morning he checked out of his hotel after consuming an Asian breakfast of *congee*, a kind of rice gruel with salted hundred-year eggs. His waitress also brought him a plate of fried bread sticks. In Chinese they're called *youtiao*, or grease sticks, he thought, as he wiped the oily residue off his hands. He paid his bill and looked for a taxi to take him to the train station.

He arrived in Chengdu at nine-forty-five, just missing the nine-forty-two train to Mianyang. The next one was at ten-eleven. Logan bought a soft seat costing one hundred RMB for the hour-and–a-half trip.

There was an older Chinese couple in his compartment, as well as an Australian biologist who was traveling on to the Wanglang National Nature Reserve, home of China's giant pandas. Her name was Zoe McAllister. She was on loan from the Australian Wildlife Conservancy and would be in the field for the next year studying the endangered species. Logan was distracted as he listened to her go on about saving the giant panda from extinction. He was more worried thinking about saving the U.S. economy from destruction.

He and Wellington were scheduled to begin their initial recon of the university that afternoon. They were meeting at the Mianzhou Hotel, downtown on Linyuan Road, at twelve-thirty.

The train wound its way through a lush valley. It was late October but the verdant landscape gave evidence to the region's humid, subtropical climate that produced over forty-five inches of average annual rainfall. In the distance, atop a craggy peak, Logan could make out the lines of an ancient temple silhouetted against a cloudless sky. Twenty minutes later the conductor announced their imminent arrival in Mianyang.

The Mianzhou Hotel was only a ten-minute cab ride from the train station. Getting out of his taxi, he spotted Wellington through the glass doors, waiting for him in the hotel lobby.

"How was your trip?" Wellington asked. He gripped Logan's outstretched hand.

"Not bad. Lots of mountains. How's the hotel?"

"It's all right. Nothing to write home about. How'd it go last night?"

Logan looked around the lobby. "Fine. I'll tell you about it at lunch."

"Why don't you check in? There's supposed to be a good noodle place just down the street. We can grab a bite there and catch up."

Fifteen minutes later the two men were sprinting to get out of a drenching downpour. The sky had opened up without any warning when they were just a block from the hotel. Laughing, they jostled past the people queuing up at the take-out window and found a table for two. Their waitress recommended the spicy beef noodles.

Logan sat back and took stock of their surroundings. He and Wellington were the only Westerners in the restaurant. Most of the clientele were Chinese, a mixture of college students, housewives and workers. No one seemed to be paying any attention to them, which was unusual because Mianyang didn't have that many foreigners.

Logan hadn't realized how hungry he was, as the waitress delivered steaming bowls of noodles. The piquant aroma of the spicy beef made his mouth water and he and Wellington were silent as they dug into their meal.

"What did our man have to say?" Wellington emitted a satisfied burp and set his chopsticks down.

"He wasn't that keen on me doing it. I didn't mention that there were two of us. He offered to go in for me. Obviously I couldn't tell him the whole point of me going in is that we don't trust him enough to handle it on his own." Logan shook his head. "At some point we're going to have to trust this guy. He's taken some pretty big risks just reaching out to us."

"It'll take time. Headquarters always seems to be asking 'What have you done for us lately?'"

"That's because we've been burned in the past. There have been times where we were so pumped about the Intel that we got lazy and forgot to run a tight operation. Look for CI problems. Test the asset. Your basic tradecraft.

"Oh. I forgot to mention. He wants out after this is all over. Apparently his wife committed suicide."

"What? Did this just happen?"

"I didn't get the specifics but it sounds like it."

"Shouldn't be a problem to get him in, should it? Parole him into the U.S.?"

"It's not that easy. Headquarters would like it if he just took a big chunk of money and walked. It's not easy getting someone into the country. Besides, once they're in, the Agency's responsible for them forever."

They paid their bill and went outside. The line at the takeout window had dwindled to a few stragglers and the rain had tapered off to a light drizzle. An old man standing beneath a frayed umbrella eyed them suspiciously. He sucked on a toothpick and watched them as they walked by.

"The university is about a twenty-minute cab ride from here. It's six miles north of the city center, just west of the Fujiang River," Wellington said.

"I'm thinking we should head up there and just stick with our cover story. We can locate the Chinese language school and see if we can get some information about language classes. What do you think?"

"When do you want to try and get into the lab?"

"We'll have to figure out what time they close up. Li seemed to think they knock off around six. If we get stopped at any point after we've talked to the people at the language school, we can tell them that we're checking out the campus. If anyone catches us in the computer lab though, we're hosed."

Wellington hailed a cab and they piled in. Minutes later they were out of the city proper, rolling by fields of rapeseed plants with their bright yellow petals. They rode in silence past the Northeast Gate where, just west of the Fujiang River, the driver pointed out the Thousand Buddha Rock.

"You want to stop? Have a look?"

"How far are we from the university?"

"Five minutes."

Logan looked at his watch. It was after three. "No thanks. We should get to the university before it gets too late."

The driver shrugged and drove on in silence.

"There," he said, pointing ahead. Logan looked out at the sprawling campus. With over 29,000 students situated on seven-hundred-some acres, Southwest University of Science and Technology was one of the premier public universities in western China.

"Where do you want to go?"

"The Chinese Language School. It's on Qinglong Avenue."

Moments later they pulled up to a new building with a fountain in front. Logan paid the driver and they went inside, where they were greeted by the head of the Chinese Language program, Ms. Wang. She invited them into her office and listened to Logan's cover story about his search for a Chinese language program for his employees.

She didn't seem to think it odd that they had come all the way from Hong Kong in search of Chinese language instruction.

"Most of our students come for the semester," she observed. "But we can also tailor our programs to meet the individual needs of the student."

"The tuition is 12,000 yuan per year. Students have the option of living in a student dormitory or university apartment. The dorms cost about two dollars per day and apartments rent for about twice that. Meals are separate."

"When is your deadline for applications?"

"We have rolling admissions, particularly for the individualized Chinese language program."

"And you have classes for all levels?"

"Yes, from beginner to advanced conversation. Would you like a tour of the campus?"

"That would be nice. Thank you."

Ms. Wang gave them a tour of the school. Logan was impressed with the modern language lab and classrooms. After they had finished she handed them off to a student assistant, who took them around to look at a typical student dorm and apartment.

The accommodations were modest, but adequate. Logan and Wellington professed interest in what the student was saying, but they figured neither one of them would be taking up residence there anytime soon so they didn't ask him any questions.

When they were finished, they told him they were going to walk around the campus to get a better feel for the place. They thanked him for taking time out of his day to show them around.

The Language School was about three-quarters of a mile from Pan's computer lab. It was five-thirty. Sunset was at six-fifteen. Li had told him that Pan's people knocked off by six for the most part.

The plan was to reconnoiter the immediate area around the lab to determine if anyone was still working after six o'clock. From what Li had told him he was fairly confident that there were no security cameras in the building although the doors were alarmed. He wanted to check it out himself before attempting to break in.

As he and Wellington walked towards Pan's computer lab he could feel the adrenaline start to kick in. A big part of the challenge they were facing was that they had minimal tools to get the job done. Because they were under business cover they weren't carrying any spy gear unless you counted the software bug he hoped to put on Pan's computer. The only thing he had on him was his Leatherman tool.

Wellington had picked up a set of lock-picking tools at a hardware store in Chengdu. They were not spy gear per se, but having them in his possession would raise eyebrows if he was stopped and searched by the police. Logan planned to have him dump them in the river when they were through.

"That's the building the lab's in," he said, pointing to a five-story block building ahead on the left. "It's on the back side so let's circle around to see what it looks like."

Lights were on in some of the classrooms, and there was a fair amount of sidewalk traffic as students and professors headed home for the day. The rear of the building was not well lighted and, unlike the sidewalk out front, there were no pedestrians walking around. They crossed a parking lot that had a smattering of vehicles and a bicycle rack with two bicycles leaning against it.

There were no security cameras mounted in the usual positions on the corners of the building's exterior walls. Pan's lab was on the fourth floor, towards the middle of the structure. The entire floor was dark. He and Wellington found a cement bench in a grassy area with shrubs and trees on the far side of the parking lot. It afforded them a view of the building without having to stand exposed in the nearly empty lot.

Logan had learned long ago that it was harder for one person to remain inconspicuous than two. The interaction between two people is somehow less threatening than one person by himself.

He and Wellington gave the appearance of chatting easily, although they were on high alert. As the shadows lengthened the air was filled with a loud humming noise.

"Cicadas," Wellington offered, as the buzzing sound swelled.

"Hard to believe they do that just by rubbing their wings together," Logan said.

"Yeah. Most of them actually vibrate this organ called a timbal to make that sound."

"Just the males do it, right?" Logan asked.

"Yeah. It's their mating song."

They listened to the rising and falling sound of the humming in the trees. It was eerie sitting in the shadows of the trees as the cicadas reached a crescendo before falling off, the din drowning out other night sounds.

Fifteen minutes later, two men exited the rear door of the building and got into the last remaining vehicle in the parking lot. They sat there for a minute, lighting cigarettes; their muffled voices carrying through the open windows across the lot to where Logan and Wellington waited. Then the engine cranked, sputtered and roared to life. The sound faded as the driver shifted into gear and edged out of the lot, turning left onto Qinglong Avenue.

After a few minutes they left their spot beneath the trees and walked across the grounds towards the building. Logan had considered waiting until early morning to make their foray into the lab, but that would leave them with hours to kill, increasing the likelihood that they would be discovered.

They reached the building and Wellington went to work on the door, which had a zinc-alloy glass door lock. He pulled his lock-picking tools out and knelt down in front of it.

"It's hard to hear the tumblers on this thing." He had his ear pressed up close to the mechanism as he jiggled his tools. "Tension's really light." He remained that way for several minutes of intense concentration and then grinned as the last tumbler fell into place and the lock opened.

They slipped inside. There was a central stairwell leading to the upper floors. They climbed without talking, intent on getting to the fourth floor and tackling the security system.

Following Li's directions, they exited the stairwell on the fourth floor; hugging the wall they crept down the corridor, passing classrooms and offices. Midway down the hallway they stopped in front of a half-glass steel door. The glass was frosted, preventing outsiders from seeing inside.

"Cylindrical lock," Wellington muttered.

Logan knew from what Li had told him that the door was alarmed. There was a keypad ten feet inside the door on the left wall. Li had given him the entry code, a six-digit sequence that had to be entered within thirty seconds or an alarm would go off. He'd said that the alarm was not centrally monitored, but that it would emit an audible alarm, which eventually would attract the attention of one of the roving security patrols.

Logan held his breath as Wellington toyed with the lock. It took him less than five minutes. He exhaled as the door swung open and they burst in. He had a pocket flashlight in his right hand, which he shone against the left wall, illuminating the keypad right where Li had said it would be.

"Breathe," he muttered.

He shifted the flashlight to his left hand and examined the security system keypad. He punched in the six-digit code and waited for acknowledgement that the system was disarmed. Nothing happened. His pulse quickened. "Shit! Forgot the pound sign." He entered the six digits once again, followed by the pound sign, and a reassuring system-disabled indicator appeared. Logan exhaled as he realized that he had been holding his breath for the last thirty seconds.

"Whew. That was too close for comfort. Let's get to work."

Chapter 23

Logan flashed his low-glare Maglite around the room to get his bearings. The lab had eight desks with computer gear, a workbench and two small offices near the door they had just entered. There was a sofa against one wall.

Wellington began moving around the room with a camera, documenting everything in sight. Each desk had a desktop computer with dual screen and its own printer. A quick look showed them to be Chinese-made workstations. While Wellington concentrated on photographing the contents of the main room, Logan went into the first small office. This was probably Pan's office, he guessed. The other looked as though it was a server room.

Bingo. There was a sheepskin on the wall. Pan's PhD from Stanford. Next to his desk was a filing cabinet. On the desk was the same computer setup; Chinese-made PC with dual screen monitor and printer.

Logan sat down at the desk and withdrew a USB flash drive from his pocket. Fumbling around in the dark, he managed to locate the small recess on the computer panel and insert the USB into it. He booted Pan's computer, the whirling noise of the PC's fan loud in the quiet room. A single blinking cursor from the monitor felt like a beacon in the otherwise darkened space.

Logan entered the password he'd been given by Langley, a safety mechanism in case the thumb drive fell into the wrong hands. The decrypted contents began to execute a program on Pan's computer, surveying the network, collecting data files and, lastly, installing a Trojan, a Trojan from Langley that would allow headquarters to gain remote entree to Pan's hard drive. This access could be expanded into other computers or servers on the network, access that could retrieve documents, take a photograph from the webcam, or even shut the computer down entirely.

The technology had been around for years. Hackers had mounted successful attacks all over the world by giving away innocuous looking flash drives infected with hacker tools like Switchblade and Hacksaw. All the intruders had to do was sit back and wait for the unsuspecting dupes to plug the USB into their PC and watch the treasure trove of data come home to Mama.

Some computer geek at Langley had customized Switchblade, he was certain, but the technology was similar to the original software and served the same purpose. The Trojan he was installing on Pan's computer would be invisible to him. It wouldn't modify anything on the network except on the storage drive, where a hidden encrypted log file was being created.

Wellington poked his head into the room. "How's it going?"

"Good. I'm just about done with this. It'll be mailing home directories, passwords, network configurations, machine-specific information, everything you'd want to know, before we're even out of here."

"You going to do the other machines too?"

"I might as well, although in theory if they're all on the same network, we should get everything from this one, but just in case we lose access to this machine, headquarters will be able to access the others."

"How about just installing it on their server?" He inclined his head towards the room next door.

"We should be able to handle that from Pan's computer, but I'll take a look."

"Do you want to survey what's in the file cabinet?"

"Check it out, but if it's full we'll be here all night trying to copy everything," he warned.

"What's that?"

Logan cocked his head and could hear the sound of voices in the hallway. He pulled the USB drive from the computer and nodded his head towards the server room next door, mouthing the word "Security." He and Wellington flattened themselves against the wall, barely breathing as the voices drew nearer.

Logan tensed as the door rattled. They had locked it behind them when they came into the lab. The lock jiggled, as the two men stood outside conversing. Logan could not make out what they were saying. Their voices were muffled through the walls. Satisfied that the lab was locked up, the two security officers moved on down the hall performing their security checks.

Logan breathed more easily. The success of the operation depended upon the two of them getting in and out of here without being detected. If they had to take out two Chinese security guards this whole thing could blow up in their faces.

They waited five minutes and continued working. Logan's flashlight pierced the darkness, finally resting on the server's physical console, the keyboard connected and a small monitor up and running. It was still logged on as admin, giving him the access needed to load the files from his USB drive.

Moments later Logan was finishing his installation of the Trojan on the server, when Wellington let out an exclamation.

"Will you look at this?"

He had pulled several photos from a file marked "Ashburn." Logan recognized them as pictures of the buildings in Virginia that housed the Internet relays for key U.S. financial institutions. There were pictures inside the garage and the green cabinet housing the optical fiber for the network.

"Weird seeing these here. I saw some of the same pictures taken by the Bureau when they set up video surveillance on this team. Unbelievable."

They decided to spend another hour documenting files from Pan's office. Logan reasoned that security wouldn't be back anytime soon, and they would have cleared the building by the time he and Wellington were ready to leave.

It was almost eight o'clock by the time they re-armed the alarm system and let themselves out of the lab. Li had told him that there was a feature with this system that would allow him to modify its cache history. He scrolled through the menu and found the event viewer and then located the event log. An action menu appeared and he was able to clear the history, wiping clean his and Wellington's visit.

Both men crept down the stairs to the first floor. The building was quiet; there was no sign of the two security guards. They decided to walk the two miles east to the river so that they could dispose of the incriminating lock-picking tools. Once they got rid of these, the only compromising evidence on them would be Logan's USB drive and Wellington's flash drive with the pictures. Both of these drives employed hidden features, making the files invisible to the casual observer. Even skilled computer experts would be hard pressed to break their encryption algorithms.

The two men walked through campus to the river, unchallenged. Although it was relatively early, there weren't that many people out and about. When they reached their destination, Wellington looked around to make certain that they were alone. He undid the knot securing the plastic bag holding the lock-picking set. One by one he removed the tools from the bag, and flung them far out into the river, where they landed with a splash. It would be impossible to tie them to him now.

"What do you want to do for dinner?" Wellington asked, as he tossed the last lever into the swirling current.

"Why don't we catch a cab back into Mianyang? We can go to the hotel and clean up, and then see what there is." He squinted in the dark to read his watch. "Eight-thirty. It'll be after nine, nine-thirty before we get back."

"We may have to settle for the hotel restaurant. Most of those places look like they close up pretty early."

They walked for fifteen minutes before they were able to flag down a passing taxi. The ride back was harrowing, although made in record time. Their driver had missed his calling as a drag strip racer, as he sped by every conveyance: motorcycles, semis straining with their overloaded trailers, and the occasional passenger car.

Logan was thoughtful as they rode back into the city. "Did you know the *China Daily* did a poll a few years ago and named Mianyang as one of the top three livable cities in China?"

"That's hard to believe. What were the first two?"

"Dalian and Xiamen."

"What happened to places like Beijing and Shanghai?"

"People are tired of the crowding and pollution. And Beijing is like Washington. All kinds of bureaucracy. Remember that *chengyu* they taught us in language school?"

"*Tian gao, Huangdi yuan?*"

Their driver turned around to look at them when he heard Wellington utter the familiar expression.

"Heaven is high and the emperor is far away."

"I'll bet they took that poll before the earthquake. Remember? 2008? There were over 89,000 people killed or missing in this area. The epicenter wasn't far from here."

They rode in silence back to the hotel and agreed to meet in the lobby in twenty minutes.

Logan showered quickly, wrapped himself in a bath towel and called home. He'd been thinking about Zahir all afternoon, wondering how she was doing. The phone rang a couple of times before she picked up.

"Hey. I miss you."

"I miss you too. How you feeling?"

"Better. I had my follow-up exam today."

"How'd it go?" There was a moment's pause and Logan could feel his heart racing.

"Everything's all right."

He felt a flood of emotion. He'd steeled himself for the worst. But now it looked like things were back on track.

"I was worried about you."

"I know."

They talked for a few more minutes.

"I'll be home tomorrow. Are you still on bed rest, or can you be up and around?"

"I'm good to go. I think I'll start classes again Monday."

"That's great. I'll see you tomorrow, sweetheart."

"Bye. I love you."

"Love you."

Logan hung up. He was elated that Zahir was all right and that they weren't going to lose the baby. It was the best possible outcome. He dressed and went down to the lobby. Wellington was already there talking to the concierge.

"There's an English pub not too far from here. Flags. About fifteen minutes walking."

"Let's do it."

Ten minutes later they walked into a little bit of England. Flags' interior was a smorgasbord of textures, with stone floors, wood-beamed ceilings and brick walls. A smattering of expats and locals were drinking beer and laughing. A couple was playing darts against one wall.

Logan ordered a Fosters draft and Wellington asked for a Guinness. Their beers arrived a few minutes later. There wasn't anything on the menu that appealed to them, so they decided to make it a liquid dinner.

As they sat there watching the crowd, Logan reviewed the day's activities. Things had gone about as well as could be expected. Kept a pretty low profile. Got in and out without getting caught. The only thing that remained was to see if the Trojan started mailing home like it was supposed to.

He'd checked the USB drive before they'd left the lab. Sure enough there was a new file on there with all the data it had copied from Pan's F drive. There'd probably be some feedback for him from Langley by the time they got back to Hong Kong. Worst-case scenario, if there was a glitch in the program, there was enough information on his USB drive to allow headquarters to take control of Pan's computer and find out what that squirrely bastard was up to.

Logan smiled in satisfaction. Not only had they pulled off an intelligence coup by breaking into Pan's lab, possibly averting a major cyber attack against the U.S., but their success should also seriously elevate Li's standing with Cyber Division. It would have been a lot more complicated getting into the lab without his help.

He and Wellington tipped their beers in a silent tribute to the PSB officer. He'd have to find the right time to raise Li's request for asylum with headquarters. They'd read about it in his write-up anyway, but this merited a separate piece of correspondence. He planned to support Li's request, but he needed some time to think through their options before running off half-cocked to Langley.

He and Wellington drained their glasses, paid their bill and headed out the door. They had an early flight via Chengdu in the morning and right now a little bit of shut-eye was in order.

Chapter 24

Lois Caldwell left her car in the visitor's parking lot at Langley and walked along the tree-lined path to the main entrance. Normally she would have taken the inter-agency shuttle that services headquarters, but she had personal errands to run after work.

At the security desk she scanned her Intel Community badge and punched in the four-digit PIN. The barrier slid open and she flashed a smile at Mike, the security protective officer who had been manning the post for fifteen years. He waved and returned her greeting.

She paused just inside the foyer to gaze at the Memorial Wall. A new star had been etched into the marble the week before. There were a hundred and thirteen stars carved into the white Alabama marble. One for each Agency officer who had died in service to the U.S.A. Just beneath the stars in a small case rested a book with the names of the officers memorialized in the constellation above. Some of their names were never revealed because those officers, even in death, remain under cover. Instead of their names, a golden star marks their place in the book.

Lois took the north elevator up to the fourth floor and walked down the hall to the China Cyber Team's spaces. She had been amazed at how quickly they were up and running once the Covert Action Finding was approved. Over a weekend, office space had materialized, high-speed lines had been installed, phone runs, computers and office furniture had been brought in, and by Monday morning they were in business.

She punched in the code on the Simplex lock and let herself into the office. Frank was on the phone. There was a cardboard tray with four coffees on his desk. He motioned for Lois to help herself as he listened to the voice on the other end.

"Look, Clarence. I don't give a damn if you're so backed up that whatever it is, is starting to crawl up your ass. I need those files and I need them yesterday!" He slammed the receiver down in frustration and then grinned at Lois.

"We know that 'Jake' and one of his officers got into Pan's computer lab yesterday. We haven't actually heard from them but our Trojan started calling home late last night."

"What's the problem? We were set up to conceal Langley as the final destination, right?"

"Right, just as we discussed. The data passed through hundreds of Internet hops, and got into the building, but someone didn't get the memo on the final destination, so it's just been sitting there all night."

"We're still using The Onion Router for this, right?" Lois asked. TOR directs Internet traffic through randomly selected proxy computers, sometimes hundreds, or even thousands of times, to conceal the identity of the user. Like an onion, TOR has multiple layers of encryption, making it virtually impossible for anyone to determine the identity of the user. TOR encrypts not only the content of the message, but the destination IP address too.

"Yes. The garble wasn't actually with TOR. We managed to get the file relayed to the Agency's unclassified network enclave."

"Who's Clarence?" She took a sip of her coffee and smiled.

"He's one of our IT guys. Mainly assigned to Special Access Programs."

"Oh."

There was a buzz at the front door, and their secretary, Roberta, let in a burly, unkempt man in his late forties. He was wearing baggy jeans secured with a pair of red suspenders, and a Grateful Dead t-shirt. Red Keds completed his ensemble.

"That wasn't funny, Frank." He thrust a computer disk at the cyber chief and stomped out of the room.

"Clarence, meet Lois," Frank announced to the retreating back.

Clarence waved his hand and kept walking. Lois tried to keep a straight face.

"He'll get over it," Frank said. He waved the disk Clarence had delivered. "Why don't you take a first crack at this and see what we've got?"

Lois took the proffered disk and walked into her office. She stuck her head back out the door and waved the cup of Starbucks. "Thanks for the coffee, Frank."

Lois's pulse quickened as she sat down at her computer. She ejected the drive and slipped in the disk Clarence had delivered. Standard protocol called for the IT staff to scan outside media on their stand-alone system for any viruses. Only when they were a hundred percent confident that it was clean would they clear it to upload onto the Agency's internal network. Even then, distribution of the material was very limited.

Their project was so sensitive that only a handful of people were read into the Special Access Program. Maybe a dozen at the most inside the Agency. The White House, FBI, NSA and the Gang of Eight on Capitol Hill brought it to another twenty.

She sipped her coffee and nervously tapped her foot as the computer whirred. It stopped humming and a file opened on her screen. She called over the team's Chinese linguist and asked him to sit with her as she started going through the folders.

"That's the root directory," he said, pointing to the uppermost file. The root directory is a kind of electronic file cabinet that organizes all of the folders and their respective files on the network.

"That means the Chinese must be using Linux as their operating system," Lois surmised. "Pan's unit is probably using the Filesystem Hierarchy Standard to organize all the folders and files on the network."

As the linguist began reading out the subdirectory names, Lois could see that there was a treasure trove of information they would be able to access. There were configuration files, libraries, home directories, log files, users' mailboxes, passwords, etc.

They worked until lunch when someone came around to take orders. Lois asked for a chicken Caesar salad and an iced tea. They had a small conference room that doubled as a break area, and ate their lunch in there. Afterwards she and one of the NSA officers took a twenty-minute walk outside. It was overcast and the temperature had dropped several degrees. Lois was glad that she had brought a light sweater.

Frank had called for a one o'clock all hands to get the initial dump from Lois. Everyone was assembled in the conference room when they got back. She gathered her notes together and took a seat at the table.

For the benefit of the computer geeks in the room, she spent the first ten minutes describing the network configurations and providing machine-specific information. "The most interesting thing about their set-up, big picture-wise, is that they have direct connectivity to the Institute for Applied Computer Science, so theoretically we should be able to get a lot more on what they're up to."

"Like what?" one of the NSA techs asked.

"Well, the Ministry of Public Security's computer network defense program, the CND, for one. Just because Pan's institute is mainly focused on cryptology and information security technology, doesn't mean they're the only ones interested in computer network exploitation.

"I saw some link analysis done by a DI analyst last year that showed how concerned China's leadership is about information security. They've named a cyber czar and there are several other organizations focused mainly on CND that interact heavily with the Institute for Applied Computer Science.

"Places like the military's Communications Security Bureau and the National Information Center. We are seeing indications of leadership interest as well. Central Committee and provincial leadership. There are others too."

"That's all good," Frank interjected. "But how about our immediate problem? Are we going to be able to stop this Zero Day cyber attack?"

"I can't answer that right now, Frank. What I do know from this directory is that we have passwords for each of the accounts on the network and access to what looks like shared libraries at the computer lab. I recommend that we prioritize what we think is most important and then start systematically surveying everything."

The group spent the next hour poring over Lois's notes, weighing the pros and cons of focusing on one target set over another. At the end of the day, they decided to begin with Pan Chengong's account and then survey the shared libraries to determine where they should allocate their resources.

To go through the back door Logan and Wellington had installed on the Chinese network, the team was using Cryptcat, an encrypted version of the Netcat tool, which hackers use to read and write data over TCP/IP and user datagram protocol connections.

"Pan seems to be working in the Linux environment," Lois said. Linux uses something called Bash Shell as the command line interpreter. Most hackers prefer command line interface to get control of a program or an operating system to graphical user interface. From their analysis of the network, Lois also determined that the Chinese were sending unencrypted Internet traffic over port 80. The team would be able to hide the Cryptcat data amongst the Chinese unencrypted Internet traffic and no one would be any wiser.

The techs conducting the daily attacks on the Chinese network would have to adjust their workday hours so that they were on Beijing time. That way they would be able to exploit the network real time.

There were groans around the room when Frank explained this to the team. "You know, China's big enough to span five time zones. But in its infinite wisdom, Beijing decided that everyone was going to be on the same time zone, so there's only one.

"We have reporting from Phoenix that Pan's lab keeps a fairly regular schedule – nine to six. They're twelve hours ahead of us, so that means our graveyard shift is going to run from nine p.m. to six a.m."

Lois spent the next two hours typing up her notes and reviewing the material she and the linguist had cataloged. She realized as she looked at all of it that they were going to need more translation assistance, if they were going to plow through all the material.

She got up from her desk and poked her head into Frank's office. "I don't know if you've thought about this, but we're about to be inundated with reams of Chinese language material."

Frank held up his hand. "Already on it. I've asked the East Asia Mission Center to loan us two linguists for the duration and NSA has two more coming over tomorrow. I'll have to find some more office space to house them."

"Great. I'm going to call it a day. I have some errands to run. See you tomorrow."

She returned to her desk and secured her notes and files in the safe assigned to her. Headquarters had a clean desk policy, meaning that even though they were in a vaulted area inside the main headquarters building, sensitive classified information could not be left out unattended overnight.

The parking lot was half-full, even though it was five-thirty. The people at Langley work long hours, she thought. There's always a crisis going on somewhere in the world.

She pulled out of the parking lot and turned south onto Dolley Madison Boulevard. Traffic was already beginning to back up heading into the District. She took a left onto Chain Bridge, crossed the Potomac River and took a right onto Canal Road.

Ten minutes later she pulled up in front of Director Mitchell's Foxhall Crescent, Tudor residence. Although she had attended George Washington University for undergraduate school and had lived in Georgetown for four years, she had rarely strayed into the tony enclave housing many of Washington's power elites.

Lois was conflicted about this meeting with Mitchell. She had received a call from his chief of staff a day after the CIA had stood up the China Cyber Team, and had been advised that she was expected to brief the director once a week at his residence on the status of their effort.

The fact that he had asked her to brief him at his residence and that she was bypassing her own chain of command to do so left her feeling somewhat uncomfortable. She knew that Mitchell attended NSC meetings, but he wasn't on the President's short list for dinner invitations to the White House.

An FBI agent on Mitchell's security detail let her into the residence and escorted her to a wood-paneled library. He left her there and said that the director would be with her shortly.

Behind the mahogany executive desk were row upon row of law books. Rich leather chairs flanked the desk and a Tabriz carpet covered the parquet floor. She walked over to look at some photos on Mitchell's desk and was struck by a picture of a young woman sculling on the Potomac. The photographer had captured her at that fraction of a second between driving the oars into the water and her recovery. Her eyes were looking straight ahead and her long blond ponytail trailed down her back.

"That's Alex," the director said as he strode into the room.

"Oh!" Lois turned and blushed. Then she remembered. Alex Mitchell, the only daughter of then-U.S. Circuit Court of Appeals Judge Greg Mitchell, had been brutally murdered in her Georgetown apartment almost ten years ago.

Alex had been an Olympic rowing hopeful. The popular co-ed had regularly appeared in the *Post's* Style section, often attending Washington soirées on the arm of her father.

The killer had never been found, and the stress from losing their only child and all of the attendant publicity had derailed the Mitchells' marriage.

"I'm sorry, sir."

Mitchell walked over to where she stood and took the photograph in his hands. "It's been ten years since we lost Alex. There are some things that you just never get over." He set the photo down and gave her a tight smile.

"Now, let's sit over here and you can fill me in."

Lois spent the next thirty minutes briefing him on the task force's activities. Mitchell asked her a number of probing questions and she had the sense that he was much more comfortable with the material than he had been when she first briefed him. Still there was something strange about the whole arrangement. As she was preparing to leave she decided to voice her concerns.

"Sir?"

"Yes, Agent Caldwell?"

"I was just—"

"Wondering why I was having you brief me here instead of at my office?"

She stuttered as she searched for the right words. "It's just…"

"Don't you worry, Agent Caldwell," he replied. "I have my reasons, which will become apparent in due course. But for now I must insist on your discretion."

"Of course, sir," she stammered.

He walked with her to the library door. "Agent Harris will see you out, Agent Caldwell. Good night."

"Good night, sir," she replied. As she walked out to her car, her mouth was set in a resolute line. There was something strange going on here and she was determined to get to the bottom of it.

Chapter 25

Li and young Zhang, the designer of 2004 Tsunami, were on the early morning train to Chengdu. Li had been surprised when Sergeant Shi came into his office late the day before, and advised him that Commissioner Fang required his presence in Chengdu the next morning. He had specifically ordered Li to bring Zhang along. They were both lost in their own thoughts as the train departed Chongqing Station.

Li was thinking back to an earlier conversation he had had with one of Xiao Mei's colleagues and close family friends, Sung Xiaohe, who had dropped by the apartment to pay his respects. He was a respected economist who had written extensively about the U.S.-China economic relationship.

Ever since he had been briefed on Pan's operation, Li had been trying to get his arms around the notion that it was in China's interest to take down the U.S. financial system. He had asked Professor Sung to give him some background on the economic ties between the two countries.

"It's complicated," the professor had replied, accepting a cigarette. He lit it and inhaled, closing his eyes in pleasure before continuing. "Many of today's international economic policies can be traced back to the Bretton Woods Conference, held during World War II. You may recall that's when the allies set up what eventually became the IMF, the International Monetary Fund.

"After the war, the U.S. established itself as the dominant economy in the world, and it followed that the dollar became the dominant currency. In those days the dollar was pegged to the gold standard. Richard Nixon changed that

186

when he took the U.S. off of the gold standard in 1970. Still, the dollar was so strong that it became the world's reserve currency, almost by default.

"As you know, we had a rocky relationship with the Americans after '49. It wasn't until later, when Deng Xiaoping began instituting economic reforms, that we began to generate foreign currency reserves because of expanding trade with America. That's when we started buying up U.S. debt."

"How much do we hold?" Li asked.

"Almost $1.5 trillion. We've been their biggest single foreign creditor since 2008."

"That's all based on trade?"

"Primarily trade. And trade with the U.S. continues to grow. Most of our companies trading with the U.S. put money into short-term Treasuries, which they then convert to pay their bills. But don't forget that the central government probably owns most of that debt. At least a trillion."

"And we keep buying dollars today because the currency's so stable?"

"Historically it's been in our interest to keep the value of the dollar high. For one thing, when it's high, the *renminbi* seems a lot cheaper. That works to our advantage in foreign trade because our exports to the U.S. end up being less expensive."

Li stroked his chin, and pondered what Sung had just said. "So it's actually in our interest to keep the dollar strong?"

"For now, I would say yes. I've heard arguments from some American economists who believe that China could bring down the U.S. by dumping all of its Treasuries on the secondary market.

"The U.S. national debt is over $19 trillion. Foreign countries hold about thirty-four percent of that, with China holding roughly eight percent. That's not enough for us to take down the U.S. economy.

"It's in our interest, at least in the near term, for the dollar to be strong. The fact that there is high demand for the dollar has encouraged many exporters to the U.S., including

China, to invest in Treasuries. These generally have low yields, but more importantly for us, they are also very low risk."

Sung paused to light another cigarette before continuing. "There are some who believe that the Americans have run their course. With the housing collapse in 2008, rise of U.S. debt, and the dollar's decline against other world currencies, many believe that conditions are ripe for the dollar's demise."

"But what would that take?" Li persisted. "It seems to me that something disastrous would have to happen to make the dollar fail." He couldn't help thinking of Pan's Zero Day attack as he spoke the words.

"It's not necessarily something that has to happen overnight or even be catastrophic. Many economists believe that the IMF should be more proactive in finding a replacement for the dollar as the international reserve currency.

"Have you heard of the SDR?" Sung paused and then went on. "It stands for Special Drawing Rights, and the IMF created them in 1969 primarily as a means of supplementing members' reserves. There are those who believe the role of the SDR could be expanded for a broader purpose. As they see it, the SDR, whose value is determined by a basket of currencies, not just one, could become the international reserve currency."

"How do they decide which currencies are included in this so-called basket?"

"The IMF's executive board reviews the basket every five years. Currently it's comprised of the U.S. dollar, the euro, the Japanese yen and the British pound."

"How would this affect China?"

"China has been making the case that the yuan should be included in this basket of currencies. The IMF approved its inclusion late last year, and it's set to take effect at the end of this year."

Li was startled to hear the conductor announce that they were twenty minutes outside of Chengdu. He had been so immersed in revisiting his conversation with Sung, that he had lost all sense of time. He glanced over at Zhang, who was dozing next to him.

He nudged the young hacker. "Zhang, wake up."

Zhang cocked one eye, his face sluggish. "Huh?" He straightened in his seat and eyed his boss. "What's going on?"

"We're almost there. We need to make a good impression on Commissioner Fang. He doesn't suffer fools. I'm assuming he wanted you to come along because he's interested in your work on Blue Waters. Make sure you're comfortable talking about your Trojan and what it can do."

Li wasn't sure how Fang planned to handle this meeting. Zhang wasn't read in on Pan's project, and he doubted that he would be. The operation was about as tightly held as they come.

It was ten o'clock when the two men alighted from the train. Li hailed a taxi and minutes later they were walking into Fang's office. An assistant asked Zhang to wait outside, while he escorted Li into the commissioner's office.

Fang was seated at his desk when Li entered the room. He had a reputation for being a hard ass. He had been the political commissar at Tianjin Municipal headquarters up until last year, when he was transferred to Chengdu after he was caught screwing the commander's wife. He came from a prominent family with connections in Beijing, so his career had not suffered despite his indiscretions.

"Have a seat, Li. Smoke?" He opened a red lacquer box on his desk and offered him a cigarette.

"Thank you, sir." Li withdrew a cigarette from the box and sat down opposite his boss.

Fang eyed him as he tamped down his own cigarette on the desktop and then lit it from an antique green alabaster table lighter. When his cigarette was lit he nudged the lighter in Li's direction and waited until he had settled back into his seat before speaking.

"How's the translation work coming from Pan's operation?"

"We're making a dent in it, but there's so much there, we'll be translating the material for months. It's one of the downsides from these technical operations. If the language resources are not allocated from the outset you run the risk that the Intel will be overtaken by events."

"I thought the software program we developed to prioritize requirements based on key word searches was supposed to alleviate that problem."

"It helps, but it doesn't make any difference if you're still drowning in data and you have limited personnel to do the work. My linguists say it's like drinking from a fire hose."

"I don't see it getting any better soon. In fact, for you it's going to get worse."

"Sir?" Li eyed Fang with apprehension. What was the cagey bastard up to?

"I wanted to hear how the work's going from you personally." He pulled another cigarette from the red box and then offered a smoke to Li, who declined. "But that's not the real reason I wanted to see you. Pan wants that young hacker of yours, Zhang I believe it is, for his operation."

"But, sir—"

"No use fighting it, Li. This operation gets what it needs, and right now Pan thinks he needs Mr. Zhang. Ever since he read your report on Zhang's operation against Blue Waters he hasn't stopped talking about him."

"Perhaps by the end of the month?"

"You're not hearing me." Fang's mouth tightened. "In fact, Zhang is on his way to Mianyang, even as we speak."

"I just left him outside your office!"

"Not to worry. We've already called Chongqing and arranged for his things to be transferred to Mianyang today. He'll be working out of Pan's lab at the university; we've arranged a place for him to stay on campus."

"Is this temporary then? You know he's not one of our professional staff. He's one of our so-called involuntary workers. He's been read into a couple of programs but he has had limited exposure to our most sensitive operations."

"I know. I read his file."

Li masked his concern. He'd had plans for Zhang, who already had shown great promise. But if Pan was ready to turn him loose on his Zero Day operation, the full weight of Blue Waters' computing power in a DDoS attack would be devastating.

His reverie was broken. "That'll be all."

"Sir." He turned and made for the door. True to Fang's word, Zhang was nowhere to be found. He hurried out the door. Somehow he had to get word to Logan.

Chapter 26

Des was restless as he waited for Judge Petrie to enter courtroom three. Petrie was the Stafford County Circuit Court judge assigned to preside over Fred Liang's arraignment.

Des had driven down to Stafford early for the nine a.m. hearing. He glanced around the room, recognizing Jim Baylow's wife from the funeral, and a smattering of friends and family members of, he surmised, the other two victims from Liang's rampage.

Liang was seated alone at the defense table. He was wearing prison garb and his right arm was in a sling. There was no one seated in the rows behind him. On the other side of the aisle the Commonwealth attorney for Congressional District 1, Todd Smiley, and his assistant, Karen Defoe, sat waiting for Judge Petrie to make his entrance.

"All rise." The bailiff swung his head around to survey the courtroom as Judge Petrie swept in and took a seat. There was some shuffling as everyone who had stood, sat back down, and the judge began inspecting the file before him.

Peering over his bifocals the judge spoke to Liang. "Mr. Liang, have you obtained counsel?"

"No, sir."

"Do you plan to do so?"

Liang squirmed in his seat. "I can't afford one right now."

Judge Petrie massaged his brows as he appraised the defendant. Finally he spoke. "You know that under the 6th Amendment you have the right to counsel. If you cannot afford to retain counsel on your own, the court will appoint counsel to represent you. Do you wish to avail yourself of this?"

"Yes, sir."

Petrie leaned down to speak to the clerk. "Ms. Allison, let it be noted that the defendant requests a public defender."

"Yes, your honor."

Petrie then turned his attention back to Liang. "Mr. Liang, you are charged with three counts of first degree murder, use of a firearm in the commission of a felony, and two counts of assault with a firearm with the intent to kill. How do you plead?"

"Not guilty, your honor."

Petrie let his gaze rest on the accused for a moment before responding. "I order you remanded to the Rappahannock Regional Jail without bail. I'm scheduling a preliminary hearing two weeks from today." Petrie searched his calendar. "Yes. November 8. Mr. Smiley, does that provide the State sufficient time?"

Smiley rose to address the judge. "Yes, your honor."

Petrie turned his attention back to the defendant. "Mr. Liang, the clerk will see to it that you have access to counsel as early as this afternoon. That will be all. Mr. Smiley, I'd like to see you and Ms. Defoe in chambers." He rapped his gavel with a resounding thump and court was adjourned.

Des scratched his stomach and peered around the courtroom. Arraignments were ordinarily routine matters, and this one had been no different. He was surprised that Liang had not retained counsel, given his earlier bravado in the hospital. He watched the deputies hustle Fred, in his faded jumpsuit, handcuffed and shackled, out of the courtroom.

This case was a slam-dunk. Although no one had seen Fred actually shoot the three victims, he and Jack Nolton would testify that Liang had fired shots at them moments after the murders, with the very same weapon used to kill Jim Baylow, Janet Price and Juanita Aquino.

"Hey, Des."

Craning his neck, he spotted Nolton sliding out of a back row. "Jack! I didn't see you back there." He stood up and met his old firearms instructor halfway.

"I snuck in right before Petrie came in. Fred's not looking too good. I heard his parents essentially disowned him after they found out what happened. They told Fred he's on his own. He's brought dishonor to the family name."

"This whole thing's screwed. Fred's a loser and he took his frustrations out on three innocent people who had everything to live for." Des hitched up his pants. "You have time for a cup of coffee or breakfast?"

"Yeah. Let's go to Dott's. She still makes the best cup of coffee in these parts."

Jack led the way out of the parking lot. He was driving a Ford F-150 with a rear window gun rack. Des poked his head inside the truck to inspect Jack's weapons. On top was a Winchester Model 70. Des knew that Jack prized this gun. It was one of the original weapons Winchester manufactured when they first introduced the 70 in 1936. It had belonged to his father and had been passed on to Jack when the old man had passed away.

Below the 70 was a Remington Wingmaster shotgun. "You doing much hunting this year, Jack?"

"I plan to. First time out will be next week. Duck hunting should be pretty good this year. Game and Fisheries came out with a new split season format – three days in October, two weeks in November, and then about five weeks in December-January. Looking forward to getting my grandkids out in the woods."

Des pushed back from the truck. "I'll follow you down to Dott's."

Later over coffee and a stack of blueberry pancakes and side of sausage, Des asked how morale was at Quantico in the wake of the shootings.

"It's still pretty raw. We're in a violent business and you know people are going to get hurt. Killed even. But when it happens like that it seems so pointless. No one here really knew Baylow, but Janet and Juanita had worked at Quantico for years."

"I wouldn't mind it if Fred fries," Des commented as he chewed on a piece of sausage. "I told him that I'd speak to the prosecutor if he helped me out. He was cooperative when we met," he admitted. "I mentioned it to Smiley, like I promised, but I'm not pulling for him.

"I had this crazy idea that maybe the Chinese were gunning for Baylow and me because of our cyber investigation and that they'd recruited Fred to take us out. We found out from Langley that the Chinese believed they'd recruited Fred, but in fact he never did anything for them. He led them along while he was in China so they'd stop pestering him."

"How's your investigation going?" Jack wiped his mouth with a napkin and signaled the waitress to refill their coffees.

Des was briefed on the goings on of the task force implementing the covert action plan, but he was not at liberty to discuss it with Jack, so he spoke in general terms.

"The Chinese are eating our lunch. They're going after everything from our missile design technology to your grandmother's recipe for rhubarb pie. They're just sucking it all up like a big vacuum cleaner."

When they'd finished their coffee, Jack motioned to their waitress to bring the bill. He shook his head as he eyed his friend. " I'm just a damn firearms instructor. All that stuff's over my head. If you get some free time, why don't you come hunting with me and the boys one Saturday? Get us some mallards."

"What's the bag limit this year?"

"Six ducks a day. But only four mallards."

"I might just do that. Haven't been out in the woods in a long time."

They said their goodbyes outside. On his way back to Washington, Des phoned Rick Wheeler's office, but all he got was voice mail. He frowned. Normally, when Des was out of the office, Rick would arrange his schedule so that they weren't both out at the same time. He phoned Lois and she picked up on the second ring. "Lois, Des. Have you seen Rick this morning?"

"No, he hasn't been in."

"When he gets in have him give me a call on my cell."

Des looked at his watch. It was going on eleven. Where the hell was Rick? Standard protocol if you were going to be late was to call in. He called Rick's cell phone but it immediately went to voice mail.

"Rick, call me when you get this," he growled.

Next he called Rick's home number. No one picked up. He remembered Rick telling him that Marge had recently gone back to teaching second grade at West Springfield Elementary School. There better be a good reason for this, he fumed.

Des stewed all the way back to Washington. He stormed into Rick's office to chew him out, and was surprised to find the lights off. Asking around he discovered that no one had seen Rick Wheeler all morning.

Des's cell phone alerted him to an incoming text message as he entered his office. It was an alphanumeric SMS message from his buddy, Ji. Des squinted as he tried to read the text. Ji was calling for an emergency meeting at two p.m.

Damn! When it rains, it rains boatloads of shit, he grumbled. It was almost time for lunch but he wasn't that hungry after Dott's blueberry pancakes.

Des preferred to meet Ji after hours, away from the prying eyes of the massive Chinese community in Washington and its environs. He wasn't as fanatical as the spooks over at Langley, with their five-hour surveillance detection runs, sneaking around in the dark. But he grudgingly admitted that their tradecraft was pretty effective. Hell, if the case officer he'd met, Jake, could pull off a meeting with that volunteer in the middle of China without getting himself killed, there was something to be said for it.

Des checked a folder he kept in his safe containing Ji's communications plan. His next meeting called for him to pick the Chinese Embassy officer up in an alley behind an Ethiopian restaurant on 18th Street in Adams Morgan. He would be driving his Bureau vehicle. They would drive out of town and when they were through, Des would drop him off near a metro station so that he could get back into the city.

What the hell was so important that Ji had called for an emergency meeting? He wondered. This was the second time in the last two months. Maybe there were new developments on the Chinese hacking operation. He stuck his head into Lois's office before he left and told her that he would be out for a few hours.

Des picked up his vehicle and took 9th Street to Massachusetts Avenue northwest. He cut up 15th and then turned onto U Street, which took him over to 18th. The timing was going to work out just fine. The Ethiopian restaurant was about a mile up 18th; he was less than ten minutes out.

Traffic wasn't too bad. The lunchtime rush had died down and it would be a couple of hours before afternoon rush hour traffic kicked in. Minutes later he saw the Ethiopian restaurant up ahead. He took a right and a hundred feet down took a left into the alley.

Ji was standing right where he was supposed to be. He was wearing a jacket and had on a baseball cap that helped to conceal his features. Des braked and Ji jumped into the front seat, slouching down so that his face was barely visible above the dashboard.

Des turned back onto 18th Street and then took Adams Mill Road over to Calvert Street where he was able to get onto Rock Creek Parkway. This would get him out of the area.

He picked up speed and then turned briefly to look at his passenger. "What's going on?"

"I had an interesting visitor this morning, that I thought you should know about."

Ji's words piqued Des's interest. Maybe the Chinese were getting ready to launch their big cyber attack. "Does this have anything to do with those people renting the commercial property in Ashburn?"

"No. This is something different. This person was an MPS officer from Beijing. He's not based here in the U.S. I didn't even know that he was coming to Washington. He used my office to cover his trip so he wouldn't come to the attention of the security people.

"I found out that he was sent here to help an American agent that had come under suspicion and was in danger of being arrested."

"Is this something you've briefed me on before?"

"No. Normally in my position, I wouldn't know about this. We get asked to help out from time to time to cover these trips, but they don't tell us anything. It's usually just between the security people.

"Anyway, he was bringing some travel documents for this American but they didn't have a current photo and needed to obtain one from him and have it inserted into the passport. I have a technical person on the S&T staff at the Embassy who helped with it.

"My visitor met with the American last night and they were able to get the photo done this morning. Our technician was the only one to see the travel document, and for obvious reasons I couldn't ask him about it. When I went by his office while he was out I noticed that there was some trash in his burn bag. In there was a copy of the agent's picture. When I saw it, I didn't need a name or information about where this person works. I understood why Beijing is going to all this trouble to protect his identity."

"Did you bring the photo with you?"

"Yes, I have it here." Ji dug into his coat pocket and withdrew a small envelope. Inside was a passport photo, which he handed to Des.

Des glanced down at the photo and felt a gut-wrenching stab of pain. Staring back at him was the smiling face of his deputy, Rick Wheeler.

Chapter 27

Logan logged onto his Agency email account to check for incoming messages. There was an Eyes Only cable from Frank Sisler, which he read with mounting anger and growing trepidation.

"FBI advised us today that one of their Special Agents has, in all likelihood, been spying for Beijing. His name is Rick Wheeler, Des Magarity's deputy in Cyber Division.

"CIA and the FBI have launched an investigation based upon preliminary evidence provided by the FBI. FBI has a cooperative contact working out of the Chinese Embassy in Washington, who Thursday revealed that an MPS officer from Beijing had traveled to Washington to assist in Wheeler's exfiltration. Their contact gained access to a photo of Wheeler that had been taken for his alias passport and shared this with Magarity, who immediately notified his superiors."

Logan seethed as he contemplated Wheeler's treachery. His eyes narrowed as he began to contemplate the ramifications of Wheeler's spying. He turned his eyes back to the computer.

"For the present, we are launching a damage assessment in tandem with our investigation. Wheeler had been assigned to Cyber Division for just two years, but in that time he had access to pretty much everything the Bureau was doing on China cyber, and most of the Bureau's cyber operations with CIA and NSA.

"He knew that CIA was trying to get to the bottom of the Chinese operation against Sec State, but he would not have had many details. He would have had access to Intelligence from the operation and it's possible that, if he passed that information on to the Chinese, they would have been able to narrow their search for penetrations of their own organizations.

"One puzzling question is why Cyber Division's contact in the Chinese Embassy has not been compromised. In his position, Wheeler would have known the actual identity of this person and could have easily informed Beijing that he had unauthorized contact with the FBI. If he did provide this information to them, why would Chinese security allow him to remain in place? Logically, he should have been recalled, where in all likelihood, he would have been summarily executed.

"Wheeler did not show up for work two days ago. It turns out that FBI Director Mitchell's office had initiated an investigation of Wheeler two months ago, based upon some anomalous spending patterns by him and his wife. Someone must have tipped Wheeler off that he was being investigated or in some way he became cognizant of the Bureau's probe.

"For now, we do not assess that you or Phoenix have been compromised. As a precaution though, we are going to ask you to stand down on any travel to China for the next couple of weeks, while we try to gauge how much damage Wheeler has done."

Logan scanned the rest of his morning email. There was nothing else urgent that needed to be addressed for now. A National Intelligence Estimate entitled *The Outlook For Sino-India Relations*, and several intelligence reports on Chinese efforts to combat terrorism at home, could wait until later.

He sat back from his computer and contemplated the view of Victoria Harbor from his office window. For a moment it made him homesick. Alexander Maritime's main office was on the waterfront in south Boston. His thoughts wandered back to Frank's message. It never failed to amaze him the extent to which some people would go to betray their country. FBI agents take the same oath CIA officers do, he reflected.

"I do solemnly swear that I will support and defend the Constitution of the United States against all enemies, foreign and domestic; that I will bear true faith and allegiance to the same; that I take this oath freely, without any mental reservation or purpose of evasion; and that I will well and faithfully discharge the duties of the office on which I am about to enter. So help me God."

Who knows what was going on in Wheeler's life when he decided to cast his lot with the Chinese? Maybe he was cheating on his wife, or he was gay and hadn't come out of the closet, or he was over his head in credit card debt. Some Intel officer had spotted him, identified his particular vulnerability, and pitched him.

Logan's blood boiled. As galling as it was, he had to admit that China wasn't doing anything different than all the other intelligence agencies around the world. He recalled a case that had broken in Washington when he was there. A senior State Department officer had been accused of having an affair with a Chinese Intel officer and mishandling classified information.

He pleaded innocent and denied working for China. Later, under a plea-bargain agreement, he was sentenced to a year in federal prison for lying to investigators and mishandling classified information.

At the time there were howls of indignation from senior Administration officials over this episode. There were cries of foul play from the intelligence community and Congress. Washington issued a démarche, and the offending Chinese official was declared *persona non grata* for activities unbecoming her diplomatic status. She was given two days to leave the country.

Meanwhile, the U.S. and every other country with an intelligence service were doing the same thing.

Bruce Wellington poked his head into Logan's office. "We still going out for Indian?"

"Yeah. Let's do it. Find out if Norm wants to go." Logan logged off of his computer and joined the two men in the foyer.

"Alicia, you up for some Indian food?"

Their raven-haired office manager looked up from her computer and wrinkled her nose. "Thanks, but Indian's not one of my favorites. Besides, I'm training for the Dragon Boat races."

"But that's eight months away," Logan protested.

"I know. But we did so bad this year, we want to win the next one."

There are dragon boat races all over the world, and the Hong Kong International Dragon Boat Festival is one of the biggest. The races commemorate the death of the famous Chinese poet, Qu Yuan, who lived during the Warring States period (475-221 BC). Coming from a noble family, Qu became enmeshed in court affairs, where he strived to stamp out rampant corruption. He made a lot of enemies in the process, who eventually succeeded in having him exiled. Banished, he continued to write and fight against corruption, but when his native Chu State was conquered by the more powerful Qin State, he became depressed and committed suicide.

Legend has it that on the fifth day of the fifth month of the Chinese lunar calendar, 220 BC, Qu threw himself into the Miluo River, where he drowned. Today's dragon boat races recall the unsuccessful search for Qu's body on that fateful day.

Logan looked doubtful. "All right. But remember, you can't paddle those things if you don't keep up your strength." Alicia was always on some kind of fad diet.

"I know. But I'm the drummer. Remember? I don't have to paddle."

"Oh yeah, I forgot. See you in about an hour."

Minutes later Wellington, Stoddard and Logan were on their way to their favorite Indian restaurant, really just a street stall, located in an alley off of Ice House Street, behind the Foreign Correspondents' Club.

They sat down beneath a faded awning and when the waiter came over, ordered the set lunch. The eatery specialized in Punjabi cooking. Within minutes they were feasting on tandoor-baked naan, succulent tandoori chicken and three mouthwatering curries.

Noise from the traffic on Lower Albert Road was muted. Nearby tables were occupied by office workers and shoppers. No one was paying attention, so Logan, speaking in hushed tones, conveyed the gist of Frank's message about Wheeler.

"I heard from Frank this morning. Looks like one of the Bureau's special agents went over to the other side. They don't think it's going to impact us here, but we won't know for sure 'til Cyber Division finishes its damage assessment." Wellington was in the middle of shoveling a fork full of rice into his mouth. He set it down. "Is this anybody we know?"

"I doubt it. His name's Rick Wheeler. I met his boss on my last trip home. We should be okay, but not everybody pays attention to 'need to know.' If this guy sat in on certain meetings or was able to pick people's brains he might have heard some things he wasn't cleared for."

Logan looked grim as he contemplated what would befall Li if his bosses found out what he was doing. The Chinese are very efficient when it comes to dealing with traitors. Typically there's a pro forma mock trial followed by a mandatory double appeal. Justice is more often than not meted out in the form of a bullet to the brain.

"Washington's asked us to refrain from any travel to the mainland for the next couple of weeks while they try to sort this out."

"How about meeting our 'friends' outside of China?" Wellington asked.

"You mean your ambassador?"

"Yeah. He's a little gun shy anyway, but if the Bureau decides to go public with this, he'll assume the worst."

"I can't see the Bureau going public with this now," Stoddard said. "I mean, what would it buy them?"

"And what was this guy thinking about, anyway? Committing espionage. And now where's he going to go? China? He'll never be able to go home."

"Yep," Wellington agreed. "There's no statute of limitations for espionage. Mr. Wheeler might just as well become Chinese."

"Either that or go home and face the music," Stoddard retorted.

"We don't even know where Wheeler is for sure," Logan interrupted. "From what Frank said, it looks like the Chinese were giving him an alias passport to get out of the country. But where to is anybody's guess."

203

"I'll bet he's already gone. The alias passport was there to buy him some more time and conceal his ultimate destination."

"Remember Howard? Spied for the Russians back in the '80s? Never went back home. Lived in Russia for almost twenty years before he died." Wellington shook his head in wonder.

"Couldn't happen to a nicer guy," Stoddard said.

"Howard actually got out of the country on his own passport, right under the nose of FBI surveillance. Used a jack-in-the-box to escape from his car and then later that night had his wife make a phone call using a recording he'd made earlier, so the Bureau would think he was still at home. Meanwhile, Howard was already on his way to Moscow."

"What the hell are they going to do to find Wheeler?" Wellington asked.

"I'm sure the Bureau and the Agency are already working their liaison contacts. They probably have Wheeler's photo watch-listed, and an APB out. Most likely they'll paint it as a missing person case. They don't want to burn the guy that tipped them off," Logan pointed out.

"I'll bet he's nervous," Stoddard declared. "Imagine, you're that guy, sitting in the Chinese embassy, meeting secretly with the Bureau, and you find out about Wheeler. I'll bet he asks for asylum. He can't go home."

"If Wheeler was doing it for money, he probably told them everything he knew. Those guys don't have a conscience. You can bet the first thing the MPS asked him was who the spies were."

Wellington nodded in agreement. "For all we know, the MPS found out this guy was spying and doubled him back against the Bureau. They could feed him bogus Intel. And they could try to find out where the Bureau has intelligence gaps."

"I'm not so sure. What's to keep him from asking for asylum?" Stoddard asked.

"Family," said Logan. "He may or may not have family with him in Washington. Senior diplomats can bring their spouses with them on foreign assignments, but they may still have a child in China. His parents could still be living, too. If he were to ask for asylum, their lives would be destroyed."

"I hadn't thought about that," Stoddard frowned.

"These are not nice people," Logan commented. "It does make me wonder about a couple of security anomalies I've noticed in the last two months though."

"Like what?" Stoddard asked.

"That PSB patrol showing up the first time I tried to meet Phoenix outside of Chongqing. I don't believe in coincidences, and even though we had Intel reporting that the MPS was sending out patrols to track down Uighur sympathizers all around Szechuan, what are the chances they'd be right there?

"The other thing is that goon that's been following us around and broke into our apartment. Zahir almost lost the baby."

"How's she doing?" Wellington asked.

"She's better. Her doctor cleared her to go back to work this week. I think it helped that she's in such good shape."

"You have a point though, Logan. Why's the PSB interested in you?" Stoddard signaled their waiter for the bill.

"Maybe it's a fishing expedition. If Wheeler gave them anything it would have been something general, not specific."

"Like what?" Stoddard persisted.

"I don't know. It could be anything."

"They can't believe that every American businessman works for the CIA. Besides, I doubt they have the resources to go after everybody. No, their priority targets are going to be in the embassy. They suspect the Agency uses diplomatic cover, and all the locals working in the embassy have to meet with their security people every week." Stoddard frowned at the thought.

"Even though the locals don't work in sensitive positions, I imagine they still pick up gossip and pass it onto the authorities," Logan added.

"At least we're not dealing with that. We may never know."

They paid their bill and headed back to the office. Logan decided he would ask Frank to send him Wheeler's photo. Who knows? Wheeler might come through Hong Kong and maybe they'd spot him. If he and Bruce couldn't travel to China for two weeks, at least they could make themselves useful. There was a glint in Logan's eyes as he thought about what he'd do if he got his hands on Wheeler's sorry ass.

Chapter 28

When they returned to the office, Logan checked in with Alicia for messages.

"Mr. Gao, from Abercrombie and York, called to invite you for drinks at the Yacht Club next week."

Logan was a member of the Royal Hong Kong Yacht Club. He used the main Kellet Island clubhouse in Causeway Bay for occasional entertaining with clients. Besides the Kellet Island facility, the club also maintained a small fleet of dinghies at Middle Island, between Deepwater Bay and Repulse Bay, and a marina at Shelter Cove in Sai Kung.

He had taken Cooper and Zahir out to Middle Island several times to teach them how to sail. Cooper was still too young to enroll in formal sailing classes but he had enjoyed their outings.

"Sure. Let's say yes. Is it couples or stag?"

"Couples."

"Let me check with Zahir first. She should be free."

He moved on to his office. He was thinking about contacting Frank Sisler, proposing that his team be on the lookout for Wheeler passing through Hong Kong, when he noticed an Immediate Eyes Only message in his queue. It was a follow-up from Frank that included an attachment – a photo of the FBI spy.

"The Bureau has received intelligence reporting that Wheeler is on his way to Beijing. There is reason to believe that he is going to transit Hong Kong and go up through the New Territories. Hong Kong is working this for us, although as you can imagine, they haven't raised it with the Hong Kong police.

"If your team could spend some time on the street over the next two days it would give us additional eyes on to try and locate

Wheeler. Be careful not to stumble into any of our people. Also, we anticipate the MPS will get its people in Hong Kong involved to guarantee Wheeler's safe passage. It's a priority to find Wheeler before he gets to China. Happy hunting."

Happy hunting, he murmured to himself. When Frank used that phrase in official correspondence it was a euphemism for "take the gloves off." In other words they were being given authorization to do whatever it took to get their hands on Rick Wheeler.

He called Stoddard and Wellington into his office and gave them a rundown on Frank's missive.

"I don't think headquarters trusts the Hong Kong Police," Stoddard snickered.

"We used to have a pretty good relationship with Special Branch, when Hong Kong was under British rule," Logan replied.

Prior to 1995, when the U.K. still governed Hong Kong, Special Branch had intelligence and security wings that shared information with CIA. But in 1995, during the lead-up to Hong Kong's reversion to Chinese rule, they shut them down. All the old Special Branch officers transferred out and they took all their records with them. The Royal Hong Kong Police became the Hong Kong Police in 1997. Now they all come under Chinese control.

"Are you assuming we haven't gone to the police with this?" Wellington asked.

"That would be my bet. If the PSB is involved escorting Wheeler to China, and they're coming through Hong Kong, they've probably reached out to the Hong Kong Police to smooth the way.

"I think we should get out on the street and see if we pick anything up. Take a good look at Wheeler's picture. If you spot him, follow him discreetly and see if you can find out where he's holed up, if he's staying here. But remember, he probably has local protection. They may not even let him out in public. It's too risky.

"They probably feel pretty comfortable since they're this close to home. The story hasn't broken in the international press yet. Have either of you spotted anything in the local press?" Logan asked. Wellington and Stoddard looked at each other and shook their heads in the negative.

Logan pulled out a map of Hong Kong. "Bruce, why don't you take Kowloon? Norm? How about Hong Kong Island? I'll cover the airport."

"What's the plan if we do spot him?" Wellington asked.

Logan's eyes flashed. "If there's any way we can pull it off, we're going to make sure Wheeler never makes it to China."

"What do you have in mind?"

"I'm still working it out. I doubt if we'll be able to just snatch him off the street. But if they do put him up in a safehouse or try to move him on the ground, we may be able to get our hands on him."

"Are we clear with headquarters on this?" Stoddard asked.

"They don't want Wheeler to get to China, period. Who knows how much he's given them already? But if their security people can sit him down for in-depth debriefings, he could do some real damage. We're clear. We have the go-ahead to stop him at all costs.

"All right. Let's move. Keep in mind, Wheeler may be using some kind of disguise."

The three men dispersed. Logan planned to visit the air cargo facility at the airport as a ruse for spending some time there. Delta, United and American Airlines all had flights arriving from the U.S. in the next few hours.

Going out there was a shot in the dark, he admitted. If the MPS was running things, Wheeler wouldn't even have to go through customs and immigration. He'd be escorted around those checkpoints and whisked away.

Logan spent an hour talking to personnel in the airport's air cargo operations department, explaining that his company was exploring options for shipping U.S. manufactured components for its boats. The air cargo setup was impressive. They had handled over four million tons of freight in the previous year and were expanding their cargo handling facilities.

After he had finished talking with them, Logan wandered over to the baggage claim area in Arrivals. He was glum as he assessed the prospect of spotting Wheeler as next to nil. He checked the Arrivals display and noted that flights from American and Delta had landed. The trouble was he had no idea what airline Wheeler was flying on. He decided to station himself at Arrivals Hall B, since that's where passengers on flights from the U.S. disembarked.

As he was scanning the throngs of weary passengers, Logan felt his phone vibrate. There was a text message from Bruce.

"Got him."

Logan felt a surge of excitement. "Where?" he texted.

"I'm just north of Mong Kok East subway station on Mong Kok Road. There's a big flower market up ahead."

"Is he alone?"

"No. There are two guys with him. They just went into an apartment building."

"Do you have an eye on the building?"

"Yeah. I can see the front entrance. Don't know about the sides or back."

"Sit tight. I'll be there in thirty minutes." He relayed the gist of Wellington's texts to Stoddard and told him to meet them in Mong Kok ASAP.

Thirty minutes later the three men met to reconnoiter the area. Logan and Stoddard piled into Wellington's vehicle to assess their options.

"My guess is that we don't have much time," Logan said. "I don't see them holding Wheeler in Hong Kong for very long. Their safest bet will be to get him into China where they can control the situation."

"Do you think they'll fly out of here or drive up through the New Territories?" Stoddard wondered.

"I imagine they'll fly. They can bypass all the security and keep him out of the public eye."

"Why would they even bring him into the city? It seems like it would've been easier for them to fly direct or catch a connecting flight right at the airport without the trouble of coming into Hong Kong."

"Could be anything," Logan offered. "Maybe he got cold feet. Told them he needed more time. Hell, maybe he's got a medical issue and they had to get him to a doctor."

"He was walking without any help," Wellington replied.

"All right. Here's what we're going to do." After he'd outlined his plan, he instructed Wellington to keep an eye on the building while he and Stoddard left to pick up the items they would need.

They were taking a chance confining their surveillance of the building to the main entrance. There were no side entrances; however, there was a rear entrance that appeared to be for service personnel and deliveries.

Four hours later they were back. Wellington reported that there had been no movement from the apartment building other than what appeared to be local residents coming and going. Logan was driving a mini-van that a local support asset had rented for the day. Stoddard was driving a Mercedes sedan that a station officer had procured using an alias passport.

"Bruce, why don't you bury your car in one of those parking garages near the stadium? I think they have long-term parking and that'll get it off the street. Meet us back here as soon as you can."

Wellington left to dispose of his car and Logan turned his attention to the apartment building. He'd prefer to take Wheeler down inside, but the six-story building probably housed close to fifty apartments. It was anybody's guess where he was holed up.

Logan checked the time. It was just after eight-thirty p.m. It was dark and he was concerned that they might miss the fugitive in the low light.

He reviewed the ops plan in his mind. It had come to him as he explored their best chances for secreting Wheeler out of Hong Kong. He was going out on a U.S. Navy warship.

Logan had remembered reading in the *South China Morning Post* that the 11th Marine Expeditionary Unit was in Hong Kong on a four-day port call. Three ships from the Bowes Island Amphibious Ready Group were berthed in Victoria Harbor. The USS Bowes Island, the group's flagship, was berthed pier side just off of Kowloon.

The group had been conducting hurricane evacuation operations near Midway Island and was calling at Hong Kong for some much needed R&R.

The plan was simple enough in concept, but was fraught with risk in its execution. Ideally they would be able to intercept Wheeler when he exited the building, although they were prepared to go mobile if he did get into a vehicle. This would pose significant challenges because they had no way of knowing his destination or where they could snatch him.

Once they had him, he would be gagged and bound and within ten minutes would be transferred to the trunk of the sedan driven by Stoddard, and taken to a second rendezvous point with a station officer. There he would be given a sedative and driven to a third rendezvous where he would be transferred into the custody of the Office of Naval Intelligence. They would see to it that he was securely brought aboard the berthed vessel, where he would remain in the brig until they reached Yokosuka, Japan. There he would be transferred into the custody of the FBI.

Meanwhile the team would reposition the rental cars on the street in Kowloon, where station personnel and the support asset would retrieve them and return them to the rental agency the following day.

Logan had drafted his operational plan and submitted it to Langley, Immediate Night Action (NIACT), because of the time difference. Sisler had come back within an hour, telling him that headquarters would work out the details with Hong Kong and the Navy. The operation had the highest priority and approvals had come back almost immediately. Chief Naval Operations himself had authorized the USS Bowes Island's participation.

Wellington slid into the driver's seat of the mini-van. Moments later he sat up and pointed towards the entrance of the building. "There." Two shadowy figures had emerged from the building and were standing just outside the door. One of them lit a cigarette.

"Let's go." Logan checked the sound suppressor on his Glock 23. He felt an adrenaline rush as Wellington stepped on the gas and then screeched to a halt in front of the entrance. The two men looked up in surprise as Logan exited the van. He recognized Wheeler from the picture. He appeared fatigued and disheveled.

The other figure was reaching for his coat pocket. Logan recognized him as the suspect PSB intruder who had knocked down Zahir in their apartment building.

"Drop it," he ordered in Chinese. The man continued reaching for his coat pocket. Logan leveled his Glock at the PSB thug and drilled one round into the middle of his chest. He went down hard and a handgun fell out of his hand, clattering to the pavement. Logan looked around. The street was empty; in the evening shadows he was optimistic that no one had witnessed what had just transpired. He bent down and felt for a pulse. There was none. Just as well. He couldn't afford to have his identity exposed.

He turned his attention back to Wheeler, who had his hands up in the air and was staring at the young CIA officer in shock. "All right, asshole. Get in the van. Now!" He shoved Wheeler into the van, jumped in behind him, and slid the door closed as Wellington screeched away from the building. So far, so good. There had been no one else in front of the building. Maybe this was going to work out after all.

"Who the hell—?"

"Shut up." Logan wrestled Wheeler onto his stomach on the floor of the van. He pulled his arms behind his back and secured his wrists with plastic restraints, then pulled a cloth from his pocket and made a blindfold, which he secured to the FBI agent's head. He patted him down. Aside from a wallet and a New Zealand passport, Wheeler's pockets yielded nothing else of interest.

Traffic was light. Wellington sped down Boundary Street and turned onto Prince Edward Road East. Wheeler was hyperventilating but otherwise he remained motionless on the floor. Wellington was headed towards an area known as Hammer Hill Park. The park is a sports facility with swimming pool, soccer fields, and an all-weather track, managed by the Leisure and Cultural Services Department. Stoddard would be waiting for them near a fast food kiosk that at this hour would be closed.

Five minutes later Wellington pulled even with Stoddard's rental car. He opened the trunk while Wellington and Logan wrestled Wheeler out of the van and into the Mercedes. The blindfold had slipped down on one side and Wheeler stared at them with a confused look on his face.

"Who are you guys?" He choked.

The three men stared down at him for a second. Then Logan spoke. "Let's just say we're friends of Des Magarity. When he mentioned you'd gone missing, he asked if we could help him track you down. It wasn't that hard."

"This is a misunderstanding. Where are you taking me?"

"You're going for a long ride, Wheeler. And when it's all over, you'll likely spend the rest of your life staring out of some shitty jail cell." Logan slammed the trunk lid closed.

"I'm going to ride with Norm to our next meet-up. Bruce, you're clear on where to drop the van?"

"Yeah. I'll drop it behind the Pedder Building near Yan Yip Street. Key on the rear tire."

"Don't forget to wipe it down. Everything. I'm pretty sure we didn't attract any attention, but you never know. We don't want to give away anything."

Wellington took off to take care of the vehicle. He knew of a twenty-four-hour detailing service about two miles from the drop-off spot, and decided to have the van cleaned there.

Logan and Stoddard met their station contact fifteen minutes later behind a Buddhist temple just off of Tai Po Road. Stoddard flicked his high beams twice as they approached the car.

Logan recognized the officer as Gary Murphy. He had seen him around Hong Kong at the American Club, but they didn't socialize overtly, the better to protect Logan's cover.

"So you got the son of a bitch?" Murphy exclaimed. "What were the chances?" He shook his head in wonder. "The chief almost pissed his pants when we got the word from headquarters that you had spotted him."

"Yeah. I was happy you guys could fast track this. Must be some kind of record."

Logan opened the trunk, and Murphy reached into a bag and withdrew a loaded syringe, which he handed to Logan. Logan wasn't squeamish about doing this. He'd seen a lot worse as a Navy SEAL.

Wheeler began to protest when he heard the trunk open.

"Shut up, Wheeler. We're going to give you a sedative to make you comfortable while you're in transit. When you wake up you'll be all comfy and a guest of the United States Navy." He poked the needle into Wheeler's thigh, as Murphy and Stoddard held him down.

They transferred him to the trunk of Murphy's car. A moment later the two cars sped away in opposite directions. Murphy had about twenty minutes before he was scheduled to rendezvous with the Office of Naval Intelligence (ONI) officers. When he had left the office, ONI was still working on a scenario for getting Wheeler onto the ship. One plan was to keep him sedated, dress him in a Naval uniform and lug him aboard in plain sight, feigning drunkenness. The other was to bag him and bring him aboard as cargo.

Logan and Stoddard breathed more easily as they drove away. They both knew that they had been incredibly lucky to nab their prey. Everything had fallen into place for them. When they were some distance from where they had made the transfer, they stopped to wipe down the vehicle. Stoddard dropped Logan off at Nam Cheong Metro station. Norm would dispose of the car as planned, and catch a taxi home.

Logan relaxed for the first time that night. It was ten-thirty and he was looking forward to seeing Zahir. He hadn't been able to talk to her all day, but she was used to his absences. He frowned as he thought about the man that he'd killed. He'd spare her the details. There would be an investigation, of course, but he wasn't concerned that it would lead to him.

With the number of triads, those international criminal organizations, on the loose in Hong Kong, there would be plenty of criminal suspects for the Hong Kong Police to pursue. Just last week, a senior member of the Wo Shing Wo group had been hacked to death with a meat cleaver in front of witnesses in broad daylight.

His thoughts turned back to Wheeler. When Cyber Division got their chance to debrief the FBI spy, maybe they could get to the bottom of what he had told the Chinese about Li and the China Cyber Covert Action plan. What he'd revealed could make all the difference between success and failure.

Chapter 29

Li Jiang and a dozen other senior PSB officers fidgeted as they waited for the political commissar, Commissioner Pei, to come into the briefing room. They had all been called to Chengdu's Provincial PSB headquarters for a meeting with the party committee secretary.

Li looked around. He recognized most of the men, all PSB officers that he had served with at one time or another. Something must be going on, he speculated. A door opened and Commissioner Pei bustled into the room. Li tried to read his face, but couldn't.

Pei walked to the front of the room and withdrew a briefing packet from a folder that he was carrying. He scanned it for a minute before beginning to speak.

"Good morning, comrades. I'm sure that you're curious about why we've brought you here today.

"Three days ago, a PSB officer escorting a sensitive agent from Hong Kong to Beijing was murdered in Kowloon, in front of the safe house where the agent was being sheltered. Since then, the agent has disappeared."

The room erupted as the men turned to their neighbors, voicing their surprise at Pei's announcement. He waited for the noise to die down before continuing.

"MPS Headquarters has launched an investigation. A team from Beijing has traveled to Hong Kong and is working with their counterparts to see if they can locate the missing agent." Pei paused before continuing. "The agent was a senior American FBI special agent working in the China Cyber Division."

There was a collective gasp from the attendees. Pei flipped through a few pages in his packet, scanning the

217

contents, before looking back up. "For some reason, that is not yet clear, we know that two months ago, the new FBI director launched an investigation into the personnel in Cyber Division at FBI headquarters.

"At some point the investigation narrowed down to our agent. He signaled to Beijing that he believed he was under suspicion and asked for help leaving the country.

"An MPS officer traveled to Washington a little over a week ago and assisted the agent in getting out. To conceal his travel route the agent crossed into Canada on an alias passport and from there flew to Hong Kong. The plan was to take him directly to Beijing, but he got cold feet and wanted a day or two to think it over. That's why they were laying over in Hong Kong."

One of the men from Chongqing, a Superintendent Fu, known as "Pockmarked Fu" because of a severe case of childhood smallpox that had left him scarred, raised his hand.

"Mr. Pei, this is all very interesting but how does this agent specifically concern us?" He gestured towards the group at large.

Pei regarded his questioner with patience before responding. "MPS headquarters was looking forward to full debriefings with him, because he had extensive knowledge of the U.S. program to counter China's Cyber War against them. Obviously they were unable to have that discussion.

"However, while the MPS was helping to get him to Canada, he told his handler that the CIA had recruited a Chinese cyber expert. A PSB officer."

Li's attention had wandered, but when he heard Pei's pronouncement, his heart began to beat at a furious pace. He looked up to see if anyone had noticed, but no one was paying any attention to him. Indeed, Pei's comment had sparked an outburst from the group as they digested this information.

Logan had assured him that only a handful of people would know that he was cooperating with the CIA. Had he lied? Could there be someone else from the PSB or the Cyber Executive working for the Americans? He trembled inside as he gnawed on the questions that flooded his brain. He kicked himself as he thought about the consequences of being discovered. Prison for certain, and perhaps even death. Dishonor for his family. It would be the final nail in his mother's coffin.

As he grappled with his emotions, it occurred to him that Beijing did not suspect him. No. He would not be sitting in this meeting if the leadership had any doubts about his loyalty. He breathed again, as he explored this line of reasoning.

Of course, the CIA would have shared the intelligence he provided with the FBI. After all they had some responsibility for investigating cyber crimes committed against American officials. The FBI would have concluded that the information came from inside China, but they would not have known precisely where.

He relaxed as he went from the brink back to normal, or what could muster for normal for someone playing this dangerous game. He turned his attention back to Pei, who had picked up where he left off.

"One theory is that the Americans have the FBI spy back in their control. The MPS has not detected any indication from overt sources that the FBI was even looking for the man. And for them to get him out of Hong Kong under the very nose of the authorities would be no easy feat. It's the kind of operation the CIA is capable of pulling off."

Li raised his hand. "Have they ruled out the possibility of a third party? Perhaps this spy was working for someone else besides us."

Pei looked thoughtful. "And that would be...?"

Li shrugged. "The Russians?" he suggested.

"I don't discount anything," Pei replied.

"You should know that the Minister has vowed to get to the bottom of this. They've ordered our complete cooperation with the investigation. You may have some MPS investigators visiting your units in the coming weeks. They will want to speak with you and your people. Please extend them every courtesy.

"Any questions?" There were none. "Dismissed."

There was a clatter as the men pushed back their chairs and filed out of the briefing room. Li was thoughtful as he departed the headquarters building. He would have to take extra precautions in the future. With the investigators breathing down everyone's necks he couldn't afford to make any mistakes. It occurred to him that the CIA would know about the FBI officer on the lam, and would be concerned about what he might have revealed to his handlers.

As he purchased his return ticket on the bullet train to Chongqing at Chengdu East Station, Li speculated that this development could impact Pan's timetable for the Zero Day attack. Of course the Americans already knew about the plan because of the information he had provided them, but no one in the PSB was aware of his betrayal.

Now though, they had reason to suspect that the FBI agent was in American hands and he was certain to be interrogated. Had he been briefed on the Zero Day attack? Li remained thoughtful as the train whizzed past fields and towns at two hundred-fifty mph.

Two and a half hours later he hurried into his office. "Bai, in my office."

Bai followed him in with a puzzled expression on his face. "Sir?"

Li got right to the point. "We've got a problem." He outlined what he had learned in Chengdu. "I doubt if those MPS officers knew very much, if anything, about our Zero Day attack. They would not have been in a position to reveal anything to this missing FBI agent.

"More troubling though is Pei's report that the CIA has recruited a PSB officer in the cyber area."

"That covers a lot of people, sir."

"I know. We've already been advised that we can expect a visit from the MPS investigators in the next couple of weeks. I want everyone to be one hundred percent cooperative when they do come. Meanwhile, let's begin our own internal scrub to make certain that our house is in order.

"Have security interview everyone separately. In particular I want updates on each person's foreign contacts and any foreign travel since our last security review. Make certain that our reporting procedures are compliant. If you discover any anomalies bring them directly to me."

"Yes, sir." Bai exited the office with a determined look on his face.

Li knew what he was doing. If he could demonstrate that he was serious about security, the MPS would have less reason to suspect him.

He wasn't overly concerned that they would be interested in him personally. He'd been very careful to mask his anger over his father's treatment. For all outward appearances he was a model PSB officer. And, although the Bo Xilai clique had shamed his father, none of that had tarnished his reputation.

After he had caught up on his email correspondence, he left his office to visit with some of the young hackers. He had been traveling quite a bit of late and wanted to see how they were settling in.

He stopped by the workstation of a pimply-faced youth named Song that the others had dubbed "Dirt Dumpling" because of his poor hygiene habits. Despite his slovenly appearance, Song was a gifted technician.

"Mr. Song, what is it that you are working on?"

The young man leapt to his feet and stuttered as he replied. "I've found a backdoor into the U.S. defense contractor, DCAS Marine Systems. One of the engineers at their facility in Syracuse, New York, has been using his office computer to search pornography websites. I was able to place a Trojan on his computer and the information we're gathering will be of great value to our Navy." He pushed his glasses back and wiped a sweaty hand on his pants.

"We've been monitoring this particular site with a small banner ad 'web bug.' From it we got his IP addresses, type of operating system he was using, the browser version and the page he visited.

"We matched the log file's IP address with DCAS, and were able to install a Trojan on their system.

"This engineer is one of the leads on a new contract DCAS has with the U.S. Navy's Surface Electronic Warfare Enhancement Program. With the work DCAS is doing, the Navy will be able to detect any hostile forces using sensors to track the movement of their fleet."

"And how do you think our Navy will use this information, Mr. Song?" This was a test. Li wanted to see if Song was actually thinking about the information he was collecting.

Song considered the question for a moment and then responded. "If our Navy has the specifications for the upgraded system, they may be able to modify their tracking sensors so that they will not be detected by the U.S. warships."

Li appraised the young man. He might be a "dirt dumpling" in appearance, but he had a head on his shoulders. He slapped Song on the shoulder. "Nice job, Song. Keep up the good work."

Song beamed and resumed what he had been working on as Li continued walking around the facility talking informally with his charges.

By six p.m. he was ready to call it a day. He remembered that Xiao Jun was competing in a district *taiqi* exhibition. If he hurried, he might get there in time to see him perform.

Huiling had convinced Xiao Jun to resume classes at a *taiqi* school in their neighborhood. He needed some activity to take his mind off of his mother's suicide. Huiling had, herself, been a devotee of *qigong*, the ancient Chinese practice of breathing techniques and physical postures designed to increase health and vitality, for years.

Many believe that *taiqi* has its roots in the ancient Taoist form of *qigong*, which is partially true, but it's very difficult to trace back *taiqi's* origins because of the number of styles and forms that developed over thousands of years.

Xiao Jun was particularly interested in the martial arts aspects of *taiqi*, thus Huiling had wisely refrained from emphasizing the health and therapeutic benefits of daily practice. They had both noticed that in less than a month he seemed calmer, less stressed.

When Li arrived at the gymnasium, the *taiqi* students were just marching out onto the floor. Xiao Jun noticed him as he passed by and gave his father a surprised wave. Li spotted his sister and brother-in-law sitting in the bleachers. He joined them there.

"Huiling, Wang. How are you?" He greeted them. Huiling gave him a hug and Wang nodded his greeting. He sat down next to his sister and looked out at the crowd.

"So many students!" he exclaimed.

"Xiao Jun has fifty in his class," Huiling replied.

"I have noticed a change in his attitude," Li admitted. "I wasn't sure if this would do any good."

Huiling nodded with satisfaction. "It takes time."

The students were practicing a form of *taiqi* known as *yang* form and for the past month had been learning the twenty-four-form style. Eventually their familiarity with the movements would allow them to add to their routines to the point where a single routine would incorporate a hundred and three forms.

Li watched with pride as Xiao Jun and his classmates executed the steps in fluid, sinuous movements. He could visualize the routine – part the horse's mane; white crane spreads its wings; repulse the monkey; grasp the sparrow's tail, and so on. As he watched his son, his tensions from earlier in the day began to dissipate. Perhaps there was hope for them after all.

Chapter 30

Des was waiting on the tarmac at Bolling Air Force Base when the C-40A Clipper from Yokosuka touched down. It was unseasonably chilly and a light drizzle had turned the runway wet and slick. He fastened the top button of his trench coat and shivered as the plane lumbered over to its parking spot and the pilot killed the engines.

In the abrupt quiet, the chatter of the small crowd gathered there seemed deafening, and they glanced around self-consciously. Des had been talking to one of the Federal marshals who would be escorting Rick to the Central Detention Facility in Southeast D.C. His arraignment on espionage charges was scheduled to take place in Federal District Court the next day. That's when the Chinese would find out that Rick was back in American hands. "Let 'em bitch," Des smirked.

He didn't know why he was there. He had no official role in the proceedings. But the fact that he had so completely misjudged Rick nagged him with such tenacity that, even if he wanted to, he could not physically turn away. No. He was drawn to that spot and couldn't leave.

He had been intrigued by the rapidity of the CIA and Navy's successful capture of the fugitive. He wouldn't be surprised if that operations officer he'd met a couple of months ago, Jake, had something to do with it. He looked like a Special Ops kind of guy. Tall, broad shoulders, slim waist, and a confident demeanor that had "don't screw with me" written all over it.

The ground crew was hurrying over to the aft door with a mobile stair ramp. After they had maneuvered it into place, the flight attendant opened the hatch. There was a pause, and then several uniformed personnel began exiting the aircraft down the stairs. Sandwiched between them shuffled Rick Wheeler.

Des was shocked by the appearance of his former deputy. He seemed to have aged twenty years since he had last seen him less than a week ago. Unshaven with hair uncombed, he was wearing an olive green jumpsuit and a pair of Navy flight boots. His hands were handcuffed behind his back and he was shackled in leg irons.

Rick's head hung down, partially masking his features. He looked up once and his eyes met Des's. There was a flicker of recognition, but he looked away without acknowledging him. As Rick walked closer to where he was standing, Des couldn't control himself.

"What happened to you, you bastard?" he shouted.

Rick kept his head down. "Look at me," Des screamed. He surged forward in anger, but several in the crowd reached out to restrain him. One of the MPs stepped up to him and bored into his eyes.

"Everything all right here, sir?"

"Yeah. No problem," Des muttered. He shrugged and turned away, embarrassed that he'd let his emotions get the best of him. It was unprofessional. This hit close to home, though. He and Rick had worked together side by side for two years. How could he have missed what was going on under his very nose?

Later, as he drove back into the District he thought about what Rick was facing. The courts had handed down harsh sentences in several recent espionage cases. Robert Hanssen, the FBI agent who had spied for the Russians for twenty-two years, got fifteen consecutive life sentences. Solitary confinement. Rick would be lucky if he ever saw the light of day again.

When he reached his office, Lois was waiting to speak with him.

"I just got out of a meeting with the director's chief of staff." She went on to explain that she had been briefing the director weekly on the China Cyber program at his residence.

"What?" Des tried to mask his surprise, but the incredulous look on his face gave him away.

"I was under orders not to talk about it with anyone in the office. I guess they figured someone here was working with the Chinese, but they weren't positive who it was. They didn't want to take the chance that they would pick up something about the program. Anyway, now that Rick's been arrested, the briefings will be back in Mitchell's office."

Looking out the door into the corridor, Des noticed a number of faces he didn't recognize. "What's going on out there?" He gestured.

"Sweep team. They're going through everything. They said that they'd be here all week. Tech support is coming in tomorrow to replace everyone's computers. They're going to do forensics on all of them."

Des sighed, shaking his head as he watched the sweep team setting up their equipment.

"Why'd he do it?" Lois asked.

Des pondered the question. "I've been asking myself the same thing all morning," he grunted. "I keep blaming myself for not seeing it."

"How could you know? It sounds like even his wife didn't have a clue."

"My first reaction was money. That used to be why Americans spied. But it's gotten more complicated than that. Some people still spy for money, but nowadays more often than not, it has to do with ideology."

"But how could Rick be ideologically aligned with the Chinese? It just doesn't make any sense."

"Therein lies the mystery," Des responded. "If Rick comes clean with the prosecution, we may find out. If not, we'll never know." His glum face matched his mood.

"Oh. I forgot. Frank Sisler wants you to give him a call on the secure line."

"When did he call?"

Lois looked at her watch. "About an hour ago."

"I better see what he wants. And Lois? Keep your chin up. We'll get through this."

Lois grimaced. "Thanks, boss. I'm headed over to Langley now."

"All right." He sat there in the silence for a moment after she left, then punched in the number for Frank's secure line.

"Frank. Des here."

"Hey, Des. Thanks for getting back to me. I called to let you know that we're sending a memo over later today but I wanted to give you a verbal heads-up. It looks like your man, Ji, is being recalled to Beijing."

"What?"

"NSA intercepted a Ministry of Foreign Affairs message to the Chinese Embassy in Washington ordering him to return to Beijing without delay for consultations."

Des felt his pager vibrate and absently looked at the number as he tried to digest what Frank had just said. He was startled to see that it was Ji's number with an alphanumeric code calling for an unscheduled meeting.

"I just got a pager message from him asking for a meeting."

"If he wants to stay, we can help with the asylum request. We'll want in though. Debriefings. Tell him before he burns any bridges he needs to bring out everything he can. He won't be of any use to us once their security people figure out he's skipped town."

"I can't imagine he'd go back. It would be a death sentence," Des exclaimed.

"The other thing we should start thinking about is damage control if he does decide to jump," Frank offered. "The Chinese will flip out if they find out we have him. They'll démarche State. As soon as you know something we need to give them a heads-up that this is coming their way."

"Do you know if his family's here?"

"Wife. I think they have a son studying in Beijing."

"That'll be a challenge. Not much chance of getting the kid out before this thing blows. The wife may not go along with it. She knows it's all over for the kid if they ask for asylum."

"Ji's screwed either way. If he stays, his family's toast. If he goes back, he's dead." There was a pause as both men considered the difficult decision Ji would be confronting in the hours and days ahead.

"Oh. One other thing before I let you go. Did Wheeler know anything about our ops officer, Jake?"

The Special Ops type he'd met with Lois at the Vienna safehouse. "Nothing specific. He was aware that the Agency was meeting a volunteer in China though."

"What did he know about the volunteer?"

"He sat in on our initial briefing for the director. So he was aware that the volunteer is a PSB officer. We didn't see the original reporting from the field so we don't know where he's from or where they were meeting."

"OK. Thanks, Des. I'll let you go. I imagine you've got your hands full without a deputy and dealing with Ji. Let us know if we can do anything."

"All right. Thanks."

Des let Lois know that he was going out. He had about two hours before his meeting with Ji in Rock Creek Park. They were supposed to get together on a bicycle trail just south of East-West Highway.

Traffic was light as he pulled out of the parking garage. He headed north and eased onto the parkway, checking his rear view mirror to see if he had any unwanted company. All clear. He ditched his car in a small parking lot off of Beach Drive, north of Meadowbrook, and hiked into the park. There were few people out at this hour on a weekday. An occasional jogger trotted along the paved path, pushing against the chilly wind.

Des reached the meeting spot a couple of minutes before Ji. When he did get there, Des saw that he was dressed in office attire and was wearing an overcoat to ward off the chill. His face was tense.

"What's going on, Ji?" He stuck out his hand. Of course he knew why Ji had called for the meeting but he couldn't let on that he did.

"I have a problem. Beijing has called me back for consultations."

"Why's that a problem?" Just as the Bureau hadn't advertised that it was looking for an FBI agent on the lam, neither had they advertised that they had him in custody. The Chinese press had also been mum on the subject.

Ji eyed him suspiciously. "You know, don't you?"

Des gave him an impassive look and waited for him to continue.

"Wheeler made it as far as Hong Kong and then he disappeared. The PSB officer who was escorting him was killed in front of the safehouse where he was staying."

Des professed surprise. "After we met last time, we put out an APB and tracked Wheeler to Canada and Hong Kong. It wasn't in the press, just law enforcement channels. But then the trail dried up. We assumed that he had crossed over into China and your security people had him."

"No, he never made it to China. They're looking for him all over Hong Kong, but the talk at the embassy is that the CIA took him off the street there and he's back in American hands." They were walking north on the trail and a gust of wind blew swirling leaves around them.

"I don't know how long Wheeler has been working for China. But I do know that one of the first things his handlers would have asked him for is the identities of the people working for the Americans." Ji paused to light a cigarette. The wind kept blowing out the flame. Des cupped his hands around the lighter and Ji was able to get it going.

"It's not clear why they would have left me here if they knew about our relationship, unless he only recently revealed this to them. If he had told them earlier and I was recalled, it could have brought suspicion down on him. He knew this. Maybe it was his decision. Maybe it was Beijing's." He shrugged his shoulders.

"Why do you assume that he told them anything?"

"I don't know for sure. But it's very unusual for Beijing to call me back for consultations. This is the first time they've done anything like this since I've been in Washington."

"What do you want to do?"

"I've talked about it with my wife. We want to apply for asylum."

"What about your son?"

Ji blanched at the question. "We have to do this. If I go back, I'm a dead man."

"But won't they take it out on him? Kick him out of school or send him to the Chinese Gulag?"

"I have a plan. But I need your help." He spent the next fifteen minutes outlining a scenario that had Des thinking Ji had been watching too many spy movies. But he had to admit that it just might work. It would require setting several moving parts in motion, and soon.

"Let's be clear. The price of admission to this party is steep. We want everything you've got, but for this to work, your challenge is to leave everybody at the embassy and back in Beijing thinking you didn't suspect a thing." He admonished Ji to be careful, and hurried back to his car.

Ji and his wife were scheduled to attend an after-hours reception at the Smithsonian's Udvar-Hazy Center near Dulles Airport the following evening. He was scheduled to leave for Beijing the next day, a Saturday. He never made it.

Saturday's *Washington Post* and local news stations carried the story of a fiery single-vehicle crash on Route 29 late Friday night. Alcohol was believed to be a factor. A Chinese Embassy officer, Ji Gong, and his wife, Meiling, were killed instantly. By the time emergency vehicles reached the scene, the occupants of the vehicle were burned beyond recognition.

It had taken some doing on Des's part. The hardest piece had been finding two corpses, an Asian male and female roughly the same size as Ji and his wife. He wasn't too worried about DNA testing of the remains. Because of an intentionally bungled communication between the Chinese Embassy and the coroner's office over the weekend, the remains were released to a local funeral home and cremated for transport back to China.

Meanwhile, Ji was keeping up his end of the bargain. He and Meiling had been whisked away in the back of a van Friday night and taken to a private airfield in Leesburg, Virginia. There they boarded an FBI jet and were transported halfway across the country. They were now ensconced in a safehouse in Saint Paul, Minnesota, where Ji was undergoing intense debriefings. He had brought out a treasure trove of information, and analysts from FBI and CIA headquarters were methodically working through it.

In the coming months, Ji and his wife would be given new identities and relocated somewhere in the Midwest or a third country, if they so chose. While they were both devastated that they had to put their son through this deception, they felt confident that at least this way they would be able to reunite with him before long.

After the dust settled, someone would be reaching out to the young man to let him know that his parents were alive. There would also be provisions to get a stipend to him for his living expenses until he could join them. They would have to be cautious with this so that it didn't draw any unnecessary attention from the authorities.

Des had been in touch with Frank throughout the weekend. From all appearances the Chinese had bought the ruse all the way. The Chinese ambassador had rebuked State's East Asia Pacific Bureau, EAP, over the cremation issue. EAP Assistant Secretary Jarvis had countered by explaining that funeral services for foreign diplomats of Ji's level did not fall within the purview of the State Department, but rather, were a private matter.

By Monday evening things had calmed down and Des was holding court from his habitual perch at the Emerald Lounge. The events of the last week had taken their toll on him. "I'm getting too old for this shit," he thought. Six draught beers and a plate of nachos supreme later, as things were beginning to get a little bit fuzzy, Des had a sudden revelation. He no longer had a penetration of the Chinese Embassy. He'd have to start looking around for someone to take Ji's place.

Chapter 31

Logan and Zahir strolled into the Compass Room at the Yacht Club's Kellet Island facility. They had accepted Andrew Gao's invitation for drinks but it had turned out to be more than that. The club was hosting Renata Sabatini, from the famed Tuscan winemaking House of Sabatini, which was celebrating the sesquicentennial anniversary of its founding by her great-grandfather, Andre Sabatini.

"No wine for me tonight," Zahir sighed, patting her swollen abdomen.

The club had gone all out. Billed as the Sabatini Wine Dinner, the menu featured pairings from Sabatini wines that had been recognized by the Instituto del Vino Italiano – Grandi Marchi, for their excellence. The menu featured Corvina ceviche, blackened scallops, and Kobe beef.

"Abercrombie and York must be doing pretty well," Zahir whispered to Logan.

"I'll say," he said under his breath, as he spotted their host standing just inside the door.

"Logan, nice to see you again. Thank you for coming." Andrew Gao clasped Logan's hand in a firm grip.

"Thanks for inviting us, Andrew. This is my wife, Zahir. Zahir, Andrew Gao."

Gao turned on the charm as he took her hand. "So pleased to meet you." He gestured towards a svelte Chinese woman dressed in traditional silk *qipao* straight out of Shanghai Tang, standing by his side. "This is my wife, Teresa."

Teresa took Zahir's hand in hers. She was unusually tall for a Chinese woman, with high cheekbones, wide eyes and skin as smooth as silk.

Her voice, in lightly accented British English, was soft-spoken. "How are you enjoying your stay in Hong Kong?"

"It's been fun getting to know the city. I grew up outside of Washington, D.C., so I'm used to the diversity you get in an urban setting."

"Where are you living?"

"We're on the Peak. Near Barker Road."

"Oh. We're almost neighbors. We live on Pollock's Path, just down from where you are. We'll have to get together."

The couples chatted for a few more minutes and then Logan and Zahir moved on to circulate among the other guests before dinner. There was a cross-section of Hong Kong business and political elites present, many representing the travel and entertainment industries.

When Logan and Zahir found their places, they discovered that they were seated at a table with a popular Chinese actress and her business tycoon husband, who had made his money in the casino industry in Macau, as well as two other couples in the shipping industry, and the Hong Kong Police commissioner and his wife. Conversation during dinner was light, although at one point Logan was caught off guard when one of the men raised the recent murder of an unidentified man in Kowloon.

From his description, Logan immediately recognized the victim as the presumptive PSB officer he had killed. He feigned ignorance and asked what had happened.

"No one knows. These things happen from time to time. The rival triads are always looking for a chance to stir up trouble. They're so busy killing each other that we don't have to worry about our own safety." He chuckled at his own joke.

The police commissioner, a seasoned career cop originally from Guangzhou, scowled at the man's levity. "We have a pretty good handle on triad activity in Kowloon," he spat out.

"This was not a triad hit. For one thing, the person killed was not a triad member. He was an employee of the security service," he conceded.

"He was a police officer?" the businessman asked in shock.

"Public Security Bureau."

Chatter at the table melted away as everyone gawked at the lawman in surprise.

"But why would someone kill a PSB officer?" the actress asked.

"We don't know. But we'll find out," the top cop replied in a decisive tone. "He was on a sensitive mission, escorting a foreign asset to Beijing, when he was ambushed. The asset disappeared, and our man was killed.

"We have been searching for the asset since he disappeared. There was no sign of him until this morning when we were advised by our embassy that he had been arraigned in Federal District Court in Washington."

There was a gasp from around the table. Logan expressed surprise along with the others, although he had already received a heads-up from Frank Sisler that Wheeler's arraignment had taken place.

Hong Kong's top cop continued. "We are pretty confident that the asset did not return to Washington of his own accord. Our working theory is that he was captured and spirited out of Hong Kong by the CIA. They are capable of such a thing." He glared at Logan.

Logan didn't take it personally. He figured the commissioner was venting his frustrations because he and Zahir were the only Americans in sight. He'd probably been getting a lot of heat from Beijing to find their man. He'd have to be careful not to get on the man's wrong side, although a part of him wanted to rebut his allegation about the CIA.

"Will your office be lodging a complaint?" he asked, without guile.

The commissioner regarded him with amusement. "Given the circumstances, I think it's unlikely that Washington would acknowledge how this asset came to be in their custody. It's even more unlikely that Beijing will complain because that would be tantamount to admitting that they were engaged in espionage.

"But someone must pay for the death of our officer. We have opened an inquiry and will be questioning residents in the neighborhood who may have seen something. It will take time but eventually an eyewitness will come forward."

Logan felt a warning tremor race up his spine. He kept his features impassive, and simply nodded. This investigation would bear watching. They had taken every precaution to avoid detection, but in a city as dense as Hong Kong, someone, somewhere, was always paying attention.

Midway through the second course, Renata Sabatini, the guest speaker, rose and walked to the lectern that the club staff had set up. Logan's dinner companions seemed eager to abandon the brutal details of the PSB officer's murder and turn their attention to more civilized matters.

Logan had actually visited the Sabatini vineyards on a family trip to Italy when he was in high school. He had been too young to sample the wines at the time, but he remembered being impressed by their museum and restaurant. During the tour of the wine cellars he had marveled at the rows of enormous chestnut casks lining the walls of the underground vault. His reverie was interrupted as the legendary winemaker began to speak.

"The House of Sabatini is pleased to be partnering with the Hong Kong Chamber and the Royal Hong Kong Yacht Club to bring you this selection of our finest wines. As one of the leading vintners in Tuscany for over one hundred and fifty years, we are delighted to share that heritage with you here tonight.

"Italian wines are world renowned, but it is the Tuscan wines, especially those bearing the *indicazione geografica tipica* appellation, otherwise known as Super Tuscans, that are truly extraordinary.

"Our family's estate is near Montalcino. Forty years ago, my uncle, Peter Sabatini, replanted sixty percent of our vineyards in Sangiovese grapes. He believed, and time has proven him right, that we could produce an exceptional Super Tuscan from this single grape variety.

"Climate and soil are what make our wines so special. The results are wines that have been described by wine connoisseurs as luxurious and silky."

Renata spoke for fifteen minutes and remained afterwards to take questions. It was eight-thirty and guests began leaving soon after the dessert and wine pairing. Logan and Zahir stopped by to thank the Gaos for the invitation, and made plans to get together soon.

Gao pulled Logan aside as they walked together towards the club entrance.

"In the spring, when the weather is warmer, we're going to put together a group of industry leaders and their spouses to take a Yangtze River cruise on one of our ships. We'll be going from Chongqing to Wuhan. I'd like to invite you and Zahir to join us."

"That would be fun. I think Zahir would enjoy that." Inwardly he ticked off the months and came to the conclusion that they would be welcoming the newest member of the Alexander clan into the world in the late spring, early summer, making it unlikely that they would actually accept the invitation.

The evening air was comfortable, so Logan and Zahir decided to walk to the Wanchai Subway via Gloucester Road. They held hands as they walked and Logan felt a warm glow. Zahir had come into his life at a time when he was plumbing the depths of despair. His younger brother had just been killed in Iraq, and his own career in the Navy had been cut short after a battlefield injury. She had filled that void and then some.

As they crossed over the highway, Logan pointed out the Harley-Davidson dealership. "I can't believe they do as well as they do here. Wellington's been talking about getting a bike, although I don't know where he would ride it. He says there's a local Harley owners group that rides on Sundays."

"What's Adèle have to say about that?" Zahir asked. Adèle was the Swedish Ericsson employee that Wellington had been dating for the last couple of months.

"Turns out she's a big biker. Used to have a BMW she rode in Sweden."

They stopped to look at the showroom window display, which featured Sportster and Softail Deluxe models. Logan's eyes took in the rich detail on the bikes. He'd never owned a bike, but a number of his Navy buddies had. He felt Zahir looking at him and turned to see what she wanted.

"I hope you're not getting any big ideas," she warned.

"Me? No way," he reassured her. "Someone in the office has to be responsible." He gave her a comforting hug. He didn't bother to mention the fleeting image that had flitted across his mind of himself on the Sportster taking a tight hairpin turn at high speed.

"Speak of the devil. Look who's here." Wellington and Adèle were leaving a Mongolian barbecue just ahead of them.

Bruce had approached Logan the week before to see if it would be possible for him and Adèle to move in together. Logan was sympathetic, but the rules for Agency officers on the subject of co-habitation with foreigners were pretty straightforward.

It wasn't that he suspected Adèle of any subterfuge. Headquarters had already run traces on her through their own vast databases as well as those of the Bureau. There had been no derogatory information.

The difference between a one-night stand and a long-term, intimate relationship was that, with the latter, the foreigner would gain insights into the CIA officer's patterns, associations and activities that could be his or her undoing if their love interest had a hidden agenda. In the past, operations and assets had been compromised because people had failed to follow these simple reporting requirements.

There was an approved path for these situations, though. Typically it involved the employee curtailing his foreign assignment and requesting permission to marry his or her foreign love. One proviso, which many found difficult to swallow, was the Agency's insistence that employees accept the final judgment or face separation from the service.

For its part, CIA would conduct extensive background checks and do its best to vet the marriage candidate. Sometimes these investigations could take as long as a year, during which time the officer was forbidden from serving abroad.

"Hey, Logan, Zahir. What are you up to?" Wellington had his arm around Adèle's waist. She smiled a greeting at them both.

"Hey, Bruce, Adèle. We had a dinner at the Yacht Club. Good wine pairings with an Italian vintner. Sabatini."

"Nice. We just did the all-you-can-eat Mongolian."

Adèle pouted. "I can never eat more than one bowl, so it's wasted on me."

"That's all right, baby, I make up for both of us." Wellington patted his stomach.

Despite his bravado, even Wellington had failed to meet the restaurant's standing challenge to its patrons. Eat five bowls of their barbecue and your meal was on the house. The last time they had gone out for barbecue as a group, the most anyone had managed was three bowls.

"I agree with you," Zahir said. "One bowl is more than enough for me."

The couples walked together towards the subway. Zahir and Adèle were walking ahead of the men.

"A couple of interesting messages came in after you left today," Wellington said in a conversational tone, glancing behind him as he did so to make sure that no one was within earshot.

Logan glanced sideways. "Anything I need to know?"

"Apparently someone saw ONI escorting Wheeler onto the ship last week, and became suspicious when the story that he had been missing came out after the arraignment yesterday. Beijing apparently decided to go on the offensive before the U.S. has a chance to complain.

"Their ambassador in Washington is going to démarche the State Department today. He plans to say that Wheeler approached Chinese officials in Hong Kong asking for asylum. They were only doing the humanitarian thing by agreeing to provide him safe haven."

"How'd you find this out?"

"My guy in Manila was in the same ambassadors' class as the Chinese ambassador to Washington, Ambassador Hu, so they're good friends. This was going to be his first démarche, and my guy has probably done a half-dozen, so Hu gave him a call to ask for his advice about how to handle it.

"Anyway, he reached out to me to give us a heads-up. First time he's used his new commo system."

"You're doing a good job with him, Bruce. Building trust. I like it."

They walked on a few more paces in silence. "What a bunch of assholes," Logan exclaimed in exasperation. "There are more Chinese Intel types running around the U.S. than we know what to do with. Maybe Wheeler's conscience will get the best of him and he'll come clean. Show them to be the lying bastards that they are.

"Humanitarian. That's a joke if I ever heard one.

"The Agency's not a big proponent of defending itself in the court of public opinion. That's why we usually get a bad rap. People make unsubstantiated allegations and we keep quiet."

"It's a slippery slope once you start down that path," Wellington agreed.

Zahir and Adele were waiting for them near the entrance to the Wanchai subway station.

"Let's take a double-decker up to the Peak," Zahir suggested.

"Why not? It's a nice night," Logan agreed.

The two couples took the subway to Central and walked over to Exchange Square, where they waited for the next bus. Hong Kong has thousands of these double-decker open-air buses that have been around since the late 1940s. Many are a throwback to the original Routemaster London bus, which was popular in the United Kingdom from the early 1950s until 2005, when service was discontinued.

Logan rarely used these buses when he was working. The routes were too predictable. During an SDR it gave surveillance the opportunity to get ahead of you and deploy numerous foot surveillants, making it impossible to "make" them because you rarely saw the same person twice.

They would get on and off, staying in touch with their team leader via cell phone to report if you'd gotten off and what direction you'd gone. You never had to worry about being alone.

As the bus ascended the steep hill, Logan searched Zahir's face. Her hair was blowing in the wind and her eyes sparkled as the driver down-shifted, the guttural response from the engine making it hard to carry on a conversation.

Their life in Hong Kong was pleasant enough, he thought, as he smiled at her. Both of them enjoyed what they were doing and life here was easy. But his gut told him that things were about to get interesting. They were going to have to double down on their defensive measures.

And just as important, this wasn't the time to go to ground. Headquarters needed to lift its ban on travel to the mainland. He needed to contact Li to find out when China was planning to launch its Zero Day cyber attack.

Chapter 32

Lois Caldwell stepped off the regional JetBlue carrier at Syracuse Hancock International Airport. She was glad she had remembered to pack a warm coat. There was a brisk wind blowing off the Finger Lakes, causing the temperature to plummet to the low forties.

She hurried to the Hertz counter, where they had her car waiting. It was only ten miles from the airport to DCSA Marine Systems' Ocean, Radar and Sensor Systems Division. The facility was one of a dozen legacy divisions that dated back to the days before DCSA and the ATI Defense Systems Group merged.

Jerome Blackburn, the special agent in charge of the Albany Field Office, had contacted FBI Headquarters earlier in the week, requesting technical assistance in evaluating a suspect hacking operation against the defense contractor in Syracuse. It had the earmarks of a Chinese operation, according to the Albany Division chief.

The Syracuse Resident Agency, which was subordinate to the Albany Field Office, was up to its eyeballs in a federal corruption probe, and Blackburn, who had once worked with Lois in Kansas City, had specifically asked for her.

Lois planned to meet Joe Fry, the supervisory agent in charge of the satellite office, before going over to DCAS. She exited I-81 onto Clinton Street and found the building where they were housed.

Joe's secretary buzzed her into the third-floor office suite. Joe, a fifteen-year veteran of the Bureau, greeted her in the foyer and ushered her into his office. "How was your flight?" he asked.

"Not bad. It was direct, nonstop so I didn't have to worry about making the mad dash for a connecting flight. Plus, it helps not to have any checked bags." She planned to be there just for the day.

"Nice. Thanks for coming up. We're swamped and thought it would be a big help to get someone with technical skills to help us figure out what we're looking at.

"The company is cooperating with our investigation but they're somewhat defensive because they didn't pick up on the hacking attack until it came to light after we approached them."

"That's surprising," Lois said. "These high-tech companies usually have a pretty sophisticated IT department. There's been so much in the news about foreign hacking and the Dark Web that they've been investing in top-of-the-line firewall software and have been sensitizing their employees to the cyber risks out there."

"That's only as good as your weakest link. In this case it was an employee by the name of Jerry Morrison. Morrison was an engineer in the Sensor Systems Division. And, according to his supervisor, he was damned good at what he did.

"The problem is that Morrison is one sick bastard. Kiddie porn. He was part of a ring in the Northeast trading in child pornography. We've had an ongoing sting operation against this group for six months. We nailed him when one of our Asian undercover officers convinced him that she was thirteen years old and he solicited sex with her.

"It turns out he'd been using his office computer to access these child porn websites, and arranged his liaison with the undercover from the same computer. Apparently his wife was suspicious that he'd been abusing their daughter for years, but she was in denial and never reported it.

"He knew that his wife suspected something, and figured that if he used his home computer, she would eventually discover his dirty little secret. So he limited his preying activity to work. We might not have caught him if he'd confined himself to Internet searches, but when he set up a date for sex, that's when we nailed his ass."

"So what made you think that there's a Chinese angle to this?"

"Well, to tell you the truth, we have an intern working for us this fall semester, and she came up with it.

"She's at Syracuse, getting a master's in database systems. She came in last week and mentioned that she'd gone to a seminar on network security the day before. One of the speakers presented a paper on the methods that the Chinese are using to target U.S. corporate networks.

"As you well know, hackers have been putting up pornography websites for years. But this site was particularly well done and lured these sickos in more effectively than anything we've ever seen. That's not to say that your average employee in a corporate setting is going to use their office computer to search for porn. But, if you're a Chinese hacker, you only have to get lucky once. Boom. Open invitation to dump a little malware into your target's network."

"After we arrested Morrison, we subpoenaed his computer, files, everything. It's all stored in our evidence lock-up back there," he waved towards a caged area down the hall. "We'll get you set up in an office and you can go through it.

"Jerome says you're making quite a name for yourself on Chinese cyber hacking. You working with Des Magarity?"

"Yep, Des is my boss."

Joe gave her a thoughtful look. "Too bad about Rick Wheeler. He was in my new agent class at Quantico. I got to know him pretty well the five months we spent together. I never would have taken him for a spy. What the hell happened to him?"

"I don't know. Des can't get over it. Everybody that knew him said the same thing. Upstanding guy. Dedicated. Family man." She shook her head. "I've only known him for a few months. He was nice to me. According to Des, he's not talking. He was just arraigned the other day.

"One quick question before I get started. Do you think it's worth going over to DCAS to talk to their people?"

"Could be. I know they've contracted with an outside computer security firm." Joe searched his desk drawer and pulled out a business card. "Cereus Data Forensics. I talked with one of their guys, Bill Plante, who's leading the effort with DCAS. He said the way they typically work is to bring in a team that does malware analysis and evaluates the intrusion to pinpoint weaknesses in the target network. They'll come up with a plan to beef up their network security. I know they're working over there today if you want to talk to them."

"Let's see how much progress I make here."

Joe showed her to a vacant office where the support staff had set up the contents of Jerry Morrison's office. "Coffee pot's back here. If you get hungry, someone will probably make a sandwich run around eleven-thirty. Just let Nancy know." He nodded in the direction of his secretary.

"I've got a meeting with the mayor at ten o'clock, so I'm going to head out. If you need anything, Nancy will take care of it."

After he'd left, Lois set about looking at Morrison's computer. The support staff had provided a stand-alone Internet connection to prevent the malware from spreading to the Bureau's internal LAN.

Joe hadn't mentioned it, but she knew that his officers would have already removed the hard drive and made a forensic copy to be used in Morrison's prosecution, an exact bit-by-bit duplicate to preserve the evidence from accidental tampering, evidence that was witnessed to by a chain of custody slip the moment the computer was seized and copied. Afterwards they would have reinstalled the hard drive on the computer to examine it as a complete unit.

Her initial goal was to establish a timeline of Morrison's illegal activity, which would help build the Bureau's child pornography case against him. For this she was going to use a commercial software program known as Forensic Toolbox.

The software allowed her to examine emails and chats that Morrison had sent or received, providing a date and timestamp for each communication. This made it fairly simple for her to document his activities.

It appeared that his illegal use of DCAS's computers had begun almost two years ago. Because the company had no internal audit system in place, Morrison had used their network to satisfy his porn addiction with impunity, until he'd advanced from being a strictly online voyeur to a predator soliciting sex with a minor.

When Nancy came around to take sandwich orders, Lois ordered tomato and Brie on a baguette, and continued working at her desk. She had most of the timeline done by two o'clock.

She set the timeline aside and got down to what she was personally most interested in, analyzing the Chinese malware on Morrison's computer. It took her several minutes to figure out that the malware was not running in the computer's random access memory, or RAM. She concluded that although the Trojan was stored somewhere on the computer's hard drive, it wasn't currently active.

Lois backed out of the program she was running and launched the Windows Task Manager to confirm her initial assessment that the Trojan wasn't running in RAM. She clicked on the processes tab and began to scroll through the list of applications to see if there was anything out of the ordinary running. Nothing leapt out at her, but then again applications can be renamed to suit the hacker's perverted sense of humor.

If it was the Chinese, she expected that whatever they had used to attack Morrison's computer would be fairly sophisticated. The typical approach would be to lure the target into a particular website, promising freebies like training videos, software, or pornography, if the user registers with an active email address. Once they register, they're sent a confirming email in which they are asked to click on a link to log in to validate their registration.

Once the target does that, the Trojan scans the computer for open ports or other vulnerabilities and attempts to install malware. If successful, the hacker is able to monitor the user's activity, copy and download files, and execute other damaging actions.

Lois decided to run a full scan on the computer. The problem was that, assuming that it was infected with malware, there was a good chance that the existing virus scanner was already infected. To defeat that possibility she used EnCase software to create another forensic copy of the hard drive, which she then isolated from the Internet environment. Then she set up a virtual environment to simulate DCAS's system, and over the next several hours ran multiple commercial virus scanners against the computer.

While the scans were churning away she organized her timeline and examined the other files from Morrison's office. She was prepared to re-scan his computer as many times as necessary, but when she looked at the results, there it was; a root kit hiding in a registry file.

Probably the best-known example of a root kit designed to target the command and control systems of a large enterprise was Stuxnet, the malware that in 2010 destroyed twenty percent of Iran's nuclear centrifuges at the Natanz Fuel Enrichment Plant.

It would take her some time to decrypt the virus's payload, but based upon what she'd seen thus far, she'd bet even money that this attack not only was Chinese, it had Pan Chengong's handiwork written all over it. What were they after?

Lois stretched and checked the time. She was surprised to see that it was already seven o'clock. Joe had stuck his head in once, after he got back from his meeting at City Hall, to see if she needed anything. They must be getting ready to close everything down, she thought.

She had copied all the files she needed to finish the job onto a thumb drive, which she would take with her back to Washington. She gathered her notes and walked into Joe's office.

"All done?" he asked.

She nodded. "For now. Got time for a quick out-brief?"

"Sure. Grab a seat. You staying overnight or heading back to D.C.?"

"I've got a nine p.m. flight. I don't think I need to talk to DCAS, although I'd recommend you stay in touch with them to see to what extent their network has been compromised."

She handed him the timeline from Morrison's computer. "This lays out Morrison's misuse of his office computer. Looks like it started about two years ago and continued right up until his arrest."

Joe took the packet from her and shuffled through the sheets of paper. He finally looked up. "I don't know how he found time to get his job done." He waved the stack of paper.

"The other thing is that this is definitely a Chinese operation. It has all the earmarks of a group of cyber hackers that we've been following. I can't go into the specifics, but I'm interested in finding out if this ties into a bigger effort that they have underway right now."

"Bastards," Joe uttered. "One day they're going to go too far."

He stood up. "We better get you on your way. Don't want you to miss your flight." He came around from behind his desk and shook her hand. "Thanks for everything. This is going to help us put Mr. Morrison away for a long time.

"I had a call from the wife this afternoon, and she's trying to convince the daughter to testify against him. She doesn't want to but the mother thinks she'll eventually come around."

Lois said her goodbyes and walked out of the office. Traffic was light on Clinton Street. As she pulled out of the parking spot and pointed her car towards the airport, her thoughts returned to Pan Chengong. She couldn't wait to get back to Washington so she could spend more time analyzing the virus. Where was this all leading? Her mouth was set in a firm line. "We're going to take you down," she blurted out loud. "We have to."

Chapter 33

Two weeks had passed since Alexander Maritime's Hong Kong office snatched Rick Wheeler off the streets and dispatched him to Washington, courtesy of the USS Bowes Island. Aside from Logan and Zahir's brief encounter with the Hong Kong Police commissioner at Andrew Gao's soirée, there was no indication the team was getting any scrutiny from local authorities.

Logan had ordered everyone in the office to conduct daily surveillance detection probes to see if they were receiving any unusual attention from Chinese security. Thus far there had been nothing out of the ordinary.

During this period of down time Logan had begun working on a proposal to dispatch the team to China for a month. It required approval from the DDO. In reality the President had already approved their covert action plan and from his way of thinking, this proposal was the best way to implement it. Their goal was to shut down Pan Chengong's operation.

He wasn't surprised when the approval came in two days later. This was risky business, but it was also the kind of operation that was CIA's bread and butter. Three operations officers and a support officer deep inside of China mounting a covert operation so vital to the nation's national security that their failure could adversely affect the U.S. economy for decades.

Separately, but equally significant, Langley had finally concluded that Li was the real deal. Although he hadn't been fully validated or issued one of those ironclad source descriptions you could take to the bank, headquarters was prepared to assign him a covert communications plan that

248

would make it possible for him to communicate securely with the team real time, while they were in China. This was critical because of the operational role he would play in the days and weeks ahead.

With the approvals in hand, Logan had reached out to Ms. Wang from the Chinese Language program at Southwest University of Science and Technology. True to her word, she was prepared to run a month-long intensive language immersion program for the four of them beginning the following Monday.

Logan, Norm, Bruce and Alicia had all studied Chinese with private tutors in the Washington area before deploying to Hong Kong. They were roughly at the same level, although Logan's listening comprehension and speaking ability were somewhat better than the others. Alicia had demonstrated a flair for reading, and enjoyed writing Chinese characters so much that she had enrolled in a calligraphy class at the Hong Kong Calligraphy and Arts Center.

The week before their departure raced by. During that time, Washington dispatched a pouch to Beijing with the tools they would need to accomplish their mission. A separate team had scouted out a cache site on the outskirts of Mianyang, no small feat given its remote location. Their supplies would be emplaced Saturday evening. It was a substantial cache, and needed to withstand inclement weather and the scrutiny of casuals.

One of Logan's challenges would be securing the cache contents once they had moved onto campus. At his request, Ms. Wang had arranged for them to lease two university apartments for the month. He recalled that the furnishings there were spartan, but those accommodations would give them more privacy than they would have living in a student dormitory.

Still, privacy was a relative term in China. They would be under some scrutiny as foreigners; security would have access to their living quarters during the day while they were in class. They couldn't leave anything incriminating lying around that would alert their minders to their covert mission.

The team planned to fly into Chengdu on Saturday. There they would split up, with Logan continuing on to Chongqing to meet with Li, while the others made the short bus trip to Mianyang.

The first order of business for Logan would be to ascertain whether Li had in any way been compromised by Wheeler's treason. He and the PSB officer had, of necessity, been incommunicado for weeks. He thought back to their last meeting in Chongqing, just before he and Wellington had broken into Pan Chengong's computer lab. Everything had seemed much simpler then. Now, the looming prospect of Li's seeming compromise hung over the operation like a foreboding cloud.

If he could establish with reasonable certainty that he was in the clear, Logan's challenge would be to convince him to go along with the proposed operational scenario and his role in it. As an inducement, Logan had secured approval from headquarters to offer Li and his son asylum in the U.S., at the successful conclusion of the operation.

If Li agreed to those terms, the next order of business would be to give him covert communications software to install on his computer so that he could send and receive encrypted messages. To the casual bystander, the program he had brought with him looked like off-the-shelf PGP encryption software, but it was PGP on steroids. Once installed, it would be undetectable to anyone with access to Li's computer, or anyone monitoring his communications.

This brief meeting on the street wasn't ideal for teaching Li how to use the software program, but there was a very good help note on the startup page that would walk him through the encryption and decryption process for sending and receiving encrypted email. Because of his computer smarts, Logan was confident that Li would master the routine with little difficulty.

Finally, he needed Li to come up with a safe site for their cache materials. For now the cache could remain where it was, but soon enough they would need to have more ready access to it.

When he had put the proposal together, Logan knew that the team would have to be largely self-sufficient on the ground in China. It would be a long lifeline to help if they found themselves in a jam. At least they would have good communications with headquarters, he reflected. Foreign businessmen had been using PGP-encrypted communications inside China for decades, and although it had raised more than a few eyebrows from Chinese security in the early days, it barely got their attention today. It was a key component of China's own encrypted communications nowadays.

Zahir had not objected when Logan told her that he would be in China for a month, although it would be their longest separation in the five years they'd been married. He knew that she would be worried about him, but she masked her feelings well. He would miss her and Cooper. They were giving up spending Thanksgiving together, but he'd make it up to them in December. Maybe take a week off when his folks came to visit and go to Bali or Phuket.

On Friday they all went out for Thai food at a family-run restaurant in Wanchai with the playful name KGB. The proprietor, a grizzled Thai septuagenarian by the name of "One-armed Kiet," never would reveal the source of his inspiration for the restaurant's name. Kiet had lost his left arm in a trawling accident while working on a shrimp boat in his native Thailand. Somehow he had migrated to Hong Kong with his family where their savory Thai curries had been tickling the palates of Hong Kong residents for decades.

Rumor had it that Kiet had been a gun-runner for the Russians during the Vietnam War, but this had been many years ago and besides, Kiet was mum on the subject.

"Everybody good to go tomorrow?" Logan asked. The restaurant was humming with customers, and the clatter of dishes and conversation had reached such a pitch that he had to shout to be heard.

The four of them would be traveling to Chengdu on the same early morning flight. No need to conceal their relationship to one another on this trip since they would be living and studying together the entire month.

"I'm not finished packing," Alicia complained. "It's hard to pack for a month," she pouted.

"You can always buy stuff there if you need anything," Norm piped up.

"I'm not taking that much," Bruce said. "We're going to be students. Jeans and tee shirts are pretty much all I'm packing."

They kept the conversation light. Zahir and Adéle were both present and neither of them was cleared for a classified discussion. Besides, this wasn't the best venue for talking shop. There was some truth to the World War II saying, "Loose lips sink ships."

Despite the relaxed conversation, Logan began to feel a trickle of adrenaline creeping into his system. Just the thought of what lay ahead of them got him pumped. They were finally going to take the fight to the Chinese instead of sitting back and taking the equivalent of cyber shots to the head day in and day out.

After they'd finished their main meal, Logan ordered a platter of mango sticky rice, one of his favorites, for the table. When it came, he tipped his drink to the rest of the table. "Fair winds and following seas."

"Safe travels," replied Stoddard and Wellington.

"You know, I've been around sailing for years and I think I get it, but where does that expression come from?" Alicia asked.

"Old Navy saying," Logan explained. "Sort of a farewell and a wish for ideal conditions."

"Oh."

"We have something like that in Swedish," Adéle offered. "*Sâ länge.*"

"Sounds like 'so long,'" Bruce replied. Adéle leaned over and whispered something in his ear, causing him to laugh.

Logan smiled seeing the two of them together. He liked Adéle and thought she was perfect for Bruce. It would be nice if things worked out between the two of them. He glanced at his watch and was startled to see that it was already ten o'clock.

"I'm ready to call it a night," he said. "Our flight's at eight-thirty so we'll need to be at the airport by seven at the latest. Looks like a six a.m. wake-up call."

Logan picked up the tab. After he'd paid, they all filed out of the restaurant and stood on the sidewalk chatting for a few minutes before walking up the street to the nearest taxi stand. There was a queue, but with the steady flow of incoming taxis they only had a five-minute wait.

As Logan and Zahir settled into the back seat, she rested her head on his shoulder. Looking up at him she whispered in his ear. "Be careful, my *delbar*." The Persian word for soul mate was a term of endearment that she often used with him when they were alone.

Her lips brushed his cheek and she snuggled closer to him as they sped through Wanchai and made their way up the twisting road to the Peak. Logan held her hand as they raced up the steep mountain. In the days and weeks ahead he and the other team members would face hardships and unknown dangers, but this feeling, with the woman he loved, would be the essential thing to sustain him, regardless of what lay ahead.

Chapter 34

Logan and the others had just emerged from Terminal One at Chengdu International Airport. It had been a bumpy ride most of the way from Hong Kong. Alicia's complexion matched that of the UC Santa Cruz mascot logo, a slimy yellow banana slug, emblazoned on her sweatshirt. She had purchased a bottle of water inside and was gingerly sipping it.

"You going to be all right?" Logan asked.

"I think so. That was pretty rough though."

"See if you can find some soda crackers. That'll settle your stomach."

"I'll be fine." Her face brightened. "This is my first time on the mainland. I'm going to make the most of it."

"Atta girl." He patted her on the back.

"I'll try to catch up with you all later tonight, but I'm not optimistic given the time constraints. Worst-case scenario, my friend can't make it and I'll have to try again tomorrow. Whatever happens, I'll definitely be in Mianyang to start class Monday."

"It'll be better once you get his commo up and running," Bruce commented.

"You can say that again," Logan nodded in agreement.

"All right, we better get going," Norm suggested. "There's a bus to Mianyang in half an hour." The trio was taking a direct intercity bus to the university town from the airport. Bruce was taking Logan's luggage off his hands so that he'd have more flexibility moving around Chongqing before his meeting with Li. Norm had enlisted a baggage handler to help them with the bags. Logan watched for a moment as they headed towards the bus station about two hundred yards away.

He turned back towards the terminal and strolled towards Gate 3 on the lower level. There were shuttle buses servicing several routes to downtown destinations. He was looking for Line 2, which would take him to East Railway Station, where he planned to catch the bullet train to Chongqing.

Logan was in surveillance detection mode now. Had been all morning, actually. Not that he'd expected to draw surveillance en route to the airport in Hong Kong. And, just as he'd predicted, no one had tailed him. But then why would they? He hadn't made a secret of his travel plans. If the Chinese were interested in what he was doing in Mianyang, they would have already contacted security there with an official query.

Other than the scare with that PSB patrol at his first meeting with Li, he had been surveillance-free on all of his trips to China. He wasn't expecting any special treatment here in the "City of Hibiscus," but the big unknown was whether Rick Wheeler's treachery had compromised their volunteer. Logan reminded himself that, although he might not be a target at the moment, if Li were compromised all the Chinese had to do was sit back and wait for him to make a move. He'd lead them to the person they were really interested in. His handler.

As he located the Line 2 shuttle and climbed aboard, Logan cursed the way this whole operation had unfolded. Under ideal circumstances, the Agency would have had more time to evaluate Li's suitability for the role he had taken on. What was he? Logan asked himself. Volunteer, agent provocateur, or pawn?

When he reached East Station, Logan hurried inside and purchased a ticket for the twelve-ten p.m. train. That would put him into Chongqing a little after two. The more he thought about it, he realized that he wouldn't make it to Mianyang tonight. By the time he'd executed a thorough SDR, it would be after ten p.m. The last train to Chengdu was at nine-fifteen.

It was raining and in the low sixties when he stepped off the train in Chongqing. He sniffed the damp air. SEALS love this kind of weather. He needed to call Li, but he wouldn't do that until he was several hours into his SDR. His first order of business was to get away from these crowds so that he could begin sifting what, if anything, was out there. He flagged down a cab, all the while scanning the street around him. So far, so good.

Twenty minutes later he directed the driver to drop him near the Days Inn Business Center. He'd have to find a hotel later. He couldn't risk raising his profile by checking in before he'd made his meeting.

From the Days Inn he struck out in the direction of a teahouse west of Chating North Road. He worked the side streets and back alleys for four hours, cataloging faces, license plates and vehicle types. It was mind-numbing work, but he was confident after four hours that he was "black."

He pulled a "clean" cell phone from his backpack as he was walking and dialed Li's number. It rang several times and went to voice mail. He hung up. "Damn. Where is he?" It was a little after six p.m.

Logan decided to put some distance between him and the area he'd been traversing for the last four hours. He hailed another cab and instructed the driver to cross the Jialing River at the Shimen Bridge. The route created a choke point, but if there were any trailing vehicular surveillance, they would be hard pressed to stay with him unless they followed the cab across, thus exposing themselves.

Logan craned his neck to look behind as they crossed the bridge, but he didn't see any suspect vehicles. The driver turned north on Hongshi Road and at Logan's direction, pulled over near the south entrance to Shimen Park. Logan paid the fare and began walking north through the park. He did a light clothing change, reversing his jacket and donning a baseball cap. The rain had tapered off but the raw weather had discouraged pedestrians, so he had the trails to himself.

He pulled up under an immense banyan tree with its distinctive leathery leaves, and tried Li's number again. This time Li answered on the second ring.

"Hello?"

"Hi. It's me. Is this a good time to talk?"

"Just a minute."

Logan could hear street sounds and a flapping noise in the background. A moment later Li resumed talking.

"I'm on my way home. It's raining, so I pulled over to avoid an accident. Where are you?"

"Here. Are you free to meet me?"

There was a pause. "Yes. We have a lot to discuss."

"You remember where?"

"I do."

"Eleven-thirty?"

"I'll see you there." Logan hung up. The call had lasted a total of twenty seconds. He exhaled as he realized that he had been holding his breath. The meeting would actually take place at ten p.m. The hour-and-a-half time difference was just an extra precaution in his smoke and mirrors world, designed to throw off anyone who might somehow be listening in.

Logan pulled a bag of peanuts that he'd bought at a corner stall out of his backpack. He scooped a handful of them into his mouth and considered his next move as he chomped through one, and then another handful. He realized that all the walking had made him hungry. He washed down the last of the nuts with a swig from a bottle of water and then put the remnants of his snack back into his pack.

He resumed walking north and exited the park on the east side near a bustling open-air market. Pedestrian and bicycle traffic had picked up and he realized that it was getting close to dinnertime and people were doing their last minute shopping.

He skirted the market to avoid the throngs and then boarded a mini-bus with a placard displayed in the window announcing Panxi Road as its destination. The bus was crowded but he found a vacant seat next to an elderly looking woman who eyed him with suspicion as he sat down. She clutched her bags closer to her body and stared at him, mouth agape, exposing a set of nicotine-stained teeth, cracked and chipped. She licked her dry lips and then seemed to shrink within herself as she edged away from him, plastering herself against the window.

Logan shrugged. The woman was typical of the uneducated peasants who inhabit much of rural China. Many of them never leave their villages, and seeing a foreigner is a rarity. She'd have a story to tell around the dinner table tonight.

Logan exited the bus thirty minutes later at Panxi 4th Branch Road. He crossed Panxi Road and walked west, weaving behind a ramshackle tea factory and a classical Chinese furniture store housed in a timeworn building whose façade sorely needed a coat of paint.

Three hours later he emerged from a neighborhood comprised mostly of apartment buildings. Up ahead was a small park opposite a bicycle repair shop where he could crouch down in the shadows to watch Li's approach to the area. It was twenty minutes before they were scheduled to meet; enough time to develop a feel for the place without heating it up.

Traffic was sporadic. There were few pedestrians on the street. Twenty-five minutes into his wait, Logan spotted Li riding a bicycle a half-block from the bike shop. He parked his bike on the sidewalk, and then leaned against the outside wall of the shop while he waited.

Logan could see the glow of a cigarette as Li struck a match. Moments later he tensed as he observed two men turn the corner and walk down the street towards the waiting agent. When they reached him, they stopped to converse. Logan could not hear their conversation from where he was, but they seemed to be asking directions. Li listened and then gestured back in the direction they had come from. They waved, turned around and walked back around the corner.

What the hell? Logan gritted his teeth and considered whether he should abort the meeting. Those two could have been casuals simply asking for directions or worst-case scenario, they could be Li's MPS handlers, issuing him last-minute instructions.

He decided to wait a bit longer to see if anything else developed. He was beginning to feel conspicuous because he'd been in the same spot for almost thirty minutes. He'd have to make his move pretty soon one way or the other.

There was too much at stake not to go through with the meeting. He'd come too far. He stood up and began walking through the park. Li spotted him as he crossed the street and approached the bike shop. As he reached the curb, a delivery vehicle sped by him. He kept his head down and reached the shadows of the building.

Li stood up to greet him. "Logan, when did you get here?"

"I just flew in to Chengdu today."

"How long will you stay this time?"

"That's what we need to talk about." He looked around. The street was quiet, but they would attract less attention if they were walking. "Let's walk. Why don't you bring your bike so you don't have to come back here?"

Li retrieved his bike and continued pushing it as they walked down the street.

"I saw those two men talking to you."

"They were lost. I know this neighborhood, so I was able to help them out."

"How are things with you?" Logan searched his face for any signs of nervousness or evasion.

"I'm concerned about my security. I'm not sure I can continue."

"What's changed?"

Li described the meeting at his regional headquarters with the political commissar, Pei. "He told us that the CIA had recruited a cyber expert. He knows about me!" Li gave Logan an accusing look and his voice trembled as he uttered these words. He stopped and fumbled in his pocket for a cigarette. He lit it, inhaled deeply and resumed walking.

"It's only a matter of time."

"Until?"

"Until they come for me."

Logan wracked his brain for a response. He had to walk Li back from the ledge. He was on the verge of walking away.

"It doesn't seem to me that if they suspected you, that you would have been invited to that meeting."

"I thought of that. Maybe it's a trick so that I drop my guard."

"Have you noticed anything unusual since then?"

"We were inspected by the MPS investigators. They interviewed everyone in our office."

"And?"

Li told him about the steps he'd taken to tighten up his unit's security posture before the inspection. "If they found anything, they didn't share it with me," he said.

"How did the FBI agent know about me?" He gave Logan a penetrating look.

"He didn't know about you personally. What he did see was the intelligence reporting about the cyber attacks that the Agency shared with the FBI. He was smart enough to figure out that it came from someone inside the cyber world."

"I don't know, Logan."

Logan decided that it was time to pull out his big carrot. "What about your plan to take your son to the U.S.?"

"I guess I'll have to forget about it."

"I got approval, you know. Headquarters values what you're doing and they want you to come to the States when we finish this operation. You and your son," he emphasized.

Li groaned. Logan went on before he could reject the offer outright.

"I've brought you a secure communications system so that we can stay in touch real-time. I'm going to be living in Mianyang for the next month."

"What!" Li turned to look at him, mouth wide open. "What are you going to be doing for a month?"

Logan explained about the intensive language program. He did not mention that three employees had accompanied him to China. Some things were better left unsaid. "In my free time I'll be finalizing a plan that will neutralize Pan Chengong's cyber attack. But I'll need your help."

They had turned into an apartment block and the street here was not well lighted. Logan tried to read Li's face, but his features were obscured by the shadows.

"What do you want me to do?"

Logan felt a surge of relief. Li might be having doubts, but at least he had not rejected his offer of asylum. "Here's what I need." After he described the plan in broad terms, he laid out the requirement for a safe site near Mianyang, where he could store the cache.

When he was done explaining what he needed, Logan trained Li on the covert communications system. He was a quick study, grasping the essentials with little effort. After Logan showed him how to access the help note, he was confident that he would be able to send and receive secure communications from his home computer. He asked him to send a test message the next day and cautioned him on the need to operate the system only when he had complete privacy.

Li told him that because of his work, he had a high-speed Internet connection in his apartment. It wouldn't be suspicious for him to send and receive encrypted email because of his need to securely communicate with his hackers 24/7.

They shook hands. Li mounted his bicycle, but before taking off he scrutinized Logan's face for a long moment.

"My life is in your hands, Logan Crowley."

Logan watched him pedal away. He turned in the opposite direction and began moving with some speed away from the neighborhood. It was going on eleven p.m. and he had three miles to go before he reached a place where he could catch a cab.

It began to rain again, a steady downpour. Despite his exhaustion, the foul weather did little to dampen his mood. In fact, he couldn't wipe the grin off of his face. They were back in business.

Chapter 35

Logan groaned as the fog cleared from his brain. He reached over to turn off the buzzing alarm. As his eyes focused, he remembered that it was Monday morning and his Chinese language class would begin in two hours.

It was still dark outside. He and Norm were sharing one of the student apartments and Bruce and Alicia had the other. They hadn't been able to get housing on the same floor but they were in the same building. The units were modest, but adequate for their needs. They wouldn't be doing much of anything but sleeping here anyway, he reflected. They'd take most of their meals in the international student cafeteria.

He decided to check his email to see if Li had figured out how to operate the software he'd given him.

He was surprised to see two messages from him. One was the test message that he'd asked for. He smiled when he read it. *"Wan shi kai tou nan,"* which, when translated, meant that "everything is hard in the beginning; it is the first step that costs." Li hadn't lost his sense of perspective despite his misgivings, he mused.

Chinese like to express themselves through pithy idiomatic expressions called *chengyu*. Many times these phrases are made up of only four characters and are often derived from ancient literature. Foreigners have a hard time figuring out how to use most of these expressions correctly because they often fail to understand the historical context of the phrase from which it is derived. There are thousands of *chengyu*, and the average native speaker peppers his conversation with them.

Logan opened the second message. Li had been doing his homework. He was proposing two potential scenarios for concealing the cache materials. One was at the home of an old family friend, and his father's comrade in arms. He was a widower who had retired to Mianyang and lived a short distance from the university where he was teaching a course in military science.

Li explained that the elderly veteran and his father had fought together against the Japanese, and much like his father, he too had grown weary of the rampant corruption amongst the higher-ups in the party and provincial leadership. He had been outraged over the treatment of the elder Li, which had led to his early demise. Li was certain that he would help, if approached.

The second scenario was more promising, from Logan's perspective. Li explained that he had a student apartment at the university assigned to his unit. His hackers often needed to hone their English language skills and he would dispatch them to Mianyang for intensive language immersions. No one was scheduled for language study until December and the apartment was available until then.

Logan pondered the two choices. It was too risky to bring in an unknown quantity like Li's family friend. It was a big leap to go from indignity over a fallen comrade's mistreatment to committing espionage. Besides, if Li had miscalculated the old soldier's sentiments, and they were to approach him, it could doom the operation.

The second scenario was enticing, although it was not without its own risks. Li claimed that he controlled the on-campus apartment, which would make it convenient to stage the materials they would need to mount their operation against Pan Chengong. But was he truly the only one with entrée to the flat? How difficult would it be to move the materials from the cache site to their hideaway without being observed? How secure would it be to leave the safe site unattended?

As he weighed the risk of exposure, Logan recalled Frank Sisler's parting words on the importance of concealing the U.S. hand in China. It was one of the basic tenets of covert action operations. The President must have one hundred percent deniability. Even the gear they would be using was either Chinese or Russian-manufactured. There would be no "made in the U.S.A." materiel to expose their connection.

Logan sent an encrypted message back to Li notifying him that he would like to use the apartment and within thirty minutes received a reply. The rooms were in the basement of a building on the other side of campus. They were equipped with a code lock on the front door because his hackers had an annoying habit of losing the key.

He went on to write that there were front and rear entrances to the building, and as of his last visit, there were no nearby security cameras or other security measures. Access to the building was unrestricted.

"Hey, what's going on?" Norm poked his head into Logan's room.

"Getting ready to study a little Chinese," he said. "Already got some homework to do." He pointed to his computer, but did not elaborate.

Norm nodded his understanding. They wouldn't be talking operations in the apartment. The assumption was that the Chinese owned the space they were living in, and it would be a simple matter for them to have audio, even video surveillance inside. If the MPS considered them a threat, no expense would be too great to contain them.

Logan recalled a story that had been circulating around Langley for years. A State Department officer in Beijing was attending a New Year's Eve party at a colleague's apartment, and was heard making a sarcastic remark to the effect that he felt bad for their MPS surveillance "friends" who were missing all the fun. Moments later the phone rang, and the only sound to be heard on the other end was the popping of a champagne cork.

"Want to get something to eat before class?" Logan asked.

"Yeah. I told Bruce we'd stop by around seven-fifteen."

Logan consulted his watch. "Okay. Give me fifteen minutes."

After they had picked up Bruce and Alicia, Logan gave them a run-down of his communications with Li. "Looks like he's good to go in the commo department. I want to recon this place he's proposing, today. I don't think all four of us need to go. Bruce, why don't you and I plan to check it out after class? If it's workable, we can start planning to retrieve the cache and transferring everything there."

"How much gear's in the cache?" Alicia asked.

"I think we have about a hundred pounds in there. We'll have to work out how we're going retrieve it. I checked out the cache site from imagery. It looked pretty remote to me, so I'm not too worried that we'll be spotted digging it up. It's getting it into the apartment without attracting attention that has me concerned."

"When do you want to pick up the cache?" Bruce asked.

"Let's make sure the apartment works first," Logan replied. "We can't make any plans until we've got that locked down."

They reached the student cafeteria. Most of the students were foreigners studying in the Chinese language program. It had the feel of a mini-United Nations – Africans, Middle Easterners, and Latin Americans mostly, with a smattering of Europeans and a couple of young women who looked to be Canadian or American.

"How's the food?" Logan grabbed a tray and got into line.

"Sucks." Norm wrinkled his nose. "You might want to consider switching from coffee to tea. They serve coffee but you wouldn't recognize it by the taste."

Logan had arrived late Sunday, so this was his first meal on campus. The others had been there since Saturday and knew what to expect. He knew that it wasn't going to be Zahir's home cooking, but then again, he wasn't here for the food.

They filled up their trays and found an empty table by a window looking out on the grounds. There was no daylight savings time in China. Everyone was on Beijing time. At this time of year it meant that sunrise was about seven-fifteen. It was beginning to brighten and Logan could see the sluggish forms of students on their way to their first classes.

Their morning classes set the routine for their next month at the university. Two hours of advanced conversation, an hour-long newspaper reading class, an hour in the language lab devoted to listening comprehension and an elective class.

Logan's head was spinning by the time they finished at one o'clock. Even though he had been living in Hong Kong for several months and used Chinese in his job and around the city on a daily basis, this amount of immersion took it to a different level. His brain ached from having to think in a foreign language nonstop.

He and Bruce dropped their books off at the apartment and began walking in the direction of the building Li had identified. Logan estimated that it was about ten minutes walking distance from the Foreign Language School. They struck out across campus. Pedestrian traffic was light; it was lunchtime and as a rule, Chinese do not like to miss meals.

It was overcast, with temperatures in the low sixties. Still it was pleasant to be out in the open air. Logan felt a sense of anticipation as they approached the building. It was just as Li had described it, five floors with wings on either end. Logan scanned the corners of the building for security cameras, but saw none.

"Let's go around back. See how it looks."

He and Bruce walked around the side of the building. There were a couple of workmen standing outside the rear door, replacing a broken window. They paid scant attention to the two foreigners, but Logan and Norm continued walking. No sense raising their profile by venturing inside while the two workers were there. It looked like about a twenty-minute repair job, so they decided to continue walking and then swing back around.

By the time they returned half an hour later, the workmen were gone. Logan and Bruce let themselves in through the rear door and in seconds were down a flight of stairs. The basement corridor was dimly lit. The two men walked by a utility room, a self-service laundry and a trash room. Li's apartment was at the end of the hall.

"I like it that there's nobody down here," Bruce whispered.

"Not now, anyway," Logan replied. He jerked his thumb back in the direction they had just traveled. "People must come down here to do laundry and dump their trash. We'll just have to figure out when it's quietest."

The apartment was at the end of the hall. The two men stood outside the door for a few seconds listening, but all was quiet inside. Logan punched in the code that Li had given him and turned the doorknob.

They crept into the room, and cleared it in seconds. No one was there. Logan relaxed for the first time in forty-five minutes. The apartment was not unlike the one where they were staying, only smaller. There was a modest bedroom, bath, functional kitchenette and study. Furnishings were monastic in their simplicity. A bed and nightstand in the bedroom; desk, chair and lamp in the study; and a wobbly card table and four chairs vied for space in the kitchen.

There were no windows to the outside; it appeared that the door they had come through was the only entry into the apartment. That could be good but it had its down side too. They'd be trapped if they were found out.

Logan was going on the assumption that there was no technical surveillance inside the apartment. Even so, they were better off keeping the chatter to a minimum. He signaled to Bruce that they should head out. They turned off the lights, paused at the door to listen for voices, and then eased out of the apartment, back down the hall and out the rear entrance.

As they walked back to their quarters, Logan and Bruce reviewed their survey of the building.

"I think our biggest problem is going to be getting in and out of the building without being seen," Logan pointed out.

"I like it that there aren't any other apartments in the basement, but those community rooms down there have to get some use," Bruce said. "We need to develop a legitimate pattern of coming over to this part of campus."

"I've been thinking about that. You know that elective class we're supposed to take? Something cultural? One of the choices is a martial arts class. The dojo where they work out isn't too far from here.

"I'm thinking we should sign up for *taiqi*. That'll get us over here and when we need to, we can spin off and go to the apartment."

"That's a good idea," Bruce agreed. "How about this? We could also just get into a running routine and make this one of our routes. We could easily run by here two, three times a week."

"I like it. So we'll get a pattern going. That'll also give us plenty of opportunities to monitor our surveillance status and check out patterns of activity around here."

"Yeah. Not a bad plan."

"One other thing that has me second-guessing myself is that we don't have a clue who lives in that building. I mean, the PSB has this apartment available for Li's guys when they come down here for language brush-up. Does that mean they have other people living in the building too? That would not be a good thing."

"This is the hand we've been dealt," Bruce offered.

"I just hope it doesn't turn into a goat rope."

"When do you want to pick up the cache?"

"Let's get a couple of days under our belt here. Get that pattern going. From the site description, headquarters estimates the cache could stay down there for months, so there's no pressure to retrieve it right away."

"You want to aim for Wednesday or Thursday?"

"That's what I'm thinking. Just the three of us. I don't think we need Alicia for this."

They were back at the apartment. "Time to hit the books," Logan said.

Bruce groaned. "I forgot how hard this is. We've probably got at least four more hours of studying to do."

Chapter 36

"Logan's made contact with Li." Frank Sisler turned from the message he was reading to look at Ellen Sanders.

The two of them had been going over Lois Caldwell's most recent situation report, revealing new details from the Pan Chengong operation. She had identified a series of communications between Pan's office and Taixun, the Chinese Internet company that had leased the target property in Ashburn.

Lois had also made the connection between one of the IP addresses used in those communications, and another that had been probing the computer network at DCSA Marine Systems, where the luckless Jerry Morrison had essentially unlocked the vault and invited the Chinese in.

Ellen perked up. "I was just reading it before I came in."

Frank looked over the document on his computer. "Seems as though Li is on board, although he was initially hesitant to commit. There's been some blowback on the Wheeler operation over there. MPS has been nosing around, investigating the Cyber hacking units to see if they can suss out where the penetration is."

"Imagine if Wheeler had made it to China. Who knows what they could've gotten out of him." Ellen looked grim.

"Logan says that he trained Li on his covert communications software. He tasked him to send a test message when he got back home. We should be seeing that pretty soon."

"Once he's up and running, it'll cut down on the need for as many face-to-face meetings."

"I agree."

Just then, Clarence, the IT technician who supported their special access programs, poked his head in the door.

"Just got these in for you," he said. He handed Frank an envelope and continued down the hall.

Frank pulled out two sheets of paper. The first was Li's test message, and the second laid out his proposals for storing the Mianyang team's cache. Frank handed the two sheets to Ellen and stroked his chin as she read them.

She had a frown on her face when she looked up. "I don't think much of his plan to use the family friend's apartment. We don't know the first thing about him. It could expose the whole operation." She leapt up from her seat and began pacing around.

"My read is that was Logan's reaction too. The other idea has its own risks, but I like it a lot better.

"Logan and Bruce went over to the apartment yesterday and checked it out. Logan's cautiously optimistic that it will work, but he admits that they run the risk of being spotted coming and going. Apparently it's not one of the foreign student apartments.

"They've already started building a pattern that will take them into the neighborhood several times a week."

"I saw that. Running routes by there and taking a martial arts class that meets nearby. I like it. I think it's the best we can hope for." Ellen handed the paperwork back to her boss. "You think they're ready to retrieve the cache?"

"They said they want to do it sometime this week."

"Good."

"Getting back to Lois's situation report, what do you make of Taixun advancing its move-in date?"

Lois looked thoughtful. "They're coming off of a successful IPO in the U.S. and this gives them a chance to showcase the company to their new shareholders. But I don't think it's just about that.

"We know from the Bureau's technical op that Pan's group is interested in the fiber optic trunk line that runs through there. What's not clear is if Taixun is just providing cover for Pan to do his thing or is an integral part of their doomsday scenario."

"Let's get an update from Des on the Bureau's tech op."

"I'm already there," Ellen said. "I asked Des for a read-out late last week. He said the landlord was being very helpful. He's giving them unrestricted access to the place. It's wired."

"Do you ever wonder if the Ashburn part of this is just a smokescreen?"

"How so?"

"That whole operation just didn't strike me as the 'A' Team in action. They came in here, bumbled around, and left clues all over the place. Maybe they want us to think Ashburn is where it's all going down. Meanwhile they're off doing something else."

"That's not substantiated by the exchange we see taking place between Taixun and Pan's lab. And there's no way they can suspect that we're reading their communications."

"Really?" Frank looked skeptical.

"What? Li?" Ellen's hand went up to her mouth. "You don't think...?"

"I'm just saying. We need to keep an open mind. Not fall in love with our agent." Ellen nodded in agreement.

"I want to send a note to Logan highlighting the impor-tance of a thoughtful and rigorous testing regimen for Li. We take nothing on face value. We should incorporate a test in everything we task him to do."

"He's going to think we're micro-managing him."

"We're just doing our jobs. Look, Logan's good. There's no doubt about it. How many first-tour case officers have the President reading their reporting? But let's not forget, he's a first-tour officer. He may be in his thirties, have war zone tours and command experience, but he's still a junior operations officer.

"Changing subjects. Was Lois going to stop by?" Frank was hoping to talk to the computer whiz about her report.

"She called in. Director Mitchell asked her to accompa-ny him to a cyber security briefing he's giving on the Hill."

"Is it just the FBI going?"

"I think so. I checked with our Office of Congressional Affairs. No one from the Seventh Floor is scheduled to be on the Hill this morning."

Frank looked worried. "I hope Lois knows not to get into anything having to do with covert action. Only the leadership is read in."

"Give her some credit, Frank. She's smart. She knows where to draw the line."

"Yeah, but it can be intimidating for someone who's not used to being in the hot seat."

"I think she's just back-benching him. She's not doing the briefing."

Frank nodded. "Let's talk to her when she gets in."

* * *

Des Magarity sat in the austere Justice Department offices and looked around. He'd been invited to attend a meeting between the lawyers for the defense and the D.A.'s office in Rick Wheeler's espionage case.

He'd been to hundreds of these meetings before. A windowless, cheerless conference room, filled with lawyers, not one of whom was pulling in less than six figures a year, and that was just the government lawyers. Clerks wheeled creaky carts crammed with file folders into the room and distributed them.

There was some commotion outside and Des was startled to see Rick Wheeler enter the room. Rick was wearing an orange jump suit. The dull look in his eyes gave way to recognition and then pleading as he walked past Des and took a seat at the table. He turned to look back at his one-time boss, but Des's stony stare was the only greeting he received.

Des hadn't realized that Rick was going to be at the meeting. From the murmuring going on around the table he deduced that he wasn't the only one surprised by Rick's unexpected appearance.

It turned out that Rick's attorneys had convinced their client to cooperate with the prosecution. Key in his conversion was the prosecution's promise not to seek the death penalty or go after his wife's pension benefits in exchange for his full cooperation. The government had already determined that Marge was an innocent victim in this affair. Despite her husband's perfidy they had no interest in adding to her woes by denying her money she needed now and would continue to need in the years ahead.

It must have come as a relief, too, to know that as part of the plea deal, his lawyers had secured the government's pledge not to seek the death penalty. He might never see the outside of prison again, but at least he wasn't going to fry, Des thought.

The meeting stretched long into the afternoon as Rick recounted his years of spying for China. It became apparent early on that there was no ideological basis for his treachery. It was simply a matter of greed. In the years since his recruitment, the Chinese had paid him $200K. Not chump change for sure, but, considering the price Rick was going to pay, it hardly seemed worth it.

There would be days if not months of debriefings to learn what the disgraced FBI agent had divulged. CIA was already doing an all-out damage assessment because he had been exposed to all but their most sensitive operations. Fortunately Rick wasn't privy to the true names of CIA's sensitive assets or clandestine field operators.

He could have given them the names of headquarters personnel that he knew, like Frank and Ellen, but they weren't working undercover in the field anymore, so that would be of marginal concern to Langley.

Des had always pooh-poohed the Agency's preoccupation with the use of pseudonyms and aliases to conceal the identities of its clandestine operatives, but he had to hand it to them. They were looking pretty smart now, from where he sat.

The prosecution moved to adjourn for the day. It was five o'clock and Des, for one, had a raging headache. He called his secretary to let her know that he wouldn't be back in.

The afternoon rush was on. He was going to avoid the Beltway and take back roads to Springfield, where the lure of a frothy cold one took his mind off the day's mind-numbing revelations. An hour later he was pulling into the parking lot of the Emerald Lounge.

The bar was just beginning to get busy. Moe slipped a cold brew into Des's hand and pushed a bowl of mixed nuts in his direction. Des hitched up his pants and draped one leg over the barstool as he surveyed the crowd. He almost knocked over his beer when he recognized Marge Wheeler seated on a stool at the end of the bar. He hadn't talked to Marge since Rick's arrest. She was sitting by herself and from the look of it had been there the better part of the afternoon.

Des was getting ready to go over and say hello when he noticed a florid-faced man eyeing Marge from the other side of the bar. Just then he made his move, sidling up to her. Des was sitting close enough to hear their conversation and decided to remain put.

"Hey, little lady, mind if I join you?" Before Marge could respond he turned to Moe.

"I'll take a vodka, straight up, and whatever the lady's having."

Moe turned toward Des with a questioning look as he poured the two drinks. Marge wasn't a regular, but she had been in with Rick often enough that Moe recognized her.

"Been in here all afternoon," he said out of the side of his mouth. "Shame about Rick."

Des grunted. "Yeah." He kept an eye on the action at the other end of the bar. Marge hadn't noticed him. She was belting down mai tais almost as fast as Moe could mix them. After about an hour of this Des could tell that the red-faced Romeo was getting ready to move in for the kill.

"Sweetheart, what do you say you and me blow this joint, and get something to eat?"

Marge stood up, swaying slightly. She gripped the bar to steady herself. "Sure," she slurred her words. The man grasped her arm and began to steer her towards the door.

Des sighed. He stood up and barred their way.

"Hey. What's this?" The man pulled up just short of Des and stuck out his jaw.

"Why don't you just let the lady go?" Des spoke in an undertone.

"You're kidding me, right?" He sneered. "I been buying the lady drinks all afternoon, and now you want to waltz in and take her away?" He moved as if to go around the burly lawman.

Des's voice finally registered with Marge. She gazed at him and without warning, burst into tears.

"Now see what you done?" the man growled. "You got her all upset. Get out of my way, or—"

"Or what?"

The man seemed unsure of himself. "Or else I'm calling the police!"

Des pulled out his credential and waved it in front of the man's face. "I am the police, scumbag. Now get the hell out of here."

He released Marge's arm and slunk away.

Des turned his attention back to Marge. She was swaying on her feet, and he thought she was going to fall. He caught her in his arms. She was limp and reeked of alcohol. She was in no condition to drive.

"Let's get you out of here, Marge. Moe, I'll send someone for her car later.

Marge slumped against him as he guided her through the door and out to his car. He held her with one arm as he wrestled with the lock and managed to swing her inside and get her buckled in.

His kids and ex-wives would get a laugh out of this, he thought. He didn't have a rep for being the caring type.

The Wheelers didn't have any family in the area that he could call. He made the decision to take her back to his place. He had a spare room where she could sleep it off.

Thirty minutes later he was home. It was well past the dinner hour and traffic had been light. He had some difficulty getting Marge up the stairs and into his apartment.

She was out cold. He pulled off her coat and shoes and slid her out of her dress. He found a pajama top and struggled to get her into it.

He rested for a moment on the side of the bed, looking down at her. Even in her disheveled, drunken state she was an attractive woman. Red-haired with impish blue eyes, she was always turning heads. Des sighed as he pulled up the covers and turned out the light. She had a tough road ahead of her.

It was three a.m. when his bedroom door creaked open. He reached for his weapon but recognized the shadowy figure of Marge. She was whimpering.

"Can you just hold me, Des?" She sniffled.

He threw back the covers. "Come on," was all he said.

She slid in next to him and buried her face in his chest, sniveling until she fell into a fitful slumber. Des eased his arm under her head, cradling her in an awkward embrace, until he too fell into an uneasy sleep. Morning would be soon enough to talk about the man who had betrayed them both.

Chapter 37

It was late Saturday afternoon. Logan, Bruce and Norm had been on the move under the pretext of sightseeing since mid-morning. They had joined Alicia for lunch at a hole-in-the-wall restaurant in town that specialized in fried dumplings.

After they'd eaten, Alicia went off on her own to explore a silk fabric market in Mianyang proper, and the men continued with their sightseeing, spending the afternoon visiting two Buddhist temples, an ancient city gate and an architecturally significant bridge spanning the Fujiang River.

Late in the day, as the sky began to darken, Logan estimated that they were less than five miles from the cache site. They had been paralleling the river for over an hour, keeping it to their east as they walked north. This area was fairly rural. It was six-thirty, and as day turned to dusk, their senses sharpened. They could hear the hum of vehicles on the G-5 National Highway to their west.

Before they'd left the city, the men had visited a hardware store, different from the one Logan and Bruce had frequented on their first trip to Mianyang, where they purchased two entrenching tools and a couple of flashlights. Logan knew from the site description that the cache was buried three feet below ground.

The Agency doesn't use caches much these days. This resupply method is a relic from WWII, when the OSS cached materiel for resistance fighters in Europe. Some of those caches were immense, large enough to stockpile weapons and ammunition, even a tank in one operation in France! Conventional wisdom nowadays is that it makes little sense to put sensitive materials into a hole in the ground over which you exercise no control, and pray that it will go undetected until the intended recipient digs it up.

Although they had been walking for eight hours, the men were feeling energized by the prospect of retrieving the cache. That would put them one step closer to achieving their mission – putting an end to Pan Chengong's Zero Day intentions.

"We must be about there," Norm said.

Their eyes had adjusted to the dark. They also had the good fortune of a cloudless sky to help light their way. Logan was searching for the landmark that would guide them into the cache site. It was a distinctive rock formation two hundred meters west of where the G-5 crossed the river.

"There," he said pointing to the left. Rising up out of the ground was a massive karst limestone formation. The cache was buried at the north end of their landmark. The instructions directed them to pace off twenty steps north of the formation and ten steps west. The cache would be three feet down.

"That should do it." Logan said, as he stepped off the measurements. He took one of the entrenching tools out of his backpack and began to dig. Bruce did the same, and soon all that could be heard was the methodic movement of earth and the occasional grunt under the strain of digging.

After thirty minutes they still had not located their supplies. "We're definitely down three feet," Logan grumbled. "Where the hell is this thing?" He stopped to wipe his face and take a sip of water.

"Could be the person who originally paced it off was a shorty," Norm offered.

The three of them were all over six feet tall. "Okay, I'll buy that," Logan said. Let's modify the pace to simulate a shorter person, and see what we come up with."

Norm measured off the distance, using an adjusted pace. It put them three feet from the hole they'd already dug. He took the entrenching tool from Logan and began to dig. Ten minutes later a loud thud told them that they were in the right place.

Logan gave Norm some relief and began to widen the hole. Thirty minutes later they were able reach in and pull out two large sea bags. They opened them up and began transferring the contents into the backpacks they had brought for this purpose.

"What do you want to do with these?" Norm pointed to the empty bags.

"Bury 'em. They're too bulky to haul out. I'm not worried about anyone stumbling on them out here. They should disintegrate over time." The men tossed the bags back into the hole and covered them. Afterwards they did their best to restore the site to its original appearance.

"Now comes the tricky part." Logan shouldered his pack. It wasn't too heavy — maybe forty pounds. "I estimate we're two and a half hours out from the university. That should put us in around ten, ten-thirty at the latest. It's going to be key to get in and out of the apartment without attracting attention."

"We've got a pretty good sense of the traffic patterns around there. It's normally pretty dead after ten, but this is the weekend so we could be dealing with a whole different dynamic." Bruce hefted his pack and adjusted the straps. "Damn. Feels like the good old days."

"Oh yeah," Norm joined in as he eased his pack onto his back. "I've been missing this," he chuckled.

The three men set out in a southwesterly direction. The night was quiet as they trekked through the countryside. They cut a wide swath around several settlements in their path, to avoid the curious eyes of locals. Best to be careful and avoid unwanted attention. An occasional dog picked up their scent and howled a warning. A door to a nearby farmhouse opened and a man came outside and stared into the darkness. They stopped moving and watched him as he scanned his yard. He scratched his head, said something to the dog and went back into the house. They breathed a sigh of relief.

As they got closer to the university district, traffic began to pick up. There were farm vehicles on the way into town with produce for the Sunday farmer's market, and an occasional long-distance transport rumbled by. But for the most part, there were few of what could be classified as "private vehicles."

In the last decade private car ownership in China had skyrocketed, escalating from a handful to over 154 million privately owned cars nationwide. Predictably, most of these were in major cities like Beijing, Shanghai, Chengdu and Tianjin, but Mianyang had its fair share too.

Municipal governments, concerned about overcrowding and pollution from exhaust, were making it impractical for the average person to own a car though. Registration fees of $10,000 were not all that uncommon, and parking charges in urban areas often exceeded ten dollars an hour.

Just as Logan had projected, by ten p.m. they were on the outskirts of the university. He signaled the route they were going to take to Li's apartment. They began walking in that direction, remaining alert for any threats.

A half-dozen Chinese students walked by them, but they did not acknowledge the three Americans. They were too busy discussing a foreign film they had just seen. Logan picked up the pace. He didn't want to invite attention by moving too fast, but he was eager to stow the backpacks.

They approached the student apartment building from the rear. There were lights shining in many of the upper floor rooms, but there was no sign of life as they slipped in the rear door and down the stairs to the basement. Logan breathed a sigh of relief as they reached the door to the apartment. They'd made it inside without being seen. He punched in the door code and the three men slipped inside.

There was a light on in the small study. Funny. He remembered that he and Bruce had turned the lights off when they'd inspected the place earlier in the week.

He heard the scraping of a chair against the floor and the hairs stood up on the back of his neck. Damn! He motioned to Norm and Bruce, but it was too late. They were already inside and the door was closed. It must be Li.

"Hello...?"

Li came out of the study. He had a puzzled look on his face.

"Logan? Who are these men?" He nodded in the direction of Bruce and Norm.

"Two friends. Bruce and Norm. They're with me." The men took off their backpacks and shook hands with Li.

"I didn't know you were going to be in Mianyang." Logan tried not to let the trace of anger he was feeling creep into his tone. He had hoped to avoid exposing Bruce and Norm to the PSB officer. Well, Logan sighed to himself, if anything were to happen to him there wouldn't be any scrambling around trying to turn Li over to a new case officer. These would be familiar faces.

"I sent you a message before I left Chongqing. Didn't you get it?"

"No, we've been out since this morning. What's going on?"

"Commissioner Fang got word from Beijing that the leadership wants to escalate the date of the Zero Day attack. Pan has come to the conclusion that with the penetration of Blue Waters, there will never be a better time. It's set to begin next week."

Logan cursed. This was moving way faster than he had expected. What was behind Beijing's decision? Maybe it had something to do with the Wheeler operation. If the Chinese felt that Rick was on to their operation, they could be concerned that he would buckle under interrogation and expose their plans. That didn't make any sense, though. Wheeler had been a Chinese asset. He was working for the MPS. What were the chances they had given him tasking related to the Zero Day attack?

"What's your role going to be?"

"That's what I'm here to find out. Pan is going to brief the scenario tomorrow morning. I suspect we will be conducting a unified hacking exercise on the target date."

"Will your men be working here, in Mianyang?"

"It's not necessary. We have the capability of conducting our part of the attack in Chongqing."

"Will you have time to meet with me after your briefing?"

"Yes. We're meeting at eight-thirty. I doubt that it will go for more than an hour, maybe two. I have to catch an early afternoon train back to Chongqing, but that should leave enough time."

Li seemed to notice the three backpacks for the first time. "So this is why you needed the apartment?" He gestured towards the gear on the floor.

"Yes," Logan replied. He explained that he had sourced everything to China and Russia, and that no one happening upon the equipment would be able to figure out that there was a U.S. connection.

Li nodded. "The likelihood of anyone coming in here is nil," he commented. "But, if someone were to discover it, there is no good reason for me to have this equipment stored here."

"I've been thinking of a cover story," Logan offered. "You said that you have your men coming to Mianyang for intensive language refreshers. How about the idea that you have this gear here so that they can keep their skills sharp? For training. They must have some free time after class, and this gives them something constructive to do."

"It might work," Li replied. "It wouldn't stand up under intense scrutiny, but for anything less than that, it just might.

"How do you intend to implement your counter-attack?" Li asked.

Logan knew that he was going to have to get back into Pan's lab one more time. A computer scientist at Langley had developed a technique using a complex algorithm that essentially created a boomerang effect, directing the attack back at its originator and a new target set. Logan knew that he could ask Li to load the software onto Pan's system, but headquarters wanted absolute assurance that it had been done. For this they needed Logan to be there in person. He could imagine the shock that would rocket through the ranks when the perpetrators realized that their attack had turned against them.

"I need to get back into Pan's lab," he replied. "I have to access his computer one more time." He didn't fully understand why the software couldn't be loaded remotely. The Trojan he'd installed on Pan's computer had gone undetected and Langley was reading everything it mailed home as though they were sitting right next door.

"You must be careful, Logan." Li's face was tense. With the attack just days away, Pan's people may be working around the clock."

"Try to find out what they'll be doing. Don't ask too many questions though. You don't want to draw attention to yourself," Logan warned.

The men talked for a few more minutes and then said goodbye. Li was planning to spend the night at the apartment. Logan and the others headed back to their own lodging.

The first thing Logan did when he got in was to check his email; the message from Li was there as well as a lengthy message from Frank Sisler. Headquarters had seen Li's message and already knew about the Cyber hackers' plan to move up the date of the Zero Day attack. They dropped another bombshell.

"Pan's lab isn't the only game in town," Frank wrote. "This became more clear to us, particularly after you were able to place the Trojan on his network. Since then, Lois Caldwell has developed information about an important telecommunications node in Szechuan that functions much like the Ashburn node does in the U.S.

"What's interesting about this is that, historically, it mirrors a tactic China's leaders employed in the late 1930s when they were trying to protect key infrastructure from the Japanese. They moved over five hundred private factories to western China to avoid Japanese destruction. China is hiding part of its key IT infrastructure inside a mountain.

"Our target is located midway between Mianyang and Chengdu near a city called Deyang. Deyang's geographic coordinates are 31.1333 degrees north by 104.4000 degrees east. The target is an IT node that services communications nationwide. It is located in a rural area called Yinghua Mountain.

"After Lois pinpointed this location, we went back and did a historical search of imagery and found clear evidence that a major construction effort was underway there in the early 2000s. It showed that for over two years there was significant earth moving and delivery of materiel into the area. We believe that the node is located inside Yinghua Mountain. Your mission is to penetrate that node just before Pan launches his Zero Day attack."

Logan got up from his computer and paced around the room. This was an unforeseen development. Getting into Pan's lab with the help of an inside asset was one thing, but penetrating a sensitive IT node in the middle of nowhere took the challenge to a whole new level. The look on his face was determined. Whatever the cost, his team would get this done.

Chapter 38

Logan spent Sunday morning working on his Chinese. Later he took a walk over to the library and began looking for information on Deyang and its environs. If the team was being tasked to target an IT node near Deyang, in all likelihood their best bet for getting close, without arousing attention, would be to pose as tourists, or businessmen. Deyang isn't a large city by Chinese standards, with a population of just over four million. Its major enterprise is the China National Heavy Machine Corporation. The company has a significant presence in Deyang, Chengdu and Zhenjiang. With their extensive shipbuilding and heavy machine building capabilities, they would be a logical contact for Alexander Maritime.

From Deyang it would be a short thirty-five-minute drive to Shifan City, which would be their jumping off point for Mount Yinghua. This county-level municipality borders the Himalayan Plateau and is the closest city to Hongbai Town, which is the gateway to Mount Yinghua.

In his reading, Logan had discovered that the likely explanation for the placement of a major IT node in this far-flung outpost was the fact that Hongbai Town had been destroyed in the 2008 Wenchuan earthquake. This natural disaster had flattened the surrounding area and killed tens of thousands of residents. By 2010, money from Beijing had begun to pour into the region, and the rest was history.

As incongruous as it seemed, the juxtaposition of the latest communications technology in this backwater was a stroke of genius. No one, except perhaps the CIA, would come here looking for serious IT infrastructure to mess with.

He set those thoughts aside as he left the library and walked over to Li's apartment. They had agreed to meet there at eleven o'clock so that Li could bring him up to date on the details of Pan's briefing. Li was not there when he arrived, and since he needed to inventory the contents of the cache anyway, Logan set to work doing that while he waited for him to return from his meeting.

He was still stewing over the fact that Bruce and Norm had been unnecessarily exposed to Li the night before. It probably wasn't that big a deal in the big picture, but headquarters would read all kinds of sinister motives on the part of the Chinese asset, into why he had shown up in Mianyang unannounced.

Logan had checked out Li's story when he got back to the apartment the night before. True to his word, he had sent an encrypted message advising that he had been summoned to Mianyang for consultations, so it wasn't as though he had tried to spring a surprise visit on him.

The other thing headquarters wouldn't care for was the fact that Li had unfettered access to the cache materials. Cost of doing business, Logan thought to himself. It's not as though Langley had the resources needed to pull off an operation this complex in a place so far removed from its allies. This was the longest logistical tail he'd ever had to grapple with.

He tensed as he heard someone at the door, but it was only Li. He took off his coat and tossed it onto a chair, taking note of the equipment strewn out on the floor, but did not ask Logan any questions.

Li lit a cigarette and then sat down on one of the other chairs at the table in the kitchenette. He looked thoughtful but took his time before saying anything. Logan knew that he was concerned about the Zero Day attack, especially the damage that he perceived would visit U.S. financial institutions, once the cyber hackers harnessed the computing power of Blue Waters and unleashed it on them.

What he didn't know was that the U.S. had already taken countermeasures designed to thwart the Chinese attack. After Li had briefed Logan on China's Blue Waters compromise, the response from headquarters had been swift. An intergovernmental cyber security task force had been formed to counter the threat. Not only had they been working around the clock to remove the Trojan from the supercomputers, they had crafted a defense that mirrored the Trojan attack in such a way that anyone monitoring it would believe that the Trojan was functioning as intended. In reality, the Blue Waters component of the attack had already been neutralized.

"It's set to begin November 27th."

"Thanksgiving? That only leaves us four days!"

"Yes. The thinking is that there will be fewer people on hand to deal with the attack because they will be caught up in the Thanksgiving holiday. Ceremonies, parades, travel. That sort of thing. Also, there is some concern that the MPS spy captured by the U.S. may have known about the attack. If he talks it could derail the entire operation.

"The offensive will begin as a multi-pronged denial of service attack against dozens of major U.S. financial institutions. Initially we believe this will go undetected because most of these businesses will be closed for the holiday, and it will not be apparent that there is a large-scale disruption of service attack underway. This element of surprise is important because the longer it goes undetected, the more pervasive the assault," Li said.

"Once the financial institutions realize that they are under attack, we anticipate that emergency measures will come into play and a high percentage of financial communications will be rerouted through the Ashburn node. If the U.S. thinks it will be able to point the finger at China by investigating the activities of our Internet company there, Taixun, they will be disappointed."

"Why's that? I thought Taixun was some kind of intelligence collection platform instrumental to the operation."

"Initially we used them that way. We were simply trying to determine to what extent the financial institutions rely upon the Ashburn node as a conduit for their communications. Once we established that data point, Taixun reverted to its actual commercial role. Everything it does now is within the scope of U.S. law.

"But getting back to the plan. At the same time we are attacking the financial sector, a large-scale cyber espionage effort will commence against the U.S. Cyber Command, the Department of Defense, and defense-related civilian organizations. While it may be that some useful intelligence will come out of this effort, our main purpose is to create a diversion. The idea is to keep those people so preoccupied with their own internal affairs, that they will be unable to devote resources to help thwart the financial sector attacks."

"Who's going to handle that part of the operation?" Logan asked.

"My unit," Li replied. He paused for a moment and then continued. "When news of the attacks hits the press, China, if pressed, of course will deny any complicity. It will be virtually impossible for the U.S. to pin any of this on China. By the end of the second day, we anticipate that U.S. markets will be in complete chaos.

"China, as a respected member of the keystone international economic organizations, will call for calm, and at the same time will begin making representations to its allies in the World Bank, the International Monetary Fund, and the General Agreement on Tariffs and Trade."

"Does China really believe that our allies are going to abandon us because of this?"

"The idea is to present a safer alternative. We'll point to new institutions such as China's Asian Infrastructure Investment Bank as more secure alternatives to traditional U.S. financial organizations. We'll lobby U.S. allies, whose allegiance to the dollar may be waning in the face of financial risk in the U.S.

"It might not happen overnight, but the goal of this operation is to undermine confidence in the U.S. economy and raise concerns over present day international monetary policy. China wants to weaken the dollar so people will begin to question its suitability as the world's reserve currency."

"But that's crazy," Logan responded.

"Maybe, if your perspective is a post-World War II western orientation. For decades U.S. hegemony has been the norm in international affairs. But in recent years, the rising powers have begun to question the status quo. China, India, Brazil, Russia, South Africa. They all want to take their rightful places in the world."

"What do you think, Li?"

"Me? Personally? The U.S. has been the dominant player for decades. There's no question about it. It's the only superpower left in the world. But China thinks in terms of millennia, not decades. China has over three thousand years of history. And the U.S.? Less than three hundred!

"Long ago China understood the virtues of patience and determination. There's an ancient proverb about an old peasant who lived on one side of the mountain but worked his fields on the other side. He and his sons spent hours going back and forth every day. One day the old man convinced his sons that they could save time by removing the mountain. This meant that they would have to dig it up. All of his neighbors laughed at him and said that it couldn't be done. He replied that they might not accomplish it in his lifetime, or perhaps even the lifetime of his sons. But eventually, with patience and determination, his family would be able to remove this impediment from their lives."

Logan looked thoughtful as he digested what Li had just said. He knew it was true that China tended to take the long view while the West tended more towards instant gratification.

"So, what do you need me to do, Logan?"

"I have to get back into Pan's lab. I'd rather handle it myself so that you're not implicated if anything goes wrong. Do you know if the security situation there is the same?"

"As far as I know."

"How about the work schedule?"

"They're following a regular schedule for now, but once the attack begins on the 27th the lab should be manned twenty-four hours a day."

"Any chance that they'll want to use this apartment?"

"No. It didn't come up. Pan's people don't have access to it. He has all the resources he needs. You can feel comfortable storing your things here."

"One more thing." Logan reached into one of the bags and extracted a thumb drive. He double-checked to make sure that he had the right one. "Can you load this onto your work system in Chengdu? It will make it possible for me to follow the attack from your end."

Li took the thumb drive and studied it before slipping it into his pocket. "You're certain that this won't be detected on our network?"

"Trust me."

Li looked at his watch and jumped up. "It's already twelve-thirty. I have a two-thirty train to catch. I should be going." He paused before continuing, unaware that he was clenching his fists. "Next time we meet, I want to talk to you about going to the U.S."

Logan had been expecting this conversation for some time. "I've been giving it a lot of thought ever since you brought it up," he replied. "One thing is that I don't think you should plan to leave right after this operation is over."

Li's expression was one of complete shock. "Why's that?"

"Assuming we're successful, we don't want the authorities here to jump to any conclusions about their failed operation and link it to your disappearance. We may want to wait six months, maybe a year."

The look on Li's face betrayed his feelings. "So long?" he asked.

"We'll talk about it. But don't do anything to jeopardize your position. We want to keep all of our options on the table."

Li nodded, put on his coat, and then slipped out of the apartment. Logan finished inventorying the contents of the cache and waited an additional fifteen minutes to make certain that Li had cleared the area. As he walked by the laundry room on his way out of the basement he noticed a couple of students washing clothes. They had their backs to him, and did not observe him as he hurried past, up the stairwell, and out the back door.

The rest of that day flew by. Logan crafted a draft plan and ran it by headquarters for their approval. There had been some revisions in the back and forth of messages but by Tuesday for the most part, his initial plan remained intact.

It called for the four of them to take a road trip to Deyang on Wednesday, where they would meet with representatives from the China National Heavy Machine Corporation, to discuss their machine building capabilities. The representative from their international division had been intrigued by Logan's call, and had readily agreed to set up meetings for them.

That would give them a good reason for being in Deyang and would give them easy access to the scenic area known as Mount Yinghua, where the IT node was located. They would reconnoiter the area on Wednesday evening, and if things went as planned, they would infiltrate the facility housing the IT node late Wednesday night or early Thursday morning.

They would be renting a mid-size SUV from Ace Car rentals to handle their transportation needs. Logan had found a good deal online that included unlimited mileage. Headquarters had also reached out to a long-term vetted asset who arranged to leave a panel truck in an alley not far from their hotel with the keys hidden in the undercarriage, no questions asked. They had a twenty-four-hour window in which to pick up and return the vehicle. This would give them better cover than using the SUV, which, if used, could tie them directly to events in Hongbai.

Logan had also spoken with Ms. Wang at the language school about their field trip because they would be missing a day of classes. She had been supportive, particularly when Logan pointed out that they would be meeting the corporate representatives in a Chinese language setting. "Good practice for all of you," she had smiled. She admonished them to practice Chinese on the drive to and from Deyang.

On Wednesday, Logan picked up their rental car at the Ace downtown lot in Mianyang. They loaded their gear into the cargo space without incident and set out on the highway just before ten a.m. Their destination was only an hour south on the G-5. Traffic was light until they hit the outskirts of Deyang, where it was reduced to a crawl. It took them almost as long as the drive from Mianyang to reach their hotel.

They had reservations at the Deyang Hotel, on Changjiang West Road, in the heart of the business district. The plan was for Alicia to remain in her room with their gear, while Logan, Norm and Bruce met with the company's International Division representatives. Their meeting was scheduled for two o'clock at their headquarters building on Zhujiang West Road, about a five-minute drive from the hotel.

The meeting and tour of the plant lasted for three hours. It was good for their cover and Logan found that there might even be legitimate business that he could do with them. Their shipbuilding operations were based at the Zhenjiang facility in Jiangsu Province, and he made a note to follow up with the shipbuilding team there on his next trip in December.

They begged off an invitation to dinner from their hosts, explaining that a colleague at the hotel was not feeling well and they wanted to check in on her. They promised to take a rain check and provided their contact information in Hong Kong in the event they had plans to visit.

The team returned to their hotel, where they remained until nine-thirty p.m. The business district was quiet at this hour, and they attracted little attention as they slipped out of a side entrance and walked ten minutes to the alley where the panel truck was parked.

Bruce initially had trouble locating the keys to the vehicle, but as he probed around the undercarriage, his hand made contact with the magnetized metal box where they were hidden. They breathed easier and began loading the truck with their gear.

When they were done, Logan and Norm climbed into the front seats and Alicia and Bruce slid into the back of the truck with their equipment. Logan navigated the truck west towards Shifan City. It was dark and there was little traffic on the highway. During the day it would be a very different scene. From there, tourist buses bound for Hongbai Town would deposit throngs of sightseers destined for scenic Mount Yinghua, where they would meander through temples built centuries ago and search the mountainsides for a glimpse of the elusive giant pandas and snub-nosed golden monkeys that inhabit this part of Szechuan.

The night sky was cloudy, with temperatures hovering just above freezing. The mountain range stood out, even in the dark, like some gigantic dragon curled up in deep slumber. Just before they reached Hongbai, Logan turned off-road and steered the truck to a forested area he had identified from satellite imagery. He pulled into the trees to conceal the vehicle and shut off the engine. "Game time," he said.

Chapter 39

Des put down the phone and massaged his temples. He had just spoken with Marge Wheeler, who had called to tell him that she'd put her house on the market and was leaving town before Christmas. It had been a couple of weeks since he'd rescued her from the clutches of that slimy stalker at Moe's. It was November 26th.

The morning after, she'd stumbled out of the bedroom and into his kitchen. He was putting a pot of coffee on when she trudged over to the kitchen counter and sat down. At first she wouldn't look at him, and her chin trembled as she struggled to control her emotions.

"I'm sorry about last night, Des." She searched his face with a plaintive look. "I just couldn't handle it anymore. With all the news, reporters, friends. Not knowing what's going to happen." She folded her arms across her chest and shivered as she fought back tears.

Des slid a bottle of aspirin and a glass of water across the counter and then reached for a coffee mug. He gave her an understanding look before responding.

"It's all right. No one should have to deal with this. I'm plenty mad at the guy and we just worked together. I can't imagine what you must be going through." He knew that she wouldn't have heard the news about Rick's plea deal, and even though the details hadn't been released yet, he decided to tell her, hoping it would help alleviate some of the pain from an otherwise dismal future.

"I was at DOJ yesterday. Rick decided to play ball with the prosecutor. You'll get to keep his pension and the government says it won't seek the death penalty in exchange for his cooperation."

She nearly collapsed from her perch on the kitchen stool. She was breathing in short little gasps as she came to grips with what he had just told her. Finally her breathing slowed and she let out a sigh of relief. "Jesus," was all she said.

"What are you going to do?" He poured her a cup of coffee and nudged a carton of half-and-half and a sugar bowl in her direction.

"I don't know." She stirred some cream into the cup, and cradled it in her hands before taking a tentative sip. "Maybe I'll just sell the house and move back to Dayton. My sister lives there."

A look of panic crossed her face. "Oh my God. The kids!" She spilled her coffee as she jumped up, but Des nudged her back onto the stool.

"They're at the neighbors'," he explained. "I called last night and asked if they could sleep over. Mrs. Prentice said she'd get them off to school this morning."

"You're the best, Des." She shuffled over to the other side of the counter and gave him a hug, holding him tight. She leaned back and searched his face. "I better get going. Damn!" She slapped her forehead.

"What?"

"My car."

He dangled the keys in front of her. "One of the boys dropped it off this morning. It's out front." She hugged him again and accepted the keys.

"You want to clean up?"

"No. Thanks. I have to go. I need to call the school. My boss is going to be upset that I didn't call in."

After she'd left, he'd showered and dressed for work. While he was getting ready he'd replayed the scene from his meeting at DOJ. Wheeler had been a productive asset for the Chinese. There was no doubt about that.

Des knew they'd only begun to scratch the surface in that session. Months, maybe even years of debriefings would take place, not only so the government could build its case against his former deputy, but so that there would be a definitive record of the security breaches and a better understanding of the compromises and risks to ongoing operations.

One thing Des marveled at was that Rick had withheld Ji's name from his MPS handlers. He had remained adamant throughout the debriefing that the MPS didn't know anything about Ji's cooperation with the FBI. Too bad for Ji and his wife, given the fact that there was no way back home for them. They'd already burned their bridges. On the flip side, there were worse things than being under the protective custody of the U.S. government and taking early retirement in some out of the way locale beyond China's reach.

Rick claimed to have been vague about specific intelligence operations and assets that he was privy to. He'd been more cavalier with information on the Bureau's surveillance capabilities, its cyber defenses, and the names and positions of colleagues across the government. That latter bit hadn't been as damaging as one might imagine, but it had helped the Chinese fill in the blanks on U.S. intelligence community staffing.

Des got up from his desk and wandered down the hall, still thinking about Marge and Rick. As he passed Lois Caldwell's empty office, he refocused on the Chinese hacking operation. She'd briefed him two days ago, and he knew that things were coming to a head. November 27. Tomorrow. That's when China was scheduled to launch its Zero Day attack, according to CIA's source. Lois was spending most of her time at Langley these days. When this thing went down, she'd be living there.

Back in his office he asked his secretary to call Jim Baylow's successor, Harry Applegate. He wanted the lash-up between DHS and the Bureau to be seamless in the days ahead. Plans had been in place for weeks to staff a joint situation room in the NCCIC'S Computer Emergency Readiness Team's spaces. When this thing went viral, he wanted to be on top of it.

* * *

Lois Caldwell pondered Logan's most recent report of his meeting with Phoenix. She was fully read into the operation now and saw all of the intelligence and operational reporting that the young case officer wrote as it pertained to the cyber threat. She assumed he managed other cases dealing with issues other than cyber threats that did not concern her. She liked him. He had the ability to drill down to the most essential elements of a debriefing and present the information in succinct, factual prose.

Everyone had been surprised by Phoenix's revelation that China was moving up the date of its Zero Day attack. There had been no indication from any other sources that the operation was being fast tracked. But then, she had come to realize that the Agency was thin on Chinese sources who were in a position to speak authoritatively on this subject. SIGINT reporting had been quiet as well.

Phoenix was far and away the most impressive source the Agency had in this area. Even their technical operation against Pan's lab had been disappointingly sparse on critical details about the operation. The Chinese were disciplined when it came to their handling of sensitive information. A careful survey of files on Pan's network revealed little that pertained specifically to the attack. There were personnel files, and libraries with theoretical papers on a wide range of cyber security topics, but virtually nothing that tied into this operation.

"How's it going?" Lois looked up to see the sharp features of Frank Sisler. He walked into her office and sat down, coffee cup in hand. She had never met anyone else who consumed as much coffee as Frank did.

"I'm starting to feel better about this," she said.

"What's making you so upbeat?" he asked.

"For one thing, getting Blue Waters back under control was huge. When I analyzed the way Pan designed this attack, it's clear that he was counting on the super-computers to accelerate the denial of service and take it to a whole different level. They'll figure out soon enough that something backfired, but by then it'll be too late.

"The other thing is that if Logan and his crew are successful in neutralizing that IT node, Pan and his crowd will be so busy trying to figure out what hit them that they'll be overwhelmed."

"What's to keep China from coming back at us in six months with something else? Our power grid; another run at our banking networks; transportation nodes. The list of critical infrastructure goes on and on." Frank looked skeptical.

"We need the equivalent of a cyber Strategic Arms Treaty, START, with the Chinese. Something like what we had for nuclear weapons with the Soviet Union during the Cold War." Frank stabbed a finger in the air to punctuate his point.

"The problem with that is, with START, you could verify how many nuclear weapons were out there. But how do you do that with computers? Nuclear weapons not only are quantifiable, but you know who has them."

"At least we used to," Frank muttered.

"With computers it's different. You can't always assume that because an attack is sophisticated, it's state-sponsored. There are some very smart, malicious, lone wolves out there who enjoy nothing more than screwing with the system.

"And what's to stop the Chinese from contracting with these loners to do their dirty work? We know they're doing it already. If they're disciplined it's very hard to establish linkages that will help us track them down and take action against them, legal or lethal."

"We have to push for stronger national cyber security legislation." Ellen Sanders strolled into the room. She had paused outside Lois's office and had caught the tail end of their discussion.

"Somehow the government has to convince the private sector that we're capable of protecting their information. If we can't, we'll never get their buy-in and in six months we'll be right back to where we are today."

"I don't think we should underestimate how determined some CEOs have been in response to the cyber threat. If you're one of the major banks or a defense contractor working on proprietary programs for the government, you've seen this threat up close and personal," Frank said. "These people may not want to cooperate with the government, because they don't want us sticking our noses into their business, but they're not just sitting on the sidelines waiting to get whacked.

"They're setting up their own cyber security departments and hiring smart computer geeks to police their networks."

"That's true," Lois agreed. "Des and I go out and talk to CEOs all the time and we see this kind of push-back. I remember one time we were pitching this to a group of CEOs from high-tech companies. We started by offering to share classified information that we had with them in exchange for their cooperation, and they just laughed at us.

"I tell them that their Internet security is only as good as their weakest link. It all comes down to individual employees exercising good judgment. Look at that case in Syracuse," Lois pointed out.

"DCAS?" Ellen had done some name traces for Lois to see if there were any hits on the defense contractor in CIA's databases.

Lois nodded her head. "Who knows what the Chinese stole from them, all because an employee crossed the line and essentially gave those hackers a license to steal?" The three of them sat there in glum silence for a moment until Frank broke the quiet.

"Changing the subject, I want to review our game plan for tomorrow. We don't have a specific kick-off time, but we know from Phoenix that Pan's launching his attack on the 27th."

"Tomorrow," Lois murmured.

"Tomorrow, Beijing time," Ellen clarified.

"Right. We're ready to go. We've been running three shifts since last week, basically monitoring our networks, reviewing intelligence reporting from the field, and liaising with our partners at NSA, the Bureau, Homeland Security, the National Science Foundation and the U.S. Cyber Command.

"We've briefed the NSC and the Congressional leadership too, every week since we ramped up the task force."

"How about the private sector?"

"Des was in New York last week to meet with the CEOs of over sixty major banks and financial institutions. Without getting into the specifics of the attack, he advised them that one was coming and that this would be a good time to review their network security protocols."

"That all sounds good on the defensive side. How do you feel about the offensive measures we have in place?" Frank drained his cup and set it down on the desk.

"We've spent the last month trying to get inside of Pan's head. I think I understand where he's coming from and, more importantly, his capabilities. What we've put together will be a proportional response to what he throws at us. That is, everything except for what Logan's team is doing. If everything goes right for them, they are going to do some serious damage."

"How deep do you think their Cyber capabilities extend? I mean, if this plays out the way we anticipate, are they just going to fold up their tents and go home, or are they going to come back at us twice as hard?"

Lois pondered Frank's question. "I don't think they have that many visionaries. People like Pan, with his unique skill set. But they can muster an army of hackers who can be quite disruptive, as we've seen in the past."

"I think the question is whether or not they'll have the political will to stay in the fight," Ellen interjected. "At some point the price is going to be too high. With the President's Executive Order on Cyber Security and Presidential Policy Directive on Critical Infrastructure Security, he now has the power to take this fight to anyone threatening our critical infrastructure like no other President before him."

"You mean military action?" Lois asked.

"Yes," Ellen replied. "Although I don't think we're on very firm ground going down that path."

"How so?" Frank questioned her.

"No one would argue the point that a sovereign nation has the right, no, the duty to protect its critical infrastructure against attack. But we're on shaky ground because we're just as guilty as the Chinese when it comes to computer exploitation operations. Don't get me wrong. I think it's a critical tool in our intelligence-gathering arsenal. But it does leave us exposed."

"It's kind of ironic that the President now has all these powers to go after cyber threats but probably won't use them because to do so would invite ridicule from the Chinese. They've started pushing back whenever the White House talks about Chinese hacking."

"It's really no different from any other form of espionage," Frank said as he stood up and headed out the door. He paused and looked back at the two women. "Everybody's doing it, and everybody knows that everybody's doing it. The thing is not to get caught."

Chapter 40

Before they began unloading, Logan issued instructions to the team. "From this point on we'll keep it quiet. Try to use hand signals. We're not that far from town, and it's a good bet that sound will carry out here."

They opened the rear doors and began pulling their gear out of the truck, lining it up on the forest floor. It was quiet, except for the gurgle of rushing water from a nearby waterfall, and the stirring of wildlife foraging in the woods. They worked in silence with practiced competence. Alicia had never served in the military and didn't share the men's special ops expertise. But she had gone through the CIA's paramilitary operations course, designed to help CIA officers without military backgrounds better support troops deployed to war zones.

Logan had pinpointed the location of their target. It was about three miles from where they'd parked. He knew from intelligence that the IT node had been built into the mountain and was accessed via a secure entrance on the fringes of Hongbai Town.

In keeping with their operational mandate to conceal the U.S. hand, they began pulling on the disguises they'd be using for the rest of the night. These included Russian-made clothing, masks, Russian-manufactured weapons (Yarygin-made Grach semi-automatic pistols) and additional props that would support their identities as Russian technicians.

Besides their disguises they were carrying alias identification showing them to be employees of the Moscow-based high-tech firm, Yantronics. None of them was carrying U.S. documentation. Aside from their Russian IDs, they bore pocket litter to support their cover legends.

A bar tab from POD Moskovye, a library card from the Russian State Library, a receipt for an electronics purchase at the Gorbushka Market, and a chit for dry cleaning from Laundry No. 25 on Vavilova Street. These props might help them bluff their way through an unexpected encounter with a local citizen, but for all practical purposes, would be useless in a confrontation with police or a military patrol.

The initial plan of attack was to determine the accessibility of the facility from its main entrance. Despite weeks of planning, intelligence on security measures they might encounter, had been thin. Historical imagery had shown security vehicles at the installation while it was under construction, but in recent years none had been observed there. Several satellite images from the previous week had depicted half a dozen civilian vehicles parked in front of the entrance during the day. Headquarters had been reluctant to fill in the gaps by tasking Li to provide information on the target, preferring to compartment the operation from him.

When everyone was dressed, Logan gave the signal to move out. "We'll parallel the road, but stay in the trees. We don't want to draw any unnecessary attention if anyone's in the area," he whispered. It must be freezing, he thought. His lungs complained as he inhaled the frigid air. His breathing was even as they began walking, producing little white puffs that hung there for a moment before surrendering to the frosty night.

They tramped single file just inside the trees. There were mostly spruce and Chinese white pines along here. The sweet-scented fragrance was pleasant, and for Logan, evoked memories of hiking into the Vermont woods with his father and brother at Christmas time in search of the perfect Christmas tree.

Forty-five minutes later the woods began to thin and they found themselves on the outskirts of Hongbai Town. Logan squinted in the dark to check the time. It was eleven-thirty p.m. There were some lights up ahead, casting shadows that played with the imagination. At this hour the town was dead, locked up tight. Lucky for them, the nearest police station was in Shifan City. Hongbai had such a small population, it didn't even merit a sub-station.

A hundred yards ahead, Logan could see the outline of a chain link fence that secured the way into their target. Access to the facility was via a sliding metal gate that opened onto a concrete pad in the shape and size of a basketball court. There were three civilian vehicles parked inside the enclosure, to the left of the entrance.

Inside the fence, where it butted up against the mountainside, there was a heavy-duty metal door that was flush with the rock. It was painted a dull gray and was windowless.

They moved to within thirty feet of the gate. As they crouched down in the dark, masking their faces, Logan surveyed the scene before him. He was puzzled by the fact that for such an important IT node, there was no obvious security.

Bruce must have been reading his mind. He edged over to where Logan crouched. "What gives? I thought there'd be cameras, guards or something."

"There weren't any visible on the imagery we looked at. I doubt they're expecting any trouble way out here. It looks pretty laid back. And remember, it's not a military installation.

"I wish we had a better idea who's inside." He tilted his head towards the parked vehicles.

The sputtering of an approaching car broke the silence. The team ducked into the shadows, pressing to the ground to reduce their profile. Logan eyed the vehicle as it approached. It was a Russian Lada that had seen better days. It coughed and misfired as the driver climbed out to open the gate. It was hard to guess his age because he was bundled up in a bulky down coat and wore a scarf that covered his mouth and nose. By the way he was moving though, Logan estimated that he was middle-aged and in reasonably good shape.

The man got back into the car and drove it through the gate, parking next to the other vehicle inside. As he was getting out of his vehicle, Logan nodded to Norm. The former Navy SEAL from Burnt Cabins, Pennsylvania, leapt into action. Crouching low he sprinted through the gate and was on top of the driver before he realized what had hit him. He struggled briefly, but was subdued without putting up much of a fight. He stared in disbelief as Logan joined them. Norm slid plastic restraints on his wrists, hands behind his back.

Logan had decided to position Bruce and Alicia outside where they could radio in an early warning if anyone else showed up. These radio units had been field-tested in New Mexico and had the capability of penetrating through all that rock.

He was also thinking ahead to the morning when the day shift discovered their colleagues, tied up inside. When the police arrived to investigate, they would get descriptions for two Chinese-speaking Russian males traveling on foot. By then, if everything went according to plan, the four of them would be having breakfast back at the university in their true name identities.

"Who are you?" their captive stuttered. "What do you want?"

"Just do what we tell you, and you won't get hurt." Logan jabbed his 9-mm into the man's stomach. He shrank back, his eyes wide with fright.

"How many people are inside?"

"Three. I make four."

"Is anyone else coming?"

The man hesitated, shifting from one foot to the other. "No. Not until morning."

"What time?"

"Seven."

"What time is your shift supposed to start?"

"Eleven p.m."

"What happened? It's already midnight."

Their captive nodded towards his car. "I couldn't get it started. It doesn't like the cold weather."

"Is there any security inside?"

"The man looked confused. "Security? No. Just technicians." He licked his lips and looked back and forth at the two men.

Logan decided to move. They were exposed standing in the parking lot and the sooner they got off the "X" the better off they'd be. "Let's go." He nudged the man again.

"How do you get in?"

"There's a keypad on the door."

"What's the number?"

The man hesitated and Logan made a menacing gesture with the gun.

"27-86-19," he mumbled.

"Where are the others?"

"They'll be doing their routine maintenance schedule. Checking the equipment, backing up the servers."

Logan nodded. He reached into his backpack and pulled out a roll of duct tape. He tore off a strip, and before their terrified hostage could protest, pulled it taut across his mouth. He struggled, trying to squirm away from them but settled down when Logan jabbed the pistol into his ribs.

"All you have to do is relax. Keep quiet and nothing will happen to you." He pulled the man to his feet and pushed him towards the entrance. He stumbled but then regained his footing and plodded across the expanse of concrete. He hesitated in front of the door.

Logan punched in the code to the lock. What happened in the next thirty seconds was critical to the success or failure of the operation. There was one way in and one way out. He didn't want to think about what would happen if anyone managed to sound an alarm.

He pushed open the door and shoved their captive inside. He and Norm crouched down low and swept their weapons right and left. A security guard was standing beside a table pouring tea into a cup. His head jerked up and a confused look crossed his face before he reached for his weapon.

"Hands up," Logan ordered. But the watchman continued fumbling for his gun. Logan shot him and he slumped to the floor.

Just beyond him another man scrambled away, sprinting down a corridor towards a telephone on the wall.

"Stop," Norm shouted, but the man reached for the phone. Norm took aim and dropped him with a single shot to the head. He slammed into the concrete, blood spattering on the wall behind him. As his legs gave out, he collapsed onto his side on the floor.

They swept through the center, clearing server rooms, offices with desks and workstations, and a workshop piled high with technical gear, spare parts, and tools. There was also a break room, a small kitchen and a lounge with half a dozen cots.

They found the third employee cowering behind a rack of servers. He trembled in fear as they yanked him to his feet and searched his pockets. They found a few personal belongings, but nothing of interest. There was no phone in this room, and the man didn't have a cell phone on him.

"Did you call anyone?" Logan shoved his pistol in the man's face. He stuttered as he spoke.

"No."

"Don't lie to me. Did you?" He waved the pistol.

"No." He began to sob. "Don't kill me. My wife and daughter need me."

"Tie him up," he instructed Norm. He was pretty confident that the man was telling him the truth, although that bastard from the parking lot had sandbagged them by lying about security. What else might he have lied about?

They shoved their sniveling captive into the lounge area and lashed him to a cot. Logan put duct tape across his mouth, covered his eyes, and stuck earplugs into his ears. Deprived of his senses, he would not be able to communicate with his co-worker after they left, which might make it harder for the police to corroborate their recollection of events.

They moved back to the hallway, double-checking the technician Norm had shot. He was dead. They hurried back into the entryway to check on their other prisoner. He was sitting where they had secured him. His eyes were fixed on the dead security guard. He looked guardedly at Norm and Logan when they entered the room.

"Why'd you lie about security?" Logan asked. The man couldn't answer, even if he wanted to, because his mouth was taped shut. For good measure, Logan placed plugs in his ears and covered his eyes.

They had a lot to do in the next six hours. When they were done with this place the Chinese would have to gut it and start all over. Before the night was over they had to take out the IT node, hike back through the woods to their escape vehicle, dispose of any incriminating evidence, resume their true name personas, dump the panel truck, check out of the Deyang, and make the drive back to Mianyang. Just in time for Zero Day.

They began to unpack the equipment from their backpacks. The idea for destroying this place had come from Lois Caldwell. It wouldn't devastate China's national cyber infrastructure, but the losses here might make them think twice about the wisdom of their offensive cyber program. They were smart enough to figure out that this was just a warning shot over their bow.

When they were assembled, the two weapons looked like something out of a Sci-Fi movie set, but gave no hint of their true destructive power. Lois had purchased the basic units from a company in Rochester. Working with physicists at the Department of Energy, and two weapons scientists from Los Alamos, they had modified the basic design to include a one-hundred-kilovolt DC power supply tied into a series of stackable capacitors that would produce a high current discharge. The elevated output from these two devices would take out everything electronic in their path.

Logan had practiced assembling and disassembling the weapon blindfolded for hours. As he was checking them one last time, he noticed that one of the capacitor stacks had come apart, breaking the connection to the power supply.

"Damn!" he muttered.

"What?" Norm looked up from what he was doing.

"This capacitor's screwed up."

Norm came over to examine it. His eyes lit up. "If they've got a soldering iron back in that workshop, I think I can fix it."

"See what you can do. I'll get started with this one." Norm hurried off to the workshop with the defective weapon.

Logan secured their radios inside an improvised Faraday cage, an EMP cover bag made out of thin polyester film that would shield their radios from the electromagnetic pulse.

After he had placed the bag near the entrance, he lifted the weapon off the floor and moved into the server room. The EMP device was basically a radio frequency weapon that could operate on either a narrow or broad bandwidth. When engaged it emitted an electromagnetic pulse traveling at the speed of light. The result was that any electronics within its range would be fried. This particular weapon had an effective range of twenty feet.

Logan began working his way through the server room, rack by rack, destroying hundreds of thousands of dollars worth of computer equipment in the process. There must have been fifty racks holding ten servers each. Norm joined him fifteen minutes later and they continued their path of destruction around the room. When they finished there, they moved to the next server room.

It took them two hours to finish the job. Given the hour, Logan doubted that their activity had set off any alarms, but he didn't want to hang around to find out. He and Norm disassembled the EMP devices and repacked their bags. They checked on the two prisoners, who were still lying where they had left them.

They let themselves out and hurried across the concrete slab, their footsteps echoing in the still night. Bruce and Alicia were waiting in the shadows.

"How'd it go?" Bruce asked.

Norm gave him a thumbs-up. "Mission accomplished," he said. "Two casualties."

Alicia's eyes widened. "What happened?"

"There was one security type who went for his gun when we came through the door, and one of the technicians tried to get to a phone," Logan explained. He shrugged. "It was us or them. Anything out here?"

"No. It's been quiet."

"All right. Let's move out."

They retraced their steps back to the panel truck. They were going to bury their equipment in the woods. Norm and Bruce pulled two shovels out of the back of the truck and went fifty feet into the woods, where they began digging. They worked silently for twenty minutes, widening a hole that would hold the equipment.

While they were working, Logan and Alicia took stock of everything they were leaving behind. They wanted to make certain there were no tell-tale clues that could lead back to the U.S. if the cache was ever found.

Satisfied with their inspection, they hauled the gear over to the hole and began tossing it inside. Minutes later everything was buried and the ground raked over with pine needles so that there was no sign of any disturbance. They raked their way back to the truck, and Norm and Alicia smoothed over the truck tracks, following behind Logan as he backed out of the clearing to the road.

It was five o'clock when they dropped off the panel truck at the agreed location in Deyang. They slipped back into the hotel, cleaned up and by six a.m. were on the road to Mianyang.

Chapter 41

Li awoke at dawn on November 27. He didn't know precisely what time Pan planned to initiate his attack against the financial networks. There was a window between eight and ten a.m. in which his own team was to launch its assault on the U.S. Cyber Command and DoD.

Normally an operation of this magnitude would get a lot of attention, but with Pan's operation taking primacy, the Chongqing component was little more than a sideshow, a diversion at most.

He'd installed the software that Logan had given him on his office network, and then gone back in to see if he could detect the malware on the system. It had taken him over two hours to find it, in spite of the fact that he already knew that it was there. He'd employed his best proprietary malware scanners to search directories, database logs, operating system logs, and firewalls, but had come up empty-handed.

It was only a matter of luck that he'd discovered the malicious application hidden inside the PSB logo. The image was on everybody's start-up screen. "Very impressive," he admitted. It was the first time he had seen polymorphic malware concealed within an image used in this way.

He checked in on Xiao Jun before leaving for work. He had an early *taiqi* class and was already up and getting ready for school. Li credited *taiqi* with giving him back his son. Of course Xiao Jun continued to have occasional bad days. After all, it had been less than two months since Xiao Mei's suicide. But the mental and physical discipline of the sport had helped him deal with the loss. He'd also been spending more time with his aunt, whose affection had helped ease his pain.

"What are you working on today?"

"Flying Wild Goose."

"Ah." Li faced his son, extending his arms so that his palms faced up. He then crouched low, bringing his arms down to his side. Inhaling, he rose onto the balls of his feet, while lifting his arms above his head. Breathing out, he lowered his arms back down to his side. The effect was not unlike a goose flapping its wings in flight.

"Maybe we could practice together sometime," Li said. "It's been awhile since I've worked out."

Xiao Jun looked skeptical. "If you say so, *Ba*," he joked. "I have to get going." He grabbed his school bag and headed for the door.

"All right. Don't forget, you're eating dinner at Auntie's tonight. I may be late so don't wait for me."

"OK. Bye." He left the room and Li followed him out ten minutes later.

Li made his usual breakfast stop, opting for a fried bread stick and a bowl of hot soybean milk. He gulped his food down. He didn't want to be late but he knew he would need the energy for the long hours ahead.

By the time he got to his office, Sergeant Shi had just finished preparing his reading board. As a senior PSB officer, Li had daily access to a wide range of reporting. As he rifled through it, he recognized a number of finished reports, because the raw intelligence had come from his office.

The most interesting piece was a SIGINT intercept from the Royal Thai Police, urging the government to lobby Beijing for greater security cooperation. Their analysts had figured out that Beijing was attempting to drive a wedge between Thailand and the U.S. and concluded that Bangkok could leverage this desire to get more security assistance from China.

Just then his deputy hurried into his office, a worried look on his face. "Sir, you'll want to see this." He handed Li a report. As he read it his mouth dropped open in surprise.

"When did this come in?"

"Just now. I brought it in as soon as we received it."

It was an initial report from the Public Security Bureau branch office in Shifan City about an incident at the IT node in Hongbai. Two employees had been killed; the security guard and one of the technicians. Two others had been roughed up and discovered when the morning shift arrived for work. They were shaken by the attack but had been able to describe the attackers as two foreign males, probably Russian.

"Is this all we know?" Li looked up from the report, his face grim.

"I spoke briefly with the operations center in Chengdu. They had just finished talking with the PSB commander in Shifan. It's a bad time for the system to be down since Chengdu depends on it for backup if their primary comms go down.

"The two men who were killed were shot, probably with a 9-mm weapon. Their bodies have been taken to the morgue for autopsy. The facility itself was clean, although they did find a receipt from a bar in Moscow crumpled up next to one of the corpses, which supports the idea that the Russians could be behind it."

"But why would the Russians do this? It doesn't make any sense."

"It's a good question. The entire system is down. There's no obvious damage to any of the equipment, but the operators haven't been able to bring it back up. Technicians from Chengdu are heading out there as we speak."

"Is our office involved?"

"Two of our technicians in Chengdu are standing by to assist if they ask for help."

"Keep me posted if you hear anything new. I'm assuming we're still scheduled to initiate our attack on the Americans per our orders. We should also stand by to offer assistance if we're needed in Hongbai."

"Yes, sir."

Li folded his hands and rested them under his chin. He massaged his jaw as he thought it through. His body trembled as a chill ran down his spine. Logan. And one of the other two men he'd met? Could they be behind this?

The order to initiate the attack on the U.S. Cyber Command came down at nine-thirty a.m. Li pushed the incident in Hongbai to the back of his mind as he ordered his hackers together for one last briefing.

As he gathered his thoughts, Li recalled when the U.S. Secretary of Defense had announced the creation of the Cyber Command, which was to be located at Fort Meade, home to the National Security Agency.

Li had always been amused by the amount of information the U.S. Government shared about its most secretive organizations. Cyber Command's Office of Public Affairs had dutifully issued a press release after the command was formed in 2009, and Beijing's military attaché in Washington had faithfully forwarded it home.

The announcement was emblazoned with Cyber Command's blue and gold seal. An eagle in attack mode was perched on a shield bearing crossed swords, a lightning bolt, and a key, against the backdrop of a revolving globe etched with interconnected lines of communication.

He and his colleagues had looked for meaning in the new symbol. The eagle stood for vigilance and the swords showed that the Americans planned not only to defend the nation but also conduct offensive attacks against their adversaries, as necessary. These would be expedited with the knowledge that Cyber Command's mission was to protect the nation's cyber infrastructure.

The young men in the conference room were becoming restless. Li began speaking. "In a few minutes we will begin our attack against Cyber Command. We will be successful, not only because you are the best at what you do, but, because the Americans are consumed with command and control, and jurisdictional battles that make it impossible for them to respond effectively in real time to what we're doing.

"We have a long day ahead of us. Superintendent Bai and I will be here if you need us. Let's begin."

The operation commenced at precisely nine-forty-eight a.m., the middle of the night in Washington, D.C. Li felt a stab of guilt as he ordered four of the men to initiate the attack, using command and control servers to direct thousands of slave computers infected weeks before with malware that took advantage of vulnerabilities in their operating systems. Li would have liked nothing more than to sabotage the attack against Cyber Command. He was not divided over where his loyalties now lay. But if he appeared reluctant to hurt the Americans in any way, it could alert his bosses or subordinates that something was amiss. He had to press forward.

"Sir, we're beginning to see a response."

Li looked up. He wasn't surprised. Beijing's military attaché in Washington had attended this year's Intelligence Threat Assessment briefing for Congress. The briefing is open to the public and is where America's top Intelligence officials provide Congress with an assessment of the threats facing the nation. He had reported that as a response to the rash of cyber attacks they had been seeing, Cyber Command was beefing up its offensive cyber capabilities and planned to establish more than a dozen teams of cyber experts who would be able to retaliate against a foreign cyber attack.

"How are they responding?" He really didn't know what to expect. Although his hackers had been launching cyber attacks against the U.S. for several years, the nature of this attack was more severe. And then there was the example of the U.S. response to North Korea's cyber attack against the entertainment giant, Sony Pictures in 2015.

It had begun with condemnation, but quickly escalated to a directed denial-of-service attack on Pyongyang's Internet, shutting them down completely for several days. If the U.S. was prepared to abandon diplomacy for cyber retaliation, no one knew where it might eventually lead. This was uncharted territory.

And, to further complicate matters, there was no reason to believe that the U.S. response would be limited to an official U.S. government response. Even the private sector was getting in on the act. They were busy setting up offensive cyber capabilities and itching to get into the fight.

"It's looking defensive for the most part. We're seeing

them take down affected unclassified networks, but it's still early. Wait. They've just initiated a malware analysis procedure, and it looks as though they're beginning to do some deep packet inspection activity."

"All right. Keep me updated."

One hidden asset that no one in the building was aware of, except for him, was an MPS source working as a civilian in the logistics center supporting the U.S. Army Cyber Command. He had been there for less than a year, recruited during a hiring blitz, when the military had put out a call to hire civilians.

He had not been activated to date. But it was possible that he might get pulled into this operation. The MPS had recruited this source because they recognized that one of the weakest links in cyber security is the supply chain. With globalization, everything from software and hardware procurement to the parts and services the government uses to maintain its networks is at risk of being compromised.

Li rubbed his hands together. They suddenly felt cold. "Sergeant Shi. Bring me a cup of tea."

"Yes, sir."

It was going to be a long day.

Chapter 42

Des Magarity had arrived at NCCIC at eleven p.m. Thanksgiving eve. He'd checked in after receiving a call from DHS's Operations Center, advising that the Computer Emergency Readiness Team was reporting a major attack against U.S. Cyber Command. They were also beginning to receive initial indications that the Zero Day attack was underway.

Des was on his third cup of coffee. He needed something to calm his stomach. The acid from the caffeine was giving him heartburn. He looked around the room and concluded that there was nothing to eat.

"How's it going at Cyber Command?" he asked one of the specialists glued to a computer screen.

"So far it doesn't look like anything out of the ordinary. Typical Chinese hack. Pretty intense DDoS." He didn't look at Des as he spoke, but kept his eyes fixed on the screen in front of him.

"Any word from Langley?"

"Oh, I forgot. Agent Caldwell called on the secure line about five minutes ago. She asked you to call her back as soon as possible."

Des walked over to an empty desk and dialed Lois's number at Langley. "Hey, Lois. Des here. What's up?"

"Hi. I think I've figured out what Pan's after."

Des could tell by the edge in her voice that she was pumped up. "Our financial networks, right?"

"No. I think that's just been a smokescreen all along."

"What?" Des's voice registered his surprise. "What makes you say that?"

"I've been trying to figure Pan out since day one. He

understands the security protocols in all these different sectors we worry about. One thing he knows is that the financial sector has probably spent more money on cyber security than anyone else outside of the government. While they've gotten some bad press, all in all they do a pretty good job of protecting their networks. I think he's after a softer target."

"If not the financial sector, then what?" Des asked.

"I think Pan's going after our power grid."

"Our power grid?"

Lois sound excited. "Yep. I've been in touch with one of his professors from Stanford," she explained. "We know from our earlier investigation that Pan did research on network protocols when he was there. But one of the things they didn't mention at the time was that he did a study of California's Energy Commission. In many ways, California's like a lot of the rest of the country; it has a patchwork of private sector and public utilities. It's a perfect target."

"Go on."

"They've got a half-dozen investor-owned utilities, forty-six-some public utilities, a bunch of electric service providers, rural electric cooperatives and Native American utilities. It's complicated. And there's no standard security protocol when it comes to their network. That makes them defenseless to an attack.

"Anyway, there's been a lot of theorizing that the U.S. power grid is vulnerable to cyber terrorism. There are doomsday scenarios out there that have the lights going out all over the country, essentially destroying our economy and way of life in one fell swoop."

"Is that even possible? Sounds farfetched."

"Not entirely. Industry and security experts did a study earlier this month that spelled out the impact of a cyber attack on the energy sector. They concluded that there would be disruption of service, and damage to equipment that would be costly to replace. The outcome could be significant, but it's unlikely such an attack could be mounted nationwide."

"How do you see this playing out? Can't we stop this guy?"

"I think I figured out why we haven't seen anything coming out of Pan's lab over the last couple of months. He's been keeping it under the radar, because that's where the attack is coming from. He's probably using machines that aren't tied into his network."

"How do you know?"

"Partially from data we got when we mapped their network. I'm ninety percent sure this is what he's doing."

Just then, one of the NCCIC analysts observed that he was beginning to see widespread power outages in Los Angeles and San Francisco. "There haven't been any storms or other severe weather indications that this could be attributed to," he observed, checking the weather channel feed.

"We have to stop Pan," Lois cried. "I've got to go, Des."

"All right. Thanks for the update." Des hung up and immediately dialed the number for the Los Angeles Field Office.

"Harry? Des Magarity in D.C. We gotta talk."

***

At Langley, Lois got off the phone and turned to Frank Sisler. "Can Logan get back into Pan's lab?"

"The team should be back in Mianyang. What are you thinking?"

"We should be able to stop this attack, using the tools we installed on their network, but I'm afraid Pan has something else up his sleeve. This first phase, causing power outages in LA and San Francisco, is possible because Pan got into the computers that control the cities' distribution systems."

"Are we sure this is Pan?" Frank asked.

"No doubt about it," she replied.

"All right. Tell me what we need to do."

Chapter 43

The drive back to Mianyang had been uneventful. Logan was still pumped from the evening's activities. He needed to get a message to Langley, detailing how the operation had gone down, and then grab some shut-eye.

He was surprised to see a message from Frank Sisler in his incoming mailbox when he opened his secure email account. As he read through the email, he was stunned by Lois Caldwell's analysis of Pan's Zero Day attack. Phoenix hadn't reported anything about an attack on the nation's power grid. Had he misled them on purpose, or was he out of the loop too?

Just then he noticed that a message from Phoenix had appeared in his email queue. It was marked urgent. "ATTACKING U.S. CYBER COMMAND, NOW. PAN ATTACKING U.S. POWER GRID, NOT BANKING SECTOR. I CANNOT LEAVE HERE." Phoenix must be transmitting from his office in Chongqing. That was risky.

He re-read Frank's message with growing concern. According to Lois, Pan was definitely going after the power grid. She didn't think he had the ability to take out power nationwide, but he could do some damage locally. Frank explained that they were already experiencing power outages in Los Angeles and San Francisco. As he finished reading Frank's message, a plan was already beginning to take shape in his mind. He went looking for Bruce and Norm.

They met near their apartment. Logan outlined Frank's message and told them what he had in mind.

"We're just going to walk in there?" Norm asked.

"Pretty much. Even though Phoenix reported that the lab would be manned 24/7 once the attack commenced, I'm banking on everybody being out to lunch. We just need fifteen, twenty minutes."

"What makes headquarters think this will work?" Bruce asked. "We see the Chinese shut down hacking operations and pop up somewhere else all the time."

"I think it's just as much about sending the Chinese a message as it is putting an end to this attack."

"What do we do if anyone's in the lab?" Norm gave Logan a knowing look.

"Too bad for them for being over-achievers," Logan replied with a steely look. "No one can know that we're behind this. If anyone's in the lab, they're dead."

Chinese treat meal times with a certain amount of reverence. To miss a hot meal is unheard of. Most workers like to eat lunch by eleven-thirty, because they tend to eat breakfast early. They never eat at their desks. With any luck Pan's entire crew would be at lunch when they went in. Given the importance of the Zero Day attack, it was also possible that they'd be working around the clock, so they needed to be prepared for that.

Norm and Bruce nodded. They split up to procure what they needed and agreed to meet back at the apartment in an hour.

It was just after eleven when the three men turned onto Qinglong Avenue in the direction of Pan's lab. When they reached the building, they skirted the west wall until the reached the rear of the building. The coast was clear and they covered the ground to the entrance without being seen.

They were surprised to find the outer door unlocked. It had taken Wellington several minutes to jimmy it open on their first trip. They must leave it open during working hours, Logan figured.

The men let themselves into the building and crept up the stairway to the fourth floor. Just as Logan had predicted, there was no one around. They paused outside the lab and listened for voices inside to be sure. It was quiet. Bruce went to work on the door with practiced ease. This time they were inside in two minutes.

The lab was empty. One look around told them that Lois Caldwell's hunch was spot on. The lab was set up like a war room. There was a map of California mounted on one wall with pushpins in select urban areas. There were a dozen laptops strewn around the room and a television monitor tuned to CNN. Extension cords and power strips were strewn haphazardly around the room.

"Our job just got a little easier," Norm said. He pointed to a space heater in the middle of the room. "These things are notorious for starting fires."

Norm had been exploring the lab, and came back into the main room. "They've got great computer gear but no smoke detectors or fire alarms."

"That should work to our advantage. But our biggest challenge is getting this thing to burn hot enough to destroy the lab before help shows up," Logan pointed out.

They began by shorting out wall outlets in the server room and Pan's office. The outlets had surge protectors with several pieces of equipment plugged into them. There was a crackling sound and sparks began to arc. Soon the walls began to smolder and the plastic plugs began to melt.

As they began working on the space heater, Logan heard a sound at the door. The three men moved to the wall behind the entrance and remained motionless, as it swung open.

A man stepped inside and as the door swung shut, Logan recognized Pan. He looked just as he had in the FBI video coverage of the Taixun technical operation in Ashburn. He was alone.

Pan sniffed the air and a look of panic crossed his face. It turned to confusion as Logan stepped into view and confronted him.

"Who are you? What are you doing here?" He looked anxiously back and forth as Norm and Bruce stepped away from the wall.

"It doesn't matter who we are, Mr. Pan. What matters is that we know who you are and what you're up to." Logan gestured towards the wall map and computers.

Pan sniffed the air again. "What's that burning?"

"We got cold and started a little fire to get warm," Bruce said.

Pan jerked away from them and sprinted for the door. Logan tackled the computer scientist before he could get there. Pan struggled, attempting to kick his attacker. Logan got him into a chokehold and the man began thrashing around as his air supply was cut off. His eyes began to bulge, and he tore at Logan's clothing. Logan kept the pressure on for several minutes, even after Pan went limp. If Pan's body survived the fire, he wanted it to look as though he had died from asphyxiation.

While Logan dealt with Pan, Bruce plugged the space heater into an extension cord and positioned it close to a couch along one wall. Moments later the fabric began to smolder and burst into flames.

Logan took Pan's pulse. He was dead. Logan rose from the floor and with Norm's help, picked the body up and tossed it onto the sofa. Anyone trying to figure out what had happened would conclude that Pan had taken a nap after lunch and fell asleep with the space heater running.

The fire was beginning to spread, the crackle of furniture catching fire. There was a whooshing sound as a file cabinet ignited and files began to burn. Electrical circuits began to sizzle and the random wiring from all the extension cords and surge protectors was beginning to melt.

"We better get out of here," Logan said. "The others could be coming back from lunch any minute. Besides, all hell's going to break loose if anyone spots this place burning."

The three men slipped out of the lab and hurried towards their escape. As they reached the landing, they could hear voices and the shuffle of feet as several people ascended the stairs. They ducked into a doorway and pressed against the wall as half a dozen people continued past the fourth floor, and up the flight of stairs to the fifth.

After the last person was out of sight the three men resumed their dash down the stairs. Reaching the ground floor they heard some people coming into the building from the front entrance. They rushed out the rear entrance across the parking lot and into the trees.

"We need to go someplace where we can be seen," Logan said. "We can still grab some lunch and hopefully that will give us an alibi if anyone starts asking questions." They slowed the pace and walked to the foreign students' cafeteria. Alicia was still at lunch, talking to a couple of Australian students. She gave them a knowing look.

"How was your run?" she asked, sticking with their cover story.

"Nice," Norm replied. "I'm starving. Anything good to eat?"

"The dumplings aren't bad. You can get them fried or steamed."

After the men had been served, they relaxed for the first time in two days. There was a commotion near the exit and people began running outside to see what was going on. Logan had a pretty good idea what it was, but joined the crowd outside. In the distance he could see smoke billowing from the building housing Pan's lab. Soon the sound of sirens filled the air and people began running towards the fire. Logan and the others joined them.

When he got closer Logan could see flames and smoke pouring out of the fourth floor. Three fire trucks had pulled up and were running fire hoses down the street to a fire hydrant. There was no water pressure from that hydrant, and with each passing minute the intensity of the blaze grew. The floors above and below Pan's lab were now on fire, and people could be seen running from the burning building. It took the fire department another fifteen minutes to find a working hydrant. Meanwhile two firemen had accessed the basement, presumably to cut the power off and coordinate the evacuation of the building.

"Not looking too good for Mr. Pan and his boys," Bruce whispered out of the side of his mouth. They hung around with the rest of the crowd for another thirty minutes and then went back to the cafeteria.

After eating, Logan returned to his student apartment and worked on a situation report for Langley. He advised them that Pan had been killed in their raid on the lab and expressed confidence that a blow had been dealt to the Zero Day attack. When he had completed his report, he hit the send button, shut down his computer and slept for the next ten hours.

Logan decided to keep the team in Mianyang until the 30th, their planned date of departure. He didn't want to do anything on the heels of the attacks on the IT node and Pan's lab that would make university officials or authorities question them.

There was press coverage of the two incidents, but they were not being linked in any way in the news. Damage to the university computer center housing Pan's lab had been extensive, estimated to be in the millions of *renminbi*. Details of the investigation into the attack on the IT node were scarce.

There had been a brief congratulatory note from Frank Sisler, advising that the Zero Day attack had fizzled at about the same time they attacked the lab. The team was being asked to TDY to Washington in early December to be debriefed on the operation.

Li had been quiet ever since his one cryptic message had advised him that Pan was going after the power grid rather than the financial networks. Logan did not plan to reach out to him before the team left Mianyang. Despite the fact that they now had secure communications, it was risky for them to have as much contact as they'd been having. After things cooled down he would reach out to him regarding his desire to resettle in the States.

On the 30th they got an early start from Mianyang to Chengdu. They had a mid-morning flight on Dragonair. Logan couldn't tell if it was his imagination or if the immigration official at the airport scrutinized his passport longer than normal. I must be getting edgy in my old age, Logan mused. Still, he was relieved when he was waved through and their flight boarded. As they lifted into the air he realized how much he was looking forward to seeing Zahir and Cooper.

Chapter 44

It's rare for non-official cover officers to step foot inside of CIA Headquarters; the Agency doesn't like to jeopardize their cover by exposing them unnecessarily. Logan and the others from the Alexander Maritime team had arrived in Washington on December 8 and today were accompanying the DDO to a briefing for the director of the CIA. They were presently ensconced in the DCIA's conference room.

The briefing went well. Aside from the DCIA, his deputy, chief of staff and the Agency's executive director were present. At the conclusion of the briefing the DCIA presented a special Meritorious Unit Citation to the China Cyber Task Force for their work. Des Magarity and Lois Caldwell were brought in, as well as Frank Sisler and Ellen Sanders. Later that morning the director invited Logan to accompany him to the White House to brief the President and members of his national security team.

At the end of his briefing, the President asked Logan for his analysis of the Chinese cyber threat. Logan looked over at the DCIA, who nodded that he should go ahead. Logan wasn't an analyst but he had been on the front lines of one of the worst cyber attacks ever witnessed against the U.S.

"Sir, we hurt the Chinese where it counts with this operation. They probably suspect that we're the ones behind the two attacks, but they can't be sure. They'll be able to rebuild the IT node and there's probably another Pan Chengong about to graduate from Stanford or MIT and go back to China to fight the cyber war for them.

"We can't afford to let our guard down. Right now, our cyber infrastructure is our Achilles heel, and until we fix that, we're going to be vulnerable to these kinds of attacks.

If I may say, sir, your Executive Order on Cybersecurity emphasizes the importance of securing our critical infrastructure, but until every American accepts responsibility for their role in doing that, we'll continue to have weaknesses that the Chinese and others can exploit."

"It may take us awhile to get there, Logan, but we will. Meanwhile we'll continue to rely on the brave men and women of the CIA to keep us safe. Thank you for your service." The President shook Logan's hand and then hurried away for a luncheon with the Congressional leadership.

After the briefing, Logan drove to the safehouse in Vienna, Virginia. Frank had taken him aside following the briefing at Langley to advise him that there had been a message from Li.

When he arrived, forty-five minutes later, Frank and Ellen were already there.

"What's up?" he asked.

Frank looked somber. "Read this and tell us what you think." He handed Logan a printout of the message from Li.

"12/08

Logan, The attacks in Hongbai and Mianyang have caused an intense security review here. Security teams are digging everywhere to get to the bottom of it. I am not certain, but am fairly confident that CIA was behind both of these attacks.

"I do not believe that I am suspected of anything. Because security will be digging into everyone's background, I am going to remove the secure communications software you gave me, from my computer. This will make it impossible for us to communicate securely.

"Your suggestion that I remain under the radar for at least six months is a good one. Unless I travel abroad before that time, I will not communicate with you. Please do not contact me in China.

"Your friend."

Logan looked up from the message. "He may be under duress."

"What do you mean?" Frank gave him a quizzical look. "When I issued him this commo plan I included an 'under duress' indicator."

"What is it?" Ellen asked.

"Normally, he's not supposed to include a date at the top of the message. If there's a date, it means that he's under duress."

"You think they're on to him?" Frank asked.

"It's hard to know," Logan replied. "There's always the possibility that he just forgot, and put the date in. These things aren't foolproof. He doesn't have a cheat sheet with prompts for this kind of thing. If his security people did find the commo system, you wouldn't want them to know that he had a way of warning us that he was in trouble."

"Wouldn't you think that if he was in trouble, they would be trying to set up a meeting in China so they could set you up?"

"I agree. It doesn't make sense. What do they have to gain by just shutting him down?" Logan handed the paper back to Frank. "What do you think?"

"We need to put him on ice. He's expressly asked that we refrain from any contact with him inside of China. He suggests that he may have an opportunity for travel abroad again."

"What if he's in trouble?"

"The best thing we can do at this point is to stay away from him. We'll give it six months and see if he reaches out to us from outside of China. If we don't hear from him by then, we'll put our heads together and see if we can come up with a plan to re-contact him."

Logan nodded his head in agreement. As he was getting ready to leave, a thought occurred to him. "What ever happened to that FBI spy, Wheeler?"

"Plea bargain. He's cooperating with the government. In return his wife gets to keep his pension and the government won't seek the death penalty."

"How much time will he get?"

"Twenty-five years. No parole."

Logan shook his head. "I don't understand why anyone would risk everything for money. Their freedom, their family, everything." He said goodbye to Frank and Ellen and headed back to his hotel.

Logan was able to wrap up his business in Washington in three days. He was looking forward to spending time with Zahir and Cooper. Headquarters had recommended that he not plan any travel to the mainland until after New Year's. He would have liked to pop up to Vermont to see his parents, but decided against it. They were still planning to visit Hong Kong over Christmas, so he would be seeing them soon enough.

December was busy. A good part of the month was spent on cover business, since Alexander Maritime's staff had been absent for all of November. Logan experienced some relief from his anxiety over Li's fate later in the month, when a report from a sensitive Chinese source advised that there had been a purge of the senior MPS leadership.

Deputy General Commissioner Gu Yan, Deputy Minister of the Ministry of Public Security, was the first to go. Newspaper accounts had accused Gu of corruption, but the Agency's sensitive source reported that the real reason for his arrest had to do with the failure of China's Zero Day attack and the assaults on Hongbai and Mianyang, which the leadership was now linking together. There was no mention of Li. But then again, as a mere superintendent he was small fry compared to Gu.

Most of the international news at the end of the year had to do with an increase in terrorist activity in Europe and the Middle East. An attack by Islamic State left 130 dead in Paris, and multiple threats by the terrorist group up and down the continent left European internal security officials grasping for answers.

Holidays with his parents and Millie's family were a pleasant respite from the harried operational pace he had been keeping. With no imminent crisis looming, he was able to relax and enjoy the festivities. The family attended the children's mass at St. Anne's Catholic Church in Stanley on

Christmas Eve and spent Christmas Day opening presents, catching up and feasting.

The following day they all flew to the island of Phuket, Thailand, for five days at the beach. It wasn't your standard Vermont white Christmas, but then again, you didn't hear any complaints from the Alexander clan.

CHAPTER 45

Superintendent Li had been summoned to Chengdu in late December to participate in a review of the Zero Day attack against the U.S. His group's DDoS attack against U.S. Cyber Command had been the one bright spot in an otherwise desultory operation. It had not been the MPS's finest hour.

Li had been disturbed over Deputy Commissioner Gu's sudden fall from grace. As Deputy Minister of the MPS, Gu ultimately was responsible for their success or failure. But Li had learned long ago that the purpose of these purges often reflected a hidden agenda and not the ostensible reason fed to the news media. Gu had lost his party position and was under house arrest. Word was out that the State Council was investigating the provincial leadership as well. The governor of Szechuan was a likely target given his close ties to the Minister's office and his open support for the cyber hacking program.

During evening dinners with his PSB colleagues there had been constant speculation about whose head was next on the chopping block. Li was confident that he had weathered this storm with his reputation intact. In fact, because of his unit's performance he had been advised that his promotion to superintendent 1st class was assured.

He had felt less tense in recent weeks, having cleansed his computer of the CIA covert communications software. He had also gone back into the network at his office and removed the malware that he had installed before the attack. It was unlikely that his secret relationship with the CIA would be discovered.

Life at home could almost be described as normal. Xiao Jun had emerged from his despondent state and Li had made every effort to be more of a father to him. He was grateful that Huiling was nearby and willing to step in to help him at times like this, when he had to travel.

While he was in Chengdu, his bosses advised him that a second round of meetings with the Thais was scheduled for after the Lunar New Year, in mid-late February. Logistical details would be worked out by late January.

His pulse quickened as he thought about his plan to re-settle with Xiao Jun in the West. It would be emotionally upsetting to the teenager, so soon after recovering from the shock of Xiao Mei's suicide. It would be difficult for both of them to say goodbye to Li's mother and Huiling. In all likelihood, it would be the last time they would ever see them. Of course Xiao Jun would not realize the finality of their goodbye until after they were safely settled in the U.S.

December and January flew by and before he knew it, he was on his way to Bangkok. The first thing he did after he had checked into the Sheraton was to call the toll-free number Logan had made him memorize, and leave a message that he was in Bangkok waiting to meet him. He would be there for three days, which should leave ample time for Logan to travel there. The operator repeated his information back to him and advised that he would pass the information on. Now all he could do was wait.

* * *

Logan read the message from headquarters with a sense of relief and excitement. Li had activated his communications plan, advising that he was in Bangkok, waiting to be met. Today was February 25 and Li would be there until the 28th. That didn't leave him much time.

He asked Alicia to book his flights and had Bangkok make a reservation for him in his Crowley alias at the Sheraton. He had a list of requirements from headquarters, mostly questions having to do with the ongoing purge of the MPS leadership. He also expected much of the meeting to deal with Li's desire to relocate to the U.S.

CIA would honor its commitment to resettle him in the U.S. but they wanted Logan to convince Li to work in place for a couple more years before he made the move.

Logan left that afternoon on a direct Cathay Pacific flight to Bangkok. His alias passport exchange was completed without incident and five hours later he checked into the Sheraton. It had been almost three months since he'd last seen Li. He wondered about his state of mind.

It was after midnight when his phone rang. He recognized Li's voice and simply gave him the room number. Ten minutes later there was a soft tap on the door.

"Logan, I'm relieved to see you. I wasn't sure that you would get my message, or that you would have enough time to get here before my meetings were over." Li had lost weight, and he seemed fatigued. He pushed into the room, looking over his shoulder as Logan closed the door.

"Li. It's good to see you." The two men shook hands and Logan steered him over to a couch. "I was starting to think you weren't going to call tonight."

"We had technical discussions that went pretty late and then I hosted their side to a dinner. The younger men all wanted to go out for drinks afterwards so we just finished up."

Li demurred when Logan offered him something to drink. "No, thanks. We have meetings in the morning and I need to be alert."

Logan spent some time catching up with him before getting into his intelligence requirements. These relationships tended to be more productive when the case officer spends some personal time with his asset, showing that he cares about his well being and his family.

After he'd covered that ground Logan got right into the intelligence debriefing. He spent an hour probing Li for information about the shake-up at MPS headquarters.

Li's information was consistent with that provided by other clandestine reporting, and in some areas, because of his first-hand knowledge, was much more detailed. When they'd finished, Logan asked him about his security situation.

"I was concerned when I got your message saying that you were getting rid of your communications software."

"Why? It seemed the smart thing to do. To get rid of any trace of our work together."

"I can understand that, but you used the 'under duress' signal in the message."

Li looked confused. "I did?"

"Yes. You included the date at the top of your message. Remember, you're only supposed to include the date in that format if you are under duress."

Li slapped his forehead. "I guess I forgot. I'm sorry."

"It's fine. But it gave me a scare. So, everything else is all right?"

"I was concerned immediately after the failure of the Zero Day attack. So far it seems that I'm not under suspicion. In fact, I'm being promoted to superintendent 1st class because our part of the Zero Day attack was the only success story. It may require that I transfer to Beijing. It's not what I want." He gave Logan an imploring look.

"What would you say if I asked you to take that promotion and go to Beijing?"

Li looked shocked. "But you promised..." His voice trailed off.

"I know. And I'll keep my promise. But we're at a critical point right now. Our leadership is putting a lot of emphasis on improving our cyber security, and you would be in a position to help us get there, especially if you're working in Beijing."

Li looked resigned to his fate.

"Look," Logan continued. "I know this has never been about money or anything like that. For you it's about the corruption that's eating away at Chinese society. But if you do stay for a couple of years, I'll be able to make the case for helping you when you are ready to make your move. We can put your son through college, and give you enough money to get settled in the U.S. What do you say?"

Li looked thoughtful. He got up and paced around the room as he considered Logan's offer. He stopped in front of his case officer and searched his face. "I'll do it," he said. "But only if you remain my contact. I don't want to meet anyone else."

"We can do that, although you've already met two of my colleagues."

"The two men in Mianyang?"

"Yes."

"It's decided then."

The two men spent the next fifteen minutes talking about their future communications. They decided that Li would send a message through international mail to advise Logan when he had received his promotion and to confirm his transfer to Beijing. These would be additional positive indicators that he was not under any suspicion, and give Langley some comfort in its decision to resume clandestine contact with the PSB officer inside China.

Li stood up to go. The two men shook hands and he departed. As Logan closed the door behind him, he thought of everything that had happened in just six months. In the end, China's Zero Day attack had failed. But, at the end of the day, unless the U.S. made a concerted effort to secure its cyber space, the risk of another Zero Day plot succeeding, loomed large. Logan's jaw set in a firm, hard line. Not if he had anything to say about it. Not on his watch.

The End

CPSIA information can be obtained
at www.ICGtesting.com
Printed in the USA
LVOW12s0433251016
510124LV00001B/1/P

9 780988 440067